J.K. FRANKO

TALION PUBLISHING

Published in the United Kingdom and the rest of the world by
Talion Publishing

Cambridge, UK

A catalogue record for this book is available from the
British Library

ISBN - 978-1-9993188-0-2

Printed and bound in Great Britain by
Clays Ltd, Elcograf S.p.A

This book is dedicated to my wife, Raquel.
Thank you for being an amazing partner, a loving mother, and an inspiration to me every day.
You're my best friend.

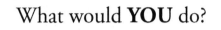

What would **YOU** do?

Thus shall you punish wrongdoers.
So that all who hear of your actions shall tremble and cease to do evil.
You must show no pity: Life shall pay for life, eye for eye,
tooth for tooth, hand for hand, foot for foot.

DEUTERONOMY 19: 19-21

PROLOGUE

When I try to piece together how this whole mess began, a part of me thinks it may have started over thirty years ago. At least the seeds were planted that far back, in the early 1980s. What happened then, at that summer camp in Texas, set the stage for everything that was to come.

Odd, how something so remote in time and geography continues to impact me here, today.

Sometimes I try to imagine her, how she felt—that eleven-year-old girl—as she ran, stumbling and tripping through the woods that night. I try to put myself in her shoes. When I do, I wonder if she was frightened.

Did she understand the consequences of what she'd gotten herself into? I imagine it felt otherworldly to her, like a dream. But not a good dream. No, one of the bad ones—the ones that make your heart machine-gun as you try to outrun some dark thing that's chasing you. But the faster you try to run, the slower you go, your legs feeling leaden, clumsy, useless. Panic sets in. Tears of frustration form. Fear takes hold and won't let go. You open your mouth to scream but realize, to your horror, that you're paralyzed. It's not that you can't scream; you can't even breathe. Not a dream—a nightmare.

Then again, all that may simply be my imagination. It could just be me projecting what I might have felt onto Joan.

Maybe she wasn't scared at all.

True, it was dark out. The night smelled of rain, but there was no lightning, only the far-off rumble of thunder hinting at a distant storm. There were no trail lights, no visibility but for the moon peeking out intermittently from behind a patchwork of clouds. But, Joan had been down this trail before. She was running toward the main cabin.

She had been at Camp Willow for almost two full weeks. She had been up and down that trail at least ten times a day, every day. Of course, that was during the day, and always with her buddy, or a camp counselor (the children called them troop leaders).

Joan had never been on the trail at night. And never alone.

Maybe I imagine Joan was scared because, as an adult, I believe that she should have been. I would have been terrified.

Adults know that evil flourishes in the dark.

The woods aren't a safe place for a little girl to be alone during the day. But at night?

Any experienced hiker will tell you that the forest changes at night. Landmarks look different. Depth perception suffers, even in young eyes.

By day, a copse of crape myrtles to the side of a trail is obvious. The bright fuchsia flowers stand in stark contrast to the greys, browns, and greens of the surrounding trees and foliage.

Turning right at the crape myrtles leads you back to the main camp. If you miss the turn, the trail continues to wind down until it reaches the scenic overlook that drops fifty feet to the river and jagged rocks below.

By day, those fuchsia flowers would be impossible to miss. But at night that landmark would simply blend into the background.

You see, there are no pretty pink flowers in the woods at night.

By now, you're probably wondering what Joan was doing out alone in the middle of the night. What could make her leave the safety of her cabin without her buddy? And why was she running?

To answer that, I have to tell you a little bit about her first.

Joan was a cute, bright little girl. Those who didn't know her well might mistake her curious nature for precociousness. But she wasn't. In fact, she was respectful and responsible, as older sisters tend to be.

She was also one of those children who aren't afraid to speak their mind. That is how her parents had raised her. She came from one of those kinds of families where the parents speak to their children as though they are adults. And the kids do the same. No pussyfooting around.

Joan was clear about what she believed, too. She didn't scare easily.

She didn't start out scared that night. She started out curious. Sneaking around after lights-out. Snooping. She called it "spying."

It's natural in young children, this behavior. Visceral. Primordial. If you have children, you know what I'm talking about. Evolution has hardwired something into kids that says: *We must learn how to spy on others. How to gather "secret" information. How to stalk. We must learn to be predator, or we will become prey.*

It's a part of growing up. It's all fun and games.

But there is a stark line that divides games from reality.

Joan crossed that line as she approached the cabin she planned to spy on.

She knew these kids. She'd been watching them for the last couple of days, eavesdropping at lunch, that kind of thing. She'd overheard them talking, but she couldn't believe what they were planning was true.

If it was, she had to do something.

You see, Joan was raised with clearly defined notions of right and wrong. She went to Bible study. And Grandma had read to her, when Mom and Dad weren't around, from the Old Testament. About Satan and Original Sin. Grandma had taught her that there were certain things that were mystical, sacred, and dangerous. You just didn't play around with them.

Joan crept up quietly, purposefully between pools of light. Once she reached the cabin, she paused. She could hear voices. Even though it was well past lights out, there was definitely something going on in there.

Carefully, she raised herself just enough to see inside the screened window, then quickly lowered herself. She'd seen them—she wasn't sure if they could see her, if they were looking in her direction or not.

She listened closely, trying to make out what they were doing. But the only thing she could hear was the hammering of her heart against her ribcage, the ringing of the blood in her ears. She placed her hands over her mouth to silence the breath that was coming so quick and shallow that she was starting to feel giddy.

She slowly peeked in the window again, and saw that no one was looking in her direction. Her eyes had already adjusted to the dark. Even so, it took a few moments for her brain to register what was going on, and a few more seconds to actually understand what she was seeing.

Joan's mouth fell open. She couldn't believe what was happening, what they were doing. She gaped, involuntarily holding her breath, staring.

There were rules at Camp Willow. What campers could and couldn't do.

What Joan witnessed went way beyond breaking camp rules. She was shocked. Stunned. And she was angry. This wasn't just wrong. It was evil.

You'd go to hell for it.

She had to make it stop.

"I'm gonna tell!"

For one brief moment, everything froze. The woods went quiet.

The three words hung in the air.

A screech broke the silence, followed by the flapping of wings as a frightened creature of some sort flew from its roost. At the same moment, the kids in the cabin turned in unison and gawked at the source of the scream.

Joan looked at them. She knew them. As she looked from one to the other, and they stared at her, Joan realized that she was outnumbered.

She turned and fled as fast as her feet would carry her. As she did, she heard a girl's voice hiss in a loud whisper, "Joan, wait!"

Joan ignored her and ran away, toward the main cabin. She felt strong, energized, full of purpose. But as I told you before, the trail was dark. The moonlight came and went. A storm was brewing in the distance. There were strange noises all around her. Shadows formed menacing shapes along the path.

And Joan was alone.

They say that when accidents happen it is usually not any one thing that goes wrong, but rather, it is the cumulative effect of multiple failure modes. For little Joan, the adrenaline, the darkness, the disorientation, and the lack of depth perception—all of these factors—probably combined and led to a very bad outcome. This is what the sheriff later told Joan's parents.

Joan was lucky at first. Despite the odds, she didn't miss the turn on the trail. She didn't miss the crape myrtles. Joan took the correct path and was headed straight for the main cabin. Until she stumbled on a root and fell, hard.

Really hard.

Her knee smashed into the ground, taking the brunt of the fall. The impact knocked off her left shoe.

Joan started crying. Quietly, so no one could hear. She tried to collect herself and rolled up into a sitting position, rocking and holding her knee. Moving it gently. Assessing the damage.

A flash of lightning startled her, but also gave her enough light to see that her shoe was only a few feet away.

She tried to stop crying.

She wanted her mommy. Wanted to be home. She wished she hadn't been spying. Wished she hadn't seen what she'd seen.

But, she also felt deep down inside that everything would be okay. She knew that Jesus would protect her because she was a good girl.

The moon peeked out from behind the clouds. In the light, Joan crawled toward her shoe. As she did, through her tears, Joan saw movement.

Shadows taking human form.

They appeared, one at a time.

The kids she'd been spying on.

* * *

The following morning, the bugle sounded as it did every day at 8:30 a.m.

Joan's camp buddy, Ann, was an early riser and was up and ready for breakfast before most. She was surprised to find Joan's bed empty.

When the other girls in their cabin told her that they hadn't seen Joan, Ann started looking for her around the campsite. Eventually, exasperated and a little worried, she sought out their troop leader, Beth.

"Are you sure she isn't just messing around with you?"

Ann shrugged.

"Maybe she's in the bathroom?" Beth asked.

"Nope. I checked."

"I bet she went to breakfast early. It wouldn't be the first time. She's probably in the mess hall."

Ann shook her head. "I found this on the trail." She held up a blue Keds shoe—left foot.

"Ann, you're not supposed to leave the campsite alone. You know that."

"I know, but I was worried," the girl responded, looking down at the shoe in her hand.

Beth took the shoe from Ann and turned it in her hands. "Are you sure it's hers?"

"Nope," she replied, biting her lip, "but I think so. Pretty sure."

Beth thought for a moment, then said, "Give me a few

minutes, and we'll go look for her together. Okay?"

Joan was not in her cabin or any of the others. She wasn't in the dining hall or anywhere else around camp. At this point, Beth advised the camp director that Joan was missing.

The camp director questioned Ann.

When Ann had gone to sleep at lights-out, Joan was in their cabin, in bed, where she was supposed to be. When Ann woke at the bugle call, Joan was gone. Her bed was mussed—it looked like it had been slept in, or at least lain in, but it was empty.

Ann had found the blue Keds shoe on the trail, past the crape myrtles, on the path to the main cabin. She even showed them the spot.

At the camp director's instruction, they performed another search of all cabins and the site.

No Joan.

This search had taken another hour, and it was at this point that Joan's absence became a serious concern.

Just before 10:00 a.m., the camp director called the sheriff's office. He and two deputies showed up shortly after and took control of the situation. The search for Joan began in earnest at 11:30 a.m.

At 1:00 p.m., the little girl's body was found at the edge of the river, broken on the rocks below the scenic overlook. It appeared that she had found her way to the edge of the canyon and fallen. She had suffered multiple broken bones, lacerations, and head trauma. Death would have been instantaneous.

Joan's family was notified. They immediately came to the camp, grief-stricken and withered.

The loss of a child is the ultimate tragedy. I cannot even begin to imagine how they must have felt upon receiving that devastating news.

The other parents, the lucky ones, were notified so that they could decide whether or not to come back early to retrieve their babies, many of whom were traumatized by the incident.

By the time Joan's body was taken away that evening, it was too late for the officers to do anything more. They agreed to return the next day.

That night at the camp, a service was held in Joan's memory for the counselors and children who remained.

The next morning, the sheriff and his deputies returned.

You will recall that this all happened almost thirty years ago. Way before the age of high-tech forensics, and long before CSI. It was a more innocent time. Simpler. The sheriff was an elected official—his main qualification for the job was his local popularity. His deputies were locals, too. Their training was minimal.

In a criminal investigation, one of the worst mistakes an investigator can make is allowing preconceived notions to taint the analysis. Unfortunately, that is precisely what happened here. The officers were pretty sure Joan had simply gotten turned around, probably lost her way, and fallen.

They still went through the motions, of course. They questioned the remaining children and the camp counselors, but learned nothing they hadn't already heard.

Suicide was discounted. Joan was a happy, well-adjusted child. None of the counselors reported any signs of depression or anything else. In fact, they remarked on the little girl's energy and personality.

Foul play was ruled out, as well. There were no signs of a struggle. Yes, there were other footprints up and down the trail leading to the overlook, but then, there would be. It was a very popular spot frequented by almost everyone at the camp.

Besides, what possible motive could anybody have to harm the little girl?

One deputy suggested the possibility of homicide to cover up another crime. But, what other crime? Joan had had nothing worth stealing. She'd been found fully dressed. She had not been molested in any way. The notion was discarded.

What made the most sense was that it had been an accident. Joan had gone out after hours, contrary to camp policy. She had been alone in the dark and become disoriented, taken a wrong turn, and fallen to her death.

It was a tragic accident. That's all. Nothing more and nothing less.

Everything was consistent with this theory, except for the fact that Ann had found Joan's shoe on the trail to the main cabin, and not on the way to the scenic overlook.

If Ann was right about where she'd found the shoe, it would mean that Joan had been on her way to the main camp, then lost her shoe, turned around, went back to the fork, headed for the ravine, and fell off a cliff to her death.

This simply wasn't logical. It made no sense.

The officers concluded that Ann was mistaken about where she'd found the shoe.

As one deputy put it, "Why in God's name would an eleven-year-old girl wander around in the woods, in the dark, in only one shoe?"

The case was closed.

CHAPTER ONE

January 4, 2018

The truth about Joan lay dormant for decades until an unexpected series of events brought it all back to the surface. These events began in 2018, in Colorado. And they began with another eleven-year-old girl named Arya Stark. She was the catalyst that brought everything full circle.

Winter had come to Beaver Creek Village. Snow blanketed the mountains and valley, and was still falling out of the night sky. Warm beams of incandescent light streaked out through the windows of nearby homes and across the ground, creating large amber triangles on the virgin white canvas.

On a gentle whisper breeze, the sound of music and laughter drifted up from the village to one of the condo balconies. Inside that condo, Susie Font and her husband Roy Cruise were cozily snuggled up on the couch in front of the TV. They were borrowing the place from friends for a long weekend. A half-finished bottle of wine sat on the coffee table between them, next to another empty bottle of the same vintage. There might even have been a third empty in the trash can.

The couple were binge-watching a boxed set of the epic fantasy series *Game of Thrones*, enthralled by the Season Six finale. In that episode, one of the main characters—Arya Stark—exacts her revenge on Walder Frey for the murder of her family. It's a gruesome yet satisfying scene that is the culmination of many episodes.

As the credits rolled, Roy said, "Damn! That was good!"

"I know. Right?" Susie agreed, pouring herself more wine.

"I didn't suspect the servant girl at all."

"Yeah. I thought she was there because she was going to become Frey's next wife or something."

"So did I!" Roy agreed.

"Frey deserved it."

"If anyone does, for sure, he's near the top of the list."

"Now that Joffrey's dead, at the top," Susie said.

"True. I hated that little fucker."

Roy sipped more wine as he absentmindedly watched the credits rolling on the television.

"How about a quick one before bed?" Susie winked at her husband, biting her lip enticingly, before nodding at the balcony.

Roy took a deep breath, smiled, and then heaved himself up. "Okay. But this is the last time tonight. The altitude up here is killing me. I can barely breathe. That and these palpitations…" He patted his chest rapidly, mimicking his heartbeat.

They stepped out onto the balcony, taking the wine with them. Susie untucked the bottom of her shirt from her pants, then reached up into her bra, retrieved a box of Marlboro Lights, and handed it to Roy.

After lighting up, they leaned on the railing and smoked in silence for a few minutes. The sounds of the night floated to them— the music and laughter from the village.

Roy watched the flickering blue hue of television sets light up the windows of nearby houses, then blew a smoke ring and said, "That show is so contagious. They really get you to hate the characters, and the medieval setting makes all that killing seem normal. Like it's okay to go around lopping off heads." He made a chopping motion. "And then they go and give you all these characters that *needs killing*." He delivered the last part with a Texas drawl, making Susie laugh.

"Crim law…"

Roy smiled at the shared memory and gave his wife a peck on the forehead. Her hair smelled of coconut.

Roy and Susie had met in law school. Although she was a bit older, he'd been a year ahead of her. They'd had a few classes that overlapped, and one of those had been criminal law. The professor, a dapper criminal defense attorney when he wasn't teaching, had told the class the story of a criminal trial in the wild west in order to make a point about "the punishment fitting the crime."

Two prisoners were brought before a traveling circuit judge in Texas. The whole town showed up for the trial. The first man was brought before the judge. He was accused of murder—of killing a man. After hearing all of the evidence, the judge found the man guilty of murder and sentenced him to thirty days in jail.

The second prisoner was then brought before the judge. This man was accused of stealing a horse. After hearing the evidence and arguments of the lawyers, the judge found the man guilty of the theft and sentenced him to death by hanging. The horse thief, needless to say, was dissatisfied with the judgment of the court.

"You sum-bitch! How can you hang me for stealing a horse when you let this asshole murderer off with just thirty days?" screamed the horse thief as the deputies took him away.

The judge replied, "I can abide that there's always some men that needs killin'. But I don't know of no horses that needs stealin'!"

Back on the balcony, Roy sat down on the small sofa, pulling a blanket over his legs.

Most would think that the sofa was put there so that the occupants of the condo could enjoy the view, but the reality was that the condo's owners put it there as a place to sit for those who enjoyed smoking—the condo-owning husband was a cigar lover himself.

Susie joined Roy under the blanket while he continued, "Frey needed killing. Sure, it's justice. But there's a revenge component to it, too. A lot of the deaths on the show have that element. Look at how Joffrey died. They could have just killed him off quickly, but instead they made him suffer from poison." He set his cigarette in the nearby ashtray.

"The same with Frey. They made him eat his kids before killing him, for fuck's sake."

Roy tended to get philosophical when he drank, and Susie sensed a "deep" conversation coming. She tried to lighten things up. "That's just for dramatic effect."

"No," said Roy. "I think there's more to it. It's biblical—Old Testament style. You know? It isn't just enough that evil people must die. It's the wrath of the angry God of Abraham. Just in case there is no life after death, no hellfire, no eternal damnation, these people have to suffer before they go. Dying isn't enough. They have to die badly. Their deaths have to be worse than, or at least as bad as, the reason they're dying—what they're being punished for." Roy looked at Susie. "They have to suffer for their sins."

Susie broke her husband's gaze and looked off into the night, before taking a drag of her cigarette and exhaling the cloud slowly.

Roy drained his wine glass and then refilled it, topping off his wife's glass at the same time. "I'm beginning to think there's something to that, you know? An eye for an eye."

Susie looked at her husband for a few seconds and then forced a smile. "You're drunk, you fool," she said, and then snuggled against him before adding, a few seconds later, thoughtfully, seriously, "Just let it go."

"No," he said. "I'm serious. I think it's inside all of us. It's human nature. After all, we're not that far from barbarism, even in this day and age. I mean, ask yourself, what keeps us civilized? A legal system that protects self-interest. Think about it. The death penalty is capitalism in its purest form."

"Bullshit," Susie said, exhaling smoke, sitting up and crushing out her cigarette.

"No, listen," Roy said as he leaned forward and grasped his wife's forearm. "Capitalism is all about creating an environment where every man—"

"Person," interjected Susie, stretching and stifling a yawn.

"Yeah, you know what I mean, Suze... every *person* can pursue their own self-interest without interference, so long as they don't infringe on anyone else's rights. So, we come up with a list of the worst infringements on other *people's* rights, the worst crimes. And, for committing those crimes, we impose the ultimate punishment— death. We have the death penalty because we believe that there are certain crimes so bad that, if you commit one of them, you are not human. You are an animal. No. Worse. Even animals deserve to live. If you commit certain crimes, you are less than an animal. You don't deserve to live. You deserve to die. You have no place in civilization."

"Babe. Come on. It's late. I'm tired and it's freezing out here. Let's go to bed," Susie said, attempting to derail her husband's train of thought, rising from the sofa and heading for the door.

He took another deep drag from his cigarette and exhaled slowly. Thoughtfully. And, just as his wife was stepping back into the condo, he called after her, a bit louder, "Suze... would you do it, if it was me?"

The words may as well have been his hand on her shoulder. She stopped and frowned. She knew what this was about. It wasn't about some shitty television show or a philosophical rant. This was about their past. Something that they had not discussed in years. She stared at him. She wanted to see his eyes, but he had turned away and was now staring out into the night as if looking for his own brand of justice out there. She asked him, to get him to look back at her, "Do what?"

Roy hesitated before responding. Distant music and laughter filled the void. "Walder Frey. If he killed me. Would you want him dead? Would you *just* want him dead? Or would you want to make him suffer?"

"Roy…"

He turned to her, tears glistening in his eyes. "Just answer the question, Suze."

Susie looked at her husband as a lump formed in her throat. "Honey, she's gone. Camilla's gone. It wasn't your fault. There was nothing we could do. We have to let her go," she said softly.

Roy turned away from her as a tear slid down his cheek. He was hurting. She hated seeing him like this.

The breeze shifted direction, carrying the music and laughter away and stirring snow from the roof, dropping bits over them in a powdery cascade.

The little snow flurry broke the moment, and Susie walked back to her husband, wiping away her own tears with the back of her hand. She stooped to kiss him on the head, then sat on the edge of the sofa next to him. Looking him in the eye, she took the cigarette from him with one hand while holding his hand with her other. She drew a deep long drag and released the smoke into the night.

"But," she whispered, "if that motherfucker had survived I would have killed him, gutted him, baked him in a pie, and fed him to his mother."

CHAPTER TWO

Roy had no idea what he had set in motion that night. That brief conversation on the balcony would have repercussions for years to come. It would change all our lives.

His plan for the trip had been much simpler. He had come to Colorado for the mountains—to snowboard. And that was how he spent the next morning.

At just after 2:00 p.m., Roy was coming down the mountain with his legs pretty well fried from a day spent snowboarding. After the snowfall from the night before, the conditions on the mountain were ideal. Half of the runs were groomed and there was tons of powder.

Roy had begun snowboarding in his early thirties. Their daughter, Camilla, was two years old at the time, and they'd come to Colorado to show her the snow.

As a latecomer to snowboarding, he was still uncomfortable with steep downhills. Powder, however, made for easy maneuvering and a lower likelihood of catching an edge. In powder, Roy could let loose: all of the adrenaline with much less risk. These were the conditions in which he felt most at ease.

Considering the ideal conditions, it wasn't crowded on the slopes.

As he came off Buckaroo and dropped into Hay Meadow, he focused on making wider, gentle turns. This was his last run of the season, and he wanted to finish upright and injury-free.

Roy believed that most people who got injured in snow sports did so on their last day on the mountain. He'd actually researched it and found that the majority of skiing and snowboarding injuries happen at the end of the day, most likely due to fatigue. Hence, he was playing the odds and quitting a day early.

Roy's like that. He's a planner. A strategist. Always thinking ahead.

He reached the bottom of the run, pulling up just to the right of the Centennial gondola lines and, as he stepped out of his bindings, he checked the time. There was just enough for one more run.

But that's when you get injured.

He smiled and removed his goggles, revealing piercing green eyes that shimmered in the dazzling light. He took a beat, then stretched his back, picked up his board, and headed toward the Hyatt firepit where he expected-slash-hoped he would find Susie.

She'd been asleep when he'd left for the mountain that morning and, after their discussion the night before, he was a bit stressed about seeing her. Dredging up the past never did either of them any good.

Fucking Arya Stark.

As Roy approached the firepit, he spotted Susie seated next to another woman. They were talking, laughing, and drinking from champagne flutes.

There is a God, he thought as he headed over to the bar for a drink. As he waited, he noticed that Susie and her friend's glasses were almost empty, so he took the initiative and ordered three fresh Veuve Cliquots.

"Ladies…" he said, setting the drinks down on a table.

"Are any available?" the blonde stranger asked, feigning looking around herself with a giggle.

Susie laughed, harder than the joke merited. "Hi babe," she said, standing up to kiss him on the lips.

Roy noticed that she was somewhat unsteady on her feet and that she'd probably already had one too many.

"Roy, this is Deb. Deb…" Susie paused.

Her companion held out her hand to Roy and finished her sentence, "Wise, Deb Wise. Pleasure."

The friend was a skier; obvious from the boots and gear. And there was a bit of a twang to her accent—sounded like Texas. What she was wearing seemed new. Very poseur. In his opinion, she hadn't spent more than an hour on the mountain in that gear.

She was taller than Susie, who is petite at five-feet-three-inches. Deb had a good six inches on her, he guessed. He also noticed the contrast between her cold blue eyes and her very animated face.

He sat on the edge of the firepit, facing their chairs.

Susie gushed, "We've been hanging out since just after lunch. And we've been very naughty. Plotting all sorts of evil." Both giggled again.

"We've had way too much to drink," Deb said.

"Although things have calmed down a bit since we switched to champagne," Susie added.

Deb laughed, hard.

Not that funny, thought Roy. "What were you drinking before?"

"Brandy," they said in unison. Something they both found equally hilarious.

"How was your day, hun?" Susie asked.

"All good." Roy smiled. "Lots of powder. Had some great runs. Hard to beat a day like today." He leaned back slightly, letting his back absorb the heat coming off the firepit.

"I bet you'll never guess how we met," Deb said.

"Beauty contest," Roy suggested. "Tied for first place."

"Oooh," Deb purred, smiling at Susie. "I like this one. He's definitely a keeper."

"Deb lives in Austin, Roy," Susie said.

"Ah. Hook 'em," Roy commented, raising the appropriate fingers.

"Roy and I met in law school at UT," Susie added.

"You told me," Deb said. "Tom went there, too. Business, I mean. Not law. His MBA."

"Roy still gets back to Austin quite a bit, on business," Susie added.

"Sure do. So, Tom is your husband? Is he around?" Roy asked, seeking testosterone. The air hung thick with estrogen.

"He's a bit under the weather actually. Altitude, I think."

"Tell me about it."

"We're thinking of getting dinner, the four of us, tomorrow night." Susie beamed.

She had worked for some time in television—journalism—and she could switch the smile and the charm on and off at will. Roy knew that. He also sensed he might still be on her bad side for raking up their past the night before. Better to go along to get along. "Sounds great. Love to meet him."

"Speaking of," Deb said, "I should go check on him." She smiled at Susie, and then, in a quick and surprisingly elegant gesture, drained her champagne flute.

Susie stood up. "Okay. Big kiss." They exchanged double cheek kisses.

"We'll touch base tomorrow. Yes?"

"Oh sure."

"Okay. See you both then," Deb said, smiling at Roy and heading off toward the hotel.

"She seems nice," Roy said.

"Very. Chatty. Funny. Kinda cute, too." Susie smirked.

"I hadn't noticed," Roy said with a grin. "So, where, for dinner tomorrow?"

Susie and Roy headed back to the condo, discussing restaurant options.

But, despite their plans, the dinner with Tom and Deb Wise the next night never happened.

CHAPTER THREE

Roy Cruise is not the spontaneous sort. He spent his last day on the mountain doing exactly as he had planned. No more snowboarding. Instead, he and Susie woke late, had breakfast, and headed to the Nordic Center to do some snowshoeing.

It was a beautiful day. The air was crisp, clean, and the sun was bright in a clear blue sky. The trails up at McCoy Park were in great shape, too. There was hardly anybody there. It felt like they had the place to themselves.

Susie was quiet. Pensive. Roy considered making conversation, but he wasn't in the mood. Besides, this was their last day of vacation. He preferred to focus on being in the moment and enjoying the beauty that surrounded them.

After a few hours, they headed back to the condo, where Susie changed to head out for a spa appointment. It was early afternoon. They agreed to meet back at the condo around 6:00 p.m. and then get a drink before dinner with Deb and her husband.

Roy showered and went shopping after dropping off his snowboard at Christy's for a wax and tune. After some browsing, he eventually bought himself some glove liners at Burton. He then returned to the condo and set about packing all his gear.

At 4:30, and with everything neatly squared away, he was bored. He pulled on his jacket and headed up to the 8100 Bar to start his pre-dinner drinks early. He ordered a Macallan 18 on the rocks, then began checking email.

He was halfway through his scotch and tapping out an email reply when he sensed another man take the seat next to him. He overheard him order a club soda, but Roy continued to focus on his email.

"Do you believe in fate, Roy?"

Roy looked up. The man was about his age, though smaller-framed, sporting neat gold hair speckled with grey. He was well-dressed—mountain clothes, Patagonia. The Submariner watch on his left wrist winked under the overhead lights. The man smiled.

"Roy Cruise, right? Miami? UT Law?"

"Have we met?" Roy asked, a bit uneasy. Roy has a good memory for faces. It bothered him that this man knew who he was, and that he was at a loss.

"Founder of Cruise Capital?"

"That's me." Roy smiled, shifting on his bar stool.

The stranger glanced around the room, then at his glass. He stopped smiling as he asked, in a lowered voice, "Father to Camilla Cruise?"

In primitive man, the appearance of spear-wielding enemies or aggressive animals triggered the acute stress response. The body responded to threats by firing adrenaline into the bloodstream, preparing for "fight or flight."

For modern man, different threats exist. Social norms define "safe" behavior. When words or gestures vary from acceptable norms, we experience uncertainty that our lizard brain equates with danger.

The mention of Camilla's name by the stranger fired adrenaline through Roy's body like an electric shock. His heart pounded. His neck and shoulder muscles tensed. He fought to control himself, eyes narrowing, jaw clenching. He inhaled sharply, and exhaling somewhat raggedly, hissed, "Who the fuck *are* you?"

The man recoiled a bit at Roy's aggression. He quickly responded, hands slightly trembling, "I'm a father, like you. Suffering, like you." His eyes still discreetly scanned the room.

Roy continued to glare at the stranger, saying nothing.

The man added, "I'm Tom Wise. You met my wife yesterday, Deb."

Roy's expression didn't change. He sat, waiting.

"The name Wise doesn't ring a bell? Wise, from Austin, Texas?" the man asked. His voice softer now. Sad.

Roy, still reeling from the man's unwelcome familiarity, vaguely recalled the name.

"Kristy Wise? Joe Harlan... junior. The senator's kid?" the man continued.

Roy remembered bits and pieces. It had been a few years before. A sexual assault. He'd read about it online. The guy, Harlan, was a UT student. Sophomore maybe. Roy wasn't sure. The girl Harlan raped was a freshman. It happened on Halloween night. There was alcohol or drugs involved. They'd had sex. She'd claimed rape. He'd claimed consent. The jury found him not guilty. There was an outcry. Claims of political interference. Tainted evidence. The father was a state senator. The young man ended up back in the news not long after—beaten up at a grocery store by the girl's father. Wise. Tom Wise. The man sitting next to him.

Roy nodded. "Yeah, it does."

The bartender was mixing drinks, out of earshot. Wise leaned in and said, "Listen, I won't take up too much of your time. Just hear me out, okay? Would that be okay?"

Roy considered the request. There was an eagerness in the man's tone that felt like desperation. He nodded, but turned back to his scotch. "Go ahead."

"Look, we're normal people. You guys met Deb yesterday. But, it wasn't an accident. That you met, I mean. We're here with Kristy. She's still trying to get over everything. It's been hard. Not just, you know, what happened. But the son of a bitch getting away with it. You can imagine. It's been hard for all of us. Hardest for her."

The man shook his head, lips pursed, as if weighing what he was about to say next. "Yeah, I beat the crap out of him. It was... just coincidence, really. Bad luck. I ran into the little fucker at Whole Foods of all places." Wise half-chuckled. "I... I went for him in the parking lot. Then security got all over me and, well, I don't remember much except the feeling of hitting him. Feeling my fist pound his face." He gritted his teeth, fist clenched. "God, it felt so fucking good. I mean *real* good, to give that little son of a bitch just... to make him suffer..." The words died in his throat as he winced. "My baby girl…"

The man wiped tears from one eye with the back of his hand. He took a breath, swallowed to recompose himself. "Well, it was kind of stupid. Spur of the moment, and I got caught." He forced a smile, waiting.

Roy was silent. He was wrestling with the knot that this man, this stranger, had stirred in the pit of his belly. His own eyes watered. He knew it wasn't just the alcohol. It was because he was also a father. Dad to a little girl who had been hurt by someone else.

"So, anyway, when I heard you guys the other night," the man continued. "You and your wife, I mean. Talking about justice. About people needing to suffer for their sins."

Roy turned and looked at him.

"Yeah. We're staying here too, next building over. Your balcony isn't that far from ours and, well, quiet night, snow. Sound carries." Wise leaned in conspiratorially. "Thing is, I know who you are. I read about you in *The Alcalde* a while back. You. Your company. *Everything.* Then I saw you in the lobby the other day. I recognized you and made the connection."

Roy leaned back. "Look, man," he said, "I don't know what you heard, but I have to tell you, I don't appreciate the eavesdropping." He signaled the bartender, who was at the other end of the bar, for his tab.

"Just one more. Please. Just one more minute," the man said, touching his arm. "It's important. I read about your daughter, what happened. It was about the same time as the stuff with Kristy. And I felt for you. We both did. Deb and I. And we took comfort. I know it's sick, it sounds sick, but we took comfort, you know, that at least Kristy was still alive. But you see, she isn't alright. Not anymore. Not how she used to be. Ever since what happened. Well. She's changed. For her, this thing, sometimes, well, it feels like it's never going to go away."

Tom Wise took a beat. Looked around the room and then back at Roy. "So, when we heard you, like I said, the other night, talking about justice. The God of Abraham. Old Testament justice. Well, I think that *was* fate."

"So, we wanted to meet you. The rest wasn't an accident.

That Deb met Susie, I mean. We're normal people. We wanted you to see that. Normal people dealing with abnormal circumstances. I mean, we wanted to have dinner and everything, you know, so you could get to know us. To see that we're like you. But I'm thinking that it's probably best we don't. Best we have... less contact, you know?"

The man's last line was delivered in a lower voice as the bartender approached with Roy's tab, then walked away. Tom watched him go.

Roy frowned. "Less contact?"

Tom looked at Roy, sipping his club soda. "Yeah. So they can't connect us."

"Connect...?" Roy's frustration got the better of him. "What the hell are you talking about, man? Actually, you know what, don't bother. I need to get going." Roy dismounted his barstool and picked up his bill with one hand, reaching into his pocket with the other.

Tom placed his hand on Roy's arm. "We're parents, Roy. Just like you. We love our daughter. Just like you. And we want justice. Old Testament justice. Just like you. Will you help us?"

There was the desperation again. It was palpable. Roy took a few seconds to study the man—chewed fingernails holding Roy's arm; droopy eyes, dark rings under them; ears flushed red; pursed thin lips slightly quivering. Desperation, but also determination.

"Help you what?" Roy asked, reluctantly.

Tom Wise stood close to Roy, furtively scanning the room, then leaned in, and in a quivering voice said, "For Kristy, and for Camilla, will you kill this fucker Harlan, for us?"

CHAPTER FOUR

"No fucking way," Susie exclaimed. "So, what did you do?"

She poured Roy a glass of red, downed the water from her drinking glass, and then refilled it with wine as well.

When she'd returned from the spa, she'd found her husband lying on the sofa staring out the window at the mountains. He'd come to the kitchen and shared what happened at the bar with Tom Wise while she opened a bottle of pinot.

"What do you think I did? I got up and left. Slung a twenty on the bar and didn't even wait for the change. It was like something out of a fucking movie."

"Holy shit..."

Susie was energized, wanting to know more details. "But you've never met the guy before. He's a complete stranger. That's crazy."

"Bat-fucking-shit crazy," Roy echoed.

They stood in the kitchen in silence.

"Well, I guess dinner's off," he said, flippantly.

Susie laughed. "Ya think?" She drank from her glass. "What's nuts is that she seemed so normal. Did he?"

"Well. He kept telling me he was fucking normal. That they were fucking normal. Normal people just like us, but then he mentions Camilla and..." Roy let the words hang in the air as he ground his teeth. "Nothing fucking normal about that," he mumbled.

Susie put down her glass. "I meant how he looked."

"You mean, did he look fucking crazy? No, of course not. Yeah. He looked like any other guy. Average height. Mid-to-late forties. Not exactly an athlete but not out of shape either."

"Did he at least offer to pay the tab?" Susie asked with a smile.

Roy laughed. But it was forced. He was staring into space, reliving the conversation in his head.

Seconds ticked. Someone laughed outside. A door slammed.

Susie picked up her glass. "Do you think you're the only person he's propositioned?" she asked, taking a sip.

Roy studied her, pursing his lips. "I have no idea." He drank from his wine glass. "I mean, maybe. In fact, I think, probably yes. He made it sound personal. By that, I mean personal to us. Apparently, his daughter went through her ordeal around about the time that *it* happened to us. And then they heard us talking on the balcony."

"You mean they heard you philosophizing after a little too much vino," Susie interjected with a smile.

Roy pulled a face and shrugged. "Well, anyway, yeah, they took that to mean that we're like them."

"But we were just bullshitting about a TV show... come on!"

"I know. *He's* nuts."

"How the hell do you go from overhearing someone's drunken conversation to asking them—a perfect stranger—to kill for you? It's fucking ridiculous!"

"You've got to admit, though, it's pretty ballsy," said Roy, indicating with his wine glass.

"They must really be hurting. I mean, it's risky is what it is!"

"Yeah... what's to keep me from going to the cops?"

Susie pondered. "That could get messy. I suppose he'd just deny it. It's his word against yours."

"It's sure as shit not the way I would do it, Suze. If you really wanted this guy dead, you'd need to approach someone you'd think was disposed to doing it, right? You do some research, some planning. You don't just hit someone up because you feel they can relate to what you're going through."

"Well, maybe they think that's enough." Susie's eyes widened. "You did tell him you weren't interested, right?"

"Of course I fucking did!" He scratched his head. "At least I think I did. Maybe I just got up and left."

"Roy!" Susie exclaimed. "He doesn't think that, maybe...?"

"Suze. I up and left. I don't think I needed to say much more than that, do you? Besides, I don't even know how to contact this guy, let alone..." Roy trailed off. He began looking around the kitchen.

"Where's your phone?" he demanded, spotting Susie's iPhone on the breakfast table by her purse. He rushed over and picked it up. "Did she give you her contact info?"

"I think so." Susie walked up to her husband and looked over his shoulder.

"You *think* so? What? You don't know?" he asked, tapping the screen.

"Hey, don't get pissy with me. You're mister 'eye for eye' Old Testament justice. What are you doing? Are you deleting Deb's number?"

"Fuck yes. We've no clue what these people are capable of. It's best not to have anything to do with them."

"There." He pressed the delete button and grunted in satisfaction.

"Make sure you delete the chat, too," Susie offered.

Roy tapped the screen a few times, then, "Done." He handed the phone back to his wife.

"Let's hope we never hear from either of them again," she said with a bite of the lip. And then she added with a shrug, "So. What do we do about dinner?"

"Did you reserve or was she going to?"

"She was going to reserve."

"Then we just don't show."

"Right," Susie agreed with a nod. Although, if Roy had looked closely, he would have seen that she was disappointed.

CHAPTER FIVE

"The senator will see you now."

Detective Art Travers stood and followed Meg, Senator Harlan's assistant, to the senator's office. The detective tried to keep his eyes up and off Meg's ass, but her skirt was of a length that made that difficult.

Meg opened the door for him and stood aside, flashing him a coy smile and a wink.

This was not the first time Travers had been to see the senator, though it was the first time he had been to this office.

The two men had met a few years earlier as a part of the investigation into Joe Harlan Jr.'s assault on Kristy Wise. Travers had been assigned to the case by the chief of police because of his reputation for diplomacy and discretion.

Senator Harlan was also a lawyer, and today Travers had been summoned to the man's law office, a very traditional space paneled in wood and cluttered with law books and prints of English foxhunts. It was barely three blocks from his office at the capitol.

The nameplate on the door read *Of Counsel,* which Travers understood meant that the senator wasn't so much a lawyer as a rainmaker. He didn't participate in the law firm's equity, only got paid for the business he brought in. Not hard to do considering that he could use the contacts he made as a senator to get clients for the firm and line his pockets in the process.

A sleazy, but perfectly legal, practice.

"Good morning, Detective," Harlan Sr. said with a velociraptor smile. The words carried a slight Texas drawl, and the senator said them while rising and coming around the desk to shake

Travers' hand. He wore a stiffly starched white dress shirt with a red tie, navy blue suit pants, and black cowboy boots. His suit jacket hung from a hook near the door, a double U.S. flag/Texas flag lapel pin prominent against the blue.

"Good morning, Mr. Senator." They shook hands.

"Stand up, son," snapped Harlan Sr., "and greet our guest."

Joe Harlan Jr. stood from a nearby couch and shook the detective's hand. The kid had a solid handshake, though his hand was moist.

Travers discreetly wiped his hand on his pant leg, hoping the slime wouldn't leave a stain.

Harlan Jr. wasn't a big guy, not as tall as his father, but wiry like him. His father stood close to six feet with his trademark boots.

"Please, take a seat," the senator offered, indicating the chairs in front of his huge oak desk. He took the power seat behind the desk, leaving Joe Junior to resume his place on the sofa.

"Now, Detective," the senator began, steepling his fingers, "we've talked long and hard on this and, as I've said a million times before, we want nothing more than to put this terrible misunderstanding behind us."

After criminal charges had been levied against his son, the senator had refused to call the sexual assault allegation what it was— rape. Instead, he referred to it as the "situation." The process, from investigation through trial, had taken almost eighteen months. It was a far cry from the rash of law and order shows that made it seem that criminals went to trial in the space of weeks. The reality was very different.

When Joe Junior was acquitted, the senator had adopted new phrasing, abandoning the "situation" in favor of the "terrible misunderstanding." Travers wondered if the senator had spin doctors who came up with this shit or if he did it all on his own.

"But the law is the law," the man was saying, "and the law has spoken. Joe must be free to go about his life as he pleases. He's been through hell and back already and the last thing he needs is to be lookin' over his shoulder and wondering if this kook is gonna ambush him again."

"So, while we don't want any more press and we want this, this," he fumbled for the words, "thing to be over, what assurance do we have that this man is under control?" The senator's voice rose. "I mean, I know that there's a restraining order and all, but how can we be sure he'll abide by it, and how can we be sure he's going to leave my son the hell alone?" The senator's nostrils were flared. His eyes were wide, boring holes in his guest. It was an impassioned delivery, one that might have impressed the average person on the street. But, it was delivered by a lawyer who was also a politician. To Travers, it was largely show.

He stifled a sigh. "Mr. Senator, the DA is looking at pushing for aggravated assault. That's a $10,000 fine and two to twenty." Travers had no doubt that the charges were being pumped up by the DA as a favor to the senator, as no weapon had been involved. Wise had only gotten one good punch in, and all Joe had to show for it was a shiner. "That's enough to make anyone think twice. Mr. Wise's lawyer has already offered to pay all medical and to provide a written apology for dismissal of the charges."

The senator pursed his lips. He was either considering what Travers had just said or pretending to. Harlan Sr. looked at his son next, who might as well have been a mannequin. He sat there looking down at his hands, avoiding eye contact with Travers or his father.

"Well, Detective," the senator replied, "we've thought long and hard on this, and we believe that the right decision is to press charges after all. I know we discussed the possibility of letting this go, but, quite frankly, I cannot see how in all good conscience we could possibly do that. This is not just about Joe. This man's actions are a crime against the people of the state of Texas. I have therefore today advised our district attorney of Joe's…" he glanced at his son, "…decision, but wanted to let you know in person, as a courtesy."

Travers looked at Joe, who just sat there. Travers had seen that look many times. Young men who were either lost, spoiled, or just high. There was no doubt in his mind that Junior didn't want to be there any more than he did, but most likely he had also been ordered to make an appearance.

The detective looked at the senator and wondered why

the fuck he'd had to come in person for this. Was it because the legislature wasn't in session? Maybe the senator needed to fill his day with *important* meetings?

The senator tapped the arms of his chair as if to rise, indicating the meeting was over.

"Well, thank you for that courtesy, sir," Travers said, mustering his best smile of appreciation.

"Don't mention it, Detective," the senator said, coming around his desk and accompanying Travers to the door. "How is Chief Manley doing?" he asked, that velociraptor smile back on his face. "Taking care of our men in blue? And the ladies, of course?" Harlan didn't wait for a reply. "Well, you tell him I said 'hello,' and don't you be a stranger. We are here to serve."

Harlan Sr. snatched Travers' hand, shaking it firmly and looked him in the eye. "I personally appreciate everything you do for us all. If I can ever be of assistance in any way, you know where to find me, Art."

"Yes, sir. Thank you, Senator," Travers replied, maintaining his forced smile. The detective was not happy. He'd hoped to be able to put this whole mess to rest. The Wise family had been through a lot. Especially the girl. Tom Wise punching Joe in the face was illegal, to be sure, but Joe probably deserved it, if not worse.

As Travers left, the senator smiled and winked at Meg. She smiled back, biting her lower lip.

Joe was still sitting in his father's office. He hadn't even bothered to get up.

CHAPTER SIX

"Sit down, for fuck's sake! You're driving me crazy!" Deb exclaimed. Tom Wise was pacing. He had been for a while.

They were still in Beaver Creek, at the condo. It was the day after Tom had met Roy at the bar.

Deb had exploded when Tom came back from the bar and explained what had happened.

"Don't you sell shit for a living? How the fuck could you not close this deal?"

They'd gone back and forth for some time, him explaining, her attacking. He'd gotten a short reprieve that evening when Kristy came back from snowboarding. She knew nothing about what her parents were up to, and they wanted to keep it that way.

Deb had given Tom the silent treatment while Kristy was there. Later, despite Tom's protests, Deb insisted had they go to meet Cruise and his wife for dinner as planned so she could show her husband *how it was done.*

Cruise and his wife stood them up.

Deb was incandescent with rage.

When they got back from the canceled dinner, they'd found a note from Kristy—she'd gone out for a while. This freed Deb to open up on Tom all over again.

Deb was now flipflopping between verbal assaults and the silent treatment. And, to make matters worse, they were both waiting for a response from that asshole of a senator and his rapist son—were they prepared to accept their settlement offer? The last thing they needed was for this thing to get any worse than it already was.

It was almost an hour later when Tom's mobile phone rang. He looked at the screen.

Harold Riviera, Attorney

"Here we go," he said under his breath. "Tom, here."

"Hi, Tom, it's Harold."

"Hey, Harold. I'm going to put you on speaker, for Deb."

"Sure."

"Can you hear us?"

"Yep. Hello, Mrs. Wise."

"Hello, Harold. Please, I've told you before, it's Deb."

"So," Tom said. "What have we got?"

"It's what we feared, folks. They're pressing charges. The DA is going for aggravated assault, which is a real stretch, as we discussed. That's on the criminal side. On the civil suit, their lawyer rejected the offer to settle. So, it looks like we're going to have to fight this thing." The words were delivered matter-of-factly, as if he hadn't just confirmed that they were going to have to go to court, with all of the stress and financial expense that would entail.

"It makes no sense," Tom whispered incredulously.

"Sure, it does," Deb spat. "Harlan doesn't give a shit about his son. Like they say, 'there's no such thing as bad press.' This'll keep his name in the papers, and it'll also serve to diffuse the bad press his son got. Makes us the villains."

"Again, as we discussed, folks, the 'why' doesn't matter so much here. The key is going to be a solid defense. There is still a ton of animosity out there against Joe Jr. It's going to be damned hard to find a jury that will fault Tom for punching this guy in the face. I know it's not what we were hoping for, but I hope you can at least put it on the back burner until you're back from Colorado. There's no point in worrying about it. After all, it's a straightforward case. The whole thing's on film. So, it's not going to be a question of what happened, it's going to be a question of whether the jury faults you for it, Tom, along with just how serious they believe his injuries were. There's a lot of sympathy for you folks out there, which means that there's potentially going to be a lot of sympathy on the jury."

Tom and Deb exchanged glances and sighed.

There was a long silence broken by the lawyer. "Like I said, try not to worry about it right now. Make the most of your time there and just come and see me when you get back."

"All right, Harold," Tom said. "Thanks for getting back to us."

"No problem, folks. Y'all take care."

Tom disconnected the phone.

"Well, hell," Deb said.

Tom was about to say something, but when he turned to his wife he noticed Kristy standing in the hallway behind her.

Deb caught his gaze and looked up over her shoulder.

Kristy had just come back from the gym. She was sweaty and glowing, healthy. The tension dissipated from Deb's shoulders at the sight of her daughter. "Oh, hi baby, you back already?" she asked with a big smile. When Kristy didn't react to her mother's greeting, it became obvious. "You heard?"

Kristy nodded. Deb expected her daughter to launch into a barrage of questions. Instead, she drank from her water bottle, swallowed hard, and then said, "Fuck. Them. I'm gonna take a shower."

Deb smiled and thought to herself, *That's my girl... What goes around comes around, sweetie. What goes around comes around.*

CHAPTER SEVEN

Three Months Later

March 29, 2018

As time passed, Susie and Roy put Tom Wise's bizarre murder proposal behind them. It was the kind of thing that, when it happened, seemed shocking and distressing, but over time decreased in importance. In the end, they came to view it as an odd anecdote.

Roy admitted to me that he thought back on it a few times over the following months. And that, the more he did, the more he began to feel sympathy for Tom and Deb. He wondered whether he might have overreacted that night at the bar. The man had probably just had too much to drink.

But then, what alternative had Tom given him? Have dinner with them and discuss killing Harlan? Or try to talk them out of it? Roy's response to the proposal was not unreasonable. At least, that's what he told himself.

As you may well imagine, Roy walking out on Tom at the bar was not the end of the story. Harlan was by no means out of the woods.

After returning to Miami from Beaver Creek, both Susie and Roy made a concerted effort to get back to their routine. To life as normal. Or whatever semblance of normality they had managed to carve from their existence after Camilla's death.

On this particular day, Roy was at the Austin Airport. He had gone on a business trip to Austin and was heading home. This trip is significant because the next day, March 30, 2018, would mark the third anniversary of Camilla's death. Though Roy didn't know it at the time, that anniversary would also mark a turning point for us all.

Roy was traveling with David Kim, a junior partner and head of due diligence at Cruise Capital. Roy had started Cruise Capital twenty years earlier in Texas when he decided to change careers from practicing law to investing in startups. Though Susie and Roy (and Cruise Capital) had moved to Miami in 2003 to be closer to Susie's parents in Charleston, S.C., Roy still returned to Texas regularly to meet with promising new startups.

David and Roy were waiting to board the last direct flight from Austin to Miami that day, departing at 5:08 p.m. and arriving at 8:49 p.m. They'd checked in online, taken the shorter and faster TSA pre-check line through security, and were waiting at Gate 14 to board when Roy's phone rang.

"Hi, Suze. On my way home. At the gate. How are you?"

"Better, now that I'm talking to you. How was the trip?" Her voice sounded huskier than normal.

"Same old, same old. You know. You gotta kiss a lot of pigs..."

"How'd David do?" Susie asked.

"Good, very good," Roy answered, glancing at his junior partner. "We saw a couple of good companies. A lot of back-end stuff. And we eliminated a few based on some of David's insights. So, yeah, very good."

"That sounds great." Susie cleared her throat. "Well, I confirmed with Roni. Everything is set for the interview tomorrow morning. And I finished up the blog post—it's in your inbox, or should be shortly. Even got my hair done," she laughed nervously.

"Hairdo? Isn't it... a radio interview?"

"So?"

Roy smiled. "How are you feeling about it?"

"It's... hard, Roy. I've cried... a lot." She breathed in deep. "I've done a lot of thinking about the interview. Writing the blog really helped. I feel like I really distilled everything I want to say in the interview into the post. So, the messaging will be consistent, but it also helped me kind of... get centered, you know, focused. I don't know…"

"Suze. Babe. I'm sure it's great," Roy reassured her, picking up that his wife was struggling not to cry on the phone.

"Hmm. Yeah. I think so. Will you read it? Please? Text me what you think, I mean, if you can, before you take off. I've still got time to make changes."

"Sure, Suze. Happy to."

She took a deep breath. Talking to her husband both helped and made her more emotional in equal measure. He was the only person who really knew her and knew how she felt, what she was feeling, and what they'd been through. "Should I wait for you, for dinner?"

"Nah. We ate a late lunch with a bunch of guys that want to be the Facebook for rescue pets. Eddie V's—I'm stuffed. You go ahead. I'll join you for a drink before bed."

"Okay. Well, try to rest on the plane, will you?"

"I'll try. I gotta board now."

"Okay, love you. Bye."

"Love you, too, Suze. B-bye."

* * *

Roy sat in business class. David was one row behind and across the aisle.

Roy has his quirks. One is that, for business travel, he prefers not to be seated next to traveling companions. He sees enough of them on the ground and would rather use flight time to read and think. As an introvert, being with people is a drain, and the only way he can truly recharge is with an adequate amount of solitude.

As the flight attendants went through the safety dance, he checked his email, but there was nothing from Susie. Then, just as he was getting ready to put his phone in flight mode, an email alert sounded.

His stomach turned, and he looked out of the window trying to suppress the unease that had washed over him. He felt hot, flushed. He loosened his seatbelt, which suddenly felt too tight, confining.

Roy knew what was coming, and the thought of it made him ill. Not the takeoff. He had done plenty of flying in his lifetime. Flying was something he enjoyed.

No, it was what he knew was in Susie's email that was making him queasy, and if he hadn't promised, if he wasn't committed to being supportive of his wife, he'd quite happily delete the thing.

But he couldn't.

From: susie.font1@gmail.com
RE: Blog Post
To: roy@cruise-capital.com

Hi Roy,
Let me know what you think.
Love you!
Susie

Then he downloaded the attachment and read.

Three Years Past, But Not Gone
By Susie Font

As a former journalist, I still remember how it felt to cover breaking news. It was an adrenaline rush. When you get the call about a new story, everything kicks into gear and the "work" begins—verify information, contact witnesses, investigate leads, and define how you will clearly and succinctly tell the story in order to inform and to educate.

What is easy to forget is that "news" starts with people: real people with real lives that have been derailed by an unexpected event. And while their story may have ramifications for us all, it is still their story. Their experience to survive and to remember.

All of that changed for me on March 30, three years ago. On that day, my daughter Camilla was driving, following the rules, going to ride her horse. Liam Bareto, a name I had never heard before but that is now seared into my memory, chose to send a text message while driving and, as he did, drifted out of his lane and into hers.

They collided head-on.

Camilla died on impact.

When the police officer came to our door and told me what had happened, there was no adrenaline rush. Nothing kicked in. Instead, I went numb. I opened that door, looked at the officer, and heard the words. Then there was nothing.

It was as if someone had turned off the volume in my world.

The next thing that I recall is my husband's face. He had just returned from a business trip. I remember him sitting next to me, holding my hand, speaking softly as I lay on the sofa staring at a spider web in the corner of the room. Just watching it move lightly as the AC blew on it.

To this day, I still don't know what my husband said to me. All I knew was that our baby girl was gone.

They say that no parent should bury their child. But to me, I haven't buried her. Camilla will now and forever live in my heart and the hearts of everyone who was blessed to know her. And, as ethereal as this may sound, I believe she watches over me. She can see everything I see and do. And, she is most likely reading these words, just as she was forever peeking over her mommy's shoulders, especially when I was writing some of my best articles.

Mommy loves you, baby! Mommy loves you so very much.

After what happened, I wanted my little girl to know how much she meant to us, that she hadn't been and would never be forgotten. So, I chose to take action.

I left journalism and now devote the hours that I used to spend on research and reporting to lobbying for changes in the laws that deal with texting and driving, along with advocating for awareness of the dangers of texting while driving.

Three years ago, my daughter was murdered by a kid who chose to put a text message before the life of another human being. A few months later, that same kid succumbed to the injuries he sustained during that act. Two lives senselessly lost—two families changed forever—and all of it avoidable.

This is my story. It is my family's story. And the Bareto family's story. But it's also the story of all of us.

By taking action, we help others to understand that when you are behind the wheel of a vehicle, you are wielding a lethal weapon just as devastating as any firearm.

We are changing the stories of many families for the good.

Thank you for your support. Together, we're stronger.

Roy looked away from his phone and out the window, discreetly brushing the tears from his eyes with the back of his hand. He felt a lump in his throat that he fought to keep from progressing into outright weeping.

As he stared through the heat shimmer on the tarmac and watched the plane next to his pull away from the jet bridge, it all came flooding back to him.

It had been a day just like this one. Bright and clear. The air filled with the afterburn of jet fumes, he had boarded this same flight: Austin to Miami. Everything had been fine in Austin. When he'd touched down in Miami, the world as he knew it had changed, forever.

Coming home.

The police car parked in front of the house.

The officers in the living room.

Susie lying catatonic on the sofa.

Him gripping the phone with white knuckles, his mind scrabbling for the right words to explain everything to Susie's parents.

From that point forward, it seemed that everything moved in slow motion. Most of it was now a blur, with the exception of the agonizing task of identifying Camilla's body. That was something he'd had to do alone because Susie was in no fit state to do so. And, to be fair, it was something that Roy managed to do with admirable dignity. It was only after he'd left the soul-crushing, gray government building and reached the parking lot that he collapsed against his car in a heap of convulsive sobs.

He was thankful that Susie hadn't seen her. Camilla's rosy cheeks and youthful dimples had been unrecognizable. Never to be seen again. He'd been sickened when he saw her, just as he was when he held her hand one last time only to find it stiff and cold. He was repulsed by his daughter. He felt guilt at his repulsion. Shame.

Roy had many memories, cherished images, of Camilla growing up. First steps, learning to ride a bicycle, her first date. It seemed so unfair for all of those images to culminate in a final, grotesque mental snapshot of her lying in the morgue.

Still, he pushed forward, and planned. He made lists: *write obituary, contact family, select funeral home, choose coffin*—a closed casket, of course. It couldn't be anything else.

He visited Camilla's school, clearing out her locker before they even had the chance to send her personal items to him, all the time ignoring the furtive glances from students and teachers. He'd canceled dental appointments, discovered her blouses mixed in with the dry cleaning, opened and dealt with all her mail.

What had been hardest for him was Camilla's iPhone. He'd brought it home as a part of her personal effects. Left it plugged in on the kitchen counter. The next morning, as he drank coffee, the notifications began to ping and they continued to do so for days as Camilla's friends exchanged messages in group chats she was once a part of. To unplug it meant letting her go. He couldn't do it. Yet, every ping was a cutting reminder that she was gone and that the world continued to turn without her.

Without her. Forever. Life marched on.

Roy remembered how Susie had been, right after. At first, just silent. For days.

He found solace in working long hours. Susie just stayed in bed. The longer he worked, the less he saw of her, and the deeper the chasm between them became.

Then, after about a month, came the anger. How crazy she'd gotten.

Bareto was in a coma, but Camilla was six feet underground. Bareto survived, but their baby was dead.

The angrier she got, the more he drank. To cope. To

anesthetize himself.

And then came the accusations. Susie began to spin out of control.

Camilla was gone because of him. It was his fault.
If only they hadn't moved to Miami.
If only he hadn't bought her the car.
If only they'd lived near the horse stables.
If only…

When Bareto finally succumbed to his injuries, Susie's anger subsided enough that she could listen to reason. She started therapy. Slowly, she began to improve. Bit by bit, she reclaimed her former self. He'd done everything he could to support her. To support them. To keep their marriage alive. He was not going to let this end them.

"Are you okay, sir?"

Roy jolted back into the present, to the whine of the aircraft as it prepped for departure, and looked up into the face of a blonde flight attendant.

"I'm fine," he croaked. Then, clearing his throat, he repeated, "I'm fine."

"I'm going to need you to switch that to airplane mode for me," the flight attendant said, nodding at the smartphone in his hands.

"I have. It is," he lied.

Then, as the flight attendant walked away, he quickly opened Messenger and sent a text.

"Blog post perfect. Love you."

CHAPTER EIGHT

The next day, I tuned in to Susie's radio interview, mainly to see how she was coping with the dreaded anniversary. It went well overall, though the way the interview ended was unsettling.

The show is called *Veronica in the Morning,* and it normally involves Veronica Rios hosting a panel of journalists who comment on the news of the week.

Although Susie studied law, she went into journalism after law school and eventually ended up working in television—first in Austin and later in Miami. It was in the early 2000s that Susie Font made her mark as an investigative reporter by scooping a story exposing the *Gang of Seven*, a group of corrupt politicians and South Florida land developers.

The story exposed her to a lot of heat as the politicians fought to cover up their scheme and identify Susie's sources, even to the point that her offices were raided by police and computer and paper files were confiscated. They didn't find anything useful because Susie had learned early in her career the importance of covering her digital tracks. In fact, Susie's technical skills are exceptional, but more on that later.

The *Gang of Seven* story also won her the respect of her peers. This credibility later added weight to her advocacy work against texting while driving. Her blog had won her a legion of fans, many of whom had also suffered loss.

Susie's credibility was one of the reasons why she had been offered the tail ten-minute slot on Veronica Rios' show as a special guest. That and the fact that the two women were old friends.

Veronica began the interview by touching sufficiently and

delicately on Susie's own tragedy, to provide the necessary context. They talked about the three-year anniversary and the weight that particular date held for both Susie and, no doubt, the Bareto family.

The interview went well. Susie was passionate but professional, grief-stricken yet hopeful.

At the end of the segment, Veronica opened the show to calls from listeners. Several people called in to share their own stories—some tragic, some with happier endings. A few called simply to thank Susie for her advocacy work.

The last caller was different.

"We have time for one more caller," Veronica said. "You are on the air."

"Hello. This is Liz Bareto, Liam Bareto's mother."

First, Susie went cold. Lightheaded. This was one call she hadn't been prepared to take. Then, anger kicked in. She felt blood rush to her cheeks and ears. Her heart began to pound in her chest.

Had Veronica set her up?

She felt ambushed, and looked at Veronica questioningly, then silently swiped a hand across her throat.

Veronica widened her eyes. She held her hands up before her defensively, shaking her head. This hadn't been her idea. She was as surprised as Susie.

"Oh, hello, Mrs. Bareto." Then, adding a suitably sympathetic tone to her voice, she added, "Let me just say, on behalf of all of us here, how very sorry we are for your loss." She glanced at Susie who was slowly shaking her head, staring daggers at her.

"I mean that, while attention is, quite naturally, focused on the victims of texting and driving—we very much appreciate that you too have suffered a loss."

"Thank you, Veronica. I certainly sympathize with Ms. Font and admire the work that she is doing, but I'd like your listeners to know that I don't think it was texting that killed my son."

As Mrs. Bareto spoke, Susie screwed her face up and made a scissor-snipping gesture at Veronica, who acknowledged her friend with a nod, but stopped short of taking action, trying to salvage the call.

"My son was injured as a result of that accident, but his prognosis was good. His condition was improving before he died, and I would like to ask—"

"Mrs. Bareto," Veronica interrupted, "we're really trying to focus on the broader issue of texting while driving. I'd rather not get into the actual details of how this has affected you and Ms. Font personally. Perhaps, on another show we could ask you both to—"

"But, Veronica, I feel it's important that your listeners hear the truth, and if you'd just hear me out, maybe they can help me. I have—"

"Again, Mrs. Bareto—"

"—tried everything, but the police—"

"Mrs. Bareto, I understand—"

The back and forth continued for thirty more agonizing seconds, during which Mrs. Bareto tried to talk about her son and his autopsy. Veronica tried to steer the call to the topic at hand, but Mrs. Bareto was relentless. Finally, Veronica gave up and signaled to her sound engineer to cut the call.

The line went dead.

"Mrs. Bareto... Mrs. Bareto, thank you so much for taking the time to talk to us today, but I'm afraid we're out of time. Before we go, I'd like to thank our special guest, Susie Font, for sharing your story with us along with all of the amazing work you've been doing to raise awareness. That's all for today from me, *Veronica in the Morning*. And, of course, if you're driving while listening to today's show, put that phone away!"

After wrapping and thanking the crew, Veronica led Susie to her office and shut the door.

"Susie, I had no idea she was calling in. I swear."

"I believe you, Roni." Susie sighed, putting her interview notes in her purse.

"I would never do that to you." Veronica opened the window and lit up a cigarette, offering Susie one, who declined. "What's up with her?"

"Long story. Short version, she's crazy. Her son's injuries were critical. But, she's deluded herself into thinking that he was on the road to recovery. She just wants someone to blame."

"For what? He was the one texting and driving."

"Exactly. It was all his fault. He caused a head-on collision. He was in a coma for a few months. And then he died. I feel for her, but she's... " Susie caught her breath. She realized that she was more agitated than she'd thought. She reached out, indicating the cigarette, and Veronica leaned over and handed it to her. Susie took a deep drag and held it, handing back the cigarette. She looked out the window for few seconds and forced calm into her voice. She exhaled smoke, and said, "She's trying to find a scapegoat. I suppose it's her way of dealing with it all. She's relentless."

Susie picked her purse up off Veronica's desk. "And she's been pedaling that autopsy shit for a while now. Claims her son died of something other than the injuries from the wreck."

"From what?"

"Fuck if I know, Roni. I don't think even *she* knows. Something about needle marks on his arm. I never got the details. She's nuts."

Susie looked at Veronica with teary eyes. "She scares me. Actually showed up at our house once and wouldn't leave. We had to call the police, get a restraining order... "

Veronica's eyes widened as she released a puff of smoke through the slit in the window, and put out the cigarette. "For real? Oh, you poor thing. As if you haven't been through enough."

"Tell me about it."

There was an awkward silence as the sound of traffic outside pushed its way in through the open window. The two women looked at each other.

"Anyway, Roni. Thank you so much for this," Susie said, hugging her friend.

"No worries. Great show, girl. You ever think of coming back? TV, not radio; I don't need the competition... "

CHAPTER NINE

Susie left the radio station and went home. She changed into running clothes—lululemon tights, jogging bra, a loose top, and a pair of Asics—and went for a run. A fast-paced three-mile loop on historic Old Cutler Road was what she needed. She felt wound up after the interview. At first, she thought it was anger at hearing from Liz Bareto. But something else was niggling at her. She wasn't sure what, but she felt frustrated, off-kilter, and she needed to burn off steam.

Old Cutler Road is a beautiful, winding thoroughfare framed by monstrous banyan trees. The branches of the prehistoric-looking banyans meet and mix over the two-lane road, forming a canopy that makes it feel as though the road runs through a tunnel of foliage. Impressive is an understatement. How many streets do you know that have their own Wikipedia page?

Susie and Roy live in a small, private subdivision off of Old Cutler Road called *Lago Beach*. Eighteen houses make up the neighborhood. Each on more than an acre. A few—like theirs—with direct access to the water.

Their house is big, a traditional Mediterranean-style home with wrought iron balcony railings, Spanish barrel tile roof, and limestone accents. The house is off-white with ivy growing up along the tower wall.

As Susie left their home and ran down Old Cutler, she thought about Liz Bareto's latest intrusion into her life. The pounding of her feet and heart and her rhythmic breathing got her into a sort of meditative state. She thought about Camilla, Roy, and herself. As she did, she began to see things more clearly. And a realization began to take shape in her head.

Upon returning from her run, she got herself a bottle of water and went out back behind the house to sit on the dock and think. Their dock is large, spanning over 120 feet of waterfront. The waters below are full of sea life, and Susie often went there when she needed to be alone. She loved the tranquility.

She sat on the edge of the dock in the twenty-foot section between their two boats. Susie and Roy have a thirty-six-foot fishing boat and a fifty-five-foot yacht. As a family, they'd spent their fair share of time on the water, fishing, lounging, exploring the Bahamas. After they lost Camilla, both boats just sat there, idle. Monuments to their grief.

Susie noticed that she had several missed calls from Roy. But she was ignoring them, for now. She needed some alone time to process what she'd been thinking, to put all the pieces of her realization together. To decide what it meant.

In order for you to understand Susie's reasoning, there is something you should know about her. I've shared quite a bit about Roy so far, but not so much about her. It's important to me that, by the time we're finished, you know everything there is to know about them both—or at least everything I know.

One thing that you come to appreciate, as a parent, is just how much of your child's personality is hardwired at birth. Some boys are athletic and others bookish, no matter how much their parents try to influence them. Similarly, some girls love playing dress-up with dolls while others prefer tree climbing and slingshots.

As a child, Susie loved baby dolls. She had the little stroller, playpen, baby bottles, and even the diapers. Babies fascinated her. She played with these toys incessantly until her brother, Chris, was born. Then, at the age of six, she gave up all of her baby toys and focused her attention on her baby brother to the point that her parents called her "mini-mom."

Susie grew into a smart, capable woman: law school graduate, respected journalist. But there's no mistaking the fact that she finds fulfillment in children. She is maternal. In my opinion, this maternal side to her is and always has been part of her nature.

Fate, being the cruel bastard it is, targeted this maternal

element of Susie's. And no, I'm not just referring to the loss of Camilla. It's more complicated than that.

When Susie married Roy, her maternal instincts kicked in. She wanted nothing more than to start a family. The subject wasn't something the two discussed at length. She simply stopped taking birth control, and he was fine with that.

Susie started a fertility calendar. She regularly tracked her cycle, ovulation, timed sex, and followed every tip on conception that her research yielded. Yet, month after month, breathless anticipation and cautious excitement culminated in a negative pregnancy test.

She knew that being unable to conceive for a few months was perfectly normal. All her research confirmed this. After six months, she began to worry. After twelve, Roy noticed a shift in her mood. She became withdrawn, distant, and when he finally confronted her, she broke down and confessed what she had come to believe, that she was in some way "defective." Roy did his best to assuage his wife, but after two more months with no results, they went to a doctor, a fertility specialist.

They got tested, confirming Susie's fears. Her condition was diagnosed as polycystic ovarian syndrome—a hormonal imbalance that makes conception difficult. PCOS is not uncommon; one in ten women have it. The good news is that it can be treated. In vitro fertilization is a common, successful solution to PCOS-related infertility.

On their second attempt at IVF, Susie conceived.

She felt like they had cheated fate.

They kept the news to themselves through the first trimester, though Susie immediately went into nesting mode: decorating the nursery, buying things she would need for the hospital and to wear on delivery day, compiling lists of suitable preschools. She checked her belly in the mirror daily to see if she was showing.

She was ecstatic.

Then came the shocker. More good news. At her twelve-week check-up, they were thrilled to learn that Susie was carrying not one, but two babies. During the sonogram, they heard the two little heartbeats, a sound Susie described as "two underwater choo-

choo trains racing each other." Six weeks later, they were told that the two choo-choos were going to be a boy and a girl.

In bed at night, Susie would hold the scratchy black-and-white-framed sonograms she kept on her bedside table and admire her little ones. She was grateful to whatever in the cosmos was responsible for their blessing, all the while trying to process the fact that, in just eighteen weeks, she had gone from thinking of herself as a barren, "defective" woman to being six months away from holding her own little boy *and* girl.

It was at this point that fate's fickle finger began to toy with Susie Font. Despite the prenatal vitamins, maternity yoga, and meditation, she suffered numerous complications. The nausea she could handle. But when the bleeding began, her doctor prescribed bed rest. Despite following doctor's orders to the letter, her condition did not improve. She spent the second half of her pregnancy in bed.

Just three weeks from her due date, fate's cruel fingers curled into a fist and punched Susie in the belly. No matter how many times they rescanned at Susie's request, the result was the same. One little heart had stopped beating. Their little boy. Their precious baby boy had died.

There followed three weeks of agonizing bipolarity. On the one hand, Susie felt joy and anticipation at being only weeks away from holding her baby girl. Simultaneously, she suffered with the grotesque knowledge that her little girl was gestating in her womb, next to her brother's corpse.

Mercifully, the delivery went off without a hitch. Their little girl came into the world without any complications. Seven pounds, five ounces. Nineteen inches long. They named her Camilla, after Susie's grandmother.

As she held her baby in her arms, Susie allowed herself to believe that, somehow, she had cheated fate. She was wrong.

Fate's next move took the form of Liam Bareto. And, while Liam paid for his mistake with his life, as far as Susie was concerned, fate won. Camilla was gone.

Now, three years later, Susie was sitting on the dock behind her house. The breeze played with her hair. She closed her eyes and imagined that it was Camilla's fingers playing with her hair. She could almost feel Camilla kissing her forehead.

Although she'd conceived two children, fate took one before birth, and the second at sixteen. And Susie felt she had failed them both.

The tears came. She let them tickle her cheek. Her mind wandered back to the radio interview and the phone call from Bareto's mother. She wiped her face and eyes and sighed.

Maybe her therapist was right. This third-anniversary thing was affecting her more than she thought. She'd been thinking a lot about Camilla, obviously.

But something had happened to Susie during the radio interview. She had analyzed it as she ran. Liz Bareto was relentless in her pursuit of "the truth" about her son's death. Three years later, she was still beating the same drum. She was driven, passionate. Susie admired Bareto's drive, even though she thought it was ill advised.

Susie did not feel the same passion. In comparison, her advocacy work felt empty, meaningless. A waste of time. And as she sat on the dock, she felt she understood, for the first time, how important her maternal side was to her own identity.

Camilla had been her purpose in life. When she died, Susie was gutted—spiritually. Camilla's death left a hole in Susie's soul.

Roy had suffered the same loss. But he had filled that hole with work. He had immersed himself in his company, and he thrived. Susie had sought to do the same with advocacy. It was her way of attempting to right the wrong that had been done to her daughter. To avenge her.

But, what did she really have to show for her efforts? No new legislation had passed. Her attempt to increase fines and penalties for texting while driving had failed. What she felt as she sat in the radio studio, and what she'd admitted to herself when she'd gone on her run, was that she was just going through the motions.

The cause was a good one. But Susie felt no passion for it. And worse, after three years, she had nothing to show for all her efforts. No results.

She lacked purpose—this was her realization. She was by

nature a mother. A nurturer. A protector. And with Camilla gone, she had no one to nurture, no one to protect.

Liz Bareto's call was what got Susie thinking about her own purpose in life.

About righting wrongs.

It got Susie to thinking about Tom and Deb Wise, and their daughter Kristy.

Susie needed a purpose.

She was a protector.

She understood, perhaps for the first time fully, that this was her path.

CHAPTER TEN

As Susie sat on the dock watching a spotted eagle stingray glide through the water, contemplating her plan, her phone "pinged."

Call me. Home soon.

A text message from Roy.

He'd called several times, starting just after the radio show. But Susie still hadn't responded. Even if her plan was feasible, what would she tell Roy?

She wouldn't have been sitting where she was if it wasn't for Roy. The two of them had built a life together. But it was complicated.

The thing is, Susie had known who Roy was long before meeting him. She had, in fact, sought him out. How Susie knew of him and how she'd found him were secrets that she would eventually share with me. But, as she sat there on that dock, if asked, she would have sworn that she would never tell anyone—ever.

Things change.

To Susie, Roy was amazing in many ways. She believed he could accomplish anything he put his mind to. That's why she had pushed him to go into business. She knew he had more to offer, and to gain, in business than in law. And, more importantly, she knew it would make him happier.

She was right.

Yet, for all his strengths, Roy was also a bit broken. At least, he seemed that way to Susie. Roy was practically an orphan. When they met, she had to really pry to get any details at all from him about his childhood. And what she got was minimal.

To say his family was dysfunctional was an understatement.

He was estranged from both of his parents. His twin had died when Roy was young, which pretty much killed his parents' marriage. Roy had been sent off to live in Galveston with his grandmother.

Now, having gone through what they had with Camilla's death, Susie could sympathize.

Susie had never met her mother-in-law. She'd drunk herself to death before Roy and Susie married.

Roy's father had attended their wedding, but only after Susie had insisted against Roy's wishes. When she'd met him, it was all she could do not to gasp. He was a shadow of a man—rumpled, twitchy, with hands that trembled when he shook hers as if he had some kind of disease.

Despite his bedraggled appearance, she could nonetheless see her husband in him. He was lean like Roy, with high cheekbones and thick black hair. He had Roy's intense, deep green eyes and perfect teeth. The main differences, aside from age, were that Roy has a crooked smile—the right side always goes up more than the left for some reason—and their skin tone. Roy had inherited his mother's light complexion. Roy's father was dark-skinned, ethnic.

Susie's phone rang, snapping her back to the present. She watched it ring, studying the word *Roy* on the screen, along with a picture of that crooked smile of his. And she came to a decision. A big decision.

"Hello."

"Hey, Suze! Where have you been? I was worried about you. You alright?"

"Hi. Yeah. Sure," she said softly.

"Are you sure?"

"Yeah. Fine."

Silence. The water sloshed just below Susie in response to something big moving just under the surface.

"So? How did it go?" Roy asked, his voice light and positive.

Susie sighed, her thoughts swirling around in her brain like a whirlpool. "Um, good. All good. I think it went okay. Except the end, I guess. How did it sound live?" She scrunched her nose.

"Okay? The whole piece was great! The end...hardly

noticeable. Roni's a pro. It sounded like you three were actually going to chat after the show." Roy paused. "You didn't, did you?"

Susie clicked her tongue. "No. Of course not. Roni is good, though. It sounded okay to me, but I wanted to get your impression—you know, from the outside."

"Well, yeah. It was smooth. Well handled. I'm really proud of you." There was another pause. "Listen, babe, you home? I'm practically pulling up to the house."

"Oh." Susie smiled. "Sure. I'm out back. See you in a bit. Um, I also have an idea I want to run by you."

"Right. Okay… well, see you in five. Bye."

Susie dropped the phone between her legs. She was sitting cross-legged on the dock. She watched the wind ripple across the water and a jumping fish freeing itself, temporarily, from the weight of its watery world. She spotted the large stingray again. Prowling. Hunting. A predator seeking prey.

The symbolism was as clear to her as the sun was warm on her face. She breathed deep and took comfort in what she saw there as an omen.

Minutes later, she heard a car door close and the sound of footsteps on the dock behind her. She didn't turn around, just waited for Roy to sit down next to her. He was still wearing his suit, no tie.

"Hey, you," he said, softly.

"Hey," she said, smiling back.

"Are you okay?" he asked, leaning forward to make eye contact with her.

"I'm good," she said, flashing another smile, but Roy could tell there was something on her mind.

"So, what did you want to talk about?"

She hesitated, feigning interest in the lapping water before saying, "You're going to think… well, I don't know what you're going to think."

"Try me," he urged with a reassuring smile.

"Well," she began, "all this has got me thinking. By *all this* I mean, it's been three years now, you know, since Camilla. And all the emotions, they're not as raw, but they're still there, you know?"

Roy nodded but didn't respond, allowing his wife to continue. She looked at him and said, earnestly, "Don't get me wrong. I know that whatever we do now, whatever happens, nothing is going to bring her back. Nothing. I know that. Anyway. It got me to thinking about the folks we met up at Beaver Creek."

"The nutjobs?" Roy asked, flippantly.

Susie scowled, then looked away, silent.

Roy noted her reaction. "Suze, sorry, but I don't understand. What do they have to do with anything?"

"Do you really think they're crazy?" She didn't wait for an answer. "I mean, hearing Liz Bareto again today brought it all back. All of the feelings. The anger. The despair. The emptiness." Susie turned toward Roy and through gritted teeth added, "The hate."

Roy didn't respond.

"Think about it. If we wanted that son of a bitch Bareto dead... just for being stupid, just for texting, can you imagine how it must feel for them? How you would feel if someone had intentionally set out to hurt Camilla. I wanted Bareto dead. I really did. I mean, I could taste it. And he was just careless. Just imagine what we'd want to do to him if he had intentionally hurt our baby girl."

Roy nodded, unable to speak from the knot that had formed in his throat.

"Think about it. I mean take a few to really think about how it would feel if someone had hurt our baby and got away with it like this guy Harlan did?"

"I... can't," Roy said, shaking his head and looking out to the horizon.

"Well, I can," Susie said evenly. "I can understand perfectly why they'd want revenge. I can understand, because *I still do*." She hesitated, and then added, "And what worries me is that you don't. There's a gap here, Roy, between us. Between you and me. An empty space. We didn't protect her. We failed her. *We* failed our daughter. And it's tearing me apart. It's tearing *us* apart."

Roy swallowed hard. Susie had hit a soft spot. She knew he had been crushed by his parents' divorce, and that he would do anything not to follow their path.

They sat in silence for a while, each processing their respective thoughts.

A long while.

Too long.

Susie looked at her husband and watched as he sat, jaw flexing, staring across the water. Then, suddenly, she jumped to her feet and began walking back toward the house.

"Suze?"

"Don't fucking 'Suze' me, Roy," she threw over her shoulder.

"I thought you wanted to talk."

She whirled back at him. "I did! I did talk. It's a two-way street, Roy. I am talking. You're just sitting there."

"What do you want me to say?" he asked, standing and facing her, but his shoulders were slouched, his hands thrust in his pockets like a naughty child.

"Fuck!" she screamed. "Something. Anything. The 'strong silent type' thing only works if there is some 'strong' to back up the 'silent.' You're just fucking *silent*. All of your fucking planning, all of your fucking philosophizing... but when it comes to feeling something, saying something, *doing something*... you've got nothing."

Roy gaped at her. He had no idea where all of this was coming from. He thought they were past this. Could he have truly been so blind? The ineptitude of his blindness seared hot shame onto his cheeks.

Susie looked around to see if anybody was listening to them and then lowered her voice anyway as she walked slowly back toward him. "Do you even care? Tell me. Do you even miss her? Camilla? Our daughter? Our only child? Our baby?" He said nothing, and her voice rose to almost a scream again, "Do you have a fucking ounce of emotion for her? For us?" she seethed, tears welling in her eyes.

"You know I do." he said quickly, in an effort to diffuse her anger.

"Well, why don't you show it?" she asked, her voice thick with exasperation, like a mother scolding her disappointment of a child. "When Camilla died, I felt empty. Hollow. Like someone had reached down my throat and ripped out my insides. I *was* dead. And when I was lucid enough to realize I wasn't, I wanted to die. And worse, I carried this suffocating belief that she never truly knew just how much I loved her. Losing her almost destroyed me. I wanted to do something to show her how I felt. To prove how much I loved her. Why do you think I quit TV? Why do you think I do all this... this advocacy shit? I thought I could show her. I thought I could channel the energy... the hate... into something good. Positive. In her memory. For her."

Roy swallowed, then cleared the lump in his throat and looked into his wife's blazing eyes. He kept his voice even and calm. "Susie. It's been three years. It's the anniversary. It makes perfect sense that you're feeling like this. I do too. But I have to keep it under control because if I don't... " the words died in his throat.

"What?" she prompted, impatiently.

"If I don't. Then I won't be able to see you clearly. To be there for you."

Hot tears burned down Susie's cheeks as she stifled a sob. "You don't get it. You just don't get it. You don't get me... " Then, she allowed the tears to come, slowly at first and then with familiar heart-wrenching convulsions as she dropped to her knees.

Roy crouched next to her, slowly at first, warily. "Susie. Babe. I've got you." He cooed, "I love you." He pulled her into his arms and was flooded with relief when she didn't push him away. "We're doing great. We're in a good place." He stroked her hair, gently. "You're going to be okay. You've come so far."

Susie stiffened. Then, suddenly, pushed him away to the point that he lost his balance and fell onto his ass on the deck. She stood and wiped her eyes and nose on the back of her arm. She was done crying. She looked at him, her face glowering. "Come so far? *You've come so far*," she repeated in a singsong voice. "What the *FUCK* does that even mean? Far from where, Roy? From crazy? So far from *fucking* crazy? At least I reacted. Where the fuck were you? At the office? In meetings?" she spat.

Roy rose to his feet. "That's not fair," he said in a measured voice.

"Fair?" She walked up to him and poked a finger into his

chest. "You want to talk about what's fair? Really? Fair? That fucker took our daughter from us, Roy. Was that fair? Her head was *crushed* because of him. Was that fair? She's rotting in a coffin right now, as we speak, because of him. Was that fair?

"Me, hating his fucking guts. Is that fair? Yes, it is. And would anyone blame me for it? No, they wouldn't. And am I happy he's dead? I'm glad he's rotting in the ground. So. Fucking. Glad." She paused to take a tremulous breath before adding, "I only wish I'd done it. No," she continued. "I wish you'd done it. I wish you'd cared enough about your daughter... our daughter... to do something about it. I wish you'd had the balls to... " she choked back tears. "I wish you'd had the balls to avenge our baby girl!"

With that, she turned and left, leaving Roy to gawk after her, shell-shocked.

CHAPTER ELEVEN

Radio show host Veronica Rios sat pensively at her desk. Her boss had just left her office. After complimenting her on the day's show, he'd asked about the last caller during the Susie Font interview.

"What was that all about?"

Veronica had blown it off as "nothing," and he'd nodded and let it go.

But she wasn't so sure.

She'd known Susie Font for years. She knew her to be a good journalist and a good person. If there's one thing Veronica was good at, it was getting the measure of people.

But, not unlike her friend, she also had a good nose for news. And there was something about the Bareto/Font exchange that was bugging her.

She was biting the tip of her pen and staring at the phone number scrawled on the yellow sticky note in front of her. As much as she tried to resist the urge, she couldn't stop herself from picking up the phone and dialing.

One ring.

Two rings.

Three rings.

"This is Liz. Please leave a message at the tone."

Veronica hesitated, but figured that she had nothing to lose.

"Mrs. Bareto, this is Veronica Rios from *Veronica in the Morning*. I'm sorry we got disconnected at the end of the show. I'm going to leave you my mobile number, you know, in case you'd like to talk… "

* * *

After Susie stormed off the dock, Roy decided to give her some space. He retreated to his study, where he now sat brooding as he listened to the distant clunk and clang of Susie preparing dinner.

He'd been in his study for over two hours. He wasn't sure what he should do next. Part of him wanted to join Susie in the kitchen and try to talk to her. The other didn't want to be anywhere near her right now. He was angry. Hurt.

But, mostly, he was worried.

He got himself a glass from the bar, poured himself a Macallan 18, and retook his chair, putting the bottle on the desk in front of him. As he gazed out the window, he saw a three-foot-long iguana slowly moving across the lawn outside. Roy envied the simplicity of the reptile's life.

Lucky bastard.

He played Susie's words back in his mind, her scene on the dock. He was pretty sure that she was proposing that they kill this Harlan kid.

Oddly, that wasn't what had Roy worried. Something else that Susie had said preoccupied his thoughts. Something more important.

Roy knew himself.

He had long suspected that he had a touch of manic-depression. He'd never sought any clinical validation of his self-diagnosis. To his mind, doctors are mostly idiots. Idiots following protocols. Glorified statisticians. There's nothing a doctor could tell him that WebMD couldn't.

Roy had researched manic-depression. He'd read up on everything he could regarding his assumed condition, and even kept a journal of his various moods for the better part of nine months.

He found that, about every sixty days, he would go into a funk that would last two to three weeks. His grandmother called it the "blues."

Roy told me that, growing up, he sometimes noticed that Grandma's mood would shift. She would withdraw, play less. She would become quiet, listless. He worried about her. One day, he plucked up the courage to ask, "What's wrong, Grandma?"

After a few moments, Grandma came out of her stare into middle distance. She turned to him, and smiled, "Nothing, sweetie. I've just got the blues."

"What's that?"

"Well, it's when you feel tired on no account. And, no matter how hard you try, nothing really gets you going. You just kind of... "

The old lady allowed the words to trail off. She could see that she wasn't explaining herself well to the little boy. So, she tried again. "You know *The Wizard of Oz*?"

Little Roy nodded.

"Well, you remember all the beautiful colors, and the munchkins, and the Lollipop Guild, and the Yellow Brick Road, and the magical witches?"

He smiled, nodding.

"Well, that's how life is most of the time, full of color. And that's how it should be. But, there's times when life feels like the beginning of the movie, all gloomy and in black and white. That's the blues."

"Is that what's wrong with Momma?" the little boy asked.

"Something like that, honey, but don't you worry." She ruffled her grandson's hair. "Everything's gonna turn out alright."

It hadn't.

Roy's mother all but killed herself. Suicide by vodka. She'd inherited the blues from Grandma, but not Grandma's strength. Roy had inherited both, or so he believed. And for this, he felt indebted to her—not just for raising him, but for her genes.

When he turned twenty-one, he legally changed his name from Roy Diaz to Roy Cruise, adopting Grandma's family name. He did it partly as a thank-you to her, but also because he was older and shrewd enough to know that a name like Diaz was a liability if you wanted to *succeed* in Texas.

While Roy may have inherited his father's green eyes, he didn't inherit his dark skin. When Roy was out and about with Grandma, who was also light complected like Roy and his mother, he was just another little white boy. The waitresses called him "young man." The men tousled his hair and called him "little buddy."

On the few occasions that his father bothered to visit his son after the divorce, he'd take him out for ice cream. When he was with his father, who was darker skinned and had more "Latin" features, Roy was suddenly the "little Mexican kid." This was the reaction, even though his father was actually Cuban.

No free extra scoop of ice cream. No friendly chitchat with the waitress. They weren't mistreated. No one was abusive. But they weren't welcomed with open arms either. They were treated as outsiders.

In Texas, there are no Peruvians, or Columbians, or Cubans. Only Mexicans. If you look "ethnically Latin" in Texas, you are Mexican. If you have a Spanish surname, you are Mexican. And, to the dominant Anglo culture, you are an outsider.

When Roy showed his grandma the court order changing his name, her milky grey eyes filled with tears and she pulled him close. Roy knew what continuing her family name meant to her. To his mind, it was the least he could do for her, and it benefited him as well.

He told me that he would never forget the look on her face that day and how good he felt. He was happy to be able to give something back to the woman who'd raised him. And it was thanks to her that, when Roy reached puberty and experienced his own blues for the first time, he wasn't caught off guard.

Right now—at this point in the story—he'd had the blues for a couple of weeks. It wasn't anything to do with the anniversary of Camilla's death. At least, he didn't think so.

It *was* probably why he'd been so quiet on the dock.

This was one big downside to fighting with Susie. She understood him and, somehow, although he had no clue how, she managed to lessen the symptoms of his blues. She gave him life. Fighting with her killed the energy.

But, when they were in sync, everything was amazing.

It had been that way ever since they had met.

Roy sighed and poured himself another scotch as he pictured Susie the day he'd first set eyes on her. It was in law school. She was wearing worn-out jeans. Stan Smiths shoes. A white v-neck t-shirt. And some kind of a jacket. Her hair was up in a ponytail. Dark, but streaked with highlights from the summer sun.

She was tanned golden. Her eyes were jet-black and her face was lively. Animated. She was wearing little gemstone earrings—studs of some sort. She had fine bones and hands, thin elegant fingers with short, polished nails, and although she was petite, she stood out.

Roy could feel her energy from across the courtyard. As though she was pulsating with life. Her eyes sparkled. Her smile beamed, lighting up her whole face.

She looked to Roy as though she lived in Oz, in the land of color, like she carried it with her everywhere she went. When they began dating, he found that her energy was the perfect counterpoint to the world into which he sank at regular intervals, that black and white Kansas that he inhabited.

Her energy had attracted him, and now it sustained him. He drew strength from her, and amazingly, rather than being diminished by him, she shone brighter as a result.

They were the perfect match.

When Camilla died, everything changed. At first, there was nothing. Susie was just gone. Vacant. Empty.

There was no energy for him. There was no energy at all.

Roy suffered through it all alone.

As he thought back, he wasn't sure if what came next had been any better. He remembered, as he sipped and savored the feeling of the scotch burning his throat. He stared across the study at the spot on the oriental rug in front of the sofa where he'd seen Susie at her worst.

CHAPTER TWELVE

It had happened several months after Camilla died. Susie had slowly made the transition from silent depression to active accusations.

In her mind, Roy was to blame. She had meticulously assembled a barrage of accusations, saddling him with blame and guilt for everything, which she would unleash with twisted zeal. She added to her list daily. Big and little things—his fault for buying Camilla the car, for letting her keep her horse so far from the house, for moving to Miami—all the accidentals—any one of which, had he acted differently, could have saved *her* baby.

Over the course of a few weeks, Susie's attacks had grown in duration and detail. She was building up to something. He could sense it.

It was her last attack, the one in the study where he now sat, that changed everything.

He remembered that it had started out as usual—Susie attacking, and him passively listening. The by-that-point-familiar crescendo of screaming and accusations grew, Roy shaking his head at intervals, but not provoking. Just playing his role.

Near the peak, when normally she would cry or add a few new insults or claims against him, she stopped. It seemed as if she'd come to a revelation. Like an opera singer getting to that final, climactic high note but not hitting it—instead suddenly stopping—and just looking out at the audience. Susie had just stopped and stared at him.

Roy had gotten nervous—this was something new, and in his life of those last few months, "new" was always "bad." He recalled shifting uncomfortably in his seat on the sofa.

Susie had walked over to the bar in his study and poured herself a drink. Scotch. She never drank scotch. She claimed it made her sick.

Then, she'd walked back to the center of the room and, in one graceful move, sat on the floor in front of the sofa Indian-style, and looked up at him.

Roy remembered the moment as if it were yesterday. For the first time in weeks, she had been smiling. The deep creases caused by her angry expression of minutes before were gone, ironed out by the warmth of her beautiful eyes. He could still feel the chill in his soul as he thought back to her words.

"You know what it is, Roy? Babe. It's not you. I know that. And I'm so sorry," she voiced the apology softly, holding her chest. "I've been blaming you. But it's not you. I mean," she swirled the drink in her glass and sniffed, looking around her, "I just... I think this has all become a bit of a habit. All the yelling. The blaming. I know it's not your fault."

She'd looked at him, shaking her head and grimacing at the realization of what she had become.

"It's just, I've been feeling so fucking helpless. So useless." She'd choked back tears. "And I can't do... haven't done anything.

"But there is something," she'd sniffed, and shuffled closer to her husband, taking a large swig from her glass, wincing at the scotch. "There is something *we* can do. As parents." She'd paused. "It's just a matter of equilibrium. Of balance. Things have to balance. They must always balance. And I think now I know exactly how to do that."

She had stared into Roy's eyes and waited until he felt compelled to speak.

"How?"

"Think about it," she'd said slowly, eyes wide as if she'd just discovered the secret to life itself. Then, she'd placed a hand on her husband's knee. "What does it say, in the Old Testament?"

Roy had tilted his head, curious.

"The law of talion," she'd said, opening the palm of her free hand, looking at it and offering it up as if it held something divine.

Roy squinted. He thought he knew what his wife was intimating, but he recalled thinking to himself at the time, *It can't be.*

"An eye for an eye, Roy. An eye for an eye," she'd confirmed for him, and then downed the rest of her drink with a grimace. She looked too happy to Roy, given what she'd just suggested. Her smile, in combination with the proposal, seemed maniacal. "The only question is," she'd continued, licking her lips, "how do we do it?"

"Susie. I don't think... "

"Don't *think*, Roy. Feel." She'd stretched the word out. *Feeeel.* "You know it *feels* right. You know it *is* right."

"Susie. Even if it was, there's a system. There's a process."

"Fuck that, Roy!" she'd barked. "You know how the system works. *If* it works. You're a lawyer. What? Negligent manslaughter? A year in jail, then parole? Community service?

"That son of a bitch," she said, and held out her arm, pointing, "going around giving speeches to a bunch of pimple-faced, fuck-tard high school kids about texting and driving? Fuck the system, Roy! I'm talking about self-help here."

"Suze, but... " he had almost whispered, "you want us to kill him?"

"You fucking bet I do."

She wasn't angry. She was smiling and repeatedly running her finger around the rim of the empty glass and then licking it. He had never seen her like this.

He felt uneasy, and something else.

"Susie, even if we wanted to... " He noted a cloud pass over her expression at his words, and quickly backpedaled, "No, I mean. I agree with you. I *want* to. But even if we contemplated doing something like this, we'd be the first people they'd look at as suspects."

"Not if the cause of death is natural," she had said, tilting her head playfully from side to side. "Not if they don't ever think to even consider it a homicide."

"*Any* investigation would start with us." Roy paused as his wife looked at him, expectantly. Then he realized, "You're saying, do it now? While he's in the hospital. In a coma?"

"Of course now!" She'd put the scotch glass on the floor, putting both hands on Roy's knees. "Now. He's in an induced coma, Roy. They put him in it, and they're gonna pull him out of it. You heard. The prognosis is good, but anything can happen. He *was* in a head-on, after all... "

"He may end up a vegetable," Roy threw back, weakly.

"Not if he's dead," she'd smirked. "He killed Camilla, Roy. An eye for an eye," she'd said, slowly.

He'd taken a few seconds to allow the gravity of his wife's words to sink in. Then, he'd stolen a glance around the room and out the window, the guilt at discussing murder causing him to confirm there were no witnesses. He'd looked back at his wife, or whoever the woman was that was inhabiting her body.

"Why not wait until he's out of it," he had offered with a shrug. "Let things play out. He might even die of natural causes or maybe even end up living the rest of his life as a vegetable. That'd be natural justice."

"Justice? Justice, Roy?! Justice is what they preach at church to children and old women to make them feel safe. This isn't about justice. This is about revenge, Roy," she'd said, eyes blazing, "Fucking revenge."

That was the moment. The look in her eyes, the spite in her voice, and the curl of her lip as she spat out the word "justice," and the sensuous, almost lascivious way Susie had mouthed "fucking revenge."

Roy's wife, as he knew her, wasn't sitting there anymore. Susie had disappeared. Gone. She'd been consumed by grief, and this malicious thing had taken her place. A primal alter ego. Someone he had never met before, but who had apparently been there all the while, lurking, waiting.

But, here's the thing. Though it wasn't the Susie he knew, he remembered feeling just as attracted to the imposter as he was to his wife. She was terrifying, but seductive. A primordial creature that was undoubtedly capable of cruelty, but possessed of such a moral clarity about what she was saying that Roy couldn't disagree. He was drawn to her. He needed her. He loved her.

"And if we get caught?" he'd found himself asking.

The question hung in the air for a while, each running through a mental trailer of what exactly that might look like.

Roy's heart had pounded against his ribcage. The thought of what they were considering had made him feel giddy.

And then, his mind had gone to work. How could they do it? What exactly would it take? It was an insane idea. The fact that he was even considering it terrified him, but it also made him feel powerful. He no longer felt uneasy, but now he knew what the something else was that he had been feeling before. He'd felt aroused.

Roy had understood back then that the burden fell to him. Susie and Camilla were his. His responsibility. Camilla was gone. Susie was in pain and had been for a long time. She needed this. He needed her.

If he denied her this, what would become of them?

He knew from his parents' experience what the death of a child could do to a family. And he had already vowed that he would never let the same thing happen to his marriage.

Susie had jumped to her feet, paused momentarily to pick up her scotch glass from the floor, and left the study.

Roy hadn't moved. He later remembered that all of his energy had been focused on fielding the tsunami of questions flooding through his brain. "What ifs" and "buts" and "hows." If they pulled this off, it would change their life.

He could do it.

He could figure out how.

He would.

Susie interrupted his thinking when she came back into the study and returned the freshly washed glass to its home on a tray by his desk. She knew how much he needed order in his workspace.

She knows you. She loves you. Do you love her?

Suddenly, as if she had only been testing him, Susie said, "You're right. It'd be too obvious. If either of us did it. It'd never work. It can't happen. Not like that.

"Goodnight, babe." She'd bent over and kissed him on the cheek. "You know something? You're a real smart guy." She'd patted his hand lovingly and then left the room.

They'd never spoken of that day or conversation again. They'd come close in Colorado. He'd wanted to, but she had put him off. Until today, on the dock.

But he had thought about it. He'd thought about it a lot.

Susie was right. It did feel empty. Bareto had left this world, but he had not been *punished*.

This had been eating at Roy and it was why he'd brought up the subject in Colorado—an eye for an eye—the God of Abraham.

They had done nothing.

He had done nothing.

Yet, after that conversation in the study, everything had seemed to improve.

Susie's attacks on him had stopped.

Bareto had never come out of the coma. He'd died. Complications from the head trauma, according to the autopsy. Justice served. But not revenge.

Shortly after, Susie had begun therapy.

Probably as a result of therapy, she'd left television and gone into advocacy.

He thought that it had worked for her.

That she was all good.

As he sat in the study, brooding, this is what had Roy worried. This is why he was preoccupied. This was important.

He'd thought that she had moved on. That the woman he had met that day three years back in his study had gone back into her cave, and returned his Susie to him.

But Susie had told him point blank a few hours earlier on the dock that it was still an issue. They had not avenged their little girl. There was still a gap between them. A space between them.

We failed our daughter. And it's tearing me apart. It's tearing us apart.

That was something Roy couldn't live with because, in his heart, he knew—as horrible as it sounded—that he could live without Camilla, but he couldn't live without Susie.

CHAPTER THIRTEEN

Liz Bareto didn't bother returning Veronica Rio's phone call that evening. Instead, the next morning she went to the radio station and waited until Veronica arrived at 8:00 a.m.

Liz had brought with her a manila folder, which was now in front of Veronica on her desk.

"Ms. Rios. I know Liam made a mistake. And I know the consequences were tragic. But he should still be alive."

Veronica, not unaccustomed to posing hard-hitting, some would say callous, questions when the story called for it, chose her words very carefully. "Mrs. Bareto, I can understand your frustration, and can't even imagine how it must feel to have lost a son, but I am a journalist. I have to deal with facts. Evidence. When you say your son should still be alive, are you claiming that the doctors made a mistake, or are you suggesting something else?" The question was posed carefully. Veronica already knew the answer. That's the very reason she had contacted this woman in the first place.

"I don't know exactly. I have three pieces of evidence and, for what it's worth, a mother's instinct. The police weren't able to make heads or tails of it all, but I know there's something here, and I'm hoping you might be able to help." She looked at the woman, eyes full of hope, and then she glanced at the folder.

Veronica made a show of hesitating, and then nodded. "Okay."

Bareto opened the folder, and began, "When Liam was in the hospital, I was with him every day. I took off work. My boss was great about it. That particular day, I had gone to get a coffee from the vending machine on the third floor—one floor down. When I stepped off the elevator, there was activity—staff rushing around—

alarms blaring."

"Liam coded?"

She nodded and said, "I rushed down the corridor toward his room—it was right at the end—he had a private room. We have very good insurance." She squeezed her eyes shut for a beat and swallowed hard. "When I got there, they were working on him." She paused, fighting off the memory of that moment. "They wouldn't let me in. Jenny—the duty nurse—pulled me out into the hall and talked to me. She tried to keep me calm." Bareto paused again. "But, um, they couldn't revive him." Veronica wanted to say something, but instead she let the woman continue. "When the autopsy report came back," she said, holding out a several-pages-long document in her hands, "it stated that Liam died 'as a result of brain trauma consistent with injuries' from the accident."

Veronica pursed her lips, nodding.

Bareto ploughed on. "I wasn't satisfied, so I hired my own pathologist and had them do a second autopsy."

Bareto pulled out a second document from the file. She flipped it to the second page and pointed to a section that was highlighted in yellow. Veronica followed her cue and read for a few seconds before speaking. "So, they found evidence of an injection in his right arm. Is that unusual considering that he was being treated at the time?"

"Well, he had an IV in his left arm. Why would anyone be sticking a needle in his right arm? And there is no record in his chart about any injections."

"Did they find evidence of anything unusual in his system?"

"No, but my pathologist said that there are a number of possibilities—different things that could have been injected that might not show up. Even just plain air could have been enough. Liam was already injured. His brain was swollen. The right amount of air might have been enough to push him over the edge. Apparently, even something as little as five mililiters would have been enough to cause harm. And it would have been undetectable."

Veronica skimmed through the rest of the report. "It doesn't say that anywhere in here."

"They'll only put facts in the report. Things they find evidence of. They found evidence that an injection had been given, but not of what was injected."

"And what was his prognosis before he... um. Before he passed away?"

"He was in an induced coma. It wasn't good, but he was improving. His doctor gave him a seventy percent chance of making a full recovery. That's why I got the second opinion and how I found out about the injection." Liz leaned forward. "I know it's not much, but it was enough for my lawyer to be able to get the hospital to pull the security footage to see who had access to his room. Or at least access to that end of the hall."

Bareto pulled a blurry black and white photograph out from under the pile of papers and placed it in front of the journalist.

It was a screengrab from a security camera. It showed a hallway in what looked like a hospital. In the center of the photo was what appeared to be a woman in scrubs and wearing a surgical mask walking toward the camera. The person was looking down, which made it difficult to identify her.

"This is from the video footage. A still frame where you can see the clues," Bareto offered.

Veronica studied the photo, but couldn't see anything unusual. "Okay. What am I looking at?"

"This image was taken about three minutes before Liam coded. Why would a nurse be walking down the hall toward his room wearing a surgical mask?"

Veronica pulled a face. There could be many reasons.

"You see the syringe? In her hand."

The radio host squinted at the photograph. Yes, the right hand appeared to be holding a small object and it could quite easily be a syringe—or a pen, or a tampon. "Mrs. Bareto..." Veronica began, shaking her head, but the woman cut her off by placing a second picture in front of her. It was similar to the first, and showed what appeared to be the same person walking in the opposite direction, away from the camera.

"Do you see it?" Bareto asked.

Veronica stared at the photo and was about to shake her head again when she spotted something. But it couldn't be. Could it? She picked up her reading glasses and examined the picture once more.

There was no question. The image based on what could be seen of the figure's outline showed a woman walking away from the camera. The left hand was down by her side and bent backwards so that it was visible to the camera, and the middle finger did appear to be extended.

"Is she flipping us off?" Veronica asked, incredulously. "Flipping off the camera, I mean?"

"Looks like it to me," Bareto answered. "This camera was near the end of the hall. There are only two rooms beyond it. Liam was in one. The other was empty."

"What did the police have to say about this?"

"Well… " Bareto straightened up and pursed her lips before speaking. "They said the cause of death was trauma and that the autopsy showed no evidence of an embolism or anything that could be remotely linked to wrongdoing. As for 'her,'" she nodded at the photo, "they have no idea who she is. But, come on. What was she doing there? And why would she do that to the camera?"

"Did they check the footage from the other cameras?"

Bareto gave a reluctant nod. "They couldn't find her anywhere else. She must have changed clothes or something."

"And so…" Veronica hesitated, "um, you think that Susie Font is this female in the photo?"

"No, oh no. Well, maybe at first. Actually, to be honest… Yes. At first, I did. She'd just lost her daughter. It seemed… plausible. But it couldn't have been her. I know that now. She wasn't even in Florida at the time. She was in South Carolina. She and her husband were visiting Susie's mother. There are plane tickets, airport cameras, TSA records. The police checked. That lady is not Susie Font. It can't be."

"Then why did you call in to the show to talk to her?"

"To see if maybe she knows something. If she has any idea who this might be. I mean, I've called and written… " She shrugged off the rest of the sentence.

"They have a restraining order against you," Veronica stated.

"Yes," Bareto admitted with another shrug. "That was a misunderstanding. You see, I waited for her, near her house, when she went on a run. I guess I spooked her."

Veronica leaned back in her chair and sighed. "Mrs. Bareto. I'll agree with you… There is something… odd here, but if the police couldn't put anything together, then I'm not sure what you expect me to do. I mean, did they interview Mrs. Font or her husband?"

"They did. But they lawyered up. They denied any knowledge."

"And they had an alibi?"

"Yes."

"Okay. Well, look. They possibly have a motive. I'll give you that. Though, I know them—well, Susie, really. I've only met her husband briefly. But, in your own words, you said that she couldn't possibly have done this because she was out of town. And beyond that," Veronica shrugged, "you don't really have much else, do you?"

Bareto's shoulders slumped. "This is all there is. I was just hoping that perhaps, maybe, if I spoke with her, you know, mother to mother… " The woman paused here and began to gather up her files in an effort to mask the emotional wave of hopelessness that had washed over her. She was alone. She'd hoped Veronica could help. But she didn't see it. She just didn't see it. She was just like everybody else.

But Veronica did see. She could see that the woman was keeping her head down to mask the tears bubbling up behind those sad eyes.

"I'm so sorry," Veronica said. That was all she could put into words. Everything else was flimsy at best, and yet... "Out of curiosity, who did you work with—at the police?"

Bareto didn't hesitate. She knew the name well by now. "Detective Garza. Eddie. Eddie Garza. He was very helpful. Very understanding."

"You wouldn't happen to have a number for him? Maybe I could follow up?"

Bareto's face lit up.

"I can't promise anything," Veronica added quickly, seeing the look on the woman's face. But Mrs. Bareto had already pulled out her phone and begun consulting the directory. She read the number out to the journalist who wrote it down on her notepad. Then Veronica showed the obviously grief-stricken mother out of the building with a promise to call if she discovered anything.

Back in her office, Veronica dialed Detective Eddie Garza at Miami-Dade Homicide.

"Go for Eddie."

"Hello, Detective, this is Veronica Rios with *Veronica in the Morning*."

"Ha! Veronica Rios... sure. Is Doug Raines still doing sound over there?"

"You know Doug? Small world. No, I'm afraid Doug retired about a year ago. Spends his days fishing now I believe."

Eddie laughed. "Fishing, not catching, I'd guess. Doug loves the gear and talking about the ones that got away."

"That he does." Veronica forced a chuckle, but the detective knew she wasn't calling to chat.

"So, what can I do for you, Ms. Rios?"

"Um, well, it's a bit delicate, actually. I've just had a discussion with Liz Bareto. I believe the name will mean something to you."

There was a pause. Not something Veronica had expected and then the detective's tone changed. "Ah, yeah, I know the lady. I don't know how much I can get into it, though—I think maybe I need to transfer you to media relations?"

Veronica forced a laugh. "Detective. Come on. Eddie. This is informal. Off the record. I'm just trying to get some background info. I don't need a source and I'm not going to quote anyone. I just want to... um, fill in some blanks."

There was another long pause. Eventually, Eddie said, "Let me call you back in a few minutes from another number. Okay?"

The journalist pulled a face as if the man could see her. "Oh, okay." She gave him her number and hung up.

Ten minutes later, her phone rang.

"Veronica, it's Eddie." The detective must have stepped outside because Veronica could suddenly hear the sound of traffic in the background. The man raised his voice in an effort to compensate.

"Hi, Eddie."

"Doug says you're okay, no bullshit, so I'll talk to you, but off the record, background only. Deal?"

"That's fine. It's just that I met with Mrs. Bareto earlier and…"

"*Ay Dios!* She showed you the lady-finger photo?"

"It has a name?"

"Yeah. Sure it does, but I've been doing this a long time and I've seen some really weird shit. Trust me, on a scale of freaky, it doesn't rank that high."

"No?"

"No. But don't get me wrong. We chased it down. You know, as a matter of procedure. Didn't find anything. *Nada.* It's like the woman was a ghost or something. I mean, I know the lady lost her kid and all, but if we spent all our time on conspiracy theories, we wouldn't get much done around here. You know what I'm saying? I mean, I can appreciate how she's feeling, but we can only work the evidence."

"What about the injection?"

Eddie sighed. "Roni? Can I call you that?"

"Sure, if it gets me an answer."

Traffic growled down the phone at her. Then, "Veronica. One hundred percent off the record?"

"Sure, Eddie."

"Off the record, the medical examiner probably fucked up. We're talking an eighteen-year-old kid in a serious head-on. That's lots of broken bones. Real bad head trauma. Real bad. He was drugged up, put in a coma for Christ's sake, but his chances weren't good to start with. So, he dies, not a big fuckin' surprise! And the ME misses the injection. This shit happens all the time. Just, in this case, there was a second opinion. And they find a needle mark, but that doesn't mean shit. It could just mean that someone else screwed up—happened to inject the wrong arm and didn't account for it. We're talking human beings, not robots. Was it unusual? Sure. Unusual enough to start a whole conspiracy thing? Nah."

"What about this… lady thing. Lady Finger?" Veronica prompted.

The detective scoffed. "You mean, why would a nurse be walking down the hall, flipping the bird at a security camera? Could happen for a shitload of reasons. Pissed at a patient. Pissed at being surveilled. Could mean anything."

"So, that's it? Nothing else?"

"*We got nothing else.* Even if there was anything to all of this, the most likely candidates were out of fucking state when the kid died. We've got no evidence, no motive, no suspects, nada."

"Dead-end, huh?" Veronica asked.

"Very dead."

"So, from your side, the 'most likely candidates' are the girl's parents—Cruise and Font, right?"

"Yep. Who else? I interviewed them personally. The lady was distraught, almost catatonic. Her husband wasn't taking any shit from us, or any chances. He brought in their lawyer. Not that it mattered. Their alibi was solid."

"Could they have had someone do it?"

"What—you mean like a contract killing?"

Veronica paused. The concept sounded ridiculous. "Yeah, I suppose."

"Sure. Anything's possible, but no evidence. They were cooperative in that regard. Finances seemed pretty legit. We found no suspicious cash withdrawals to substantiate something like that."

"So, it was never a homicide?"

"Homicide?! Roni, get real. Kid's head got smashed to a pulp 'cause he was googling Russian MILFs while driving. Anyone who does that has got a death wish. I'd say it was more like suicide than homicide." The detective was getting bored.

"Got it. Okay."

"Why you interested, anyway?"

"Nothing, Eddie. Just came across my desk. Seemed odd.

Thought I'd get an expert's opinion."

"Well, I'm afraid it's a dead-end. Sorry I couldn't be of more help."

"No, no. I appreciate your candor."

"No problem. Anytime."

Veronica heard the traffic sounds die down just before the connection ended.

She wadded up her notes from the call and tossed them into a small trash can under her desk.

CHAPTER FOURTEEN

After his fight with Susie on the dock, Roy spent the better part of three days in his study. He didn't plan it that way; it just sort of happened.

For all her clanging about in the kitchen that first evening, Susie had not popped in to say that dinner was ready. Roy had hoped she would, but she hadn't. She was obviously still angry with him.

Roy, unsure about how to approach her, stayed in the study, drinking his scotch and brooding.

Slowly, his drinking and brooding turned into something else.

Was Susie serious about killing this Harlan guy? Maybe. Maybe not. She'd pushed him to kill Bareto three years prior, in the same study he was sitting in now. Then she'd backed off.

Was Susie truly as unhappy as she claimed? Maybe. Then again, maybe it was just the effect of Camilla's anniversary.

Would killing Harlan save their marriage? Possibly. She seemed to think avenging Camilla would fix things between them. He had no idea.

But, practically speaking, none of that mattered.

Not really. Not yet.

Roy thought about Susie's proposal—killing Harlan—like he would a business deal, an investment.

The first question Roy asked about an investment was not *How much money do we invest* or *What kind of return can we expect?* He never focused on what was to be gained.

The first question was always, *Does the business work? Is the business model feasible?*

Susie had proposed that they kill Harlan to avenge their daughter.

The first logical question to Roy was, *Could they do it and not get caught?*

Was it feasible?

If the answer was "no," then what could be gained by doing it, and all the rest—Susie's motivations, avenging Camilla, and so forth—didn't matter. If it couldn't be done, if they couldn't get away with it, then he could tell Susie precisely that, with confidence. *It can't be done.* And that would be the end of it.

But if the answer was "yes," if killing Harlan was feasible, then bigger decisions would have to be made.

And so, Roy's planning to kill Harlan began primarily as an intellectual exercise. I don't think he fully appreciated where that intellectual exercise would lead.

Of course, Roy had never planned a murder before.

Where to start?

As the scotch flowed, so did his creative juices. Roy began to pace the room, studying his bookshelves. Lots of business books, an equal amount of histories, some philosophy, and a few historical novels. No *Idiot's Guide to Murder.*

Before law, Roy studied history. He is a big believer in collective wisdom. This particular subject—murder—was very well suited to "ancestral insights."

On the lower left shelf, where he kept his collectibles, autographed copies, and a couple of first editions, he spotted a dusty but beautiful volume he hadn't referenced in a while. He pulled the leather-bound tome off its shelf and sat down at his desk.

He placed his scotch on the edge of his desk, on top of a magazine, well away from the book. Then he opened the book gently, careful of the spine, to the table of contents.

Jacob and Wilhelm Grimm were philologists in the 1700s in Germany. You probably know them as the Brothers Grimm. Their study of medieval German literature spanned decades.

The brothers collected traditional stories from all levels of society, from peasants to the aristocracy. Their aim was to preserve tales that had previously existed only in oral form, handed down from generation to generation—a practice threatened by the rise of industrialization.

Many of these stories were, by the Grimms' own admission, "not suitable" for children.

This is ironic, as a common thread throughout the Brothers' Grimm collection is stories that are didactic in nature and seem to aim precisely at teaching children how to survive in a dangerous world.

After all, fairy tales are essentially how-to survival stories.

Roy had found inspiration here before. He skimmed through the collection, entertaining himself, almost losing sight of his objective, until he hit upon *The Singing Bone*.

In reading this little fairy tale, Roy unwittingly transitioned from brooding to planning.

The summary he gave me goes like this.

A giant boar was destroying the countryside, such that the king put a price on its head. Among many others, two brothers set out to try their luck at killing the boar.

The younger brother went off on his own. The older brother went off drinking with other would-be hunters—for courage. While the older brother was drinking, the younger brother found and killed the boar.

On his way back to deliver the boar's body to the king, he came across his older brother. The older brother joined him. But along on the way, the older brother killed the younger and buried him under a bridge.

Then, the older brother delivered the boar to the king, claimed the credit for killing it, and, as a reward, was married to the king's daughter.

The story didn't end there. There has to be a lesson. A moral.

Sometime later, a shepherd was passing by the bridge where the younger brother was buried and saw a bone sticking up out of the ground. He picked it up and fashioned it into a mouthpiece for a horn.

And, lo and behold, the horn magically began making music on its own.

The shepherd took the horn to show it to the king and his court. Everyone was shocked when the horn sang the story of the murder of the younger brother by the older brother. The older brother was executed by the king for his crime. (There is no mention of what happened to the princess. In all likelihood, she was married to the shepherd.)

The moral of the story: bury your bones deep, because bones can sing. Or, another way to describe it… perhaps dead men tell no tales, but their bones just might.

This story was Roy's jumping-off point. The first key element in his planning.

He sat back in the chair at his desk, and mulled.

No singing bones…

For Roy, this initially translated into "leave no body."

He pondered.

How do you best get rid of the body?

Who is going to come looking for it?

Where will they start looking?

And when?

Roy's train of thought led him from the Brothers Grimm to hide and seek. Just as fairy tales teach children lessons about life, so do games. Childhood games are a metaphor for how life works.

Hide and seek teaches children real-life skills.

The "hiders" learn the life skills of camouflage, shelter-taking, and subterfuge.

The "seeker" learns investigation, pursuit, and capture. These are skills that are useful in the roles of both predator and prey.

Or criminal and policeman.

Didn't it all boil down to this?

Roy sat and contemplated, swirling his almost empty scotch glass, his mind bouncing from point to point.

So, what does a cop look for?

Clues. Sure. But what kind?

The body, fingerprints, weapon, cause of death, evidence, connections…

What kinds of connections?

Who would want this person dead...?

He poured himself another scotch.

For Kristy. For Camilla... Tom Wise's words returned to him, as they had many times before, like a phantom haunting his thoughts. *...will you kill this fucker Harlan for us?*

What had Wise been thinking? It was insane. Fucking crazy.

Or was it?

He and Susie had considered the same thing—killing Bareto. And she had backed off—Roy believed—because of what he'd told her.

It was too obvious.

He and Susie had clearly been motivated to kill Bareto for what he'd done. They would have gotten caught.

We had a motive.

But Harlan?

This guy, Harlan, lived in another state. He had absolutely nothing to do with Roy or Susie. Hell, they didn't even know what he looked like. And Harlan certainly didn't know who they were.

Their only connection was the drinks Susie had shared with the wife—he couldn't even remember her name—and that brief conversation he'd with the husband, Tom. He racked his brains trying to picture who exactly had been in the bar with them.

Had anybody noticed them together? Possibly.

Had they spoken to anybody? Nobody but the bartender.

Would the bartender remember them? It had been several months. And even if he did, they could have been talking about anything.

It was highly unlikely that either of these encounters had been caught on any kind of video, security or otherwise. And if there had ever been any video, by now it had probably been recorded over or deleted. And how would it even come to light? Because, for anyone to look for such a video, there would need to be *a connection* between Harlan, and Roy and Susie, and Tom and... Deb, that was her name.

There was no discernible connection between any of them.

Certainly, none between Roy, Susie, and Harlan.

Hence, there was no discernible motive.

No motive.

Why would Roy Cruise of Cruise Capital, Miami entrepreneur, husband, and grieving father, want to kill a twenty-something-year-old kid, a rapist, from Austin, Texas, whom he had never met?

There was no plausible reason why he would want to.

Which was why it was entirely plausible that Roy could kill Harlan and get away with it.

CHAPTER FIFTEEN

Roy's decision to move forward was built on a careful plan.

The morning after their fight on the dock and his initial fairy tale research, Roy awoke in the study. He'd spent the evening after their argument alone, drinking. He'd slept on the sofa, not wanting to see Susie.

The night before, Roy had decided that killing Harlan was worth considering. Of course, that had been after several scotches and no dinner. You might think that this "decision" made while intoxicated would be forgotten the next day or chalked up to "the booze talking."

You don't know Roy like I do.

When he sets his mind to something, look out. So, too, when he makes a decision.

Roy was now focused on determining whether killing Harlan was feasible. Whether or not to actually do it, and all the morality involved, were questions for later.

By this point, Roy had expanded on the Grimm Brothers' lesson.

No singing bones.

In his mind, this had come to mean the elimination of anything that could tie him to the crime. If you want to murder successfully, you must leave *no singing bones.*

No body.
No weapon.
No fingerprints.
No witnesses.
No motive.
Was that possible?

What were the odds?

Roy understood business and the odds of a venture being successful. He had no idea what the odds were like for getting away with murder.

So, he did some research online.

From FBI and Bureau of Justice data, Roy learned that, starting in the year 2000 and going forward, there'd been approximately 15,000 murders committed in the U.S. every year.

In about 7,000 of those annual cases, the killer was identified and convicted.

In approximately 3,000 of those cases each year, a suspected killer was identified, but not convicted.

And, in approximately 5,000 cases, no suspect was even identified.

That meant that about 8,000 murderers out of 15,000 got away with it every year. So, by Roy's math, the odds of getting away with murder in the U.S. were a little better than sixty percent.

Not great odds. But not bad either.

Better than blackjack...

This gambling analogy may well sound flippant when you consider the gravity of what Roy was considering. But for an investor like Roy, it made perfect sense. He may not have plotted murder before, but he understood how to analyze probabilities when faced with a new investment opportunity.

All he believed he had to do was apply the same legal and business process principles here.

Roy's first successful venture was a music-streaming platform that came out shortly after Napster. It was called RamRod. Napster got all the press because it had first-mover advantage. But RamRod was a fast-follower. RamRod studied Napster's platform and learned from its mistakes—both legal and business model errors—and built a similar platform that ultimately sold for over $200 million. A big win at the time.

What Roy learned from that experience was the same lesson MySpace learned from Facebook. The first-mover doesn't always win. Sometimes, it pays to be second. Or third.

As long as you *learn from those that came before.*

He distilled this into two fundamental but related principles.

Principle Number One: *Copy others who have successfully done what you are trying to do.*

Principle Number Two: *If you fail, be original. Don't make the same mistakes others have made.*

Roy now knew that many murders *are* solved (forty percent). In each of those cases, the killer made mistakes that led to him or her getting caught and convicted.

What Roy needed to know was, *What were those mistakes?*

He could brainstorm a list. But why reinvent the wheel? If anyone knew what to look for to find a killer, it would be a killer-finder, someone who did that for a living... a homicide detective.

Roy poked around online for about fifteen minutes, then got his keys, hopped in his Range Rover and headed over to Bayside Marketplace, a shopping center that had been built in the late 80s and was regularly featured on *Miami Vice*—a 1980s crime show.

Roy found this ironic.

He parked on the street and walked to the Crocs store, where he bought a pair of navy blue Crocs, charging them to his AMEX.

Misdirection.

He was already focused on leaving no evidence.

Roy then walked three blocks west to the Miami Dade Community College bookstore and paid cash for a used copy of *Practical Homicide Investigation: Tactics, Procedures, and Forensic Techniques - 5th Edition.*

The *PHI* he called it.

He was careful to keep an eye out for security cameras. He also wore a University of Miami baseball cap, just in case. He didn't want any video to exist of him buying a how-to guide regarding homicide. Roy brought the book back to his study and started reading and taking notes.

He would decide later how much "practical experience" might add to a homicide detective's ability to catch a killer. For now, starting out by understanding how homicide detectives were theoretically trained to solve crimes was good enough.

If he could understand the starting points and processes, he would have a much better sense of what mistakes killers made and how detectives used those mistakes to catch killers.

The *PHI* was like the rulebook to grown-up hide-and-seek, with examples, case studies, and so forth. Roy built an outline, based on the *PHI*, of how an investigator would approach a murder. He read the entire book cover to cover. The outline took the rest of the first day and the whole day after to complete. He barely slept, and left his office only for light snacks.

Susie was apparently still mad at him and left him in peace, which was fine. He didn't want her to know what he was up to, and he certainly didn't want to face her until he had an answer.

After completing the outline, he condensed everything he had learned from the *PHI* into one hand-written document that he labeled *Roy's Rules for Murder*.

This left him with one final step—practical application. Roy spent the entire third day in his study planning. How could he apply *Roy's Rules* to killing Harlan and getting away with it?

At about 6:00 p.m., he put the final touches on his plan. There were a lot of details to be addressed. To be safe, he kept it all hand-written. Nothing on the computer. No digital traces. And he made extensive use of shorthand and abbreviations.

The plan was risky. It was dangerous. But, it met all the requirements of his *Rules*.

Most important, it was *feasible*.

Roy opened the half-empty bottle of scotch, poured himself a generous measure, and sat back to admire his work. There were lots of practical details, forensics, and so forth.

But, it pleased him to note that, philosophically, it all came down to hide-and-seek and the Brothers Grimm. Collective wisdom.

No singing bones.

By the time he got through what remained of the bottle of scotch, he felt he was ready to talk to his wife.

He set his phone alarm for 5:00 a.m., pulled a pillow from the sofa, and fell asleep on the floor, on the oriental rug where Susie had been sitting three years before when she had proposed to him that they kill Liam Bareto.

CHAPTER SIXTEEN

Human motivation is a complex thing. Roy Cruise is no exception. I have struggled to understand why exactly Roy went down the path he did.

Susie had her reasons. While it took her some time to reveal them to me, once she did, her choices made sense.

But, she didn't reveal them to Roy until things had gone much, much further. As a result, Roy's motivations were all his own.

And they were more complicated.

Roy is a very fortunate man. He's built a solid business. He's wealthy. He finds his work fulfilling. He has a wife he loves. He has almost everything that most people struggle their whole lives to achieve, and many never do.

Why risk it all to try to kill someone who has done nothing to you?

Was it fear of losing Susie—of his marriage failing?

Was it about avenging Camilla?

Or was he driven by the sheer challenge of it?

He is a very competitive person. It shows in his work life. I sometimes wonder whether, maybe, proving he could get away with it played some role in his decision, as well.

You'll have to judge for yourself the "why" of the path he chose.

Roy was up early the next day getting everything organized. At 7:30 a.m., he sent a text to Susie.

She awoke to the *ping* of her phone.

Good morning, babe. Meet me on the boat, please...

The couple had not spoken since the day of the radio interview. Sending her a text message this early in the morning would most likely get her attention.

Okay, came the reply. *On my way.*

As Susie approached the dock, she could hear the growl of engines. But it wasn't the yacht. It was the fishing boat, the Yellowfin. He hadn't taken that boat out in a long time. Not since Camilla. Hearing the sound of it took her curiosity level up another notch.

"Can you get the bow line, babe?" Roy shouted across to her. "I've got the springs and stern."

Susie freed the boat from the bow line and clambered aboard. She took her usual seat of the two in front of the helm while Roy stood at the controls. The seat next to Susie was conspicuously empty.

Roy eased the boat gently away from the dock and began the slow trek down the channel and out to the bay.

Much of the area around them was made up of mangroves and very shallow, so they had to follow the channel for almost ten minutes at about six knots before reaching the bay. Once there, Roy gunned the engines and the Yellowfin leapt forward like a playful dolphin.

The boat had a top speed of sixty miles per hour, and with its stepped hull, traveling at that speed—even in rough water—was surprisingly smooth.

It had been a long time since either of the two had felt the warm breeze and salt air on their faces.

It was bittersweet, as the third member of the family who'd always accompanied them was missing.

It brought back memories.

It felt good to be on the water again.

In Florida, as in most of the U.S., a license is not required to run a boat, provided that you own it. However, Roy had studied for and obtained an International Certificate of Competency, certifying him to captain boats up to twenty-five meters. He'd obligated Susie to do the same. To him, it was a question of safety—if they were out on one of the boats and something happened, he didn't want her stranded and clueless.

Roy had by this time logged almost 600 hours as a captain.

He made a few maneuvers, cutting port and starboard. Testing systems. Everything seemed to be working well. The fact that the boat had been idle for some time didn't mean that it hadn't been maintained. Roy ensured that both boats and his jet ski were cleaned and serviced weekly. He'd hired a maintenance company for that purpose.

When he was satisfied that everything was running well, in the middle of Biscayne Bay, Roy brought the boat to a slow stop, then shut off the engines.

He came around toward the bow, sitting down, straddling the coffin box in front of Susie, facing her. She was watching him keenly, but she said nothing as the water lapped gently around them.

Roy knew she was waiting for him to start the conversation, and so he got to it.

"Suze. What you said the other day. I want you to know that I heard you. I always hear you, even if sometimes it may seem like I don't. I understand where you're coming from. All of it. And you got me thinking."

He put both palms down in front of him, between his legs, and leaned forward as if needing the support. "Back with Bareto, it was just too dangerous." Susie folded her arms. "We were too close to it. We would have been prime suspects. It would have been impossible not to get caught. But this... " He looked up, as if searching for the right words, then back at her. "This Harlan guy. If—and it's a *big if*—if we choose to do it, well... I think it might actually be doable. I think we could get away with it."

Susie raised her eyebrows and uncrossed her arms. Sure, she'd been expecting a revelation, maybe an apology. But she hadn't known it would be this.

Roy thought he noted a twinkle in her eyes and held up a hand as he scooted forward, closer to her. "But I need you to hear me out. All of it. I mean really listen to me. It's important that you understand everything, fully, and I mean everything, Suze."

He was serious. Susie relaxed and settled back into her seat to listen.

It took just over thirty minutes for Roy Cruise to lay out

his detailed plan for killing Joe Harlan Jr. By the time he'd finished, having spoken his plan aloud for the first time, he was exhausted.

He also felt a bit queasy—and Roy doesn't get seasick. Somehow, putting the whole thing into words and sharing it with another person made what he had concocted seem much more real. These were no longer just musings in his study.

He felt good sharing it with Susie, relieved to have confessed why he'd been skulking around for the last few days. He sat back and looked around, letting everything he'd explained sink in.

Bay sounds were all that they heard for several minutes. The lapping of the sea against the boat. The creak of boat parts as they pushed and pulled against each other with the roll of the waves. The distant hum of faraway craft. The occasional slap of a fish hitting the water.

They both sat in silence, until Susie spoke. "Roy, are you sure about this?" She breathed. "I mean, the other day... I was pissed. I mean... I was upset about the interview, and Liz. And with the whole third-anniversary thing... " She trailed off and started to bite her thumbnail, something Roy knew she did when she was anxious.

"What?" Roy asked carefully, "You don't want to do it?"

"No... I mean... Yes... " Susie spoke through her thumb, then realized what she was doing, and lowered it, sitting on her hand. "No, I'm not saying that. I... I do feel like there's this hole... from Camilla. I don't think she got the justice she deserved."

"Stop calling it justice, Suze. This isn't justice. This is revenge pure and simple. Like you said. Call it what it is... "

"Right," she interrupted. "That's fair. Look, I don't know if an 'act of revenge' will fill this hole," she spread her hand over her chest, "in my soul, but... I feel like something is pulling me in that direction. Something's compelling me to do this. Does that make sense?"

Roy nodded. "I feel the same." Susie lifted her eyebrows and opened her mouth to speak, but he continued quickly to try to maintain control of the direction of the discussion. "Like I said, I may not show it like you do, but it doesn't mean that I don't feel it, Suze," he said, earnestly. She bit her lip in acquiescence. "I want revenge for our little girl. And if we can't get that by killing Bareto, then…" he nodded as if to convince himself, "…then, it'll have to be by avenging another wrong."

Her eyes widened as she looked at him.

"What?" he asked, looking her in the eye.

"That!" she pointed at him. "Yes! That's it! That's exactly how I feel!" she said excitedly, delirious at the fact that they both finally seemed to be on the same page.

"But should we find someone else?" Roy asked, leaning back. "I mean, why Harlan?"

Susie said nothing for a few moments, then answered, "I've thought about that, too, a lot, these last days." She leaned forward and took his hand in hers, looked into his eyes, and continued. "I mean, for me, the answer to 'why this guy' is—like you said—that we have no connection to him at all. If we pick someone that killed somebody texting while driving, that's a connection. Tenuous, sure. But still, a connection. And, the fewer connections, the better.

"Plus, we have a pretty clear idea that he did the crime. I mean, the girl's parents tracked us down and asked us to do it. And the fact that they approached us, that they're feeling the same things we felt, going through the same things we went through, that means something to me. Somehow, it seems right. It feels right. They're asking for justice—revenge, like you said—and if we can get some… something… out of that, some sort of closure, then…" she finished the sentence with a shrug, still holding his hand.

Roy sighed.

"Look," Susie continued, "I don't think it's easy to choose who. Of course, it isn't. If we were just starting from scratch, maybe we'd look for someone else, but we are where we are because of everything that's happened… because of everything that has *come to us*. This guy feels right—*this* feels right to me," she said with a determined smile as she squeezed her husband's hand.

She gave it a few seconds, studying Roy, and when he didn't respond, she sat back, releasing his hand, and added, "But if you think we should find someone else… "

"No. Babe. Listen," he jumped in, "the plan is done. I think we can do this. If he's guilty, then whether it's him or someone else makes no difference. Guilty is guilty. Revenge is revenge. Right? There's just one thing I think we have to do before we agree to do it."

"That's why you kept saying 'if we do it' before?" she asked.

He leaned closer to her and spoke softly but seriously. "We have to be sure. We have to be one hundred percent positive that he did what the Wises claim. We have to be certain that he actually did rape that girl before we do anything. Deal?"

Susie nodded, eagerly. "Deal."

CHAPTER SEVENTEEN

Susie's justification for killing Harlan, and specifically Harlan as opposed to someone else, was weak in my opinion.

I could have understood—conceptually—the logic of her wanting to avenge Camilla by killing someone who had caused a death by texting while driving. I would never have condoned it, but there would have been logic to it.

Her argument that killing someone who had committed "their crime"—texting while driving—her claim that killing such a person would create "a connection to them"—to her and her husband—seemed weak to me.

But, okay. Fine. Forget texting and driving. Why not go after a person who had intentionally killed someone and gotten away with it—someone who truly deserved it? That made more sense to me than killing the Harlan boy.

When I put this to Susie, she responded by telling me a story. Well, the beginning of a story that gave me the first bit of insight into what was truly motivating her actions.

* * *

Susie was unpacking her suitcase on a luxury cruise ship.

She was sixteen years old, and at that awkward stage that a lot of girls go through, though she had gotten there a little later than most. *A late bloomer*, her mom said.

She was all arms and legs. Her father would often tell her that she looked like a newborn fawn. He would call her his 'gangly-growing-girl.'

Needless to say, this only added to her already heightened insecurity about her body. Her breasts were too small, in her opinion. And, she was still dealing with getting the hang of the whole period thing. So, having her dad kid her about looking like Bambi really didn't help. It just added more stress.

Her mother, on the other hand, was great about it. Very supportive. In fact, the two of them were very close, to the point that Susie couldn't understand when some of her friends complained about how they *hated* their mothers. No doubt, Susie's mom wasn't perfect, but she could tell that her mom cared about her. That she was trying to help her, look out for her, and guide her. She really didn't see how you could expect more.

As she unpacked her suitcase, she felt trepidation over some of its contents. The white bikini Grandma Font had bought her for the trip stressed her out. When she'd tried it on, the bottoms had looked like granny panties and she'd barely filled in the top. She shoved it deep into a drawer and put other clothes on top, as if burying it would make it go away.

As she unpacked, she could hear the high, tinny sound of music coming from her brother Chris's headphones as he put away his own clothes. A typical boy, he was just taking everything from his suitcase and shoving it into drawers in no particular order. Filling one drawer, then the next, and so on.

When her parents had told them that they were going on a cruise, Susie had been super excited. When they'd added that they would be going with their neighbors, the Wests, less so. Though her brother got along great with Alan, the Wests' younger son, there was typical teenage awkwardness between Susie and Ben, the Wests' older son. He was only a year older than her and they went to the same high school, but the similarities ended there. He was closer in mental age to Chris than to Susie.

This meant that she was probably going to spend a lot of time alone on the trip. So, she'd planned for it, bringing several books, which, as she unpacked, she organized on her nightstand in the order she planned to read them.

While she had fantasized a bit about the idea of maybe meeting a cute boy on the cruise, when she weighed the excitement of the possibility against the stress of it, she thought she'd probably be happier just tanning and reading. The thought of meeting a cute boy while wearing Grandma's white bikini—which she would avoid wearing at all costs—made her palms sweat.

It's just a phase. You'll grow out of it.

"Easy for you to say, Mom."

On day two of the cruise, Susie went down to the pool after lunch and staked out the same lounge chair she had occupied for most of the prior day. She was wearing a blue one-piece swimsuit and Wayfarers, and had brought her first book—already half-finished—with her.

She had just gotten back into the storyline when she heard a voice say, "Hi there, stranger."

At first, she thought the words were addressed to someone else, and she just kept reading. Moments later, she felt a tug on her big toe. Susie started, then sat up and lowered her book, squinting up at the person standing over her who was backlit by the sun. She raised a hand to deflect the glare and get a better look at the intruder.

As she did, blond hair came into focus, done up in a high ponytail. The "woman" removed her sunglasses, and smiled. Susie stared for a moment, then suddenly recognized the face, the face of a girl. As she did, a surge of emotions shot through her—joy, excitement, sadness, and fear—all at once.

"Deb?"

The girl in the red bikini sat down on the edge of the lounge chair next to her.

"Small world, huh?"

Susie studied her old friend as her heart thumped in her chest. She had grown, as Susie had, since they'd last seen each other. But Deb was more developed than Susie. She had the body of a full-grown woman. Her breasts were... well, they were breasts. She looked like she was about the same height as Susie, but while Susie looked like Bambi, Deb looked more like Jessica Rabbit—at least in Susie's eyes.

"How have you been?" Susie asked.

"Good. You?"

"Good."

"Whatcha reading?" Deb still had that Texas drawl, though it was lighter now.

"*Bourne Supremacy.*"

"Ah. First one was good."

"Right? This one's okay so far."

They chatted back and forth at a comfortable rhythm. Like two kids warming up to play ping-pong. Neither taking the conversation beyond small talk.

"You here with your family?" Deb asked.

"Yeah. You?"

"Nah. Came with my Aunt Jenny. Just the two of us. She's over there." Deb waved at an attractive fortyish woman wearing oversized sunglasses. The woman offered a big smile and waved back enthusiastically from the other side of the pool. "She saw you lying here by yourself, reading, and told me to introduce myself. Wants me to make friends. I almost shit my bikini when I came over and saw it was you!"

Susie laughed. Deb had a gift for interspersing her speech with vulgarities in ways that had always made Susie laugh. Hearing her doing it again conjured up good memories.

"So," Deb said, "anyway, I gotta get going—get ready for dinner. We should hang. You have plans?"

"I'm meeting my folks, but I could try and get out of it. I'm kind of an eighth wheel anyway."

Deb laughed. "Huh?"

"I'll explain later. Where are you guys eating?" Susie asked, gathering her things.

"Lido deck."

"Cool. Let me talk to my parents and I'll meet you there. What time?"

"Seven."

"Okay. See you later."

Susie caught up to her parents and the Wests at one of the ship's bars. They were having pre-dinner drinks.

"Honey, it's great you found a friend. Isn't that great, Mark?"

"It's not a boy, is it?" her father asked with mock seriousness.

"No, Dad. It's a girl. Her name is Debra."

"You go on up and get ready for dinner," said Susie's mom. "And when you're ready, I'll take you so I can meet this Aunt Jenny. Just swing by here right around seven. We aren't going anywhere."

"Thanks, Mom."

Susie went up to the cabin to get dressed.

She opted for khaki shorts with a light blue polo and a pair of Converse sneakers. As she looked into the mirror, she saw that she had gotten some sun. Her skin was radiant. Her eyes were jet-black. She smiled, thinking she looked kind of cute—*seeing some light at the end of the tunnel, maybe...*

At seven, she and her mom walked into the Lido and scanned the area for Deb and her aunt. She spotted them at a table in the middle of the room. As they approached, Aunt Jenny and Deb stood to greet them.

"I am so glad that the girls met," Aunt Jenny said enthusiastically.

"Me too!" Theresa Font replied.

"When I saw your girl by the pool all alone, I told Deb, you have just got to go and say 'hello!' There aren't a lot of kids their age here, so they need to stick together, right?"

"It's so nice of you to ask Susie to dinner. Are you traveling alone? You're welcome to join us—though, we're just two married couples, so I don't know how much fun we'll be."

"Well, aren't you sweet! I appreciate that so much. I am meeting a *friend* later. If it's alright, maybe the two of us can join you?"

While the ladies firmed up future locations and possible meeting times, the two girls excused themselves to go check out the buffet.

During dinner, Deb's aunt read a book while the girls

continued their small talk, gradually becoming reacquainted. When the girls returned to their table with dessert, they found Aunt Jenny speaking to a man—not bad looking by Susie's estimation, though a few years younger than Deb's aunt.

"Girls, this is Stan." The girls politely greeted the new member of their party, then seated themselves. As they ate dessert, Deb and Susie stifled giggles and rolled eyes at each other as Aunt Jenny suddenly seemed much more animated than earlier. Her voice had gone up at least an octave in pitch, and she was laughing loudly at jokes that, in the girls' opinions, were lame.

"Jenny," said Deb. "Is it alright if we go exploring?"

Her aunt barely looked up. "Sure, honey. Y'all go on. But be good. Be back by 11:00."

One of the great things about a cruise ship is that teenagers can go off on their own, alone, in relative safety.

For the balance of the trip, Susie and Deb settled into a routine. They met for breakfast at 10:00. Laid about the pool until 2:00. Had a light snack around 4:00. Dinner at 7:00. And they said goodnight at 11:00.

When she thought back on the cruise later, most of the trip was a blur to Susie. She couldn't recall what they'd talked about. Or how they'd occupied so much time. It seemed to her, when she told me about it, that the three groups—her family, the Wests, and Jenny, Deb, and Stan—were the only people on the cruise ship.

Susie remembered seeing her parents and the Wests periodically. She remembered her brother and the West boys playing in the pool, and recalled one ill-advised attempt by the boys to hang out with the girls—which Deb had brutally shut down. She remembered Aunt Jenny and Stan appearing and disappearing at various times. All of them were like extras in a play.

But she couldn't recall any crew members, other families, or other children. Not specifically. They were there in her memory like a backdrop, pieces of furniture on a stage.

The whole trip was book-ended by the first day, when Deb found Susie, and the last day—the evening, really—which they'd spent saying goodbye.

Susie had just finished getting ready for dinner and was leaving her cabin when she saw Deb coming down the hall with a large macramé pool bag and a blue and white striped beach towel.

"Come on, girl. Change of plans. Follow me."

Deb led her down passages, stairs, and then through a door marked *Crew Only*. They continued down hallways and more stairs, deeper into the bowels of the ship.

Finally, Deb opened a door into what appeared to be a part of the crew quarters. There were two bunks on one wall, a sink under a medicine cabinet on the opposite wall, and a chair tucked under a small desk. The floor was wall-to-wall carpeting—mainly blue with an ugly, repetitive wave pattern in beige.

They sat down on the floor, and Deb took out a bottle of white wine. Twist-off, no cork. She opened it and took a swig, then handed the bottle to Susie, who did the same. The wine had lost its chill, though it was still slightly cooler than room temperature. To Susie, it tasted thick and sweet... too sweet, actually.

They talked until the bottle of wine was empty. Then, Deb reached into her bag of tricks and pulled out two cans of warm beer and handed one to her friend.

"You hungry?" she asked, producing a jar of nuts, a bag of crackers, a chocolate bar, and some Doritos. "I've been raiding the mini-bar. A little every day so Aunt Jen doesn't freak out. This stuff is wicked expensive!"

They chatted, and snacked, and sipped beer. They laughed about how Aunt Jenny acted around Stan, and joked about Ben West and how immature he was, and how immature all boys their age were. To Susie, it felt like they had talked about everything.

Almost everything. There was one topic they hadn't discussed.

The way Susie remembered it, one moment they were talking and laughing, and the next she realized that there were tears rolling down her cheeks.

"Susie. Dude, what's the deal?" asked Deb, concerned. "You're killing my buzz."

Susie wiped her eyes with the back of her hand, then sniffed, and sipped from her beer.

"You alright?"

"Yeah. Fine" Susie replied. "It's nothing."

Deb reached into the bag and pulled out another beer while watching Susie closely. "Last one," she said, opening the tab. "Split it?"

Susie said nothing. She could hear distant voices from the corridor. Then, closer, the sound of a stomach gurgling. She wasn't sure if it was hers or Deb's, but she instinctively put a hand on her belly and noticed that it was shaking slightly.

Susie looked down at her hand, hesitated, and then took a slow, deep breath and without looking up, asked, "Do you ever think about me?"

Deb turned to her, smiling sweetly. She reached out and gently lifted Susie's chin.

As Susie looked into Deb's eyes, her belly fluttered. Deb leaned into her, slowly. Susie felt at ease, calm, and then pulled back, suddenly, surprised when she realized that Deb was going to kiss her.

Susie crossed her arms defensively, sitting back, and looked down and away, and said, "Sorry, Deb. It's just... I'm not... " Susie took a deep breath and looked up, apologetically.

Deb leaned in again.

Susie told me that Deb's mouth tasted of Doritos and beer. She remembered Deb's hands on her. Gentle at first, then rougher, urgent. She remembered the weight of Deb's body on hers. The warmth of her skin. The sounds they made from pleasure, then giggling and shushing each other for fear that someone would hear, until they no longer cared, their passion burning hotter than the fear of being discovered. She remembered the bliss of release, something she had never experienced before—not like that. And, afterward, she remembered lying for what seemed like hours in Deb's arms.

It was almost midnight when they quietly tidied up the room and then sat, holding hands, knowing that goodbye was all that was left.

Susie began to cry again, and Deb held her in her arms and kissed her hair. Then, Deb pulled out a Velcro wallet and said, "I want to give you something."

She carefully unfolded a small photograph—a 3 x 5 print, creased vertically and horizontally, a thin white cross running through the image—and handed it to Susie.

Two little girls, suntanned and smiling. Two friends with their arms on each other's shoulders, grinning at the camera.

"This is amazing," Susie said.

"I thought you'd like it." Deb smiled, satisfied. "Hey, who knows you best?"

"Deb does," murmured Susie, studying the photo.

She remembered. She remembered the moment the picture had been taken. So long ago now. So much had happened since.

They'd been so much younger.

Still just girls.

Innocent little girls.

CHAPTER EIGHTEEN

Susie felt satisfied that she had overcome the initial hurdle of convincing Roy to plan Joe Harlan Jr.'s demise. And, once I understood her connection to Deb, I could understand why she was focused on killing Harlan.

But Roy still wasn't ready. He still wanted proof that Harlan had done what he'd been accused of.

After returning from their boat ride, Susie and Roy convened in Roy's study to discuss next steps.

"First, let's talk process. So, up to this point," he said, "I've only done generalized research on murder and conviction rates in the U.S., and I went to a college bookstore and bought a book on murder investigation—cash. I call it the *PHI*," he said, indicating the book. "All pretty innocuous. Not traceable.

"But, whatever else we do from now on in terms of planning, research, et cetera, we have to assume it can all be traced. In case we should ever come under suspicion, we need to make sure we leave nothing behind that indicates any connection to Harlan or Kristy Wise or their whole situation. I have some tech ideas to help us achieve that.

"First, I've already turned off all location services on my phone. So, I can't be tracked. Here, give me yours," he said, holding out his hand.

Susie obediently handed her phone over, and her husband instantly and somewhat expertly began manipulating the screen.

While he did, Susie said, "And if we're going to do any online research, we should use my old burner laptop, right?"

"Huh?" Roy looked up.

"My burner. That piece of shit Chromebook I have. I started

using it back when I was investigating the *Gang of Seven*. Why do you think they could never get at my research files? It wasn't for the lack of trying... " She winked at him.

Roy looked dumbfounded. "I've heard of burner phones. But a laptop... What makes it a burner?"

"Some simple stuff, and some modifications," she said. "For example, I've never loaded any email accounts on it, so it can't receive any attachments from outside sources. It hasn't been out of my sight since I bought it—except when it's locked in the safe—so no one could plant anything on it. You know, malware, spyware. Same for travel—never traveled with it, so it hasn't been through 'security checks' or left my sight long enough for anyone to plant anything on it."

"Okay."

Susie continued, "Then, I replaced the Chrome operating system with Arch Linux open source and added some security software that gives me more control over boot-up, so I can keep a lookout for the usual off-the-shelf spyware. I also opened it up and pulled the little pin off the SPI flash chip; that's where BIOS sits."

Roy frowned at her.

"You know," she continued, "the code that's underneath the operating system? Pulling off the pin makes the chip read-only so that no one can mess with my files. And then, just to be sure, I put super glue in all the USB ports, but not the power port obviously. Then, I downloaded TOR."

"Tor?"

"Yeah. TOR. The Onion Router. It's a browser, like Safari or Firefox, but it masks your IP address. Lots of people use it, journalists, activists, people who want to keep their identity secret. You know—dark web amateurs, online drug buyers, and so on. But, you have to be careful with it 'cause, well... because of its very nature, the government likes to track it. So, I do all my research via open Wi-Fi at different coffee shops. And I'm on no more than sixty minutes at any one location. And never at home."

"Fuck, Suze... "

"What?" She shrugged. "You can never be too careful. You

said it. Besides," she added, looking up at the ceiling as she whispered with a wink, "Big Brother *is watching.*"

"Okay. So…" He picked up a large, expandable Redweld folder a bit anticlimactically. "I have labeled this folder *Landscaping*," he said, pointing to the word he had written on the file. "Anything we do in writing, and there should be very little, goes in here."

He held the folder open, showing that it contained no more than ten sheets of paper. "My notes from the *PHI* and the plan."

Susie nodded.

"When we're not using it, it goes in the safe."

"Okay," Susie said. "But I assume we'll need to do a lot of online research, and if we want to be efficient, then— "

"Can you make me another burner?"

Susie smiled. "I tell you what. You take mine and get started. I'll go buy another laptop and get it set up. Takes a few hours," she said.

"Okay. Sounds like a plan. I thought we'd divide up the work into two parts. One of us needs to do what the *PHI* calls victimology. When someone is killed, the homicide detective comes up with a deep-dive bio of the victim—any and all information that could be relevant to the case. Look. Like this." He handed her the *PHI* opened to page 21. She read.

Victimology is the collection and assessment of all significant information as it relates to the victim and his or her lifestyle. Personality, employment, education, friends, habits, hobbies, marital status, relationships, dating history, sexuality, reputation, criminal record, history of alcohol or drugs, physical condition, and neighborhood of residence are all pieces of the mosaic that makes up victimology. The bottom line is: *Who was the victim and what was going on in his or her life at the time of the event?*

"I figure we should do this now, so we know what we're up against, and to make sure there isn't something we don't know about Harlan that might bite us in the ass. We should know as much about him as anyone would investigating his murder. Or at least as much as can be learned from public sources."

"Sounds smart," Susie answered. "What's the other part?"

"Guilt. Someone needs to research the actual crime—the rape. We need to know what happened and be sure that we believe he deserves what we're preparing for him. We need to make damned sure that this guy did it, at least as much as humanly possible."

"Okay. Which do you want?" Susie asked.

"I don't care," Roy said.

"Flip you for it? Winner gets victimology. I'll take heads."

Roy dug a coin out of his desk drawer and flipped. It landed on the rug heads-up.

"Okay then," he said. "Give me your burner and I'll get started while you go shopping."

CHAPTER NINETEEN

With Roy out of the house, Susie returned the *Landscaping* folder to the safe. It was a good-sized safe—a Fort Knox Legend 7261 Vault. Roy had had it installed when they'd bought the house. It stood 6' tall and 5' wide. The interior was custom finished so that there was space for important documents, some jewelry, and two locked drawers—one for him and one for her.

Susie had always thought it ironic that they owned such a large gun safe but only kept one weapon in it—a small handgun, a Glock 26 subcompact.

When they'd moved to Miami, Roy had been concerned about crime in the city. So, he'd bought the gun and attended a concealed handgun course. He'd asked Susie to do the same. For the first two months in the city, he carried the gun pretty much everywhere. After that, it remained locked in the safe and—to Susie's knowledge—hadn't been moved since.

Now, as she was about to lock the safe door, she paused to open the file and have a look inside.

LANDSCAPING FOLDER – FIRST DOCUMENT
(Roy's handwritten notes)

ROY'S RULES FOR MURDER
(Page One)

1. THE KILLER SHOULD HAVE NO DISCERNIBLE MOTIVE.

1.1 Human nature seeks cause and effect. If the killer is in no way connected to the victim, the investigator will be stymied. Murder is one of the worst crimes. To go to that extreme, the killer needs a good reason. But this reason more than often only need be as good as the killer's moral compass since there are people who will kill for $20. (They are the idiots.)

1.2 "Life is cheap." Literally. If the downside for killing is outweighed by the upside.

1.3 The more you have to lose, the greater justification or motivation you need.

1.4 To kill successfully, you should not "need" anything that the victim has.

1.5 You should not have any reason to want the victim dead.

1.6 You should have nothing to gain from the victim's death.

1.7 Think self-interest. Think capitalism. People only do things if they gain from them. People are motivated by self-interest. If the killer has nothing to gain from killing the victim, why would he do it? Why take so much risk? It makes no sense.

1.8 The typical investigator will look for reasons that someone would want the victim dead.

1.9 The typical investigator will often work to cobble together reasons for killing the victim.

1.10 Investigators are programmed to believe that all crimes require motive and opportunity. (If one can eliminate—or obfuscate—one's motive, one will cease to be a suspect).

1.11 The perfect murder is completely random. (Randomness is the kryptonite of the homicide detective).

2. THE KILLER SHOULD LEAVE NO FORENSIC EVIDENCE.

2.1 If there is no motive, then only physical clues remain (along with witnesses—see item 4 below).

2.2 According to PHI, a critical element in establishing culpability is Locard's Principle, which states:

> 2.2.1 The perpetrator will take away traces of the victim and the scene.
>
> 2.2.2 The victim will retain traces of the perpetrator and may leave traces of him or herself on the perpetrator.
>
> 2.2.3 The perpetrator will leave traces of him or herself at the scene.
>
> 2.2.4 A successful murderer will leave no forensic evidence for the homicide detective. Nothing at the scene. Nothing on the victim. Nothing on himself.
>
> 2.2.5 In a perfect murder, there is no crime scene. (No crime scene = no forensic evidence.)
>
> 2.2.6 Always remember that forensic evidence comes in many forms. Patterns of activity can be evidence. As can deviation from patterns.

Just as randomness in victim selection is kryp
tonite to the investigator, so is randomness of
behavior.

Leave NO SINGING BONES.

(Page Two)

3. THE KILLER SHOULD LEAVE NO BODY.

3.1 No body $=$ no forensic evidence.

3.2 No body $=$ no proof of death.

3.3 Without a body, all you have is a missing person. The longer it takes for investigators to shift from a missing persons investigation to a homicide investigation, the better. Any forensic evidence that exists will age. Witnesses' memories will become duller and more easily confused.

3.4 Eliminate the body. Mobsters know this. They bury bodies in building foundations. Cement shoes. Etc.

4. THERE SHOULD BE NO WITNESSES TYING THE KILLER TO THE VICTIM.

4.1 This is simply a restatement of the above points, but instead of forensic or circumstantial ties, this rule focuses on human ties.

4.2 The history of "justice" and the legal system has been built around how to deal with "eyewitness" testimony. Any good murder plan minimizes the possibility of eyewitnesses.

4.3 It is likely that, in getting the victim to a suitable location for elimination, potential witnesses may be encountered. Every effort should be made to make the victim, the killer, and the circumstances of any interaction witnessed as forgettable as possible.

4.4 Seek out crowded places. Better at night. Better where potential witnesses are drinking or under the influence of drugs. Obviously, avoid security cameras and CCTV.

5. THE KILLER SHOULD HAVE AN ALIBI PLACING HIM SOMEWHERE OTHER THAN AT THE CRIME SCENE.

5.1 This goes to the element of opportunity. If you are not near the victim at time of death or disappearance, you do not have "opportunity."

5.2 Verifiability of the alibi is critical. Multiple people—at a party or an event. On video or CCTV. Must be able to prove you weren't anywhere near the victim.

5.3 The further from the crime scene, the better, both in geography and time.

(Page Three)

6. USE UNAVOIDABLE INTERACTIONS WITH THE VICTIM AS OPPORTUNITIES TO MISDIRECT.

6.1 It is inevitable that, in organizing the murder, there will be some traceable actions that must be taken and contacts that must be made, including with the victim.

6.2 Use these necessary connections as opportunities for misdirection by implicating other individuals who have a stronger connection with the victim than you. This will take attention away from you and serve to further confuse the homicide detective.
In other words, not only do you not want to have a

motive, but you should try to leave breadcrumbs that point to other people as having a motive.

* * *

Susie smiled to herself as she closed the folder, placed it inside the safe, and locked up.

Cute. Very cute.

There were definitely good points in *Roy's Rules*. The whole idea of even making a list was so very typical of him. All planning, analysis, and strategy.

Susie knew better. You could plan all you wanted, but in the end, sometimes you just had to *do shit*. Another smile crept across her face as she recalled the words of boxer Mike Tyson: "Everybody has a plan, until they get punched in the face."

CHAPTER TWENTY

Between work, life, and going to coffee houses to use the Wi-Fi, it took several days for Roy and Susie to finish their respective research projects.

They set aside a Saturday morning to debrief over coffee, toast, and the two burner laptops.

Susie went first.

"Harlan was born Joseph Alan Harlan on April 1, 1994. His father is Joseph Alan Harlan Sr., a Texas senator and a lawyer. Mrs. Harlan died when junior was young. He was raised by Dad—an only child.

"I got a lot of the early life stuff from articles about his dad. There isn't much about the son online, at least not before the rape. Although I did find some pictures of him with Dad at different political functions. Campaign stuff. Barbeques, that kind of thing. Then there's this... " She showed Roy her screen, "A picture of him playing football. Nothing noteworthy. No mentions of honors or anything when he graduated.

"As for the rape, I didn't get into the details of the case, as that's your job, but some of the articles do contain background information on him, so I went through those. He was a junior at UT at the time. He did one year at Austin Community College, then transferred in. No indication of whether there was any influence from Daddy involved—no speculation about it, either. Which means that it may have been on merit.

"There's a bunch of pictures of him in connection with the trial. There's actual shots in court, one that looks like it came from a UT yearbook, and this one with Dad at a press conference.

"Anyhow, his major at UT was poli sci. He wasn't in any frat that I could find mention of.

"Um, he lived in an apartment north of campus with two roommates—a Frank Stern and a Marty McCall. This becomes relevant in a minute.

"He must have also been dating a girl at the time of the rape because one article says that his girlfriend 'refused to comment' on the situation.

"Since the trial, he's graduated—a year late—and finished his degree at ACC with a major in poli sci and a minor in government affairs. There was one piece in the *Austin Herald* talking about a protest at UT—anti-rape stuff—kind of focused on his case, so I'm guessing he couldn't finish his degree there because of what happened.

"He's now working at a startup in Austin called Procurex Systems. They build back-end procurement technology for governmental entities—cities, states, and so on. The company was founded by Frank Stern—the former roommate—who is also the CEO.

"But, get this, Procurex recently sued a Seattle-based firm called TrueData Technologies—founded by, fanfare please, none other than Marty McCall. The other roommate. The suit claims that a lot of the code being used by TrueData, along with part of the system's design, was stolen by McCall from Stern and Procurex. The suit is pending in federal court in Austin.

"Harlan works for Procurex as a government contracts manager. So, he's not C-Level, but that may be due to optics issues—the kid's had a shitload of press coverage. I wouldn't want him meeting with clients either. I couldn't find anything on whether or not he owns any part of the company. But, with a daddy in the Senate, I'm guessing that Joe, Jr. can give, or claims he can give, Procurex a leg-up in getting contracts with different governmental entities.

"Oh, and that's not all. I also managed to dig up some info on the Whole Foods incident. The basics are that Harlan was shopping at Whole Foods when he was confronted by Tom Wise in the parking lot. They argued. A fight started. Joe went down and security guards had to pull Tom off him.

"Harlan pressed charges. The thing actually went to trial. Pretty quickly, too—there wasn't much to it. The DA went for aggravated assault, but the jury found Tom guilty of plain old assault—which I believe is a class A misdemeanor—and he was fined a thousand dollars.

"And, get this. The *Austin Herald* interviewed some of the jurors after the trial, and quote, 'When asked if they felt justice was done, juror Mildred Crane responded, *Not really, he should have hit the little bastard harder!*'"

Roy laughed. "Go, Mildred."

"Of course, there was also a civil lawsuit for damages. It was dismissed right after the criminal case was resolved. It settled. But, there are no details—undisclosed terms, blah, blah, blah.

"Something else I also found that I think is interesting," Susie added, typing on her keyboard and turning it slightly so they could both see the screen. "Check this out."

She tapped the touchpad and a video started playing, full-screen, on YouTube. Using her finger, she scrubbed to minute 2:32, then released. After a moment of wheelspinning, the video jumped forward and started.

Joe Harlan Jr. was standing on a stage. He was wearing blue jeans, sneakers, a t-shirt, and a wireless mic. A banner up behind him read "Longhorn Startup." Then, he started speaking.

"For each of the last six years, the Government Accountability Office reports that the Pentagon has overspent its budget. This last year, the amount of overspending was $295 billion. Yes, that's billion with a 'B.'

"Most of you have probably heard stories about $600 toilet seats and $7,000 coffeemakers. But these are anecdotes. Symptoms.

A recent spot audit of the Army found that, of twenty-eight procurement contracts reviewed, eleven of the files contained no information detailing the basis for procurement decisions. The process is broken. And it is costing all of us hard-working taxpayers money.

"My name is Joe Harlan Jr. My team—Marty McCall, Frank

Stern, and I—have a solution to that problem. Our solution is Procurex."

The video continued for another two minutes, pitching Procurex and explaining how their online platform created a process for procurement decisions that could be handled, tracked, and stored online. After Joe finished speaking, the three founders answered questions moderated by Dr. Bob Metcalfe—co-inventor of Ethernet, a UT Professor of Innovation, and the moderator of the event.

Harlan was poised. Eloquent. He was funny, likeable, and he and his two partners seemed to have a good rapport. The video was a little window into their world before the rape allegation and subsequent lawsuit had set it on fire.

"Okay. So, I've seen a lot of pitches. That was a solid nine out of ten," Roy said, pointing at her screen.

"He presents very well, doesn't he? Seems like such a waste—everything that's happened," Susie said thoughtfully, and then added, snapping out of it, "Anyway, that's all I have on Harlan. But," she added, teasingly, "the investigative reporter in me did a bit more."

Roy raised an eyebrow.

"Well, I got to thinking that the issue here is around whether he raped *her*. Ultimately, it comes down to a credibility thing. So, I did a little research on Kristy Wise, as well. You know, just to see what's out there. And, there isn't much, although every little bit—"

"Seems appropriate," Roy finished for her.

"That's right," she agreed with a smile.

Despite the fact that their research was ultimately leading to attempting murder, Roy would have put money on the fact that his wife was enjoying herself in a way he hadn't seen in a long time.

"So, she is not a public figure in any way, shape, or form either. A lot of what I found on her also stemmed from stories about the rape case. Dad is in real estate investment. Mom stays at home. Kristy's an only child. Honors student at St. Stephen's. Freshman at UT when all this went down. Here's a photo." She tapped her mousepad.

"Cute girl," Roy said, looking at the photo. He saw the same ice blue eyes as the mother, sandy blonde hair. High cheekbones. Attractive. "Favors her mother."

"No boyfriend at the time. Was studying biology, pre-med. She was on the lacrosse team. Also something about the Model UN. No arrest record. No claims or mentions of drug issues, or alcohol, or any kind of prior claims of harassment or date rape or anything along those lines."

Susie shook her head. "In summary, just a nice, bright girl starting her college career at UT. Nothing to indicate otherwise," she concluded with a shrug.

"Okay," Roy said. "Good idea to do some checking on her. This is great stuff," he added enthusiastically, "but then, I didn't expect anything less." He chased the words with an admiring smile and then sat up in his seat. "So, the rape...

"From a factual perspective, it's pretty straightforward. I have some of the same stuff. Kristy was a freshman at UT. Good student, not amazing, but top ten percent at her high school, which was good enough to get her into UT.

"There was a lot of media coverage of the case, so there's a decent amount of detail there.

"Harlan and Kristy met during the first week of classes. They hung out with a lot of the same people. One of her close friend's family was friends with Harlan's. That seems to be the initial connection. Harlan Jr. was a junior at the time, as you said.

"They saw each other periodically. Never dated, but went out together as part of the same group.

"So, it's Halloween 2015. They're all out partying. Kristy calls it an early night. She says she's not feeling well. Harlan offers to walk her back to her apartment. He does.

"Security footage shows them both entering the apartment building at around 10:15 p.m. From the body language, their proximity to each other, the gait of their walk, everything still looks fine between them. But, unbeknownst to both, Kristy's roommate—a girl named Bethany Rosen—decides to call it an early night, too. Security footage shows her entering the building roughly forty-five minutes later, at 10:56 p.m.

"She states that when she entered the room, she saw Harlan and Kristy on the living room floor. Kristy's naked from the waist down. Harlan is just rolling off her. He's still wearing a condom. Then, in a stream of apologies about overstaying, he can't get dressed fast enough.

"Now, according to Rosen, Kristy is out cold. Unconscious. Not moving. Her testimony states that, at first, she 'thought she was dead.' So, she loses it. Pulls out a can of mace, starts yelling at Harlan. Calling him a rapist, murderer, and so on, and pretty much chases the guy out.

"Then, Rosen tries waking Kristy, but can't. Starts to 'freak out'—her words—and calls 911. Medics arrive. Take Kristy in. Apparently, she'd ingested roofies, but they're able to detox and stabilize her.

"Of course, she remembers nothing. The rape kit comes up with no semen although they do find some of Harlan's pubic hair on her—but that's consistent with what Rosen saw, so no surprise there.

"Given the hospital report, the girl's memory loss, and Rosen's statement, the police get involved. Harlan is arrested and charged with sexual assault.

"At trial, his lawyers try to prove consent by offering evidence of these three tweets posted by Kristy on the night of the incident.

10:22 p.m.	*Feeling better. Love Halloween. Be safe everyone!*
10:24 p.m.	*Found someone special. Chivalry is not dead! Gonna get funky tonight!*
10:31 p.m.	*Reward your prince charming. Life is short.*

"Harlan claims at trial that, when they started having sex, Kristy was conscious and consenting. He claims she was fine until they finished. And that they both fell asleep on the floor until just when Rosen came in.

"Which meant that the trial became a simple case of credibility. Did she or didn't she consent on the one hand, and did he or didn't he know that she was unconscious or unable to resist on the other?

"The jury went with him. And here's a quote from the jury foreperson that kind of sums it up. *It was very close. Very. Maybe he posted those messages; maybe she did. We don't know. But, in the end, we weren't convinced that he knew she was unconscious. Or when. How can you prove what's inside someone's head? I don't know. They just didn't prove it beyond a reasonable doubt.*"

Susie allowed her mouth to fall open and pulled a face. "Shit! What about the fucking hospital report? The roofies?"

"I know," Roy agreed with a hopeless shake of the head. "It's nuts. But you know as well as I do, the system isn't perfect."

"No wonder the Wises were so pissed off."

There was a long pause as they both processed what they had just shared with each other. Then, Roy looked up, serious. "Do you feel like we've got enough, Suze? It's a classic 'he said, she said'—and a jury heard it and then found for 'him.'"

"Fuck," Susie whispered. She was frustrated. "Where the hell are we going to get better information than what we've got?"

"Well," he said. "I have an idea."

CHAPTER TWENTY ONE

People can be divided into two categories. Some just stumble aimlessly through life, careening from event to event. They don't plan, and have no specific direction or goals. You could call them free spirits, or bohemian. I prefer "stumblers."

There's nothing wrong with being a stumbler, *per se*. In fact, because they don't think ahead, stumblers lead relatively carefree lives. They don't worry about or sweat the small stuff. They are free from thinking about the consequences of their actions. Of course, as a result, they often tend to ignore the impact that their actions might have on others. They are quick to forget those who have trespassed against them, but equally quick at forgetting their own trespasses.

Being a stumbler does have its consequences, however. For a stumbler to be successful—for life to yield a satisfactory bounty—they must have strong improvisational skills. Be able to think on their feet.

The other category of people is made up of "planners." Planners set goals, work toward objectives. They keep lists and diligently maintain them so that they can serve as a roadmap for life. Some of their goals are ambitious, others less so. And thus planners must also become "prioritizers"—something stumblers never have to attempt because, well, they don't plan.

Planners are at their happiest when they have a list of things to do, and they take great pleasure in systematically completing tasks on their list, be they big or small. (As a planner, I actually keep a second list of 'completed items' just to track what I've accomplished.)

It's very easy to get wrapped up in your objectives and ticking items off your list. And, it's hard work prioritizing and making sure you are focused on long-term goals.

XXXL Duffle bag — C
Weekend size duffle bag — C
Quikcrete bags (4) — C
1-gallon jugs of water (6)
20 ft. of anchor chain — C
Small padlocks (5) — C
Handheld GPS
Magnetic compass
Wetsuit, men's size M
Water booties, men's size 10
10-gallon gas can (full)
Handheld waterproof VHS radios (2)
Emergency locator
Hefty 13-gallon trash bags (1 box)
6-pack Michelob Ultra
6-pack Cristal beer
Ice pick — Heavy Duty Titanium Ice Pick from ASR
Outdoor, Silver — C
Piece 12" x 12" plywood
Four-foot long 2" x 6" planks of wood (2)
Medium-sized black hand towel — C

This may seem somewhat simplistic, but it's a perspective as old as time.

Over 2,500 years ago, a Greek named Aesop wrote about planners and stumblers, only he used a metaphor.

In Aesop's fable, the grasshopper is a stumbler: enjoying life, carefree, not thinking ahead. The ant is a planner: hard-working, diligent, saving up for winter.

And so, it comes to pass that when winter arrives, the grasshopper is unprepared and has no choice but to beg the ant for food, but he is turned away and dies.

Aesop was definitely pro-ant. Pro-planner.

Ultimately, stumblers and planners all end up in the same place. The graveyards are full of indispensable ants and mindless grasshoppers. Winter comes for us all. (*Fucking Arya Stark...*)

Perhaps.

But, it takes a planner to get away with murder, and Roy and Susie are planners.

They made a plan, put together their lists, and each began working toward completing tasks on those lists. To be fair, Susie's list was far simpler than her husband's, and therefore her day was shaping up to be much easier than Roy's.

They rose early because he needed to get to the airport. They shared coffee and talked about their plans for the day, oblivious to the morning talk show yammering in the background.

After yoga, Susie went shopping—buying items, many for cash, from the list they had laid out together in advance. Some of the items were for keeps and could be bought using traceable means, i.e. a credit card. But others were strictly cash only.

This is the list Susie shared with me ("C" stands for cash purchase):

While Susie was shopping, Roy slept on an American Airlines flight to Seattle, connecting through Dallas-Fort Worth. The flight arrived around noon with the time difference, which gave him most of the day for meetings and left enough time for him to catch the red-eye at 10:30 p.m., arriving home at 7:10 a.m. the next morning.

Roy had scheduled four meetings back-to-back, though only one was of any real importance to him. Due to the nature of that last meeting, he needed to make the trip alone.

David hadn't been very happy about it. Roy's junior partner was paranoid.

When Roy first met David in the offices of his own startup, he noticed a poster hanging on the wall behind David's desk. At first glance, it looked like one of those eagle-soaring motivational posters that usually have a caption like: *Teamwork. Working together means winning together.*

But, on closer inspection, the caption read: *Only the paranoid survive.* The image was of a large herd of gazelles running in all directions. Just barely visible at the top left was a cheetah who was feasting on one of them.

David suspected everyone and trusted no one. Additionally, he was coming up on a major milestone that exacerbated his paranoia: Cruise Capital's four-year-up-or-out policy.

Roy believed in only keeping talent that could step up to full partner level. In his opinion, four years was long enough to determine whether someone was fit to be partner. He also had a track record of axing more people than he kept. And, while David was confident in his abilities, anything out of the ordinary right now was bound to make him skittish. Roy's solo trip to Seattle could be interpreted in two ways: either he was giving David additional responsibility—meaning that he would be "stepping up"—or he was edging him out.

"David, it's not a question of trust, man," he'd told him. "It's a matter of efficiency. You do the Austin trip this month and I'll go to Seattle. We'll get twice as much done."

"But Roy, this is supposed to be a partnership. You're the

one who told me that 'two heads are better than one.' Now, when you've finally got me agreeing with you, you head off alone. Don't get me wrong, I can handle the meetings by myself, but I thought that was the whole point of this partnership—the whole synergy thing."

"It is. Of course it is, David. It's just a question of resources. I don't need to be in the room with a company to call 'bullshit.' Neither do you. You go to Austin and let them pitch you. I'll do the same in Seattle. We weed out the ones that are non-starters. Then, we jointly follow-up on the ones that look promising. Get more info. Work them together."

Roy could have kicked himself. David's reaction wasn't something that he had anticipated, and he should have. Nonetheless, he'd managed to persuade him that the divide and conquer strategy made sense.

Which meant that, at least for now, he'd managed to allay David's suspicions.

CHAPTER TWENTY TWO

I believe that Roy's decision to meet with McCall was probably what put their plan at greatest risk.

For Roy, it was about confirming what he believed about Harlan and the rape. So, from that perspective, it could be argued that it was somewhat honorable that he should even take the risk to ensure that they weren't planning on ending the life of an innocent young man. But then, this is Roy I'm talking about. This is what he does. In business, performing due diligence is just another part of the investment process.

Nonetheless, from a purely strategic perspective, it was a dangerous move.

The meeting was set at the Trace Bar in the W Hotel Seattle. It had been a long day—three meetings down, one to go.

He ordered a club soda with lemon and was eating bar nuts when he heard someone ask, "Roy Cruise?"

He looked over his shoulder and stood. "Hey, Marty McCall?"

They shook hands.

McCall looked slightly younger than he did in his online photos. He was taller than expected, too, wearing jeans with cowboy boots and a white t-shirt under a light, black leather jacket.

"What you having?" Roy asked.

"Beer please," he said to the bartender who was hovering nearby. "You got a pilsner?"

"Rogers okay?" replied the bartender.

McCall gave him a thumbs-up, and turned toward Roy, who jumped right in. "So, TrueData Series A. You guys are looking to raise quite a lot of cash. Where does it get you?"

McCall went into a detailed discussion of his proposed use-of-funds plan, then preached some about the inefficiencies of "government everything" and how "just fixing procurement" could save taxpayers a ton of money and make TrueData shareholders wealthy.

Roy listened to the pitch with interest, taking some notes on a small pad and asking questions.

Then, as the conversation started losing momentum, Roy signaled the bartender for another round. McCall began to try to "close" Roy, offering to send him a term sheet, have him over to the office for a tour, et cetera, but Roy dodged the offer by asking questions about the legal structure of the business and its capitalization table.

"Okay," he added, with an air of gravity, "so, obvious question: what about this Procurex litigation?"

If McCall was taken aback by the direct question, he didn't show it. Instead, he smiled. "Bunch of bullshit, man. This guy, Frank—you know we were roommates, right?"

"Yep, I read the lawsuit."

"Then you also read our Counterclaim?"

Roy nodded.

In the Counterclaim, McCall and TrueData mirrored the same claims that were being levied against them. McCall added that it was he who'd come up with the idea for the company, he who'd written all the code, and that Frank Stern was the one who was trying to steal it from him.

"The whole thing's just a ridiculous pissing match," McCall said dismissively before taking another swig from his glass, swallowing and adding, "I came up with the idea, and I've got the code to prove it. Date-stamped. I was building this thing back at the apartment while Frank and Joe were out chasing pussy. And we all know how it ended for Joe... I finally got sick of carrying the whole project and cutting them in when they weren't doin' jack. Frank was supposed to be the marketing and fundraising guy, and Joe was supposed to be our 'in' with the government, greasing the skids to get us our first contracts.

"I don't know how much you know about government contracts, but Texas is almost like its own little country. If you can land the state or some of the bigger municipalities, it opens doors all across the country. So, the plan was for me to build it, Frank to raise the money to grow it, and Joe to get us the contracts.

"Well, Joe went and fucked it all up. Kind of hard to focus on building your startup when you're on trial for rape, you know?" There was bitterness in McCall's tone. "Six months into that mess, I told them both I was done. There's no way Frank could raise any cash with all that hanging over us—understandably—and Joe was... well, he was busy. So, we cut ties. All nice and legal. All above board. I bought out their shares—a bit cheap, I'll admit, but fair and square.

"That's when I came out here. You know, implement the same plan, but this time with a focus on the West Coast. And it worked. We landed a few contracts, things were starting to turn around and then, the next thing I know, Joe gets off the hook and they're both suing me for stealing *their* idea." He shook his head and took another sip from his glass. Cheeks glowing red. "Like I said, total bullshit. They're looking for a payoff. They can't build the company because they don't have the skills, so they're trying to rip me off. Total and utter dick move."

"But won't the litigation cost you a lot of time and money?" Roy asked casually, as he signaled the bartender for another round.

"If they could afford to pursue it, yeah. But their lawyer doesn't even do this type of litigation. He defends insurance companies. He's a friend of Dad's—Joe's dad, I mean. They work together. The old fart is way out of his depth, and he's used to working for money—hourly fees and all that. He's doing this case on a contingency.

"How long do you think they'll fight before the time and expense starts to cramp their friendship? We're just going to delay and delay and delay, run up their costs, and give them nothing. You know the game. And we actually have legit claims against them."

Roy had seen this before. It was an ill-conceived game of chicken. The only winners would be the lawyers. He'd actually been one of those lawyers early on in his career, so he knew how it worked and how it would likely play out.

"You mentioned the rape thing," he said, steering the conversation to his main area of interest. "What about all that? I mean, you were his roommate when it happened, right?"

McCall shifted in his chair and then drank slowly from his glass. Roy noticed a change in his demeanor and moved to salvage the conversation. The last thing he needed was for the guy to clam up. "I'm just curious," he said, projecting his best business face. "It was all over the news," he added with a shrug. "Man, I went to UT."

"Bad shit. I mean, the lawsuit's bullshit. But I don't want to go and say anything that could get me sued for slander or something like that, you know? Let's just say that I'm living in Seattle now, and I'm happy to be here. The whole legal process down in Texas—the rape trial—I'm no lawyer, so I really can't comment on it. Fuck. It is what it is, I guess."

"But you were roommates, right?" Roy prompted, aware that he was walking a very thin line. The alcohol he'd been encouraging the guy to swallow could go two ways: loosening his tongue or making him paranoid. He was reminded of his conversation with David. "I mean, I assume at some point you were friends, right?"

"Yeah. All three of us were roommates, you know. And friends for a while. Then, you get to know people, and maybe you move on. I mean, I'm trying to build something new here. That's why I moved."

Fuck.

They were engaged in a conversational ballet—Roy recognized it, though he wasn't sure if his dance partner did. McCall was trying to bring the conversation back to TrueData, while Roy gently pushed him to open up about Harlan. Maybe that was too obvious? Roy tried another line of attack.

"Did you know the girl? What was her name… um, Kristy, right?"

"Yeah, Kristy." McCall paused. "I knew her. She's a real sweet kid. Witty. Good sense of humor. We hung out a few times. A bunch of us I mean. Group of guys and girls. That was some fucked up situation if you ask me."

"What do you think actually happened?" Roy asked, trying not to seem too interested as he asked the question.

McCall paused, scowled and then forced a smile. "Um, this is all kind of getting off topic. Really doesn't have anything to do with—"

Roy cut him off, sensing that he'd pushed too hard. He tried to backpedal—make it seem like idle conversation. Perhaps if he made as though he was ready to go, McCall would open up to keep him talking? "Sorry," he said, rubbing a fictitious ache at the back of his neck. "It's just been a long day talking business. Morbid curiosity, I guess. Read about it all online." Roy chuckled, "And I've still gotta catch the red-eye back." He straightened, stretching his back.

McCall's keen eyes observed him for an uncomfortably long time before he turned from him and stared at something back behind the bar. Roy thought he'd lost the guy and was contemplating getting the check, then heard him say, "You don't really think you're ever gonna be so close to something like that, you know? I mean, you hear about these things, date rape and roofies and all that, but it's always strangers, people you don't know. But this," McCall paused, "... this really hit close to home, you know? For me. I mean, you think you know a guy pretty well and then..." he trailed off there and it was all Roy could do not to lean over the counter so that he could look into the young man's eyes, but then McCall turned to him, eyes full of sadness, glanced around to make sure no one was listening in, and asked, "This is just between us, right?"

Roy gave him his best casual nod.

"You know, I've seen Joe get pretty wasted. Him and Frank both. A lot. Like, blackout, where-are-my-pants, I'll-never-do-tequila-shots-again wasted. And, you know, when Joe drinks, he gets that kind of good ole boy 'let's get some pussy' kind of thing going. Says a lot of stupid shit. *Does* a lot of stupid shit.

"Frank really brings out the worst in him. I mean, Joe's situation with his dad is kinda sad, but Frank comes from a real fucked up family. When the whole thing was going down against Joe, I expected any day for them to rope Frank in. Never happened.

I was surprised."

"Rope him in, how?"

"Man," said McCall, pausing as if considering whether to share more. "Let's just say that Frank was really into the whole pharma scene. I mean, Joe on his own is just a horny little fucker. But Frank was the one bringing drugs into the mix. Now, I don't know anything about the whole Kristy thing firsthand, but I heard more than a couple of people say Frank snuck her the drugs. Whether Joe knew about it or not, I can't say for a fact.

"Could he have known? Yeah, he could have. Do I think he did? Between you, me, and the lamppost—yeah, I do. Hell, Joe would fuck the lamppost if he could make a hole in it. But, did he rape her, knowing she'd been drugged? No fucking idea, man."

McCall drank from his glass. Roy was grateful for the interlude while he processed what he had just heard. Comfortable that he had gotten all he was going to get from McCall, he brought the conversation back to the investment. He told McCall that Cruise Capital was interested, and that he would circle up with his partners when he returned to Miami. Then, he paid the tab, shook the man's hand, and promised to be in touch.

Roy left the hotel and headed to a Target Mobile Store on 2nd Avenue that he'd identified in advance, just five blocks away. He paid cash for a prepaid mobile phone with 200 minutes on it. Then, he walked back to the hotel and called for an Uber to take him to the airport.

CHAPTER TWENTY THREE

Roy's flight from Seattle landed in Miami at just past 7:30 a.m. and he was home by 8:30. Susie had a cup of coffee and some toast waiting for him.

"So, how did it go?" she asked.

"Two take-aways, I think," he said, sitting at the kitchen island with his coffee. "First, I think I'm about as sure as I can be, absent a confession, that Harlan did it, and he maybe even had an accomplice on the roofies. His roommate, Frank Stern."

"No way."

He shared with Susie what he'd learned from McCall.

"So, it sounds like there's very little doubt that Harlan did it," Susie said.

"I agree."

"What was the second take-away?" Susie asked.

"Well, Harlan and Stern are suing McCall—their companies are suing each other, right? I think that gives us a good angle to get Harlan to Miami."

"Explain."

"I can make the case that it makes sense for Cruise Capital to invest in McCall's company, but for the lawsuit. The lawsuit is in the way. The trick to solving that would be getting Harlan to abandon his buddy, Stern. Not that I would do it—the investment, I mean—but I think it gives us a good excuse to have Joe Harlan Jr. come to Miami and visit with Cruise Capital."

"That sounds like a plan, but I think the less you're connected with it, the better."

"Yep. I agree. I think I can sell it to David, though. Let him initiate it. It's got to be believable in case anyone asks later. I'll talk to him tomorrow."

"Won't that make him a suspect?"

Roy thought about the question. "Possibly—I just need to make sure he has a solid alibi. That shouldn't be an issue." He raised his eyebrows. "Man, was he pissed about not making the trip with me," he added, taking a sip from his cup.

Susie stepped over to peck him on the lips. "I have every confidence that you can sell it, Mr. Cruise. And, if not, fuck him. It's your company."

"That's not the point, Suze. It's about making it seem like it's not all my idea, in case anyone ever looks into it."

"Agreed," she replied. "Now, I've got to get to yoga. You working from home today?"

"Yeah. With a shower and traffic, it'd be late by the time I got to the office. Might as well."

"Okay. See you later."

In his study, he pulled the phone he'd purchased in Seattle out of his computer case and placed it in the safe.

In my opinion, that phone and the meeting with McCall were the weak links in Roy's plan.

CHAPTER TWENTY FOUR

"So, how'd it go?" David asked as he situated himself at the conference table.

Roy was entering the room juggling coffee, a bagel (in his mouth), a napkin, his laptop, a folder with notes from his Seattle trip, and a notepad and pen.

"Interesting," Roy replied after removing the bagel from his mouth and taking a bite. "The healthcare pitch was pretty lame. The chicks with the farm-to-market delivery business surprised me, though; very sharp, and cute... you'd have liked the brunette... but too early-stage, I think.

"Then, there was the car seat company. Great product, but a very crowded space. I went to a local baby store, just to see—way too many competitors. Very hard to stand out. I think they're all passes.

"Oh, and I added one company at the last minute," he added, casually, sliding a copy of the investor deck across the board table to his partner. "Seemed interesting. They're competitive with Procurex."

David read the company name on the folder and then looked at Roy askance.

Roy tried not to groan. David's paranoia was back. Not disclosing his visit to TrueData before the trip was going to be a problem. But then, the original objective had simply been to pump McCall for information. It had only been as he was making his way home that he realized that both McCall and TrueData could ultimately form part of their master plan. Now, having putting the meeting on his schedule without any internal discussion whatsoever was naturally going to get Mr. Paranoia's attention.

"Okay. I'll bite," David said. "What the fuck?"

"How do you mean?" Roy half-smiled.

"Man, one of my meetings in Austin was with Procurex—their competition. You know that. You also know they're suing each other. We've done no screening on TrueData. Nothing. Zip. But then you go and meet with them anyway... what the fuck's going on, Roy?"

Roy widened his eyes, dramatically, as if he was surprised by David's outburst. "Well," he began with maximum composure, "David, nothing's 'going on.' It just kind of popped up. And since I was there already, and we know the space some from the work you've done on Procurex—great work, by the way—I thought I'd have a quick look. Besides, they're suing each other—doesn't hurt to hear both sides of the story."

The compliment seemed to assuage David. His posture appeared to relax.

Roy moved to drive the message home. "I had a couple of beers with the CEO. This guy, McCall, he seems like the real deal. He's taken the company from nothing to three major contracts—including L.A. County—in the nine months since he moved to Seattle. Everything is trending positive, but... " Roy paused, "...the company is on the ropes. I mean, he put up a good front, but this lawsuit's gonna kill them. And we both know how it'll end."

"Only the lawyers'll make money."

"McCall knows that, too."

"And... ?" David asked.

"Right. So, I was thinking. McCall needs cash to fight the lawsuit, and to just plain grow. He's in a weak position right now. They have a good product, revenue in place, contracts in place, and a legit business model. But, there's this fucking suit hanging out there that's basically startup syphilis. I think we could get a good chunk of the company at a low valuation because of the lawsuit—they'll go down on their stock price if the money's real."

"Okay. But what about this litigation?"

"Well, that's the thing. We'd have to be in a position to know that it's going away. Dead certain. So, what if we buy part of the company cheap while the lawsuit's an issue, then make it go away? Cha-ching!"

David smiled. He loved the strategy of the business game. He understood the numbers and business models, the SWOT analyses, all the MBA bullshit. But it was the real-world issues that really got his juices flowing. And, really, that's where the big money was hidden.

"From what I read in the court file," David said, "there's only two people that can make that happen. McCall and Stern."

"Yeah, but McCall mentioned that there's another guy on the team at Procurex that's the government connection—Dad's in congress or something, um..." He deliberately didn't speak the name and glanced over at the file.

"Harlan," David filled in, as expected.

"Right. Joe. I haven't met him, but the CEO mentioned him being really connected. Dad's also in a law firm. Apparently, the lawyer representing Procurex is a family friend; sounds like he's handling the suit as a favor—at least that's how McCall made it sound."

"So, you're thinking we make a lowball offer—real money on the table—to McCall for a big piece of TrueData, and somehow we finagle getting Procurex to drop the lawsuit by getting at this Harlan guy?"

"I'm willing to bet that this kid doesn't care if he owns a piece of TrueData or of Procurex, as long as he makes money, right? If he got a job offer at TrueData, doing his government thing, with some equity, I've got to believe that he would be disinclined to have his dad's friend suing the company. And, I'm willing to bet that his memory about 'who did what' might change as far as the lawsuit goes. What do you think?"

David smiled. "It could work. We'd have to be sure we had this guy Harlan in the bag. But, if he's willing to play ball... it's a delicate balance. McCall, though... you think he'll work with this guy?"

"If we buy enough of the company, we're on the board. We make him do it."

David thought about this. Then said, "Maybe we should see what this guy is like—Harlan? And find out if McCall will lower his price? I mean, I have some reservations, but it could work."

Roy nodded. "Makes sense. How about I contact McCall and tell him we're interested, but it's got to be at a much lower price. See what he says. While he's thinking that over, we get this Harlan guy in and check him out. Maybe even make a pitch to have him come over to TrueData, but the lawsuit has to go away... "

David glanced out of the window and Roy could almost see those cogs turning. Then he turned back to him, "That's pretty fucking good, Roy. I mean, the timing's got to work. But if it does, it could be a winner for us. And for McCall."

"And for Harlan."

"Yeah. Let's give it a go," David said.

"Cool. Okay. So, I'll get on the horn with McCall, make him a lowball offer and see what he says. Then we need to see about getting Harlan on board. Why don't we fly him down here? Cheaper than both of us going to Austin."

"Yep. I'll give him a call. Stroke his ego a bit. Get him down here for a little wine and dine, and then we make the pitch."

"Great." Roy looked at the calendar on his phone. "Let's shoot for about two weeks, the last week of April?"

"Got it," David agreed.

CHAPTER TWENTY FIVE

"Hello, Marty? Roy Cruise here."

"Roy! How are you, man? Your flight back okay?"

"Fine, Marty. Long, cramped, and bad food. Otherwise, fantastic."

McCall forced a laugh. Roy noticed this so he got straight to it. "So, listen… we're really liking what we're seeing with your company. You've got great tech. A great platform. Solid team. And the early results are good. But... I think we're going to sit on the sidelines for a while."

There was a short pause as McCall absorbed the last comment.

"Come on, Roy, everything before 'but' is bullshit."

Roy laughed. "Yeah. Well, the problem is the lawsuit, man. You know I was a lawyer before I got into investing. I know litigation. And lawsuits are about a lot of things, but the merits aren't one of them. First off, they're extremely expensive. They're distracting. They're bad PR. And, there's always the off chance that you can lose even a bullshit case.

"It just really ups the risk profile of a company. And I saw enough risk in my lawyer days to last me a lifetime. Don't get me wrong. I love TrueData. We just need the lawsuit gone before we can do anything."

"Roy. Come on. You're killing me, man. I told you how we're handling it. It's barely an issue. We've got great lawyers. I guarantee, it isn't and it won't be a distraction."

Roy didn't respond. Instead, he relaxed back in his chair, placing his feet on the desk. He wanted the guy to sweat.

The young man finally spoke, eagerly. "Listen, Roy. Just tell me what I need to do to prove to you that it won't impact your investment."

"Marty, risk has to be tied to return—the greater the risk, the greater the return. Right now, we see a lot of risk." He shrugged, as if McCall could see him through the phone line. "The only way I can see to mitigate that risk is by discounting for it."

The startup founder fell silent. Traffic rumbled in the distance. He mumbled, "Discounting by how much?"

"To be fair, it can't be any less than sixty percent."

"Shit, Roy! That's fucking nuts! You want me to sell you part of my company at a sixty percent discount because of a bullshit lawsuit? That's insane, man!"

"It may seem that way, Marty, but if this lawsuit goes south and we lose all our money, what do I tell my investors then? That we paid market price for a piece of a great company, knowing full well that it was being sued? *That* would be insane, Marty."

There was more silence.

Roy continued, "I tell you what, Marty. I appreciate that it's a difficult decision for you. Don't answer now. Sleep on it. I know it isn't the number you were expecting, but with that lawsuit out there, it's probably the best you're going to get, at least from us." He paused. "Let's talk again in a couple of weeks."

"Okay, Roy," McCall said, glumly. "And hey, thanks for seeing the value. I'm not sure I agree with you on the litigation risk, but let me have a think. Let me see what I can come up with, if I can find a way around it."

"Sure, Marty. Sounds good. Take care."

Roy hung up the phone and folded his arms behind his head. He knew the game, and he was giving Marty McCall a crash course. He'd been doing this long enough to be able to read people. He knew that Marty would get back to him. It was only a matter of time.

A few minutes later, his computer pinged. It was too soon to be Marty.

He sat up and checked his laptop. It was a new calendar

invitation. One that brought a smile to his face.

Invite:	Meeting with Joe Harlan
Attendees:	David Kim, Roy Cruise, Joe Harlan
Date:	May 3
Time:	9:00 a.m. – 11:00 a.m.
Location:	Cruise Capital, Miami

CHAPTER TWENTY SIX

Susie waited for her weekly grocery run to buy the two six-packs of beer that were the only remaining purchases on her to-do list. She packed up and stored all of the other items as planned, ensuring that the beer went into the mini-fridge on the Yellowfin. She also double-checked to make sure that the fish knife was stowed in the drawer where she normally kept it.

As she walked back to the house, she saw Roy standing on the terrace. He waved to her and they met halfway at the pool.

"Hey, lover!" she said.

Roy smiled. She only called him that when she was horny.

"Hello, angel." They kissed softly on the lips.

"Maybe we should take this into the cabana?" she purred.

"That would be nice."

As they moved in that direction, Susie's mobile phone rang. She looked at the display, at Roy, and then frowned. "It's the resort. Bimini."

Roy left her talking and went upstairs to change into his around-the-house clothes. Having grown up a step below lower-middle class—though not quite poor—Roy had gotten used to the idea of having around-the-house clothes. While Susie would come home in her work clothes, kick off her heels, and just start doing things around the house, Roy felt compelled to change as soon as he got home. In general, if Roy was home, he was in an old pair of jeans and an old law school t-shirt of some sort.

As he came down the stairs, he could hear Susie's voice. Still on the phone.

He swung by the kitchen to grab a snack, then followed her

voice into her office to find her sitting behind her desk, phone still to her ear.

"It's a sixty-foot yacht. Thirty-amp power," she said, pausing to take a delicate sip of Pinot Grigio from her long-stemmed wine glass. "Stern power hook-up, starboard side. We'll be staying on board. Yeah. Uh huh. The vessel's name is 'Lady Suze.'"

She lifted her eyebrows, smiled, and blew him a kiss. "Yes. That's right—seven nights. Fisherman's Village Marina is fine. Yes please, can you use the card on file? Yes? Perfect. No. You can just email me the confirmation. Anything else?" After a final pause, she said, "Thank you. No, that's it. Thanks very much. Goodbye."

She hung up and turned to her husband who had flopped onto the sofa, eating grapes.

"All set," she said. "Seven nights, beginning April 28." She held her glass up in a toast.

Roy smiled and gave her a thumbs-up. "Here we go."

CHAPTER TWENTY SEVEN

Frank and Joe had always been the cool roommates. Marty was the book-smart odd man out.

Marty didn't like to party. It not only rhymed, it was true.

He didn't party like Frank and Joe. Not like a rock star.

When he thought about it, Joe realized that he really hadn't partied like a rock star either—not until he'd met Frank. Frank took it all to a whole new level.

Joe blamed his tendency to repress his desires on Harlan Sr. Dear old dad was always sneaking around with women, always worried about "appearances." A complete hypocrite.

Joe still remembered when he'd had his first inkling of his father's secret life. He'd been just a kid. His mother had still been alive, but bed-ridden, already diagnosed with the big C.

She was getting chemo and having a bad time of it. Her hair had fallen out. Joe remembered because he'd given her his baseball cap from his little league team. She had cried.

Joe's father had hired a lady, Nurse Sally, to help with Mom. Joe's dad worked late, and wasn't always there for his wife—he couldn't be.

One night, a Texas-sized storm rolled in. The rain and thunder hammered against the windows and lightning made phantoms of the furniture. Little Joe wanted to go his parents' room, as he always did on stormy nights. But since his mother had been sick, their room had gotten scary. It smelled bad, like medicine and sweat.

So, Joe thought he would go to see if he could sleep with Nurse Sally. When he went to the guest room, he saw that the light was on under the door, and there was noise coming from the room—a slapping noise. The door was closed, but it was an old house, and there was a good-sized gap between the bottom of the door and the floor—no threshold.

Joe carefully laid down on the floor, slid up to the door, and put his right eye up close to the gap. He couldn't see everything, but he could make out that Nurse Sally was there. He could see her hands and feet. She was on the floor next to the bed in a crawling position. Like a dog.

He could also make out that his dad was kneeling on the floor behind her. Moving. His movements were in synch with the rhythmic slapping sound.

Meanwhile, Joe's mother was two rooms down the hall, dying.

"That's some fucked up shit," was all Frank had to say when Joe told him about it. Although, he understood. Frank's father was on his fourth wife, and Frank was pretty sure he also had at least one other chick on the side.

"Of course, I'm fucked up," Frank would say. "If it's not nature, then it's nurture. With a dad like mine, what do you expect?"

Frank stood by Joe through the whole Kristy bullshit. Of course, Frank kind of had to. The roofies had been his idea. He was the one who put them in her drink. But still, he'd been there for Joe the whole time.

What happened next only served to bring them closer. Marty bailed on both of them, and took the company with him.

That whole mess brought Frank and Joe together. True friends. Joe knew he could count on Frank. So, when Joe got the call from David Kim, he had to tell him. He couldn't leave Frank out in the cold.

"What do you think, man?" Joe asked.

"It's awesome. Miami's amazing. Have you ever been?"

"No. Not yet."

"Awesome club scene," Frank said, making a hang-ten sign with his hand. "Amazing chicks. And these guys are the real deal. Cruise Capital makes companies happen, man. If we can get them to fund us, we're golden." He paused, then asked, "Have you told your dad yet?"

Ever since Kristy, Joe's old man had been keeping a pretty tight rein on his son. If there was a deal to be done with Cruise Capital, Joe's father would need to be in the loop.

"Nah. I have to, yeah, but I wanted to run it by you first."

"Look, Joe, if these guys want to fund us, great. If it's just about a gig for you, that's cool, too. It can't hurt to hear them out. You know me, I'm all about possibilities, my man."

"Okay. But, I'm gonna tell 'em we're a package deal. If they want me, they've gotta hire us both."

"That's my boy! Bros before hos!" Frank said, initiating a fist bump. Joe bumped in return.

"Speaking of…" Joe looked at his phone. "It's almost nine, dude. Want another beer?"

"Sure."

Joe went to Frank's refrigerator. As he retrieved two Bud Lights, the apartment doorbell rang. By the time he made it back to the living room, Frank had already answered it.

"The girls are here!" he yelled.

They stepped into the living room. Small skirts, big hair, too much makeup. Frank was appraising them both from behind as he followed them in.

"Hello, ladies," Joe said, tossing Frank his beer.

Frank caught it, and then the hand of one of the girls, and led her toward his bedroom.

The remaining young woman smiled at Joe and said, "Hi, I'm Sheila." She looked young even with all the makeup. Joe wondered exactly how young.

"You over eighteen?" he asked.

"You wanna see my ID?" she asked, nervous.

"Nah. Not knowing for sure makes it more fun," he said, unzipping his pants and stepping closer to her. Then, he announced, "Sheila, let me introduce you to Big Joe."

Sheila came toward Joe, then knelt down in front of him. Her hands trembled as she reached for him.

Joe took a swig from his beer and thought, *Like a rock star.*

CHAPTER TWENTY EIGHT

At one point, I asked Roy how he was able to make the shift from *normal* person to someone who would attempt to kill a complete stranger. After thinking for a bit, he explained that, while there were a lot of factors that led up to it, ultimately it was a decision that came *to him*.

It wasn't so much intellectual as it was visceral.

He said, "It's like waking up too early. You know. You wake up one morning before your alarm goes off. Maybe twenty minutes before. You know you've got time—you can stay in bed a while longer if you want. So you lie there, breathing, thinking about the day ahead of you. What you've got to get done.

"Then... you just get up. It just happens. You don't say to yourself, 'Now I am going to get up,' and then start moving. You just do it.

"With Harlan, sure, I sat down and planned the whole thing. But then there was a moment, one instant when I thought, 'Shit, I am really going to try to pull this off.' I didn't 'think about deciding.' I just knew."

He then went on to tell me exactly when that realization hit him.

It happened on a beautiful day when he and his wife were out boating. Roy and Susie are familiar with all of the best spots in their area. And there are a lot of them. This is because most of the Florida coast is part of the Atlantic Intracoastal Waterway.

Visualize, if you can, a long, thin ribbon of islands off the Atlantic coast of Florida. The water in between the mainland and that ribbon—a series of bays, lagoons, rivers, and canals—is part of the Intracoastal Waterway, a navigable shipping route that runs all the way from Boston, Massachusetts down to Key West.

Down in Roy and Susie's stomping grounds in southeast Florida, Miami Beach, Fisher Island, and Key Biscayne are a few of the barrier islands that comprise that long, thin ribbon. Most of the islands are connected to the mainland by bridges, though a few are accessible only by ferry.

The water in this part of the Intracoastal is shallow—on average, only ten feet deep with a controlling depth of six feet. It's a safe and popular area for recreational boating, with sandbars and beaches that can be enjoyed virtually year-round. Great for swimming, kite surfing, jet skiing, and so on.

Ever since their morning outing together on the Yellowfin when Roy had explained his plan, they'd been taking the fishing boat out at least once a week. So much so that, by this point, Susie and Roy had turned Miami Gold—the boater's tan.

No matter how much sunscreen you wear, being on a boat is like spending time on a mirror under the sun. The UV rays get through everything—even SPF 100—little by little. If you sunscreen religiously, that slow tanning results in a deep, all-over body tan that you really can't get any other way.

Miami Gold.

They had just spent a lazy day anchored off Nixon Beach, one of their favorite spots on the Intracoastal, and were returning home. As Roy slowly brought the Yellowfin up against their home dock, Susie stood at the bow, waiting to hop to the platform and tie up.

She was wearing a white bikini and had that Miami Gold tan. Her hair was in a ponytail and was sun-streaked from the time they'd been spending on the water. She looked back at him for a moment as they were about to bump the dock and smiled.

Roy said it was that moment. That was when he knew.

In a flash, he saw the Susie he had first seen back at UT. The golden tan, the ponytail, sun-streaked hair, and those jet-black eyes. Her little gemstone earrings were now two-carat diamond studs. But she still had the fine bones and hands; the thin, elegant fingers with short, polished nails.

It was that same Susie. And the energy was there again. It was back. That positive energy that she used to radiate for him, for his benefit. He had missed it. Longed for it. After they had lost Camilla it was as if that warmth had been extinguished, and the world—his world—had turned dark and cold.

Roy felt an overwhelming attraction to his wife in that moment, and he was filled with joy that Susie, albeit scarred from what they'd been through, was his again. As he looked at her, he could see bits of Camilla in her, too—the fine bones, the dark eyes.

Roy isn't the religious type. He's been through too much pain to place any faith in a personal god—a god who actually knows your name and cares what you do every day. He does believe that there is an organizing force in the universe. He believes in energy—maybe even a common energy that all things share that can be tapped into and that can shape our lives.

What first attracted him to Susie was that he could feel that energy flowing from her. And at that moment, on the boat, he said that he once again felt that energy flowing between him and her, and he felt Camilla in it, as well. But all of that, he told me, flowed from Susie.

Susie was the source.

Roy believes in optionality. That there is value in having choices. So, until a decision absolutely has to be made, there is no point in making one. You can choose a path and head in that direction, but until you reach the point of no return, there is always choice.

This is how Roy approached planning the death of Joe Harlan Jr.

Feasible? Yes.

Plan it? Yes.

Do it? We'll see. He'd always thought that the final decision would be made when they had Harlan right there in front of them.

That's what he had thought until that moment on the boat.

It was for Susie that he had planned it. She was all that he had left, and he could never lose her. Never.

He knew then that he was going to go through with the

plan.

When I asked what his grandma would think of all this, of his master plan, of what he was "doing for his wife," he paused. Then, in a serious tone, he recited a bible quote that she had taught him.

Do not seek revenge or bear a grudge against anyone among your people but love your neighbor as yourself. I am the Lord.

Roy then pursed his lips, looked at me and said, half-smiling, "Yeah, well... Fuck that."

CHAPTER TWENTY NINE

"This whole thing seems a bit odd to me," said Harlan Sr., sipping from his scotch.

"Dad. You just don't know anything about startups. Cruise Capital has done a lot of investing, and they've had some big wins. Why can't you believe that they're interested in me?"

"It's not that they're not interested, Joe. They wouldn't have called if they weren't interested. But what they want—that I'm not so sure about."

"That's why we're having the meeting," Joe said, rising from his seat to fetch a drink.

The Harlans lived in West Lake Hills, overlooking the Colorado River. When Joe had transferred to UT, he'd practically begged his father to let him move out and live on his own. Not a day went by that Harlan Sr. didn't regret the decision to let his son leave the nest, only to move in with a bunch of beer-swilling idiots.

This meeting with Cruise Capital could lead to something positive. Harlan Sr. knew enough about how government worked to know that there was a genuine business opportunity here. And, he believed that he could help the boys land some solid government contracts, once they got the platform up and running.

While Joe Junior came with baggage, he also came with the senator's contacts and influence. It was conceivable that Cruise Capital might be willing to overlook one in exchange for the other.

Joe returned with his beer and sat down across from his father out on the deck.

"This first meeting is just to talk about the idea."

"Okay, Joe. Run me through what this guy David said one

more time. Think hard and try not to leave out any details."

Joe sighed. "The guy called me up and said that he met last week with Frank. That he was impressed with the company and what we've done. That he's familiar with the government sector. He said he's really impressed with our vision for the company. That they think there will be some big opportunities in the near future, and that they're looking for someone who knows the space, understands the politics of it all—especially in Texas—and that they'd like to explore the possibility of me working with them.

"I told him I already have a job. He said he understands, but that there's jobs and then there's building a future. He said if I am happy with what I'm doing, fine, but what can it hurt to talk? So, I told him I would talk to Frank about it, and he said that he'd prefer if I didn't, 'cause Frank might not like the idea. That this would be something I would do instead of working with Procurex.

"Then he said they'd fly me down, put me up at a hotel. If I'm interested after the meeting, great. If not, no hard feelings. I told him to go ahead and set it up."

"You think," asked Harlan Sr., "it might be a good idea for me to talk to him?"

"Come on, Dad!" Joe fumed. "I'm twenty-four years old. I'm not a kid anymore! Besides, I'm telling you everything he's telling me. What's the harm? I'm not going to say 'yes' without talking to you first. Frank is cool with it. And don't get me wrong, Procurex has potential, but the lawsuit's only gonna get us so far. We still need a company. We're way behind Marty.

"These guys have a ton of cash. They could either buy us the people to catch up, or maybe they want to build their own and compete with Marty. Or maybe they want to buy one of the companies—Procurex or TrueData? I don't know. What I do know is that I have nothing to lose from taking a trip to Miami and hearing them out. You always say it costs nothing to listen."

Harlan Sr. regarded his son for several seconds before acquiescing. Besides, what could he do, really? Joe was free, white, and (over) twenty-one.

"When do you leave?" he asked.

"I fly out Wednesday, meet with David Thursday, and come back early Friday morning."

"Alright, then. Sounds good." Harlan hesitated, unsure how to express himself with his willful son. He eventually managed, "You know, I am proud of you. Of what you're trying to build. With your career and everything. Just be smart out there, and keep your nose clean, okay?"

Joe nodded. "Will do, Dad."

CHAPTER THIRTY

Roy normally arrived at the office at 8:00 a.m. every day. This Monday morning, he was in over half an hour earlier so that he could prepare for his first meeting of the day.

"Morning, boss," his assistant Eve said as they met in the hallway.

"Good morning, Eve. How is everything?"

"Just about set. J.C. is waiting in the conference room. I'm just checking on coffee."

"Great. Be sure to buzz me when David gets in."

J.C. Cohen was the attorney for Cruise Capital. Roy had begun working with him on a referral when he'd decided to move the company from Texas to Florida. Over time, J.C. had come to handle all legal matters at the company, from corporate to transactions and human resources, which was the subject of that morning's meeting.

Roy entered the conference room.

"Good day, Roy."

They shook hands.

"Good morning. All set?"

"Yes, sir. All the paperwork is in order. Just need you to do a final review on a couple of terms."

They went through the documents, which were edged with yellow sticky tabs marking pages that needed final approval. They reviewed each tabbed page in meticulous detail to ensure that the final points that they had discussed had all been incorporated.

As they got to the last one, the speakerphone on the table came to life. It was Eve.

"Mr. Cruise. Mr. Kim has just arrived."

"Thanks, Eve. We're almost there. Go ahead and send him

in."

David opened the door. "Eve said I should come in?"

"Yes. Grab a seat." Roy gestured to the chair on the opposite side of the board room table.

"Morning, J.C.," David said, reaching across the table to shake the lawyer's hand. He noticed that he was in full battle regalia: pinstriped blue suit, starched white shirt with French cuffs, red tie. Then he looked at Roy. "Okay. So, what's this about?"

"I'll let J.C. explain," Roy said, glancing at the lawyer seated next to him.

J.C. fidgeted with his tie knot, put on his reading glasses, and carefully adjusted the papers in front of him so that all of their edges were perfectly aligned. Then, he picked up his pen and looked at the man across from him.

"Mr. Kim. You were hired by Cruise Capital on May 23, 2014."

David frowned. He knew perfectly well when he'd started at Cruise Capital. He didn't need it read out to him, but he nodded.

"Since that time," the lawyer continued, "you have held the position of junior partner. Your duties have included screening potential investment opportunities; preparation, collection, and review of due diligence documentation; production of due diligence reports; recommendations for investment decisions; and analysis of potential exit opportunities."

J.C. paused, peering over his glasses. If he was expecting a reaction from David, he didn't get one. The man's face was expressionless.

When the lawyer maintained his gaze, David spoke. "I'm sorry. I wasn't sure if that was a question or a statement," he said before breaking the stare-off and glancing at Roy, who at that moment appeared to be finding a peculiar interest in his thumbnail. "What the fuck, Roy?" he asked.

J.C. cleared his throat and continued, "As you know, Cruise Capital has a very strict policy regarding hiring and retention. Hires are vetted very carefully. Performance expectations are high. And partnership decisions are generally made four years from initial hire date. It is an up-or-out policy.

"If you recall…" the lawyer took the first document off the stack in front of him and slid it across the table, "your Employment Agreement, Article Seven, specifically spells out this policy. This same Article Seven also provides that either party may terminate the Employment Agreement with or without cause. Legally, this means that the Company—and by 'Company' I mean Cruise Capital—or you, as the Employee, may terminate your agreement at any time and for any reason. You understood this when you signed the agreement, correct?"

David fought back the impulse to rage at the automaton. "Sure, J.C.," he responded evenly, "I read the agreement. If you recall, you made a point of bringing this to my attention at the time. Jesus, can you please just get to the point?"

The lawyer straightened his shoulders. "I really don't see the need to take the Lord's name—"

"Really? You try sitting on the opposite side of this desk listening to you pontificate like a fucking legal messiah," David seethed, eyes flashing with disdain.

"Gentlemen, please," Roy jumped in. "Mr. Kim's right. Let's put the legalese aside for a moment. And, as you both know, I prefer straight talking anyway. So, let me be blunt…"

Roy reached over and pulled the remaining papers from in front of the lawyer, positioning them on the table in front him. He picked up the first one, glanced at it, and turned it toward his business colleague.

"This is a Termination Agreement. It provides for the end of your employment with Cruise Capital, along the terms of what is outlined in your Employment Agreement. It has the usual non-compete language, confidentiality provisions, and so forth."

Roy placed the document in front of Kim who didn't even glance at it. He'd locked eyes with Roy and wasn't going to give him the satisfaction of breaking the stare.

"Any questions?" Roy asked.

David pushed the Termination Agreement to his right.

"What's behind door number two?" he asked, indicating

the remaining sheet of paper with a quick upward jerk of his chin.

Roy paused, then finally broke eye contact to look down at the remaining sheet. He spread his fingers like spider's legs over it, then placed his fingertips on it, turned it, and slid it toward David.

David stopped it from sliding into his chest with the heel of his palm.

"That," Roy said, "is a Partnership Agreement with your name on it."

"You motherfucker!" David said.

Roy laughed out loud. J.C. dropped his lawyerly pose. Then, as if on cue, the conference door behind David Kim burst open and the other five partners of Cruise Capital streamed in. Eve followed with a tray of champagne flutes while Greg—one of the partners—popped open a bottle of Pol Roger.

Everybody took turns, alternately congratulating the new partner and making fun of his recent ordeal.

Roy then asked for everyone's attention. "So, I know that this little ritual may seem a bit sadistic, but there's a point to it. As you all know, Greg Mendez was the second partner in the firm after me. And when Greg started, he didn't know shit."

Everyone laughed.

"Roy taught me *everything* I know," Greg responded sarcastically.

"All kidding aside. When Greg and I first worked together, one of the core principles that we operated from was optionality. Any time we looked at an investment, there would come a decision point. A time where you had to fish or cut bait... "

"Shit or get off the pot!" Greg confirmed.

"Or that," Roy continued, "but we believed it was critical that the final investment decision, the commitment, be made based solely on the merit of each case. It's too easy to get emotional, to let the effort you've put into a deal, the relationships you've built with the people, affect your final decision and force you to commit too early.

"So, when the time came to offer Greg partnership, we discussed that. I didn't put on the little show that I did today... of course, there was nobody here but us two. But we talked about the decision as a fork in the road—either commit one hundred percent to the firm and all that it stands for, or you walk away, no hard feelings. In fact, every partner in this room will tell you that they were offered the same choice—admittedly, each time with a little more dramatic flair."

Another ripple of laughter.

"We get better every time," J.C. said.

"Not quite ready for an Oscar yet, buddy, but you're getting there," Roy said, patting the man on the arm.

"And so," he added, turning back to David, whose cheeks were now glowing red from all the attention, and lifting his glass, "nothing pleases me more than to propose a toast to our brand new partner—David Kim."

"To David!" they all chorused.

"Oh, actually, before we celebrate, and J.C. correct me if I'm wrong, but I don't think that acceptance can be inferred from the words 'you motherfucker,' can it?'"

More laughter.

The partners erupted into a unified chant of, "*Sign it! Sign it! Sign it!*"

This continued until David put pen to paper, then shook hands and hugged some of his new business partners.

An hour later, pastries devoured and champagne glasses drained, Roy ran into David Kim in the hallway. "Congratulations again," he said, patting him on the shoulder.

"Thanks, Roy. Really appreciate the opportunity. I'm stoked!"

"You deserve it, man," he responded with a grin. "Oh, and by the way, minor business thing. Susie's planned a getaway for the two of us next week. So I'm going to be working from the Bahamas."

"Sure. No worries. I've gotcha covered."

"I'll be on email and available by phone. Only thing is, I forgot about the kid from Austin that we're bringing in... "

"Harlan? No problem. I can push him off, or if you want, I can meet with him and then loop you in later if things look promising."

Roy made a show of thinking about the suggestion. Then, "Nah. Don't put it off. You handle it. Just call me after the meeting for a debrief and we'll take it from there."

VACATION IN BIMINI

DAY ONE

Saturday, April 28, 2018

The night before implementation of the plan began, Susie and Roy took care of eliminating all traces of their research and planning. They took out the burner laptops and deleted all files having anything to do with Harlan. Roy ran the *Landscaping* folder's contents through the shredder. Then, to be safe, he burned the shreds in the barbeque.

They woke early Saturday morning. Susie tidied the house and locked up. Roy went aboard the Sunseeker to make final preparations for their journey.

Roy is pretty meticulous about this kind of thing. Though he pays a company to maintain both boats and the jet ski, he still checked oil levels, coolant levels, fuel levels manually below decks, and all the strainers. Then he cranked up the generator, switched over from shore power, and brought up all the systems.

He already had waypoints to and from Bimini plotted on the GPS from previous trips. Nevertheless, he ran through their planned route just to be sure.

There was a storm coming in—a small system—which wouldn't be a problem as far as getting to Bimini, but might put a crimp in their plans. He'd been watching it carefully, checking the NOAA—the National Oceanic and Atmospheric Association website—every couple of hours for updates.

Roy was a believer in the adage that "A good sailor weathers the storm he cannot avoid, and avoids the storm he cannot weather." On this occasion, the weather was something they'd have to work with as best they could.

He was finishing his departure checklist when Susie came

aboard and joined him on the flybridge.

"All set, Captain?" she asked. "Ready to cast off?"

"Yep. All good to go. You want to do the honors, or shall I?"

She smiled at him. "It's been a while, so let me."

"Sure," he said, stepping aside.

Susie took the captain's chair and started the engines as Roy went below to the deck level to cast off.

She turned on the bow and stern thrusters and tweaked each gently against the dock to make sure they were operational.

"All clear!" Roy shouted from below.

Susie gently pulsed the thrusters, and the boat slowly glided away from the dock. Once clear, she began to manipulate the two throttles, alternating between port and starboard engines to keep the boat moving straight down the coffee-colored waters of the channel. It was a bit of a trek out to the bay, which—running at six knots—offered plenty of time for the engines to warm up.

Once they entered the green waters of the bay, Susie set course for Biscayne Channel, which would take them just past the tip of Key Biscayne and out into the Florida Straits.

Roy always got a kick out of passing through Biscayne Channel and the view of Stiltsville. Though it was down to only seven houses, at one point there'd been almost thirty wooden buildings in the middle of the bay, lining the sand flats on either side of Biscayne Channel. The destination had been dubbed Stiltsville after the wooden pilings—stilts—on which these buildings were constructed.

Construction of Stiltsville began during Prohibition. The first building—Crawfish Eddie's—started the whole thing. He sold bait, beer, and food off his shack to local boaters. Others soon followed.

By the 1940s, a number of invitation-only member clubs were operating in the flats—gambling, black market whisky, celebrities. Ted Kennedy had his bachelor party out there.

The exciting days of Stiltsville ended in 1965 with Hurricane Betsy. After that storm, the state declined to issue any new permits for construction and placed restrictions on the rebuilding of existing structures. Commercial operations in Stiltsville were banned altogether in 1969.

Roy marvelled at how something so rustic could have been considered desirable—supply and demand was always his conclusion. Even at its peak, there'd been very few buildings out there, and you could only get there by boat. The exclusivity and remoteness had made them desirable.

Of course, that was then. Hurricanes and government regulation destroyed the businesses. Roy chuckled to himself and wondered which of the two was the more destructive force.

Once you're out past Stiltsville and through the channel, the path to Bimini is almost due east. The distance is about forty miles. Traveling at twenty knots in good weather, the trip takes about two hours.

Susie set the autopilot to ninety-five degrees, about five degrees south of where she actually wanted to end up in order to compensate for the Gulf Stream current, and then she and Roy sat back to relax.

Crossing the Florida Straits can be simple or deadly. It all depends on the weather. Think of the Florida Straits as a giant oceanic river running from south to north through the deep trough between Florida and the landmass of the Bahama Banks. The water in that trough reaches depths of over 6,000 feet. Ocean liners navigate the surface while all manner of sharks live beneath.

Because the water in the straits flows from south to north, a north wind creates wind-against-tide conditions, resulting in steep waves that can make crossing dangerous. The best crossing conditions are in light to no wind, or with a southerly wind.

For their crossing, Susie and Roy had an easterly wind at about five knots, which made for tolerable conditions. Their greater concern was the weather over the next couple of days, since the forecast showed winds from the north at five to ten knots. Not good news.

"Whatcha thinking, babe?"

"Weather." Roy looked out to the horizon. The Sunseeker was plowing through two- to three-foot seas like a warm knife through butter. While they felt the movement below, as they were seated well above the action in the flybridge, they were spared a great deal of the discomfort. "Seas like this, it's not impossible, but the risk level definitely goes up."

"Well, all that could change."

"Yeah. We'll just play it by ear. See what tomorrow brings."

The Straits crossing is beautiful, something everyone should experience at least once. As you head for the Bahamas, the Miami skyline slowly recedes, fading into nothing. And just about thirty minutes after it disappears (depending on your speed), the island of Bimini comes into view.

At first viewing, the water in the Bahamas is so strikingly blue as to seem artificial, like blue antifreeze. This is because the islands of the Bahamas are really just the bits of land that peek out from under the water, and are all actually part of a massive limestone shoal called the Bahama Banks.

The submerged part of the shoal is not far underwater— twenty to forty feet on average. The Banks break the waves coming in from the Atlantic and reduce the amount of bottom sediment stirred up around the islands. This, plus the shallow depths and low levels of green-producing phytoplankton, all combine to create that super-blue water.

Susie and Roy navigated onto the Banks and into South Cat Cay. Roy preferred going through customs there because it was generally less crowded. They docked at the fuel station—not that they needed to refuel, but topping off their tank meant not having to pay a slip fee while they passed customs.

At the first port of call in the Bahamas, only the captain goes ashore to present immigration paperwork. So, while Susie handled refueling, Roy walked over to the customs and immigration house. He sat on the porch bench to the left outside the small wooden building until summoned by the immigration officer to enter the left door of the building. The tiny office was neat and well air-conditioned.

Roy presented their passports and visa forms, and answered the usual questions regarding length of stay and so forth. Their passports were stamped and they were formally admitted into the country.

Roy then went back outside the same building and sat on the porch bench to the right until he was asked to enter the right door of the same small building by the customs officer. Roy declared his boat—with the jet ski that they'd brought on the swim platform and one paddleboard as tenders—and again waited for his documents to be stamped and returned to him.

Once all of their paperwork was processed, Roy put everything into a Ziploc bag for safekeeping and returned to the Sunseeker. He then took the helm and ran the boat out of Cat Cay and up north to Bimini, where they docked at the Fisherman's Village Marina at Resort World Bimini.

While Roy ran a hose over the boat to wash off the sea salt, Susie went ashore to collect the golf cart they had reserved by phone from Sue & Joy's, the little convenience store and golf cart rental shop next to the marina. While they weren't planning on moving around much on the island, renting a golf cart was a documentable transaction that could be verified.

By the time Susie returned, Roy had already put the jet ski into the water and tied it near the bow of the boat so as to leave the swim platform clear.

They dined at The Tides that evening, had an expensive bottle of wine, and paid with AMEX, tipping well to ensure that the waiter would remember them. Then, they headed back to the boat.

They sat for a while on the flybridge, sharing a drink and a blanket. There was a cool wind blowing from the north and the air smelled of ozone.

There was an almost full moon out, though it wasn't visible through the clouds. Roy had factored the lunar phases into his planning. The moon would be full the following night, April 29, 2018 at 8:59 p.m. From that point on, it would begin waning, but would still provide sufficient illumination for what he had planned, provided there were no clouds.

Bad weather was on the way. The critical issue was timing. When would it break, and for how long? Time would tell, but for now they went down below and allowed the boat to rock them to sleep as the rain tapped a lullaby.

DAY TWO

Sunday, April 29, 2018

When Roy and Susie woke the next day, it was to rivulets of rainwater running down the boat's windows. It looked like the bad weather planned on staying.

They had coffee in the stern cockpit. Roy fiddled about on his laptop, checking emails and sending a few quick responses. It was important that this be a working vacation and that he maintain intermittent but constant contact with the office. The better he maintained contact, the better he could account for his activities and whereabouts.

While he worked, Susie read a book.

At 11:00 a.m., they got into their beach gear and drove the golf cart north where they went for a walk on the beach. They carried with them a map of the island and used Navionics—a GPS boating app—to scout landmarks that would be needed for the implementation of their plan. They did not enter any landmarks or coordinates into the app. Rather, they noted them on paper.

When lunchtime rolled around, they weren't that hungry. Instead, they went down to the master stateroom. Roy caught Susie's hand and smiled at her, mischievously, before kissing her. She responded. Her hungry kiss was his cue to slip a hand up her t-shirt and cup her bikini-clad breasts before fumbling to free them and then delicately allowing his palm to touch her nipple. They continued kissing—slowly, in anticipation of what was to come.

It wasn't long before Roy felt her nipples harden under his touch. They giggled like school children before she pulled him back onto the bed, where she crawled backward until her head hit the headboard.

"Ouch!"

More giggles as he tugged at her bikini bottoms and she pushed at his trunks.

Sometimes they would linger on foreplay, other times it was oral, and, although they never discussed it, Susie would usually lead.

Not today.

Roy climbed on top and was inside her sooner than she expected, the surprise eliciting a delighted squeal from her. He was different this time—urgent—and it excited her.

Susie raised her legs and Roy placed his arms under them, locking the fronts of his elbows into the backs of her knees, lifting them up and out. Susie's hips began to buck in synch with her groans, and Roy let one hand slip down and rub hard, fast circles against her clit, knowing the stimulation would push her over the edge. As she climaxed, he stopped thrusting and started grinding his pubis into hers. Her first orgasm was barely over before Susie whimpered and came a second time. That was Roy's cue to thrust faster and faster until he exploded inside her.

Sex on the boat always felt different to them. They could never decide whether it was the gentle movement of the craft bobbing on water that accentuated the rhythmic thrusts of lovemaking or the subconscious knowledge of proximity to the primordial soup of the sea. Regardless, it was something that they both enjoyed and had missed.

Afterward, they had mimosas and reviewed the 'Harlan plan' in detail one more time. The plan was risky, but it involved multiple points at which they could change direction and/or abort.

The key points of the plan were settled.

There was only one point they still hadn't agreed on. Whether to drown Harlan, or kill him first and then sink his body.

Roy had always been for drowning. It wasn't a question of pain or suffering. He simply felt that, if they drowned Harlan, there was less risk of any bodily fluids contaminating the crime scene. His view was purely practical.

Susie had taken a more philosophical view. She felt that just leaving Harlan to drown didn't bring them closure. They had undertaken the task of avenging Kristy, and through her, Camilla. That meant actually taking Harlan's life. Leaving the killing to a third party, even if that third party was the sea and death was assured, somehow felt to Susie like copping out.

"It's like *Game of Thrones*. When a lord condemns someone to death, he acts as the executioner. If you pass sentence, you should swing the sword."

Roy didn't get it, but in the larger scheme of things, it was a minor point. And as they say, "Happy wife, happy life." So, he had agreed to provision for a direct kill option. The question was, how?

They'd considered drugs, but the only drug available to them without creating a trail for the police was a bottle of Xanax that Susie had left from when she'd been dealing with Camilla's death. Susie felt that there was a certain poetic justice in using pills to kill Harlan. But while the Xanax could certainly tranquilize him and likely render him unconscious, they'd learned with some research that they didn't have enough of the drug to actually kill him.

In the end, they'd settled on two direct kill options. Both were very hands-on. The first was suffocation—either via plastic bag or via strangulation (which, technically, could cause death by both impeding respiration and by limiting or stopping the flow of blood to the brain). To this end, they had purchased a box of Hefty trash bags—kitchen size. Roy had tried one on, and it fit over his head nicely.

The other option was the ice pick. The thrust of an ice pick directly into the heart would cause almost immediate death. If it wasn't removed from the victim's body, the amount of blood lost outside the body should be zero. And, even if it was removed, blood loss would be next to nothing.

Of the two options, Susie was for the ice pick. Roy, again, felt that the Hefty was probably the better approach. In the end, they had decided to prepare for both, as well as drowning, and make the final decision in real time.

At five, Roy went up top and turned on the grill. He cooked tuna steaks and asparagus. They were forced to eat in the cabin, as the weather had not improved. At nine o' clock, they decided to call it a night.

DAY THREE

Monday, April 30, 2018

Roy was up early, puttering around the boat. Susie woke to the sound of him moving about and the smell of coffee. She rose, poured herself a cup, and joined him on the flybridge.

The sun was up, the air humid from the evaporation of recently fallen rain. It was cloudy and windy, but at least it was dry.

"Better weather today," Susie observed.

"Yeah. According to NOAA, the Straits are still at three to five feet. Not ideal."

"No. Well, if not today, there's still tomorrow."

"Let's see how things evolve. Maybe we give it a shot."

They decided to go for a walk, making sure to pass by the security cameras in front of the hotel. They went into the gift shop—which also had a security camera—and bought a tube of toothpaste. Then they returned to the boat, where Roy checked email and responded to messages. Then he read as Susie watched TV.

In the evening, they watched the sunset from the flybridge. The skies were clear, the wind had finally calmed, and the most recent information from NOAA put the Straits at two to three feet.

Their plan called for Roy to leave Bimini by night.

By day, jet ski activity around Bimini would be of little interest to anyone, and no one would be likely to remember what they saw or when. But a jet ski in the Straits was a different story. While it wasn't unheard of, it was rare to cross from Miami to Bimini on jet ski. The few that made the crossing did so in groups and by day, usually with a support boat. A jet ski out alone in the Straits by day was likely to draw attention and possibly become the subject of radio traffic. They did not need that kind of attention.

Hence, the night crossing. Since they didn't have running lights, a jet ski in the Straits at night would be all but impossible to see. And no one would be crazy or stupid enough to cross the Straits on a jet ski at night. Which was why Roy planned to do just that.

The biggest threat to making the crossing in the dark, aside from weather-driven waves, was other watercraft. Getting hit by or hitting a tanker was the biggest risk. Roy would keep a close eye out for other vessels, as they would have running lights. There was also the added risk of hitting virtually invisible obstacles—a floating log or a pallet of cocaine.

After sunset, they had dinner down in the cabin: prosciutto, cheese, and crackers.

"So," asked Susie, "what do you think?"

"I think we give it a try tonight. From the sounds of it, the weather tomorrow is likely to be the same, possibly better. I'd say we take a shot tonight and, if it's too rough, abort and try again tomorrow, rather than wait until tomorrow and put all our eggs in one basket. That way, I can also get a feeling for how bad it really is. What do you think?"

"Makes sense. You can always turn around and come back. But if tonight's as good as it gets, and it's doable, then you get it over with. Getting there is the critical part. Coming back isn't such a big deal."

"Yeah, but I'd just really like to be with you on the boat when we head back. Just to be safe."

"Roy, I doubt that things will move that fast. It'll take days for them to figure out he's missing. More to figure out he's dead. I don't think that's as big a risk as you think."

"I know. But it's zero risk if we're together, right?"

"True. I agree, don't get me wrong. I'm just saying, if you can't get back, we can deal with that. But if you can't get there to begin with, then the whole plan blows up... "

He nodded.

After sunset, they went to the casino. They withdrew their daily limit of cash from the ATM and went to the low stakes blackjack table, where they played until almost midnight. Susie drank white wine and Roy had club sodas. Both made sure to make eye contact a couple of times with the security camera that sat up and to the right of them on the ceiling.

At 11:45 p.m., they left the casino, returned to the boat, and went to bed.

DAY FOUR

Tuesday, May 1, 2018

The alarm woke them at 2:00 a.m.

Roy went up to the cabin, where the moonlight was sufficient for him to see what he was doing without having to turn on any of the lights in the boat. He slipped into his wetsuit and booties, and hung a pair of goggles around his neck.

While he dressed, Susie kept watch from the flybridge until she was satisfied that all was quiet. Then, she went down and pulled the jet ski up by the swim platform and tied it close. From the crew cabin on the stern of the boat, she brought out the ditch bag and the extra ten-gallon tank of gas.

The ditch bag contained a magnetic compass, an EPIRB, two quarts of water, a small mirror, a flare gun, sunscreen, a handheld VHF radio, an inflatable flotation device, a small oar with a telescoping handle, and a Miami-purchased burner phone.

She was securing these to the jet ski when Roy came out. He was fully prepped. Roy affixed the GPS unit to the attachment he had rigged to the steering column of the jet ski. He would wait until he was out of the marina to turn it on.

That was it.

"Good luck, babe," Susie said, kissing her husband on the lips and then wiping the Vaseline from her nose. Roy had generously covered his face with the stuff to protect it from the salt water.

"See you tomorrow," he said with a wink.

He straddled the jet ski and Susie used the line to pull it along the side of the boat to the bow. There, Roy released the line to Susie and pushed off, out and away from the Sunseeker.

He used the telescoping oar to paddle away from all of the

nearby boats so as not to wake anyone when he started the engine. Once he was clear, he tapped the throttle to get it into forward gear, and quietly put-putted out of the marina and into the channel.

The waters were relatively calm. Roy could feel the light breeze on his face. He hadn't yet put the goggles over his eyes. He kept to the center of the channel; even though the water was deep enough all around him, he didn't want to risk hitting a shallow patch of sand and sucking a bunch of crap up into the impeller. As he approached the end of the channel, he switched the GPS on. It booted up, and the screen map showed him his exact position.

Roy rounded the point of the island, just past Alice Town, and turned west, where the wave height increased significantly. He was riding up and down swells of three to four feet. The water was very choppy, though he knew that was in part due to the water off the Straits crashing against the island and bouncing back. He hoped that, once he put some distance between himself and Bimini, the waves would decrease since large waves prevented him from opening up the jet ski. He was still chugging along at about ten knots. At this rate, it would take him five hours to get back to the house—he'd be arriving in daylight, which was not good.

Though he could see relatively well by the moonlight, he couldn't see well enough to really gun it because the waves all ran together in the dark. He needed to be able to see which way the waves were running so he could position his body on the jet ski depending on whether he was riding up or down the waves. The visibility just wasn't good enough for that, and he wasn't even wearing the goggles yet, which would get wet and further reduce his visual acuity.

He checked the time and position on the GPS and decided to give it another thirty minutes to see if the conditions improved as he got farther away from land.

* * *

Susie was lying in the master stateroom. She couldn't sleep. If everything went according to plan, Roy would arrive at the house between 4:00 a.m. and 5:00 a.m.

After all the planning, it was hard for her to believe that the day had finally come. She touched her belly where a knot was forming and then turned and hugged a pillow, tuning in to the gentle rocking of the boat. It was calming. Peaceful.

She had spent a lot of time on the water since marrying Roy. Before that, she'd only been on a boat once. That cruise ship, when she'd reconnected with Deb. That had been decades ago—it seemed like a lifetime had passed since then.

At the end of that cruise, they had exchanged contact details, though Susie had been reluctant to stay in touch. While she'd felt a strong connection to Deb, she'd been somewhat fearful of her, as well, afraid of how she felt when she was with Deb.

Susie admitted to me that she'd seen Deb, periodically, over the years. They spoke occasionally by phone, but most of the calls were inconsequential catching up or planning a tryst. But two of the calls she told me about were significant. One took place shortly after Camilla's death, with the second coming the day after.

* * *

As a child, when the phone rang in her house, to Susie it was like Christmas day. She had no idea who was calling when she picked up. Was it Nana, announcing an unexpected visit? Or one of her mom's friends? Or one of her own friends calling to gossip about school or boys?

That old-fashioned ringing of a telephone, the kind that was connected by a wire to a wall, was an announcement of something new and amazing, full of opportunity and hope.

Then came answering machines that allowed you to screen calls before or instead of answering. Screening took away all the surprise. Susie loved taking the chance and just picking up, risking that it might be someone you didn't want to talk to—and being thrilled if it was someone you did.

She described answering machines as condoms for telephones. Safe, but uncomfortable.

Then came Caller ID. No need to answer a call without knowing who was on the line—or at least what phone number they were calling from—ever again. Why in God's name would you answer a phone call from someone you don't know? Would you have sex with a total stranger? Would you?

Susie thinks technology has taken all the mystery and excitement out of receiving a phone call. It's conditioned us all into feeling that we are *entitled* to know who is calling, especially when that one word appears on screen.

UNKNOWN.

Susie finds UNKNOWN annoying and exciting. Irritating, yet nostalgically sexy.

UNKNOWN returned some of that long-forgotten mystique to receiving telephone calls.

Who could it be?

Telemarketing?

Alumni fundraising?

The FBI?

This particular call Susie told me about was from UNKNOWN, and she answered on the third ring.

"Hello?"

"Hi there, honey," said a female voice in that unmistakable Texas drawl.

"Deb?" Susie looked around the kitchen. Luckily, she was home alone. Consuelo was upstairs somewhere, vacuuming. And yet, she still felt the compulsion to check, to make sure she wasn't within earshot of anyone.

"The one and only," Deb said.

"Oh, Deb... " Susie struggled not to cry, so many emotions

welled up inside her all at once.

"Honey. I am sooo sorry about Camilla. I just found out. It's horrible. Just horrible. Are you holding up alright? You be tough, girl. You need to be." Deb paused, but Susie knew her and knew there was more coming. "And you listen to me. It will pass. I know it may seem like the end of the world, but you're tough. You always have been. How about Roy? Is he holding up? Is he helping you through it?"

Susie breathed out slowly, attempting to control her emotions. "You know how Roy is. He's all analysis. It's all in his head. He's doing what he can. He's trying. He's in a funk... obviously. But he's been a trooper. He organized the service—I just couldn't. I'm only just now getting back to some semblance of a... " The rest of the words drowned in her throat and she began to cry.

"Oh, honey. Now, you go ahead. Get all that out of you. Oh, girl. I wish I could be there to hold you." Deb paused. She could hear Susie crying and she gave her a few moments, and then she offered, "You have to take consolation where you can, sweetie. She went fast? No pain. Is that true?"

"Um," Susie sniffed, trying to get a hold of herself. "Yes. I think so. They said it was instant... " another sob snatched the rest of the word away from her and she took a few more seconds before garbling. "Um, that, that's what they told us anyway. We... it had to be a closed coffin... because—" Her throat closed, and the tears came once more.

"Well, there you are. We all gotta go sometime. Honey, we're all dying, from the day we're born. And 'we know not the day nor the hour...'"

Susie laughed through the tears. "When the fuck did you get Jesus?"

Deb laughed, and responded in her preacher voice. Susie could imagine the Holy Roller expression on Deb's face as she said, "Now, Susie, at these times, we must all seek consolation in the Lord."

"Praise be!" she replied with a sniff and a chuckle. There was a long pause before Susie spoke again. "It's good to hear your voice, Deb."

"Oh, yours too, hun. So, tell me, are you being smart about all this? Keeping it together?"

"What do you think?"

"Well, that's what I'm scared of. That's why I'm calling. Who knows you best, hun, who knows you best?"

"Deb does." Susie smiled.

"And who knows what you need?"

Susie was about to laugh but instead her face saddened. "You know what I really need, Deb? What I really need?" she asked in a whisper.

"Why do you think I'm calling you, girlfriend? I know my girl. I read in the news that the boy's in critical condition. Is that right?"

Susie nodded as if her friend could see her. "A coma. Drug-induced. Who knows what'll happen?" Her face darkened. "I know what I want to happen," she said through gritted teeth. "Fuck, if I could get my hands on him, I'd—"

"Easy there, girl. You're way too close to it all to be thinking that kind of shit. Be smart. Even if you did everything perfect, they'd go straight from his hospital room to your front door with a warrant."

"I don't give a fuck!"

"Sure you do. You've just gotta let nature take its course."

"Bullshit! What about Camilla? What about my baby girl? Fuck nature! I think we should be the ones to do it."

"Get real, babe. You're not thinking straight. You need to get focused. What kind of life will you have in Leavenworth? Or whatever it is in Florida." Deb took a beat, then asked, "Susie, when you said 'we should be the ones to do it,' who exactly did you mean?"

Deb waited for a reply, but none came. She pressed, "Susie, did you talk to Roy about... this... about what you want to happen?"

Susie took a deep breath, before answering defiantly, "Maybe—a little."

"Oh, for fuck's sake, girl, you have lost your mind! You need to get that shit outta your head, right now. You hear me? I told you. You're way too close to this. You, for sure. You *and* Roy, worse. Honey, Roy is a lot of things, but a killer, he ain't."

"He's actually thinking about it."

Deb fell silent. She wasn't expecting that answer. "What, he told you this?"

"No... not exactly... not yet. But I know him. I can tell. I've been riding his ass, blaming him. I know it's unfair, but I can't help it."

"What did he *say*?"

"Nothing specific."

"Susie, this kind of thing, this isn't like playing bridge, honey. You can't *hint*. You can't insinuate. You don't go leaving murder magazines open on the coffee table. You gotta be specific." Deb's voice went up an octave. "But, I tell you what. It'd be the stupidest thing you could do. Both of you. 'Cause like I said, even if you pull off a perfect murder, there'll be a 'knock knock' on your front door in twenty-four hours max, I guarantee. And how well do you think old Roy'll hold up under questioning?"

They both paused, considering.

"Look, honey," Deb continued, "I get that you want to go all Ezekiel 25:17 on this kid. But these kinds of things, they got to be done with a cool head. You know that. No emotion. And, honey, that ain't you right now."

"It could be."

Deb waited for a long time, waiting to see if Susie would fill the empty space, but she didn't. "Look, hun, this payphone smells like vagrant piss. I gotta go. But you just need to leave this whole thing to Deb. I'll take care of everything. You make peace with your husband. And be kind to yourself. Remember, every day is precious, honey."

Susie remained silent as she attempted to swallow a new wave of tears.

"I tell you what, Susie. Honey, you sleep on it. I'll call you tomorrow, 'same bat-time, same bat-channel.' And you tell me then that you're gonna to do the smart thing. Okay?"

Susie bit her lip. "Okay," she said, reluctantly.

"But if you talk to Roy about this—and I don't recommend it, but I know you, right? Who knows you if Deb don't? *If* you talk to Roy about this, you gotta be di-rect. You gotta tell him that the plan is to go Old Testament 'eye for an eye' on this fucking kid. You gotta be up-front. No *hinting*, no suggesting. Draw him a picture and color it in, okay? You got it?"

Susie chuckled.

"Got it?"

"Yeah, Deb. I got it."

"M-kay. I'll call you tomorrow. And don't do nothing stupid between now and then, you promise?"

Susie nodded again. "I promise," she said. "Thanks, Deb."

"Shit... I love you, babe. But then you already know that."

Susie hesitated, then said, quickly, "I love you, too!" But Deb had already hung up.

That evening, Susie had a conversation with Roy, which I shared with you earlier. I'm speaking, of course, of the one in the study—where Susie drank scotch and proposed killing Bareto.

The following morning, as promised, Deb called back.

* * *

Susie was just dozing off when she felt a *thunk* against the hull of the boat.

She sprang out of bed and headed up the stairs. As she approached the top, she heard a tapping against the door to the cabin, metal against glass, and saw Roy standing outside, barely lit by the moonlight.

She hastily unlocked the door.

As he toweled off, he said, "Too rough out there. Plenty of light. The moon's great. You can see. But there's not enough visibility to know what's behind the next wave. Very slow going. If I'd kept up, I wouldn't have gotten there until after seven, at least. Way too risky."

Susie hid her disappointment. "No worries. We'll try again tomorrow," she said with a smile. "Right now, you need to get out of that stuff, get dry, and get some rest."

Roy was already stripping down, his wetsuit hanging around his waist, as he toweled his hair and chest.

"I'll get you another towel and some dry clothes," Susie said.

By the time she came back, Roy was naked.

She smiled. "Did the wetsuit not help?" she asked, looking down between his legs.

Roy followed her gaze and laughed. "Not very sexy, huh? You'd never have married me if you'd seen him this tiny, right?"

She handed him sweatpants and kissed his wet hair.

"No. The gear was all good. Wetsuit was fine. I was actually a bit warm. Though, I wasn't out there very long—about an hour in the actual Straits. I did feel my body temp dropping, so I think that for a longer trip the wetsuit will be a lifesaver—literally.

"GPS was good. Hard to see it through the goggles. But the spray was an issue mainly because of the waves. I think that if it's calmer tomorrow, I may not have to use them the whole time. All said, it comes down to the waves. Just too choppy."

"Well, let's get some sleep," Susie said. "You need to rest and reset. Hopefully, conditions will be better tomorrow."

They went to bed and Roy put his arm around her, pressing his body against her back. It wasn't long before he warmed up. The blood returned to his loins and Susie could feel him gently rubbing against her, hinting. She pretended not to notice, and went to sleep thinking of Deb.

* * *

Susie and Roy woke late the next day. They had slept a good nine hours. The sun was already streaking in through the portholes in the stateroom.

Susie made eggs and toast and served them with ham slices. Roy made coffee and sliced grapefruit.

While they ate, Roy tuned the VHF to the weather channel. Per NOAA, the seas were at two feet with a southwesterly wind at five knots.

After breakfast, they headed topside. It was a sunny, clear day with virtually no wind, and it was hot.

They boarded the golf cart and took a tour of the west side of the island. The seas towards the west and Miami looked extremely calm.

"If this holds up, we're golden, Suze."

"Fingers crossed," she responded.

They spent the rest of the day around the marina, being seen. In accordance with the plan, Roy went into the hotel gift shop, bought some sunscreen, and stopped just short of smiling for the security camera.

They lounged in the pool by the Mega-Yacht Marina and drank a couple of mojitos at the swim-up bar before visiting the sushi bar at the Hilton.

Roy switched things up this time to ensure that they were noticed by eating a few pieces of sushi and then sending the rest back claiming that it tasted odd.

Back on the boat, they waited for things to quiet down before Roy donned his wetsuit and took to the water once more. He slowly made his way out of the marina at just past midnight.

DAY FIVE

Wednesday, May 2, 2018

Roy made his way down the channel without incident. The channel is large, and he stayed on the Atlantic edge, far from shore. He kept the speed low, trying to be discreet.

He reached the end of the channel and made the turn, comfortable that he hadn't drawn attention to himself.

He turned west again, as he had roughly twenty-two hours earlier. There was quite a bit of chop where the channel and the ocean met, but it was nowhere near as bad as the night before. He chugged away from Bimini toward the Straits at ten knots. Then, he checked his GPS heading and aimed himself toward home.

He was gradually able to increase his speed and, at twenty minutes into the journey, the sea suddenly flattened out. To his relief, he made it past the turbulence kicked up by the islands and shallows of the Bahama Banks. Per his GPS data, the depth was 2,292 feet.

He was over the Straits.

Squeezing the throttle, he took the jet ski up to forty knots. He was skimming over the water now with virtually no resistance, which meant that the spray was minimal, so he pulled the goggles from his eyes and let them hang around his neck. He could choose between protecting his eyes from spray or some tiny bug that might be in the air versus better visibility. He chose the latter. His biggest worry was running into a cargo ship or freighter.

Roy tried to stay alert, fighting tunnel vision and scanning in front and to the sides for red, white, or green lights that would indicate another vessel. And, sure enough, at about the halfway point, he spotted some lights to the north—red to the left, green to the right. Whatever it was, the positioning of the lights told Roy the vessel was heading away from him. Just to be sure, he slowed to a stop.

He took the opportunity to move about on the jet ski. The tension was making his neck tight and his butt numb. He stretched. He even stood up a few times—carefully, of course. The last thing he wanted to do was fall overboard out there. Alone.

He drank some water. Shook his head a few times.

The GPS told him that he was sitting 2,769 feet above the ocean floor. The only thing standing between him and a half-mile fall was a shitload of seawater. Something splashed nearby as if to remind him of that. From the sound, it was most likely just a small fish. Above him, the moon, which was just past full, had skidded to a new position in the sky.

He breathed deep and took in the beauty and peacefulness of the moment.

One more swig of water.

Then, he stowed the bottle, settled back into the seat of the jet ski, checked his position and heading, and hit the throttle hard. Homeward bound.

* * *

Susie woke with a start. It was 3:00 a.m.

She switched on the bedside lamp and looked at the notes she and Roy had put together just hours before. Based on his new departure time, assuming good conditions and an average forty-knot speed, he should be home by now. She knew this. She had made the crossing with him numerous times, both on the Sunseeker and the Yellowfin.

It was beautiful if you crossed in the right conditions, but in bad weather it was a completely different story.

They had only been caught out in a storm once on the way

back from Bimini. They'd just finished a week-long trip all the way down to the Exumas and were heading home. There'd been a large system up in the Tampa area, crossing over the peninsula toward them.

They'd decided to try and beat the storm. And they had, too—pulling into Biscayne Bay just as the rain started. But they'd made the second half of the trip battling four- to six-foot waves. Camilla got seasick. Susie played nurse while Roy captained from the flybridge. It had been a nasty trip that she didn't care to repeat.

Still, that had been on a fifty-five-foot yacht. When Roy had told her that he planned to make the crossing on a jet ski, she'd told him he was crazy, and she'd meant it until she'd realized that was the point. Who in their right mind would cross the Florida Straits alone, at night, on a jet ski?

Assuming everything went as planned, she'd meet him at 4:30 a.m. She checked her alarm, again, and tried to go to sleep, but no luck. Whatever had startled her awake had pumped enough adrenaline into her bloodstream that she knew she wasn't going to sleep anytime soon.

So, she got up, fixed herself some coffee, and went back to the book she was reading, but not before making sure that her phone was on and the alarm set.

* * *

Roy arrived home at 2:50 a.m. He put the jet ski up on its floating dock and went aboard the Yellowfin.

There was no need to go into the house. Not that anyone would see him. They'd given the help the week off. But, to go in, he'd have to turn off the alarm, which would create a record with the alarm company that someone had been at the house.

Everything he needed was already on the fishing boat. He

changed out of his wetsuit into dark blue shorts and a black UV-rated boat shirt. By day, his attire didn't scream "covert operation," but it was dark enough to make him less visible at night. He took some time out to stretch in a dark part of the yard, as he was sore from the journey over.

Then, he dealt with the jet ski. He opened the bungs to drain water from the hull, and then he started the engine and ran fresh water through it to flush the cooling system. Finally, he refueled, filling the tank to the top. He needed it ready for the trip back. He'd felt that the risk of waking someone through all this action was low and was far outweighed by the risk of the jet ski not working for the return trip.

Tasks complete, he started the engines on the Yellowfin and cast off.

As he headed down the channel toward the bay, he scanned the neighboring houses. No lights on. No flickering TV lights. No one seemed to be awake. At 3:12 a.m. on a Wednesday morning, it was to be expected.

As he puttered out of the channel and into the bay, the speckled lights of downtown Miami slowly came into view. Many office and condo lights were out. It was nonetheless a breathtaking sight that made Roy sigh. He never tired of this view.

He cranked the throttle up to about twenty-five knots. It was a good speed. It would get him to Bimini in two hours, and it was an economical speed at which to run the boat.

Roy knew that the Yellowfin carried just over 475 gallons of fuel. At between twenty-five to thirty knots, he figured he could run about 600 nautical miles. That was more than enough distance to allow them to execute their plan and still leave plenty of fuel in the tank. There would be no need to refuel anywhere and attract attention, create a traceable purchase transaction, or leave behind any witnesses.

As he cruised through the middle of Biscayne Bay and headed for the channel, he was suddenly filled with a sense of awe and accomplishment at what he'd just done.

Crossing the fucking Straits alone at night on a jet ski!

He got goosebumps all over his body. And there was that primordial feeling again, welling up through his gut and bursting out all over him.

He was out in the bay now, far from land. No one near.

He screamed at the top of his lungs, "Hell yeah, motherfucker!"

* * *

At 4:00 a.m., Susie left the Sunseeker, locking the door behind her. As agreed, she left the lights on in the stateroom and the galley before checking to see if anybody was up and watching.

She saw no one. No lights or activity.

If she'd been paying closer attention, she would have smelled cigarette smoke in the air.

She gingerly stepped onto the dock from the swim platform and headed out of the marina.

She was carrying a small waterproof backpack and was wearing flip-flops, shorts, and a sweatshirt over her swimsuit. She walked north. Her pace was brisk, purposeful. To anyone passing by, she would look like a late-night reveler heading home, or possibly an early morning fisherman heading out to meet a group for a charter.

Susie walked until the she reached Bimini's Luna Beach. She took off her flip-flops and walked along the sand, away from the buildings, staying close to the water. She walked until she reached the stretch of beach where she and Roy had stopped on their walk the first day. She checked her bearings using Navionics to determine that she was at the spot that they had marked previously for the rendezvous.

She was standing on the beach at the end of a small sand road that led across the island to a large building they'd been told was part of Resort World. When they'd checked on her phone, Google had said it was Villa 210. That didn't seem right, but it didn't matter. This was where they'd agreed to meet. The coordinates were correct per the Navionics app. And the surroundings indicated that she was in the right place, as well.

One of the first lessons Susie had learned about boating from Roy was LOTFW. When running a boat, you have a number of instruments at your disposal. Charting systems provide position and course information. Radar indicates possible vessels, obstacles, and weather systems. Sonar can tell you the approximate depth of the water you are in. Even the radio provides information about the weather and sea conditions.

The Navionics app she was using there, on the beach, provided her detailed coordinates indicating that she was in the place they had agreed upon. But to be safe, Roy had reminded her she should always LOTFW—*Look Out The Fucking Window*. She confirmed that the landmarks they'd identified were all in the right places. It was important to look carefully. Because, as we know, landmarks change in the darkness.

She opened the backpack, laid a towel out on the sand, and sat down. She took out the handheld VHF radio, turned it on, and set it to Channel 68. She placed another towel like a blanket over her legs for warmth.

The time was 4:52 a.m.

She had been waiting forty minutes when she saw boat lights approaching from far offshore. She checked the radio volume to make sure it was on and on the right channel as the lights drew closer. She could just about discern the shape of a boat by moonlight. It looked like the Yellowfin.

She clung to the VHF, her heart quickening. This was all very cloak-and-dagger, and when the radio crackled to life, she actually felt giddy with excitement. It felt as if she had a bunch of minnows swimming around in her belly.

"Radio check, radio check, radio check, come back."

Holy shit! He's fucking done it...

She held the VHF near her mouth and replied, "Go to ten, go to ten, go to ten, over."

The Yellowfin's searchlight flashed briefly.

She took a quick look around to make sure no one was around. Then she jumped to her feet, picked up the towels, and stripped off her sweatshirt and shorts. She pushed everything into the backpack, sealed it, and headed into the water, where she slung the bag over one shoulder and slowly swam out to rendezvous with her husband.

The boat was about one hundred yards offshore. When she approached, Roy used a telescoping boat hook to bring up the backpack. Susie followed, climbing up the portable swim ladder. Once she was safely aboard, Roy piloted the Yellowfin around the north side of the island and onto the shallower Banks, where there would be less boat traffic, and dropped anchor.

Once the engines were shut down, Susie hugged her man before asking, "How bad was it?"

"Not very, actually. The water was fairly calm. I got a little bit of chop leaving Bimini and then at the other end, entering Biscayne Channel—abrupt depth changes and landmass wave bounce, I imagine—but other than that, incredibly smooth.

"I saw one tanker, but it was heading away from me. I have to admit, there was a point about three-quarters in where I started to fall asleep. But just the thought scared the shit out of me. Woke me right up.

"Neighborhood was quiet. No lights. I think odds are good no one saw me come in—small craft, hardly noticeable. And heading out, we've been out on the Yellowfin so much lately that, *if* anyone saw, they wouldn't look twice."

Part of the reason they'd been spending so much time out on the Yellowfin had been for their neighbors to get used to seeing it moving again. In the event that someone noticed it missing that day, it would likely just be chalked up as another day that the boat was being used. Hopefully, it wouldn't stick in anyone's memory.

Susie smiled at Roy, with admiration. "So, now comes the waiting," she said, putting a hand on her hip.

The first part of their plan was in place. Their alibi. They were in Bimini. They had passed through customs. They were officially, documentably, outside the United States. The Sunseeker would stay in the marina as a witness to their presence in the Bahamas. Silently testifying: *We are here.*

Meanwhile, the Yellowfin gave them mobility.

The next step in the plan didn't come until that evening. They had gone back and forth over what to do while they waited. They could leave the Yellowfin anchored and swim ashore. But leaving the boat alone meant that they would not know who might pass by, see it, and perhaps even recognize it. Any number of things could happen that would result in there being witnesses to the boat being in the Bahamas, and they needed to know if that happened.

So, they concluded that the safest place to be was with the boat, anchored far from prying eyes or where anyone was likely to pass.

They put up a sun cover for shade. The plan now was for Roy to sleep and Susie to keep watch. He needed to rest, recover from the night before, and gather strength for what remained.

According to their plan, in about twelve hours, they would kill Joe Harlan Jr.

* * *

At 6:15 a.m., Joe Harlan Jr. parked at Austin Bergstrom International Airport. His flight was at 9:29 a.m.

While Joe was careless about a lot of things, he hated the stress of running for a flight. He'd much rather be early and people-watch—girl-watch, really—until flight time. Truth be told, the boy hated flying. The idea of being in a metal tube 30,000 feet above ground made his balls shrivel. If he didn't think too much about it, he was okay. But if he dwelt on it, he got very uneasy.

He'd been awake since about 4:00 a.m., excited about the possibilities that his meeting with David Kim could open for him.

And he was a bit nervous about the flying. He was unsure which of the two had kept him from getting a better night's sleep.

As he headed for his gate, he stopped at Ruta Maya for a decaf coffee and lemon pound cake. He flirted with the barista. Although she was a bit on the chunky side and had crooked teeth, he wouldn't have thrown her out of bed.

As he paid for his coffee, he saw that she lingered a bit on his credit card.

A quickie in the back room before the flight?

He had time, and it had been a couple of days.

A fuck and fly—like a rock star.

It'd be a great story to tell Frank.

He put on his most appealing smile.

She was smiling back at first. But then it happened, again— what he'd seen a lot of since the whole "Kristy thing." The cashier's face changed as she registered why his name sounded familiar. She handed back the card. Smile gone.

Fucking Kristy bullshit... That one piece of ass has cost me more pussy than if I had AIDS.

He went to the gate and ate breakfast. As he waited, he considered the trip ahead. If this worked out, his luck would finally have changed. At a bare minimum, the life he'd had before the "Kristy thing" happened would be restored.

Prior to Kristy, he'd been about one year away from graduating. He'd been a co-founder of a start-up with some real potential. He'd had a hot girlfriend. He'd finally convinced his dad to let him move out on his own—with roommates, but still. Looking back on it, he kind of regretted the whole thing. Well, the getting caught part, at least. If he'd actually thought the whole thing through, he'd have planned a bit more carefully.

But the truth was that he hadn't really planned it out at all. It had just sort of happened.

Lesson learned, but at what a price. He'd had to drop out of UT—his dad's suggestion. They'd probably have thrown him out if he hadn't. He'd had to move back home. Laura—the hot daytime girlfriend—had disappeared. But the worst part really had been the impact on his sex life. Once word gets out that you're a fucking roofie-dishing rapist, it's like being a leper. He'd even had hookers take a pass on him.

That's why this deal with Cruise Capital could be a gamechanger. Miami would be a whole new world—a fresh start. In Miami, he was no one. No one, but also potentially the successful director of a very successful enterprise. They'd be lining up to blow him.

Sure, the whole dad being a senator thing had always been useful, and probably wouldn't carry that far down there, but something had to give.

One thing at a time.

So long as he could use his dad to get David what he wanted, where Joe actually lived may not even matter to them.

Joe Harlan Jr. stood when they called boarding for Group Five.

After taking his seat, he discretely took a valium out of his shirt pocket and slipped it under his tongue. No stress. A quick nap. Next stop, Miami.

* * *

Roy called David at 1:30 p.m. from the Yellowfin, which was still anchored just off the coast of Bimini. Susie had been keeping watch all day while Roy rested—nothing unusual.

"Hey, boss. What's up?"

"Hey, partner," Roy responded. "All good here. Just wanted to touch base. I sent you an email on the ArtCraft deal. I think it's a winner."

"Yep. Got it. I'm gonna Skype tonight with Todd and Gordon to go over the details."

"Sounds good. Nothing like a conference call and a nice

glass of scotch by the air conditioner." Roy laughed.

"Yeah. It's been a long couple of days. Over-celebrated the partner thing Tuesday night. Man, I am not as young as I used to be." He chuckled.

"Tell me about it."

"But, yeah. I'll check your email and send you my thoughts after the call."

"Perfect. Everything else good?"

"Yeah. Got that Harlan guy here tomorrow morning. Pushed it back to 10:00. That way, we can roll it into lunch, get a couple of beers or whatever into him. Then I'll soft-pitch the TrueData idea. See how he responds. The more I think about it, it makes a lot of sense for him."

"Yeah, but you'd be surprised how many people will choose the path that benefits them the least."

"I dunno. This guy, he seemed pretty motivated about coming out here. We'll see."

"Okay. Well, let me know what you think on the diligence stuff. Just email me. We can circle back after I see your comments."

"Will do," David answered. "Hey, how's the trip? Looked like the weather was kind of crap earlier this week."

"It was, but it's much better today. We've just been hanging out. Beachcombing. That sort of thing. But, man, something I ate last night did *not* agree me with me. I was on the can all night."

"Whoa, Roy! TMI, man."

Roy laughed. "Oh yeah. I forget. You don't have kids. Once you've had a kid, discussing puke and shit becomes pretty normal."

David chuckled. "Jeez. Is it too late to take that termination offer?"

They laughed.

"Alright, David. Talk soon," Roy said.

"Cool. Enjoy. Say hi to Susie."

"Will do." And with that, Roy hung up, then looked at Susie. "No change in plans. David's got a conference call tonight. So he'll have a solid alibi. He's not meeting with Harlan until tomorrow, so our guy is available."

"Okay," Susie stretched her shoulders, then her neck, tilting her head to each side. "Well then, let's do it."

Roy turned off his cell phone and stowed it in Susie's waterproof backpack. Susie's was already in there—also turned off.

As Roy started the engines, Susie changed into white shorts and a light blue long-sleeved boat shirt. She was wearing a ballcap with her hair pulled up in a ponytail and large dark sunglasses. They doubted that Harlan would have researched Susie as a part of any investigating he might have done into Cruise Capital in advance of his trip, but to be safe, they wanted to be sure to obfuscate her features as much as possible.

Roy had already changed into khaki lululemon shorts and a white v-neck t-shirt. He was also wearing a floppy white bucket hat and sunglasses.

He set course for Government Cut.

They were giving themselves ample time to make the crossing, just in case there were any unexpected bumps along the way. The weather had held nicely all day, though, and the crossing was even smoother than Roy's earlier voyage that morning.

They rode in silence sitting side by side, passing a few boats here and there that were headed in the opposite direction. Roy imagined they carried families, groups, and couples that were heading across to Bimini for a short vacation, or maybe just into the Straits for some deep-sea fishing. There was no reason for any of them to take note of the couple in the Yellowfin boat, let alone stop to think, *They look suspicious. Probably murderers. Remember that boat!*

Roy felt queasy anyway. Not that he was having second thoughts. Just that it was all becoming very real. After all the planning and preparation, this was it. It was *go time!*

At about 3:45 p.m., Roy could see the entrance to Government Cut, and he turned the helm over to Susie, who was playing the part of ship's mate.

Roy got the Seattle burner phone out of the backpack while Susie slowed the boat so that he would be able to hear to make the call.

In all their planning, they had been diligent about ensuring that nothing conflicted with their Bimini alibi. As they'd been finalizing things, Susie had raised the opposite point. They also needed to ensure that there was nothing connecting Harlan or his disappearance to Bimini, and therefore to them.

Based on Susie's research, they learned that mobile phone carriers keep logs identifying which cellular towers a mobile phone number has been associated with. If you make a call on your mobile phone from Colorado, the call information is captured and logged. Most carriers keep that data for at least one year. AT&T purportedly keeps it for ten years.

Armed with this knowledge, they'd turned off their personal mobile phones before leaving Bimini. And they had not turned on the Seattle or Miami burner phones at all, yet.

Now that they were back in Miami, the plan called for them to use the Seattle burner. This was the first time the phone had been turned on since Roy bought it, and he was somewhat apprehensive that the thing might fail. If it did, their whole plan was shot since there was no back-up. He should have bought two.

Roy took a deep breath. He turned on the phone. It booted up, thankfully.

He dialed Joe Harlan Jr.

Contrary to my belief that contacting Marty McCall was the weakest link in their plan, Roy believed that it was this phone call that put them at greatest risk. For their plan to work, they had to convince Harlan to come to them. That meant contacting him and giving him notice of a potential meeting.

Notice meant time—time that Harlan could use to let someone, anyone, know that Roy Cruise had called him. Let them know that he was going to meet with Cruise.

They'd tried to come up with a safer approach, but in the end they'd decided that it was a trade-off. Either they could go to Harlan—in which case they could not dictate the crime scene—or they could bring him to them, dictating the crime scene but running the risk that he might contact someone. They'd opted for the latter.

If it all went to shit and the Harlan kid did share details of the meeting with someone, their plan was simple—deny. After all, they were in Bimini. The only witness who could testify firsthand that Roy had called Joe Harlan Jr. was Joe Harlan Jr. And if everything went according to plan, he would be dead.

"Hello?"

"Joe Harlan?"

"Speaking. Who's this?"

"Roy Cruise of Cruise Capital. How are you?"

"Oh, hey, Mr. Cruise. I'm fine, how are you?"

"I'm great, Joe. Great. Did you make it into Miami, okay?"

"Yes, I did. Thanks for asking, sir. I just got into the hotel a while ago. It's really nice. Thanks for putting me up."

"Oh, don't mention it, Joe. Least we could do," Roy said. "Um, so, listen... since you're already in town, I wanted to give you a call to see if you'd like to have dinner tonight?"

"Uh, yeah. Sure. But, where are you calling from? I'm getting a weird area code. Are you in Miami?"

"Yeah. My mobile phone's dead. Borrowed my captain's phone. We're out on my yacht. We just finished entertaining some clients—investors. But David's taking it from here. Anyway, didn't know if you wanted to come aboard and have something to eat." Roy's tone was casual, relaxed, as if he'd been lounging around all day, tanning himself, instead of plotting murder. "I wanted to call you, what with you being in the city. I wasn't sure if you knew anyone down here and didn't want you spending the evening alone. If you're free, of course, I mean if you have plans, then..." he left the sentence unfinished hoping that the boy would jump in.

"Are you kidding me? Dinner on your yacht or hotel food alone? Sure! I'd love to!"

"Fantastic. How about we pick you up at six?"

"Okay."

"You're staying at the Intercontinental, right?"

"I am."

"Okay. We can pick you up at Bayside Marina. It's about a ten-minute walk from your hotel. Or you can Uber if you can't take the heat."

"Okay. Sounds good. I'll be there at six sharp."

"Perfect. There's a shopping center kind of attached to the marina. I'll meet you there, in front of the Starbucks, and then we can walk out to the boat. If you have any issues finding it, call me here. I'll keep the phone handy. And, once my phone is recharged, I'll send you a text so you have that number, too."

"Sounds good, sir. Looking forward to it. I'll see you at the Starbucks."

"Excellent."

Roy hung up. The die was cast.

* * *

At 5:50 p.m., the Yellowfin pulled into Bayside Marina. Susie captained the boat. She looked the part, and to complete her disguise, she'd pulled a white UV sun gaiter that she'd had around her neck up to cover the lower portion of her face. These are very common on the waters in Miami. All that sun—skin cancer kills.

Roy debarked and headed toward the market. As he walked, he dialed Harlan on the Seattle burner phone.

"Hello."

"Joe! How goes it, man?"

"Good, good. Just getting to the shopping center. I think I'm in the right place."

"That's great. I'm in the marina right now, but I'm heading your way. Should be there in about five minutes. Get yourself to the Starbucks and wait for me there, okay?"

"Got it. See you!"

Roy left the dock and walked over to the Bayside Marketplace. He carried a pair of sunglasses for Harlan.

As he rounded the corner, he saw his would-be victim standing in front of the coffee shop, waiting. He was dressed casually—khaki pants, a blue polo shirt, and boat shoes. He was wearing sunglasses and looking around as if expecting someone.

"Joe," Roy said, holding out his hand.

"Roy," the kid responded, shaking it.

"Right on time. I like that. Come on. We're over this way."

As they walked, Roy asked, "Those shades UV-rated?" He nodded at the glasses the boy was wearing.

"Yes, sir."

"Good. So, first time in Miami?"

Small talk came easy as they made their way back to the marina. Roy wasn't focused on the conversation, but on whether or not anyone was giving them any undue attention. The area was crowded with locals and tourists, but everyone seemed to be on about their own business. Nothing out of the ordinary.

They reentered the marina proper and walked toward the drop-off where Susie, who had been hovering offshore, was slowly puttering back to pick them up.

"This is us," Roy said as he caught the line tossed out by his wife.

"Hey," Susie said, enthusiastically. "Welcome."

"And that's Jen. First mate. She'll be running us out to the yacht."

"Hi," Joe said.

Roy gestured to Harlan to climb aboard as he held the line. Then Roy followed suit, bringing the line on board with him and pushing them off of the dock.

"This is our guest of honor, Joe Harlan Junior," Roy said, officially making the introduction.

"Well, it's really nice to meet you," Susie said before turning back to the helm.

Roy and Harlan took seats at the stern as Susie piloted them out of the marina. Once out, she pulled beers out of the cooler. She handed a Michelob Ultra to Roy and a Cristal Peruvian lager to Harlan. "I'd offer you a Michelob, but that's what the boss drinks and there're only two left," she said, lifting her eyebrows at her husband.

"No worries," Harlan said. "Thanks."

Susie returned to the helm. She was now too far from her passengers to hear the conversation over the engine noise.

"So, do you boat much?" Roy asked, taking a healthy swig of his beer and then releasing an appreciative sigh. "Wow... that's good. Thirsty! It's been a long, hot day." He raised his bottle. "Cheers, Joe! Welcome to Miami!" He exclaimed, beaming.

"Cheers!" They clinked bottles and drank deeply.

"No. Not much boating," Joe continued, "not this kind. I mean, we get out on the water down in Austin, but it's river boating. Completely different," he breathed. "Wakeboarding, that kind of stuff. Nothing like this."

Roy studied Harlan as he spoke. He looked just like he had in the YouTube video Susie had shown him. Thin guy. Lanky. Average height. A decent looking kid, in a WASPy kind of way. The kind you'd imagine pledging a frat at UT.

"Gotcha. Yeah, this *is* different. So, anyway, the plan for tonight. The yacht's out on the other side of South Beach. Chef's getting dinner prepped. Meanwhile, Jen's gonna take us around the bay. Through the Venetian. Stunning views. So, you'll be able to do some sightseeing. And, of course, if you're into that kind of thing and want her to point out any celebrity houses, just say so. She knows her stuff. Then we'll head out to the yacht for dinner."

"Sounds great," Joe said.

Roy pulled on his beer again, and saw that Joe was keeping up. "So, this boat, then—it's just your tender?" Harlan asked.

"Yeah. This is for short hops, and fishing. The yacht's bigger. Nicer and more comfortable."

"Man, it must be amazing. Being so successful. I mean, our family business is politics. That's a very different animal. Not so much about creating value as redistributing it, you know? I always had a hard time figuring out what direction to go. Follow my old man's footsteps or do something else. Did you always know you wanted to do what you're doing?"

Roy shifted in his seat. This kid was engaging. Likeable. Sure, it was flattery, but he pulled it off well—it seemed sincere. As he watched him talk, he tried to understand how this handsome, affable young man could have done what he had to Kristy.

What if he didn't?

Roy pushed that thought out of his head. He'd already crossed that bridge. He and Susie both had. The research had been done and it had been thorough. He had even sought out McCall's up-close and personal version. It was clear. No. The way this agreeable young man presented himself here today did not change what he'd supposedly done, *what he had done,* that Halloween night.

"… and you also have a law degree, right?" Joe was asking, admiringly.

Roy forced a smile and automatically gave a brief rundown of how he'd transitioned from law to business. He deliberately kept the overview short because he wanted his guest to talk more. He wanted to listen to *him*, to find reasons not to like him.

"So, how much did David tell you exactly about why we wanted this meeting?"

"David—great guy, by the way—said that you guys were looking hard at the government procurement space. That you were talking to a bunch of companies, and that as a result of those discussions, you felt like you needed some expertise on the government side. Public affairs type experience. And, since that's what I'm doing at Procurex, he said y'all thought it'd be worth sitting down and talking about how we might help each other.

"And so, I'm here to let you guys fill in the blanks. I mean, I understand the space, and I've got solid connections—in Texas, for sure—so the question is how we can help each other out."

The kid was articulate. Direct. He appeared to know exactly what he had to offer, although Roy noticed that while he mentioned his connections, obviously for effect, he didn't dwell on them. Roy imagined this was because he was aware of the limit to his father's reach.

Roy nodded. "That's a good summary. And right on target. So… um, Jen!" he shouted. "Could you bring us another round?" He looked at the young man, who nodded gratefully and promptly drained the rest of his bottle.

Jen arrived shortly after and handed the men two more

bottles; Michelob Ultra for Roy and a Cristal for Harlan.

"How do you feel about TrueData, Marty McCall's company?"

Harlan paused for a second. "Well, Marty was a friend. I'd like to think he still is. I know I'm still there for him, at least. But, when he saw an opportunity to take what we were all building together for himself, he did just that. And, um, well, I was obviously disappointed," he said, with a sad shrug. "Hopefully, one day we can put it all behind us," he added, washing down the memory with a gulp from his bottle.

Roy wanted to say something, but he was momentarily lost for words. The response seemed genuine. He felt uncomfortable, as he hadn't been expecting to like this young man who, until today, he had pegged as a spoiled, entitled prick who went about life trampling on others without any sense of decorum or responsibility.

To keep him talking, Roy asked Harlan for his views on the direction the government procurement space was heading. Harlan talked about government waste. He explained the procurement process. He explained how Procurex planned to solve those problems. It was a re-hash of what Roy had seen Harlan speak about on YouTube.

Roy listened attentively—not to what the young man was saying, but to how he was saying it. As he got near the bottom of the second beer, it seemed to Roy that there began to be a very slight slur to Harlan's speech.

They were passing Flagler Memorial Island at this point, when Susie rather abruptly began turning the boat around. "Just want to make sure we don't get back to the yacht to a cold dinner!" she called out.

"Sounds good," Roy said. While Harlan continued his monologue on procurement, Roy looked around to see what had caused Susie's change in direction. He immediately saw that, up ahead, at anchor, was a decent-sized, sky blue Viking. It looked suspiciously like a boat that belonged to their neighbors, the Foxes. From the looks of it, no one on board had seen them. Roy instinctively sank into his seat and hunched a little, trying to disguise his profile.

"Let's have one more beer," Roy said, abruptly, "then we can switch to wine onboard. Jen, two more, please!"

"You're in luck, boss, I found another Ultra at the bottom," she said moments later as she handed over the bottles.

Roy studied Harlan carefully. So far, the young man had finished two beers, which meant eight milligrams of Xanax—they'd put four milligrams of the crushed pills into each Cristal bottle. They'd had a total of sixteen pills to work with.

Based on their research, the Xanax-alcohol combination would result in lethargy and sedation. This was what they were after. There was also a concomitant loss of inhibitions, and the possibility of either euphoria or depression and irritability. Since Roy and Susie were only interested in the sedation effect, they hadn't worried too much about whether their victim would feel "happy" or "sad" for the duration.

They'd been cruising slowly for about forty minutes by now. The sun was dropping. It wasn't dark yet, but twilight was approaching. Susie raised the throttle, decreasing their speed slightly.

Joe was still talking, pausing from time to time and blinking. Roy kept him going, nodding, asking quick questions, actively listening. As Harlan continued, his speech became more hesitant. His slurring became more pronounced.

They were heading east now. The sun was rushing toward the horizon behind them, as if anxious not to see what was taking place on the boat.

Harlan reached a natural pause in his monologue and took a drink from his beer. As he did, Roy removed his sunglasses and hung them by the stem from his shirt collar. The contrast between his tanned skin and his green eyes made them sparkle more than usual. He smiled that crooked smile of his and said, "So, Joe, let me cut to the chase. Would you be interested in coming to work for me?"

"Abswolutely," Harlan said. Then he cleared this throat, chuckled, and shook his head and repeated. "Absolutely."

"Are you mobile? I mean, got a wife or girlfriend that we need to consider?"

"Come on, Roy." Harlan laughed. "I know you did your homework."

"How do you mean?"

"The whole rape bullsssshit. You think it's easssy finding a girl after that?"

He was hissing his s'es. Inhibitions definitely reduced. Roy couldn't tell if the irritability in Harlan's voice was the drugs, or just the truth. It didn't really matter.

"Tell me about that. I mean, hey, I'm a big believer in the system. You were acquitted, and that's good enough for me. But, like you say, it must still be affecting your life, no?"

"Shit, Roy. I had to leave UT, man. Couldn't walk across campus without some asshole yelling something at me, or some bitch. And this was *before* the trial. Nobody cared what really happened."

Harlan paused, looking blankly ahead. Then he continued, "They didn't wait to hear the evidence. They just assumed—privileged white boy must have done it. No way to get a fair trial."

"Wow. That must have been really hard on you."

"Fuck yeah, it was. But hey, Frank stood by me. And my dad, too, don't get me wrong... But, Frank, he was there for me like family, man. Better than family." Harlan belched. "He's my best friend."

Harlan was slurring heavily now. "Hey. By the way. I forgot. We're a package, man. Package deal. I mean, if I come to work for you, no deal unless there's a spot for Frank, too. Okay? Cool?"

Roy knew the answer was irrelevant, and said, "Yeah. Cool. We'd love to have him."

Joe raised his hand for a fist bump. "That's what I'm talking about," he said. "Bros before hos!"

Roy returned the fist bump.

Harlan removed his sunglasses and he leaned into Roy, but his eyes were on Susie. Then, voice a little lower, conspiratorially, he asked, "So—shoot straight with me, man—you tappin' that? 'Cause that is one fine piece of ass there. I don't know what she's hiding under the mask and shades, but hey—you don't fuck the face, right?"

Harlan laughed. "A little on the Latina side, no? That is *sweet*, man!"

Roy put his arm around Joe's shoulder and said, "Bro! You're going to get a great new start in Miami. A clean slate. I'm glad that everything worked out in the end for you. To justice!" he said, raising his bottle.

Harlan clinked his bottle a little too hard. "Ooops. Sorry. Man, not sure why, but... feeling a bit woozy," he said, blinking rapidly. "Normally can drain a few more beers before... shit."

Roy reacted with concern. "It's probably a little seasickness. Hey, Jen?" he shouted. "Can you slow it down a bit?"

Susie slowed the boat. They were just reaching the end of Government Cut. Soon, it would be dark.

"Yeah," Joe said, smiling. "To justice."

* * *

When Joe Harlan Jr. had boarded the boat, he'd felt fine. He'd been pumped, really. Dinner on the yacht with just the founding partner meant he was getting the VIP treatment. When he'd first gotten Roy's call, he'd worried that maybe there was some other reason for the meeting. Maybe Cruise was gay. But after meeting him, Joe's gaydar had registered a negative. This was *VIP treatment*, plain and simple. His dad would be impressed.

After a while on the boat, though, he'd started feeling a little weird.

It was hot in Miami. And humid. But with the boat rocking, and the engines droning, not to mention the beer, he'd started feeling worse. Seasick? Drowsy?

As he self-assessed, he recognized that he'd had an early start that morning. And he'd had that Valium when he got on the plane—maybe that plus the beer was affecting him. Now, everything seemed fuzzy. All he wanted to do was sleep.

He'd kept his sunglasses on as long as he could because he didn't want Roy to see that his eyes were drooping. Roy's rambling on about doing business with the government didn't help.

Harlan had tried discreetly putting his hand in his pocket and pinching his leg, and biting his tongue, to help stay awake. He even tried imagining fucking Jen, right there on the boat. Nothing seemed to help...

Joe heard a thunking sound that startled him as he tried to recover his balance. When he looked down, he saw his beer bottle rolling away from him, leaving a fizzing trail of foam as it went.

"Whoa. You okay there, buddy?" Roy asked, retrieving the beer bottle and handing it back to his guest.

"Yeah. I'm good, man. Just feeling a bit weird." He rubbed his eyes and tried to focus on what he was doing.

In Miami.

On the boat.

Heading for the yacht.

VIP treatment.

"It's okay. You're okay. It's most likely the altitude change," Roy offered. "Being at sea level, plus the heat and humidity. It sneaks up on a lot of people."

Joe nodded, swaying more than the boat's rocking demanded, and took another swig of beer. It was getting warm and had a peculiar bitter taste to it. He felt queasy, and the rocking of the fucking boat didn't help.

"I think maybe I should lie down for a bit," he said.

"Sure," Roy agreed. "Let me help you."

He led Joe up to the bow of the ship and helped him lie down on the coffin box, the boat's built-in elongated cooler, on his back, legs on either side.

"We should be at the yacht in about ten minutes. You rest. You want some water? Dramamine? Do you feel like you're gonna puke?"

Joe thought he said "No," but wasn't sure. The platform was comfortable and warm. There was a nice breeze blowing over the bow. And the drone of the engines rocked him to sleep...

* * *

Joe half-woke, feeling some discomfort.

He tried to turn on his side, but he was unable to do so. It felt as if his hands were stuck together. He tried to use one of his legs as a counterweight, but realized that it, too, felt awkward. Useless.

It was quiet. The roaring noise from before was gone. There was a nice breeze blowing over him. Cool. Beautiful.

He heard voices, conversing. Mumbling. It reminded him of when he'd been a child and he'd hear his parents talking as he fell asleep. The memory made him happy. It brought back feelings of comfort and safety.

He tried to lift his head, but it felt heavy, way too heavy. Sleep was better. Much better.

* * *

At 8:00 p.m., it had been two hours since Joe began ingesting the Xanax and beer cocktails. For the last hour, Susie had been navigating the boat back toward Bimini. They were now well clear of Miami, but still far enough from Bimini that no cell tower would pick them up.

Although their mobile phones were turned off, they could only assume that Harlan's was not. The plan called for them to stop well before getting in range of Bimini to make sure that Harlan's cell phone didn't ping off a Bimini cell tower and give his whereabouts away.

They were in the Straits floating over 2,000 feet of depth below when Susie dropped the engines to idle. The roaring of the motors gave way to silence.

While Harlan slept, Roy and Susie carefully prepared him for execution. First, they slid the plastic tarp under his body, positioning him face up. They weighed the corners down with diving weights so that it wouldn't blow around. They used zip ties to bind Harlan's wrists. They didn't overtighten, as they didn't want to wake him, but made sure that if he did come to, he would be unable to wriggle free. They also attached a line to each of his ankles, then gently tied the other ends to the boat's recessed bow rails.

Just in case, Roy put a metal mallet on the deck, next to the coffin box near Harlan's head. If he did wake suddenly and become unruly, they would use it on him. But that was only in case of emergency, as they didn't want to make a mess that would generate unnecessary forensic evidence.

Also on the deck, by the mallet, were an oversized duffle bag, twenty feet of anchor chain, and the five padlocks. Roy had brought these forward from the aft storage while Susie watched Harlan.

As Roy turned to retrieve more items from storage, their prisoner began to groan and move.

"What do you think?" Roy asked in a low voice.

"Might be wearing off. Maybe we should get it done, then bring up the rest of the stuff? What's left? Just the Quikcrete?"

"Yeah," Roy said flatly as he watched their hapless victim.

This was it. All their planning had been leading up to this moment and yet now, in the moment, he felt trepidation. Nausea. Unlike their guest, he knew it wasn't seasickness or alcohol.

"Hold on," he said. He went to the helm and took a quick look at the GPS screen. There were no boats nearby per the AIS. He turned on the radar and waited for the screen to populate. No vessels nearby. He switched the screen off and headed back toward the bow.

"All clear," Roy whispered to Susie.

"Ice pick or Hefty?" Susie asked, anxiously.

"I guess just plain drowning is out of the question?"

"Roy, we've come this far. We can flip for it if you like, but I think *we* should end him, not the ocean." His wife's words were cold. Hard. Determined.

Roy thought for a moment. "Alright, let's do Hefty. If he starts to get out of control, then I'll use the pick."

"Okay."

Roy walked around to the bow of the boat. He carefully took up all the slack in each of the lines that was tied to Harlan's ankles. While he'd be able to move his legs some, he wasn't going anywhere.

As he did this, Susie went aft and got the box of Hefty bags. She opened it and removed two. She then sat down on the bench in front of the helm, slipping one of the bags under her thigh. She should only need one, but had the extra just in case. Once she was in position, Harlan's head was just in front of her at the end of the coffin box, his feet toward the bow.

Roy held the ice pick in his right hand. He carefully straddled the coffin box, putting one leg on either side of Harlan's body. The young man was on his back with his hands bound together in front of him. Roy towered over their quarry.

Susie looked up at her husband. "Ready?"

Nervously, he gave her a thumbs-up. Then he lowered himself slowly onto Harlan's body. He ended up sitting on Harlan's hips, cowgirl style, facing his head. Roy put his weight on Harlan and leaned forward. He brought his arms in tight, trapping Harlan's arms just above the elbows and holding him down. He put all his weight onto Harlan.

He still held tightly to the ice pick.

Susie maneuvered Harlan's head into the Hefty bag, and then she pulled downward, trapping Harlan's face in the plastic.

* * *

Joe suddenly jerked awake. He was confused. He was sure that his eyes were open, but he couldn't see anything. He felt a crushing weight on his chest and torso, weighing him down.

He could move his lower body, but something was pulling on his ankles, restricting his range of motion. His legs felt leaden, clumsy, useless. He couldn't move his arms at all.

He was disoriented. His mind reeled, trying to recall something, anything that would help him understand where he was.

But his brain wasn't receiving any visual or audio cues. It was dark. Everything sounded muffled. When he moved his head, he could hear an odd crackling sound, but that was it.

Chemicals and plastic were the only things he could smell, and it was making him want to retch. He tried to breathe, tried to suck in fresh air, but nothing came. It was as if he were sucking on an empty tube.

That's when the panic set in. It wasn't as acute as it probably should have been, thanks to the Xanax in his system. Still, he felt his eyes burning—tears of frustration. He opened his mouth to scream but realized to his horror that he couldn't. It wasn't that he couldn't scream; he couldn't even breathe. His lungs had nothing to scream with.

He thought that maybe he was asleep, dreaming. A nightmare. That's what it was, a hideous nightmare. That made sense. He tried to wake himself up.

He struggled. His heart machine-gunned as it fought harder and harder, trying to get oxygen to his starving organs. His chest was on fire. He wanted air. He needed air.

Though his higher brain functions were still being impacted by the Xanax, his lizard brain began to take over. His body bucked and convulsed against the weight on his torso. His head fought against the pressure that he felt on his face.

What the fuck was going on?

Then they came. Flashes of memory. He had travelled to Miami. Cruise had called him—for dinner on the yacht. VIP treatment. He'd boarded the boat. There was that chick, Jen. He'd spilled his beer. Had he made it to the yacht? He couldn't remember. Had he gotten drunk at dinner? Was he back at his hotel? Or still on the yacht?

* * *

"Aw, fuck!" Roy groaned, disgusted.

"What?"

"He pissed all over me."

Harlan had convulsed for about twenty seconds. Then stopped. Then convulsed one final time, and then stopped again. They'd been counting to sixty, just to make sure he was dead.

"You think that's it?" Roy asked, flushed and sweating from the exertion of holding the bucking body down.

"Yeah. Eww, I think I smell shit," Susie said, screwing up her nose.

"Ya think?" Roy puffed, gingerly getting up off the corpse.

Susie looked to see if her husband's shorts were wet, but it was too dark. Although, from the way he was moving, he was obviously soaked.

Roy got off the coffin box, stripped off his shorts and underwear, and tossed them overboard. "I'll be right back."

Minutes later, Roy returned wearing the blue short shorts he'd arrived in that morning in Bimini. It seemed like ages ago.

Susie was already gathering the edges of the plastic tarp up over Harlan to try and contain the urine and any other bodily fluids that might be leaking out of him and making their way to becoming evidence on the deck.

Roy untied the lines that held Harlan's feet and dropped them on the body. Then he picked up the duffle bag and, starting at the feet, they began to wrestle Harlan's body into it, tarp and all.

Eventually, the two of them managed to get the full body inside.

"Wait," Susie said quickly, before reaching into the duffle bag and retrieving Harlan's mobile phone. She tapped on the home button, then used Harlan's right thumb to unlock the screen. She scrolled to recent calls. He had received two from:

Cruise Captain

"Goddammit. He created a contact." She clicked on the icon to bring up the contact with the Seattle phone number:

206-576-1324

Roy looked over her shoulder as she hit "Edit," changed the contact name to "Marty McCall," and saved. Then she carefully wiped the phone down on Harlan's shirt to remove her fingerprints and put it in the duffle bag next to him.

"Good catch," Roy commented. "I forgot all about the phone."

"Yeah. Okay, listen," Susie said in her no-nonsense tone. "Why don't you get the bags of Quikcrete up here? I can get the anchor chain wrapped around him."

"You sure you don't need help with the chain? It's heavy."

"I've got it, Roy. Just get the fucking Quikcrete up here," she snapped, a bit more harshly than seemed necessary.

"Whoa." Roy raised his hands defensively, stepping back.

"Sorry," she added, changing her tone slightly. "Not trying to be bitchy. I just don't want to have him here like this any longer than necessary. He fucking stinks. You get the bags. I'll get the chain around him, okay?" It wasn't really a question.

Roy went aft for the four bags of Quikcrete. In order to save time, he removed all four from storage before beginning the process of bringing them to the bow.

As he brought over each bag, Susie helped him place it in the duffle bag with Harlan. There was no need to open them as water would seep in and set the concrete inside the bags.

As they placed the bags, Roy noticed that the body now had the anchor chain wrapped around it, secured with padlocks and looped through the victim's belt.

But Harlan was no longer on his back. The lower body was on its side, his upper body twisted even further, facedown.

"All secure?" he asked.

"Yeah. I had to do some twisting and such, but he's tied up tight," Susie said, casually, as if she was talking about prepping the Sunday roast.

Roy pulled on the chain. There was no slack. Of course, once the flesh rotted off the bones, the chain would loosen, but the body would still be in the duffle bag, which would still be weighed down by the anchor chain and, shortly, the Quikcrete.

After putting the Quikcrete in the duffle bag, Roy added the lines that had held Harlan's legs, the three empty beer bottles, and the fourth untouched bottle that contained beer and Xanax, plus the Hefty bag. As he held the sides of the bag together, Susie zipped it almost shut.

"Final check," she said.

"Yep."

Roy went to the console and came back with a small piece of paper and a flashlight. He read from the paper.

"Duffle bag contents: Tarp?"

"Check."

"Hefty?"

"Check."

"Leg lines?"

"Check."

"Anchor line?"

"Check."

"Padlocks?"

"Check."

"Quikcrete?"

"Check."

"Beer bottles?"

"Check."

"Sunglasses? Scratch that. He had his own shades."

"Yep, check."

"Phone contacts and phone in bag."

"Check."

"Ice pick?"

"Shit."

They fumbled around for about a minute before they found the ice pick on the deck up against the base of the coffin box. It had fallen during the process.

They placed it in the duffle bag.

"Ice pick, check."

"Burner phone," Roy said, and headed back to the stern of the boat where he had left the Seattle phone on one of the seats.

As he placed it in the bag, Susie said, "Details, details."

"No kidding. I'm glad we made the list."

"Okay. That's it," Roy finished, and placed the list in the duffle bag. With the anchor chain, they had calculated that the duffle bag would weigh approximately 180 pounds fully loaded—not including Harlan.

They retrieved the two four-foot, 2x6 pieces of wood from storage and placed them between the coffin box and the side of the boat, creating a small ramp.

Then, between the two of them, they heaved the duffle bag up and across the two boards. They shuffled it to the edge, and paused to look at each other before giving it a shove into the water. It sank immediately.

Both knew that the ocean depth below them was approximately 2,000 feet. That was exactly how they had planned it.

* * *

The trip back to Bimini took just under an hour. Roy pulled up about fifty yards from the beach where he had picked Susie up that morning. There were no other boats around. Susie, now wearing a wetsuit, kissed her husband before lowering herself into the water via the swim ladder. Roy handed her the backpack containing their two mobile phones in a Ziploc bag.

Roy waited until he saw his wife make it to shore. Then, he started up the engines and headed back to Miami.

* * *

It was almost 11:00 p.m. by the time Susie reached the Sunseeker. She took a quick hot shower and emptied the backpack. She put her wet clothes out to dry and hung the wetsuit in one of the showers. Then she went down to the galley, taking the mobile phones with her.

Though they had location services turned off, any calls that they made or received would register with the mobile carrier based on where they were located. That was why both phones had been switched off since they'd left Bimini. Susie now switched them both back on and plugged them in to charge.

As per their plan, she used Roy's phone to call her mother. Although she didn't answer—she'd probably already taken out her hearing aids and gone to sleep—that made no difference. Susie didn't even leave a message.

But now, somewhere in AT&T's database, there was a call placing Roy's cell phone in Bimini on the night of Harlan's disappearance at 11-ish p.m.

Meanwhile, Susie was famished. She pan-fried herself a small tuna filet and steamed some broccoli. While the broccoli cooled, she popped open a bottle of red and ate at the dining table.

It was done.

And if Susie was completely honest with herself, she had expected more. She hadn't expected to feel joy or happiness, but something. Vindication maybe. Satisfaction. Or at least some kind of sense of relief. She had imagined the whole thing would be much more dramatic. That she would maybe have said something like, *This is for Kristy* or *This is for Camilla.*

Yet, when the moment came, she'd been much more concerned with making sure that no air got in through the Hefty bag, and that he didn't manage to somehow fight his way off the coffin box. In fact, as she thought about it, she had expected more of a struggle. Again, more drama.

Nothing.

She blamed the drugs.

When she'd tightened the Hefty over his face, she'd tried

to time it with an exhalation, so that there would be less air in his lungs and he'd die more quickly. She hadn't done that to spare him any suffering... just to kill him with less risk of him getting loose somehow. Once she had put the Hefty over his head, she'd counted to ninety-eight before he'd stopped moving.

He had struggled some, but less than she'd expected. With Roy sitting on top of him, he hadn't had much room for maneuvering. And with his legs tied to the rail—that had been Roy's idea—the guy hadn't stood a chance. His legs had been Harlan's only point of leverage. When he'd tried to pull with them, he'd just lifted his face up into the Hefty and his body up into Roy's.

Susie confessed to me that what they'd done felt very clinical to her. Heartless. Without emotion. She had no sympathy for the victim, but no joy at the killing, either. It was an empty feeling.

Though maybe, in a way, the feeling was appropriate. What they had done was about punishment. Punishing Harlan for what he'd done to Kristy. Making something that was so very wrong right again. It was, in reality, an execution.

And execution, if done correctly, is about the executed, not about the executioner.

The whole thing felt very anticlimactic. Maybe her feelings would change over time. However, then and there, at that moment, she just wanted to unwind and forget about everything.

Susie opened the wine fridge and reached into the back left corner. Voila! A full pack of Marlboros. She took the pack with her up to the flybridge and lit up. Susie smoked and tried to clear her mind. She didn't want to do any more thinking that night.

She was sitting in the back corner of the flybridge on the sofa, sipping wine and smoking. As she exhaled a giant plume of smoke and watched it dissipate in front of her, a voice startled her.

"Hey there!"

She followed the direction of the sound down to the bow of the boat in the slip next to theirs. It was a woman. There wasn't enough light to really see her, or gauge her age, class, or anything useful, yet Susie found herself responding, "Hey!" into the darkness.

"You got an extra smoke?" the voice asked.

"Um, sure," she replied, gathering her thoughts as she tried to extract a smoke from the pack. She also realized it was taking her a bit too much effort to pull out a cigarette.

Clearly, I'm a little drunk.

"Can I come up?" the voice questioned.

"No problem," Susie replied, forcing a smile into her voice when she really wanted to tell the stranger to fuck off. She wasn't in the mood for guests and she was feeling imposed upon. She put a cigarette on the table and waited.

A head and then a pair of shoulders appeared at the top of the stairs to the flybridge.

"Hi. I'm Toni," the woman said.

Susie didn't get up. "Hi Toni. I'm Susie."

Susie's new unwelcome friend picked up the cigarette and lit up.

She was a fiftyish looking woman. Chunky, attractive in a "used to be athletic but gave in to crème brûlée" sort of way. She wore shorts and a long-sleeved boat shirt. Barefoot, as boating protocol demanded, with a little ankle bracelet on her left leg.

"Thanks," she said. "Thought I had another pack, but I was wrong. Must have smoked more yesterday than I thought."

"No worries."

"I've seen you guys before. Up at Compass Cay. Few years back. You have a daughter, right?"

Susie recalled the trip. The summer before Camilla died. She didn't feel like correcting Toni and opening a can of worms, though.

"Yep. That *has* been a while. You have a good memory."

"Beautiful boat—Lady Suze—hard to miss. I guess you're Suze?" Toni took advantage of the question to take a seat across from Susie.

Susie smiled. "A nickname my husband uses."

"We're in I Sea U." Toni made a face that said, *He didn't name her after me.* "Roland's a surgeon."

"Got it. Cute."

They paused for a moment.

Smoking.

"You look tired, girl," Toni commented.

Susie let out a short laugh. "Wow… that's pretty direct."

"No offense. I just mean that I've seen you around the last couple of days, and today, you look tired. Up since early this morning, no? Like 4:00?"

Susie's heart skipped. Toni knew way too much about their business. Like the proverbial duck that paddles frantically beneath the surface, Susie's face remained impassive.

She couldn't have seen anything. She didn't see anything.

"Yeah," she said, "Rough night last night. At dinner yesterday, Roy—my husband—ate something. Bad sashimi, we think. It hit him around 2:00 a.m. this morning."

"Ugh. Vomirrhea?"

Susie nodded.

"That's tough on a boat. Close quarters."

"Tell me about it. Around four, I couldn't take it anymore. So, I went out to get some air."

"I hear you. Roland—my husband—snores. It's not the end of the world given that I'm a bit of an insomniac. I'm awake a lot anyway. I read a lot. Romance novels mainly. Thrillers. But the nights are long and sometimes he's so loud I can't concentrate. So, I go out for walks too."

"Right. It's pretty quiet around here, isn't it? I thought there would be more activity when I went out this morning. But hardly anyone was around," Susie offered in an attempt to find out if the woman had seen anything.

"Oh, you'd be surprised," Toni said provocatively.

"Oooh. Tell me," Susie answered, scooching a little closer. "I love gossip."

The woman proceeded to give her host a night owl's perspective on the last few days. Three days earlier, on Sunday, the husband and wife two boats down had gotten into a shouting match at about 3:00 a.m. On Monday, some suspicious characters loitering around turned out to be maintenance guys—Toni had called marina security on the VHF. And just last night, there was a couple making out—really making out—on the bow of the Benetti docked port side.

"Man," Susie said, "It's amazing. All that going on while the rest of us are sleeping." She paused. "I hope we haven't bothered you too much with all of our shenanigans."

"Naw. You guys are quiet. Good neighbors."

"We try to be. So, how has your stay been otherwise?"

"Real nice. We came up with some friends—they're over in the Mega-Yacht Marina. They've got a 120-foot Hatteras. So, we've been hanging out with them a bunch on their boat. They loooove their poker. You guys play? Roland and me, we love poker. Nothing high stakes, mind you, just cards, some smokes, friendly conversation. You know?"

"Sounds like fun." Susie smelled an invite coming. She was calculating whether it would be better to spend more time with these folks, or less. Before she could decide which way to respond, Toni continued.

"Too bad we head back tomorrow. Got family coming in to visit."

"Back to reality, huh?"

"Yeah," the woman said, wistfully. "Hey, your guy need any Pepto? If he's real bad, I can get Roland, have him check him out?"

"Oh, no thanks, Toni. I think he's on the mend. The worst is over. He's rehydrating now."

"Yeah… that's exactly what I was gonna say. Lots of liquids. Water, Pedialyte, Gatorade. You know the drill."

"I do. In fact," Susie said, stubbing out her cigarette, "I should probably check in on him and call it a night."

"Oh sure," Toni said, not bothering to mask her disappointment.

Susie took her pack of cigarettes and pulled out four. She handed them to her neighbor and said, "Take these. Get you over 'til tomorrow."

"Thanks, hun! Very sweet of you." Toni perked up.

Susie picked up the wine bottle and ashtray and walked her uninvited guest off the boat. She also made a mental note: a thirty-five-foot Sea Ray Sundancer—*I Sea U*—with the homeport of Ft. Lauderdale.

It was just past midnight.

DAY SIX

Thursday, May 3, 2018

Roy's crossing to Miami had been somewhat choppy. Nothing serious for the Yellowfin, but making the journey back by jet ski in those conditions would be another story.

Roy had been preoccupied with watching the weather and keeping an eye out for other watercraft. He knew that, at some point, he'd need to think through everything that they'd done that day, but for that he wanted no distractions. He'd put it on the backburner.

He approached the mouth to his home canal at about midnight. Slowing the engines, he decided to hang out in the bay for a while to allow time for the neighbors to go to sleep. He was tired, though, and after half an hour, the amber lights and flickering of televisions hadn't changed.

He started the engines and ran a bit south of the canal entrance, then dropped anchor to wait. He set his phone alarm for 2:00 a.m. in case he drifted off. Which he did.

He slept fitfully—really, he was more in that state of semi-consciousness that feels like the border between sleep and wakefulness. It was cold out on the water.

His dreams ran like a preview for a film called *Killing Joe*. The set-up, the boat ride, the drugged beer, the Hefty bag, the piss—that rancid smell of urine—and finally dumping the body. It was all bits and pieces. His mind replayed all the steps in the plan, everything they'd done, looking for mistakes.

He kept dreaming that the duffle bag had gotten stuck to the back of his boat somehow, and that rather than sinking the dead body, he'd been dragging it around behind him all night.

He awoke.

A rogue wave had jostled the boat, interrupting the natural rhythm of the sea that had lulled him to sleep.

It was 1:13 a.m.

Still early. Some of those lights were still burning bright.

As he scanned the neighborhood across the bow of the Yellowfin, his eyes settled on the coffin box where, just a few hours earlier, he and Susie had killed a young man. Roy had on other occasions sat there chatting with his daughter. Susie had lain there more than once to take in the sun while he fished.

The space was tainted now. It would never be the same again. He would wait a few months, then sell the boat.

As Roy contemplated, he felt engulfed by his surroundings. He felt buried in them, entombed.

Floating alone in the bay, as he looked to the east and south away from downtown Miami, the horizon melted—the division between the sea and the sky dissolved into one massive snow globe of darkness and water. Roy felt alone in a floating tomb.

Mercifully, when he looked to north and west, he could see the silhouette of houses along the coast—some with lights on—and all of them backlit by the lights of civilization. Light at the end of a long, dark shaft. That view made him feel connected with civilization, a part of the larger human story.

As he sat there, Roy struggled to curate and inventory his thoughts and emotions. An amazing wife. A job he loved. Financial independence. A great business. Yet, he had risked it all by crossing the Florida Straits on a jet ski at night. Worse still, he had done that to kill a twenty-something-year-old man he didn't even know. And, now he was about to risk his life—again—on the jet ski, to cover up that murder.

What the fuck is wrong with me?
Why would I ever...

A number of reasons paraded through his mind, but none felt sufficient.

To avenge Kristy's rape.
Because Harlan deserved it.
Because he escaped punishment.

Because Tom Wise asked, for Kristy, and for Camilla.
To avenge Camilla? Really?

When push came to shove, he knew he'd done it because Susie had wanted him to. No, because she'd said she *needed* him to. And because, after thinking it through, he'd believed he could get away with it and he wanted to prove it.

Did that make him an amoral adrenaline junkie? After all, that's what an impartial observer would think, wasn't it?

Maybe he needed help?

He laughed. It was a hollow laugh.

Admitting you have a problem is the first step.

"Only eleven more to go," he said out loud.

Shut the fuck up.

Practical Roy took over.

It was too late to be second-guessing what they had done. Or why. Susie had wanted it, sure. Then again, other factors came into play as well. Susie wouldn't have asked him to do it if Harlan hadn't been a bad guy. Susie wouldn't have asked him to do it if Camilla's death hadn't left her feeling useless, impotent, empty. He'd felt the same way. He'd muddled his way through it… but she needed more.

He knew that, during those months after Camilla's death, he'd almost lost Susie. Their relationship had been on the brink of collapse. And that was something he couldn't take. He'd seen his parents' marriage implode when his twin died, and he couldn't stand the thought of the same happening to him. To them.

But now, after everything they had been through, and especially after what they had just done together, Roy knew that he and Susie could weather anything. There was no doubt in his mind that this act, as callous and as outrageous as it might seem to an outsider, had brought them together in a way that nothing else ever could. They would be bonded together forever, come what may.

Were they amoral sickos? He didn't think so. Maybe their moral compass was off a bit. Okay, maybe it was off by a lot.

But, their actions were justified. They had offered a sort of twisted human sacrifice to the god of vengeance. Although their victim hadn't done *them* any harm, he had hurt someone. And they—Susie and Roy—had also been hurt by someone. They were owed some retribution. In the scheme of things, somehow, all these harms were fungible in a way, weren't they?

Wasn't that what Susie had written about in her blog? This wasn't just Camilla's or Kristy's story. It was *a story of all of us*. The harms done to Kristy and Camilla created an imbalance. Roy and Susie had only helped to restore the balance.

Susie. God, how he loved that woman.

At 2:00 a.m., the intro to "Stairway to Heaven" woke him from another light doze.

He switched off the alarm and rubbed his face as he surveyed the neighborhood. Most of the lights were out now, so he started the engines and began the slow run up the canal back to the house. And, as much as he knew it was ridiculous, he couldn't help but take a quick peek over the stern to make sure there was nothing dragging behind the boat—no duffle bag.

Thank God! He shook his head and laughed.

He bumped up against the dock at 2:20 a.m. and tied up the Yellowfin. Then, he turned on the VHF and tuned to the weather channel. Conditions had improved slightly. He opened the weather app on his phone and saw that the forecast was the same for the next several days.

Then again, the weather was fickle. A bird in the hand...

He had a decision to make. Spend the night and the next day hiding out on the Yellowfin, hoping for a better crossing tomorrow night. Or, he could take off now and go slow. He had more than four hours until sunrise. He'd just had a nap and felt okay. He'd already made the crossing once. He knew what was in store for him.

He removed the second burner phone from the console. This one he'd purchased in Miami for only one purpose—to let Susie know when he would be attempting the final return journey.

He texted her, *Gerry?*

Any word starting with a "G" meant the return trip was a Go. "W" meant Waiting and "A" was for Abort.

They'd discussed this and agreed that if the weather was too bad, Roy could stay in Miami and Susie could run the Sunseeker back alone. She was more than capable. It just added some risk. She could be stopped on her way home by the Coast Guard or the Bahamian authorities for whatever reason. If he wasn't aboard, that would become a matter of public record.

Similarly, if there were witnesses to Susie leaving Bimini, they may well notice that there was no jet ski on the swim platform. This could prompt questions about Roy's whereabouts. After all, the Bahamian authorities had documented them *both* entering Bimini *with a jet ski*.

No, Susie returning alone was not ideal, but it was workable if the return crossing via jet ski was impossible. Although Roy didn't feel that was the case. He felt the return was worth the risk.

Susie responded to his text—confirming she'd received it— with, *Sorry, wrong number.*

He pulled on the wetsuit. It was still damp and cold from his crossing the day before. He gathered his gear, screwed closed the bungs on the jet ski, started the engine, and headed out.

There was a light chop in Biscayne Bay. He could comfortably run at twenty knots. However, as he passed Biscayne Channel, the seas deteriorated. Again, the issue wasn't the height of the waves so much as how lack of visibility affected his timing and balance when rising and falling with the waves. He slowed to fifteen knots, made sure he was on course, and focused on keeping a lookout for other vessels.

Though he tried to stay alert, the droning of the engine, the cold, and the persistent undulation were hypnotic. He dozed off around 4:00 a.m. When he came to, the jet ski was running at less than five knots as a result of his grip on the throttle weakening while he slept. He was also off course.

Alert once more, he released the throttle, slowing the jet ski to a stop. Then, he sat up straight and slapped himself a few times in the face. He was out in the Straits, about a third of the way across, but the current had taken him north. He glanced over his left shoulder. He could still see the Miami skyline in the distance.

The wind was blowing really loud, and yet, oddly, there was hardly any breeze.

Then it struck him. Adrenaline. Fight or flight.

That's not fucking wind!

He looked over his shoulder again and saw them. Lights; red on the left, green on the right, and white above. All three were growing larger by the millisecond.

A boat. A big boat was bearing down on him. Fast!

Roy gunned the jet ski as he turned to face forward, pointing it away from the yacht that was about to run him over. The engine sputtered a few terrifying times and then kicked into gear. He felt the propulsion pull him back, hard, but he held on, mashing the throttle lever into the handle, willing the fucking machine to fly!

Roy felt, then heard, the boat pass behind him. He could feel its mass displacing the air around him and narrowly missing him by what must have been inches, because a split second later he felt the wake coming. It ran under the jet ski from back to front, stern to bow. As it did, the rear of the machine rose high, threatening to topple him from it. He tried to turn to run with the wake, to ride the wake. But he was too late. His reaction was too slow. The stern of the jet ski rose high, dipping its nose down until with a jolt it buried itself in the ocean, slamming to a stop and launching Roy over the handlebars and into the sea.

* * *

Susie awoke at 5:30 a.m. to the sound of an engine. It sounded close. She scrambled out of bed and headed up top, thinking it might be Roy. Yet, as she slid open the glass door and stepped out onto the rear cockpit, she immediately knew that she wasn't hearing the sound of a jet ski.

Toni, her neighbor, was down on the dock untying her stern line. Apparently, they were leaving even though it was still dark.

Susie stepped off the boat.

"Heading out?"

"Yep," Toni said. "Back to Lauderdale. Family."

"I see. Well, it was nice meeting you. Safe travels!"

"You, too. Take care. Hopefully, see you again soon. Oh, and thanks for the smokes. They were a life saver!"

Toni carried the line on board with her.

Susie watched as they left and waved as they headed down the channel.

Back on board, she made coffee and went up onto the flybridge to wait. She re-read Roy's message. *Gerry?* According to her phone, it had arrived at 2:42 a.m.

The critical part of the plan was over. They were documented as being in Bimini and out of the United States when Harlan disappeared. It would be impossible to place them anywhere near him, but getting Roy back to Bimini would seal the deal. Assuming he could do twenty knots, the trip would take about two and a half hours. He should be arriving around 5:15 or so.

At 6:00, Susie began to worry. She checked her phone. No more text messages.

The sun came up.

Susie was in uncharted waters. They had discussed the possibility that something could happen on the crossing, going or coming. The jet ski could break down. Roy could hit something— something floating in the water, an animal, a boat. Or, he could just lose control and fall off the jet ski. In the dark, with the waves, depending on how hard he fell and how far from the jet ski he was, he might not be able to find his way back to it. Sure, the kill switch would shut it off. But in the dark, with waves, he might lose sight of it, even if he was uninjured.

And, of course, there were the predators. Sharks. Susie cringed at the thought.

They'd been through all the possibilities. And they'd tried to provision the ditch bag for as many eventualities as possible. As far as Susie was concerned, they'd agreed that she was to stick to the 'Roy has food poisoning' story until the last day of their planned time in Bimini.

It was Thursday.

If, by Saturday, Roy still hadn't appeared, she was to report him missing, claiming that he'd taken the jet ski out for one final spin that day and hadn't returned.

"Plan for the worst, visualize the best," Roy had said.

So really, for now, all Susie could do was sit and wait.

She went up onto the flybridge and sat facing toward the channel, watching for Roy. For the next hour, Susie watched as boats and yachts came and went. Several jet skis went out.

Her heart skipped when she saw one returning.

Not Roy.

At 7:00 a.m., Roy still hadn't arrived. The sinking feeling in her stomach was turning to nausea. Susie went below and put on another pot of coffee. She lit up a cigarette. They never smoked inside the boat, but fuck it.

When the coffee was ready, she poured herself half a cup, then topped it off with Baileys and went back up top, taking the remaining quarter bottle of Baileys with her.

At 8:00 a.m., still nothing.

She was starting to feel ill. Her stomach was cramping, and she found herself getting angry at herself.

Are we fucking idiots?

The weight of what they had done suddenly hit her like a truck. Not killing Harlan—that needed to be done—but Roy crossing the Straits on a jet ski. Alone. At night. Twice! It was too risky. They should have called it at one crossing. He should have just stayed in Miami.

What the fuck am I going to do if he doesn't come back? If he doesn't make it? If he's...

Susie couldn't bear to think of Roy dead.

She'd seen a lot of death.

Too much of it, and too close.

This whole mess with Harlan was the second time Susie had been close to a killing.

The first had been much more emotional. Visceral. She had managed to repress that shit for years. But now, as if in punishment, her sadistic subconscious insisted on dredging it all up—bringing it to the surface like a putrid carcass that had filled with gases as it rotted and floated up from the bottom of the sea.

Susie was thirteen when it happened, but she could still hear those three fateful words as if they'd just been screamed out loud.

I'm gonna tell!

By the time Susie got her shorts back on, Deb was already out the cabin door and running down the trail.

Susie was gangly and long-legged, but she was coordinated, fast. She caught up to Deb just past the turn on the trail heading back to the main cabin. She saw that Deb was crouched down. When Susie approached, she found Deb talking in harsh whispers to Joan, who was sitting on the ground, trying to untie a knot in one of her shoes that had apparently come off somehow.

"I know what I saw!" Joan whined.

"You made a mistake. If you tell and you're wrong, that makes you a liar!" Deb said. "And you know what God does to liars? In hell?"

"I may be a liar, but you're a... a whore!" Joan yelled, awkwardly. She'd obviously heard the word before, but it sounded as though she'd never used it.

Susie wondered if Joan even knew what it meant.

"You're a little cunt is what you are," Deb hissed, eyes flashing aggressively. Unlike Joan, she was clear and calculated in her choice of words. The rage in Deb's voice frightened Susie.

She stepped in to try and calm the situation. "Hold on," she said, placing a hand on Deb's shoulder. "Let me talk to her." She could see Joan had been crying, and there was dirt and blood on her knees. She wondered if it was Deb who had pushed her down.

Susie knelt down next to Joan and looked her in the eye. "Joan, are you okay?" she asked, softly. "Did you hurt yourself?"

"No. I just tripped on that stupid root," she said, pointing with her head.

"Where were you going?"

The little girl hesitated, glancing at Deb who was still glaring at her. Then she blurted, "I saw what you two were doing. It's evil and I'm gonna tell!" she said, through gritted teeth. She was afraid, but she wasn't going to be intimidated. Grandma had told her that she should always stick up for herself, and for the truth. *God helps those who help themselves.*

"Are you sure you know what you saw? 'Cause I think you may be wrong."

"I *know*," Joan insisted, struggling to untie the laces on her shoe so that she could put it back on. "And you're going to hell," she added, petulantly. "Just like in the Bible. You're bad, bad, sinful girls!"

Susie looked down at Joan's shoe and began, "Let me help—" but the rest of her sentence was cut short when the little girl suddenly lurched forward, as if propelled by an unseen force, went limp, and then folded in on herself until she was resting on her legs.

At first, Susie thought she'd had some sort of fit—anxiety, or epilepsy, or something. Then she looked up and saw Deb standing over Joan, holding a thick tree branch with both hands like it was a baseball bat.

Slowly, it dawned on Susie that Deb had hit Joan across the back of the head with the branch. Susie was stunned. Her head began to buzz. She wanted to say something but couldn't. Her tongue was paralyzed.

Deb dropped her weapon and began arranging Joan, laying her flat on her back. Susie could see that Deb's mouth was moving, but she was unable to comprehend exactly what she was saying.

"Susie!" Deb hissed through gritted teeth while her strong hands shook Susie back to reality. "Help me," she ordered.

Together, they picked Joan up—one taking wrists, the other ankles. Deb led, and Susie followed. They trudged down the path through the woods until they emerged at the opening to the scenic overlook. Susie could hear the rumble of the river fifty feet below.

They were still carrying Joan. Deb moved closer to the edge, but Susie stopped, pulling Joan protectively back toward her.

"Wait Deb, stop! What the... what are you doing?" Susie asked, incredulously.

Deb carefully put Joan down. Susie did the same.

"Susie, if she told what she saw, you know what would happen to us? You know how it is for girls like us?"

"But Deb, you didn't even try to talk to her. Maybe if we talk to her—"

"Don't be fucking stupid, Suze!" she snapped. "You heard her spouting her Bible shit."

"Yeah, but when she comes around, I could try to…" Susie babbled in a trembling voice, but allowed the words to trail off when Deb stepped closer to her.

"Come around?" Deb put her hand on Susie's shoulder. "Susie. She's fucking dead," Deb said, flatly.

Susie looked down at Joan. She couldn't tell if she was alive or not. She dropped to the ground next to her and held her hand in front of her face. That's what they did in the movies. Or at least that's what she thought they did. She couldn't remember. She was confused. She didn't feel any breathing.

She bent over and placed her ear on the girl's chest with the hope of hearing a heartbeat. Susie later remembered the tears blurring her vision. All she could hear was the roar of the river.

She looked up at Deb.

"I didn't mean it," Deb said weakly. She was breathing hard, though Susie couldn't tell if it was from the exertion of carrying Joan or from nerves. "I think I hit her too hard."

Susie looked at Joan, then around them as she considered their predicament. She couldn't stop crying.

"Susie. If we don't get rid of her, we're going to jail. Is that what you want?"

Now, decades later, Susie took a swallow of her spiked coffee, then lit a cigarette with shaking hands as she remembered.

After they'd pushed and rolled the body over the edge of the ravine, Deb had told her exactly what was going to happen next.

"Sometime in the morning, they'll figure out that she's missing. They'll start looking. If we're lucky, the river will carry the body away. If not, they'll find her sometime late tomorrow. They'll think she fell. That's what it looks like.

"Then they'll ask around to see if anyone saw anything. All we have to do is say 'no,'" Deb said, "tell them that we were in our cabin all night. Asleep all night. I'm your alibi, and you're mine. We stick to that. Keep it simple. We *know* nothing. We *saw* nothing and then that'll be the end of it. Okay?"

But Susie was unable to reply. She just sat there staring into space, her body aquiver.

Deb tried to put her arm around her, but she pulled away. She didn't want to have anything to do with her. With this.

It didn't work out exactly as Deb predicted, but close enough. As soon as the authorities found the body the next day and told the girls, Susie called her parents to say she wanted to go home. They picked her up that same evening. She'd never even been formally questioned. Although, at the request of one of the deputies, the camp director contacted the parents of all of the girls who had left camp early. Susie's parents received a call, and they asked her if she had seen anything unusual.

"No. Why?" she had answered.

And that was it. That was the extent of her questioning. That had been the end of it.

Susie had wanted to forget all of it, as though it had never happened. She felt the same way about Harlan now. Sure, there was a difference. Complicity in Joan's murder was forced upon her. Harlan's murder had been a choice she'd made with eyes wide open. Still, she felt the same way about both deaths. Thinking about it tired her. She just wanted to forget.

She just wanted Roy back.

At 9:30, Roy was over four hours late.

Susie was beside herself. She had no idea what to do beyond drinking and smoking. She'd finished what was left of the Baileys, and as she was about to go back down below to explore her options, she saw a jet ski coming in at the far end of the marina. As with all the other jet skis she had seen that morning, her heart somersaulted.

She squinted into the distance. The rider was bare-chested —no wetsuit—and wasn't wearing goggles or a life vest. Roy had been wearing both.

Dammit!

Her heart sank. She wanted to cry. Scream. Call for help. She couldn't do any of these. Instead, she trudged down to the galley and opened a bottle of scotch.

Roy's Macallan. As she poured herself a half glass, the smell of it reminded her of Roy. Her thoughts wandered, albeit reluctantly, to what life might be like without him. She felt isolated. Alone. And those tears that wouldn't come before were starting to well in her eyes.

Maybe she should call someone. Her mother? Roni? Maybe Deb? She didn't want to be alone. She couldn't bear being alone.

She took the glass with her and began her ascent once more. She needed air.

As she emerged topside, she heard, "Hey…" She looked over, and there he was, wetsuit around his waist, clambering off the jet ski. No goggles. She could see now, up close, that he had been sitting on the life jacket.

"Oh, thank God!" She tried not to overreact. As he stood on the swim platform, holding the jet ski handle to keep it from drifting away, she rushed over and handed him a line to secure the craft.

Roy straightened up stiffly—he was sore, she could tell, but she couldn't help herself from throwing her arms around him. "What took you so long?" she demanded.

"Inside first," he said, ending the embrace and opening the door to the saloon. She followed him in.

"What a fucking night!" he began as he dropped on the floor and began stretching. "The waves sucked. Too high. So, I had to run slow. Like at fifteen. Then, I almost got run down by a fucking yacht at about the halfway point. Son-of-a-bitch didn't even see me. Probably on autopilot. I went over. Into the water. The kill switch saved me. I came up and swam like crazy to grab the motherfucker—the jet ski, I mean. Lost my fucking goggles."

"Oh God, Roy! I'm so sorry."

"Fucking stupid. I was tired. Not paying attention.

"So, I finally managed to get back up on the jet ski, then I look behind me and see two or three more boats more coming at me—I mean they were at a distance, but gaining. So, I course-corrected south, trying to get out of the direct path from Miami to Bimini. Of course, going south is just like changing lanes in traffic. On the new course, all the boats heading to Cat Cay were still behind me.

"Again, I course-corrected further south. And further, until there were no boats coming. I ended up coming over onto the Banks at Browns Channel, way south. Of course, by the time I got there, it was sun-up.

"So, I just puttered around the east side and back up to here. But I had to stop to refuel. Then, I had to deal with some crap line that got caught in the impeller. I had to shut the thing down, get under it, and cut that shit out.

"Oh, and I forgot to put on the Vaseline when I left. So, I stopped and put some on when I remembered—because of the burn."

Susie giggled. He looked like Kim Kardashian doing duck face. She was staring at him now, relieved to have him back in one piece.

"What?" he asked, instinctively raising a hand to his face. "My lips are all puffy, right?"

Susie laughed and gently kissed him.

"Was it all quiet at home?" she asked.

"Yeah, well, I got back too early. So, I anchored in the bay for a couple of hours until everyone went to sleep, then went home and made the switch. But yeah, all quiet."

They were silent for a few moments, and then Susie took a deep breath and sighed. "Well, that's it. We did it. It's done," she said with a grin.

"Yeah. Looks like we pulled it off," Roy responded. "Now, we just wait and see if they can catch us."

* * *

Roy stripped out of the wetsuit, rinsed off in the shower, and went straight to bed. Susie took care of the gear. She unloaded the ditch bag and gas can from the jet ski and then rinsed out his wetsuit and goggles. It gave her joy to do so. To care for and mother him.

Roy slept until 11:30. He was awakened by the ping of a text message on his mobile phone. It was David.

DAVID: Harlan a no-show.

ROY: Really? No phone call? Nothing?

DAVID: Nada. Called his mobile twice. Got voice mail. Didn't leave a message...

ROY: Give him a couple of hours. Maybe he went out and partied. Overslept, maybe?

DAVID: 👍

Roy got out of bed and showed Susie the texts.

Now that he was up, Susie told Roy about her conversation with Toni of *I Sea U* the night before. A snoopy slip-mate was not good news, but there was nothing to be done at this point. She'd seen what she'd seen, knew what she knew, and was gone.

And then, even though he could have slept more, they decided it was better to go out and be seen. They went to the resort casino and played blackjack for an hour, being sure to get on the security cameras. Then, they had lunch at the Big Game Club Bar—paying with AMEX, of course. Roy told the waiter it was Susie's birthday, and they brought a cake and sang "Happy Birthday." The bill was $147.29. Roy tipped the waiter—Jamie—a crisp one-hundred-dollar bill, telling him the birthday thing was a prank, but thanking him for going along with it.

They walked on the beach.

At 2:00 p.m., Roy called David.

"Hey, Roy."

"Hey. So, still nothing from our visitor from Texas?"

"Nope. Nothing," David answered. "I called one more time about fifteen minutes ago, just before you called me. Voicemail, again."

"Well, that's not very professional, is it?"

"No. But I'm not surprised I guess."

"Yeah."

"Weird thing is, he texted me last night, so I figured he got here."

Roy's stomach lurched. "Oh, really?" he asked, trying to sound nonchalant. "What about?"

"Well, that's the thing. The text didn't make sense. It said, 'Sorry we can't have dinner. See you tomorrow'—something like that."

Roy paused a moment, then asked, "You were going to have dinner?"

"No. That's what's strange. That was never discussed. Not a part of the plan."

"Humph." Roy pondered for a moment. "You think he was pissed off? Like, he expected you to take him out to dinner?"

"I don't know, man. It's weird. I saw it around eight last night. So, I wrote back asking if he was writing to me or someone else—figuring maybe he had plans with someone else he knows in Miami, but he didn't reply. Odd. Who knows?"

"Yeah. Well, if he got cold feet, he'll come back around. All we can do is wait, I guess."

"You think he just fucked us over to get the free trip to Miami and he's just out partying?"

Roy laughed. "Stranger things have happened."

"Yeah, I suppose. Hey, so I went through all the DD on ArtCraft... "

They talked through some business items they had pending for another ten minutes or so, then hung up.

After hanging up and as they walked back to the Sunseeker,

Roy shared what he had just learned.

"Shit," Susie said. "You think he texted anyone else?"

"It's possible. We knew it could happen. We should have checked his phone for text messages when we had it in hand. That was stupid."

"Wouldn't have mattered, I suppose. What could we have done at that point?"

To Roy and Susie, this was the biggest uncontrollable factor in their plan—the time between Roy contacting Joe and them meeting at the marina.

Back at the boat, Susie stretched out in her white bikini on one of the sunbeds while Roy chatted with a couple of neighboring boat owners, sharing his business card with one of them.

Being seen was a part of their plan that they could control.

DAY SEVEN

Friday, May 4, 2018

David's intercom buzzed. He'd only just returned from lunch and had barely removed his jacket.

"David?"

"Yes. What is it?"

"Joe Harlan on line two."

David smiled. *Finally. A day late, but better than nothing.* He was curious to hear what excuse the kid would offer for missing their meeting.

"Joe. Where the hell are you, man? You alright?" he asked as soon as he picked up the phone.

"Hello, Mr. Kim?"

David didn't recognize the voice. It was much deeper than Joe's. "Yes?"

"This is Senator Joe Harlan Sr."

Okay. David thought. *If the father's calling, it can't be good.*

"Oh, hello, Mr. Senator. What can I do for you?"

"Well, I'm calling about Joe. I haven't heard from him and I know he was meeting with you," the man said in a cultured Texas drawl.

For reasons unknown to him, David's heart skipped a beat. "Actually, Mr. Senator, I haven't seen Joe. We were supposed to meet at 10:00 a.m. yesterday, but he was a no-show. I tried calling him a few times, but he didn't answer."

There was an unnerving silence at the end of the line, then, "Right. Well, he's a big boy, and not having heard from him since Wednesday, I didn't think much of it. But he was supposed to be on the early flight back from Miami to Austin this morning. He was not. I called the airline and they told me he didn't check in."

"Um. Well, that is strange."

"Did y'all by any chance arrange his accommodations?"

"We did. We put him up at the Intercontinental Hotel."

"Is there more than one, or do you have an address?"

"It's downtown on Chopin Plaza."

"Thank you. You didn't by chance speak with him after he arrived in Miami?"

"No, I'm afraid not."

"Okay, Mr. Kim. If you do hear from him, could you let me know or tell him to give me a call? I'm sure it's nothing. Boys will be boys. But all the same. I just want to be sure he's okay since it's not like him to miss a flight."

"Oh, absolutely, sir. Of course."

David took down Harlan Sr.'s phone number and they hung up.

Immediately, David dialed Roy.

"Hello."

"Hey, Roy, you okay to talk?"

"Sure, what's up?"

"Just got a call from Harlan Sr. Says the kid didn't fly home. He was supposed to head back this morning, but he didn't even check in for the flight."

"Shit, that's weird," Roy said. "Are we sure he made it to Miami at all?"

"Well, now that you mention it, no. I just assumed that he did. His dad seemed to think so, too. And I guess from the text he sent me, I figured he was here. Shit." David sighed. "Harlan asked me if I'd talked to the kid after he got here. I told him I hadn't. I forgot about the text."

"Well, no biggie. He'll turn up. But it is weird that he no-showed the meeting *and* missed his flight back. Should we be doing something? I'm not sure what, but it just kind of feels like we should."

"I dunno. I got his old man's phone number. You want to call him?" David asked.

"Shit," Roy pondered. "And say what? Offer to help?"

"Maybe."

Roy sighed. "Yeah. I guess. Gimme his fucking number."

* * *

Detective Travers' phone buzzed.

He was having lunch at Jo's on Second Street. Travers was an Austin native and he loved his hometown. Although the city had changed dramatically in the forty-odd years he had lived there, and although it had more than doubled in size, to him it still felt like the small town he had been raised in.

One of his favorite pastimes was people-watching downtown—even if the place was being overrun by executive types. More suits. Also, more startup types wearing beards, torn jeans, and Vans. But there was still that funky, hippie, independent vibe to Austin that distinguished it from every other city in Texas.

Travers looked at his phone. The number looked familiar, but it wasn't in his contacts.

"Hello."

"Detective Travers."

He would recognize that cultured voice anywhere. "Mr. Senator. How are you?" he asked, forcing a smile as if the man could see him.

"Fine, thanks. And yourself?"

"Can't complain. Just finishing up lunch. How can I help you?"

"I apologize for the intrusion, Detective, but it's about Joe."

"Go on."

"I don't want to make a fuss. It's probably nothing. But you see, Joe flew out to Miami Wednesday for a business meeting. The meeting was Thursday morning. He was scheduled to return this morning on a flight arriving here around 9:30. But he missed the meeting and the flight. I called the hotel in Florida, and he did check in, so I know he made it to Miami.

"I've called him, and texted, and he doesn't answer." The senator paused. "Again," he continued, "I don't want to make a stink just yet, but, well, this is unusual. I was hoping you'd be able make some inquiries."

"Was he travelling with anyone else?"

"No. Alone."

"Who was he meeting with?"

"A gentleman named David Kim. With a company called Cruise Capital." The senator gave Travers David's phone number and the name and address of Joe's hotel, as well as the name of the young lady in reception whom he'd spoken to confirming that Joe had in fact checked in.

"Okay. Let me make a few calls."

After hanging up, Travers Googled Miami-Dade Police Department on his mobile phone and dialed the main number. He introduced himself and, after a brief explanation, he was patched through to a duty officer in Investigative Services.

"This is Detective Pérez," a woman answered.

Travers introduced himself and proceeded to schmooze his counterpart like only cops can when they need something.

Rosa Pérez seemed friendly, open, and amenable, and it wasn't long before Travers felt he could get to the reason for his call. "Listen, Rosa, I need a favor."

"I'm listening," she said, curiously.

Travers passed on everything he had learned from the senator.

"Cruise Capital, huh?" Rosa asked.

"You know them?"

"Heard of them. Nothing specific. Just rings a bell. Financial guys. And the kid's name, H-A-R-L-A-N?"

"That's right. My guess is the kid's on a bender," Travers commented, making light of the situation. "He's got a history."

"Really?" Again, Rosa's tone was inquisitive. She was eager

to know everything there was to know and Travers sensed that he wasn't going to get far if he held back. So, he gave her a summarized version of the Harlan story, including the Whole Foods altercation.

"Sheeyit!" Rosa said. "What a mess. You checked out her parents yet?"

"Nope. Just got off the phone with the senator. The dad's offices are downtown. I'm thinking of dropping by after our talk. We're on good terms. They're nice folks, and, between you and me, I don't blame him for punching the little shit."

Rosa was quiet for a short while, but then promised to make some inquiries, starting with the Intercontinental Hotel.

* * *

Senator Harlan's intercom buzzed. It was Meg.

"Mr. Senator?"

"Yes, darlin'?"

"A Mr. Roy Cruise for you on line one."

"Got it."

The senator picked up the receiver. "This is Senator Harlan, Mr. Cruise. Hello."

"Hello, Mr. Senator. How are you?"

"Well, I'm a bit worried if I'm to be totally honest with you."

"I understand completely. I'm calling because I spoke to my partner David Kim about your son, Joe. I was very concerned when I heard about the situation and wanted to see if we could help in any way. I'm assuming you haven't heard from him yet?"

"No. Nothing yet. It is concerning because it's not like him to miss meetings—or flights, for that matter."

"I appreciate that. Is there anything we can do to help?"

"At this point, no. I'm having his travel looked into. I

suspect he'll turn up sometime soon. He's a good boy, but he's young if you get my meanin'. You know. Wild oats and all... "

"I sure do. Well, if there's anything I or my firm can do, Senator, please don't hesitate to ask. I'm out of the country right now, but let me give you my mobile number—direct. That way you can reach me if you need to."

"Sure appreciate that, Mr. Cruise."

"Please, call me Roy."

Roy gave the senator his mobile number and hung up.

* * *

Tom Wise stepped out into the lobby of Highland Commercial Real Estate to find Detective Travers waiting for him.

"Art," he said with a smile, shaking the man's proffered hand.

"Tom, how have you been?"

"I'm good. Come in," Tom said, leading the detective into a small conference room with a round table for four. "Can I get you something? Coffee? Water?"

"No, thanks."

They sat.

"So, how's it going? How's business?" Travers asked with as much enthusiasm as he could muster.

Tom paused, eyeing his visitor with a skeptical grin. "Art. Come on. This obviously isn't a social call. Tell me what's the matter. Or what you need. We can get a beer some other time."

Travers laughed. He had always admired the man's directness. And he was going to afford him the same. "Well, Tom, I'm just wondering if you might have taken any trips lately."

"Trips?" Wise echoed, suspiciously. "Not really. Wait. What's this about? Should I call my lawyer, Art?" he asked slowly.

"Tom, you only need a lawyer if you've done something wrong," chuckled Travers. Then, more seriously, he added, "Look, it's nothing. Probably nothing. I'm just looking into something and, you know, it's just a formality. I just need to confirm that you weren't out of town in the last few days. That's all."

"That's all? Well, I can't see why you'd be asking me, unless this has something to do with that that... " Wise paused. He wanted to measure his words. He'd already gotten himself into enough trouble by not controlling himself. He couldn't afford, literally, any more trouble. "Harlan kid?" he finished, finally.

"As I said, just checking a box, Tom. So…" Travers waited, and then prompted the now stone-faced man, "have you taken any trips in the past week?"

"Just box-checking, huh?" He took a deep breath. "Art, I haven't been out of town since Christmas—not counting a weekend in Fredericksburg. This week, I was here all week. Worked every day. You can ask around the office. I know they've seen enough of me. Had a dentist appointment yesterday. Mid-afternoon. Then I took Deb to Fleming's for dinner. And, unfortunately or fortunately, depending on which way you want to look at it, there'll be a credit card transaction somewhere. You need more?"

"No. No. That's all right. So, Mrs. Wise was in Austin, too?"

"Like I said, we had dinner last night. She had a tennis tournament at the club early this week. Plays doubles. So, there'll be plenty of ladies that can vouch for where she was."

Travers sighed, seemingly with relief. "Okay then," he said simply, and then stood.

"So, are you going to tell me what this is about?" Tom asked, rising to show the detective out. "Should I be concerned?"

"Why should you be concerned? You haven't been anywhere or done anything," Travers answered before making for the door. Tom Wise watched him go, a thoughtful frown on his face.

* * *

The four-star Intercontinental Hotel is situated in downtown Miami. It is the kind of place where attention to detail is standard operating procedure and not just a staff-room poster. Many of the rooms feature enviable views across the bay, and for the hardened lounge lizards, the Bluewater Bar is adjacent to the rooftop pool, overlooking an oasis of palm trees and fountains that stretch out to Biscayne Bay.

Detective Rosa Pérez was standing behind the manager at the door to Room 576. It was the manager's understanding that the room was still occupied since the guest had missed his 12:00 checkout.

A swipe of the master key card made the door lock snick open and the light panel flash green. The manager pushed it open and stood aside.

"Please wait here, if you don't mind and hold the door open," Rosa requested.

"This is the Miami Police, is there anyone in here?" she called out to the room, but there was no response. "Hello? Anyone in here?" she tried again, stepping inside.

Nothing.

She sniffed the air.

Nothing.

No odd smells. The room temperature seemed normal. The shades were open.

She checked the floor around the entry for anything that might be out of place or that could constitute evidence.

Nothing.

She looked around. It was a standard hotel room. Two double beds. On one was a carry-on sized suitcase that lay open. Next to it lay a pair of blue pants and a white shirt.

One of the chairs had a few crumpled clothes items on it. Maybe dirty clothes. It was hard to tell. A green t-shirt. A beige denim jacket was draped over the back of the chair. Travel clothes?

There was a Dopp kit laying open in the bathroom. A toothbrush and toothpaste were on the counter. From the drip of the shower head and the collection of water in the pan, she surmised that the shower had been used, although the bathroom was neat. Towels folded. There was a washcloth hanging to dry inside the shower, and one of the large bath towels was folded, but not like the others.

Nothing seemed out of the ordinary.

Rosa checked the closet, which was half-open. Empty. She looked under the beds.

Nothing.

"Any charges to the room?" she asked the manager.

"We can look," he said, "but when I charged the extra night after he didn't check out, I don't remember seeing any charges other than the room."

Rosa continued looking around the room and only when she was satisfied that there was nothing else to see did she speak without turning. "I'd like to take a look at your security footage?"

Five minutes later, they were all squished into a small box of a room in the basement of the building.

Rosa asked an overweight man in a security uniform to cue up footage beginning fifteen minutes before Harlan's check-in time—which the computer check-in system indicated as being 2:28 p.m.

They spotted Harlan entering the building at 2:19 p.m. There was footage from the camera behind the front desk showing him checking in. Finding footage of Harlan leaving would be more complicated. He had changed clothes, and the hotel had over twenty security cameras in common areas and entrances.

She asked the security guard to preserve all security footage from Harlan's check-in time forward and then got to work.

* * *

"Art Travers on line one," Meg said.

"Art."

"Hello, Mr. Senator. I guess you haven't heard anything?"

"No. I've called repeatedly. Still getting voicemail."

"Right. So... " Travers explained that he had paid a visit to the Wises. While the alibis had to be validated, and could be if necessary, he felt reasonably sure that both husband and wife had been in town.

"No nervousness. No curiosity. No long-winded, convoluted explanations. He was working. Saw the dentist. Wife played in a tennis tournament. Easily verifiable stuff."

"And the girl?"

Shit.

He hadn't thought of checking on her. Travers had followed the Harlan-Wise situation closely, and he'd developed a sense for who Kristy Wise was. He did not see her as capable of malice, much less murder, and hadn't even thought to verify her whereabouts.

"We're verifying her whereabouts, as well," he lied, "but we have every reason to believe that she was in Austin. As far as the hotel, Joe definitely checked in. Miami PD is conducting a full, detailed review of all security footage. Normally, we wouldn't do that so early, but... " He trailed off there, unsure how to word the rest of the sentence for fear of tormenting the senator more than necessary.

"I appreciate that, Detective. Thank you."

Travers had not requested the review as a favor to Harlan Sr., but more because of the son's history. The chances of something happening to the guy were much higher than in normal circumstances. But he wasn't going to tell the senator that.

"Does Joe carry a credit card?" he asked. "One that you have access to, I mean. Like a second card on your account?"

"That's a good point. Hold on." The line went quiet, then he heard the muffled voice of the senator shouting, "Meg!" followed by muffled discussion. After about a minute, the senator was back on the line.

"Um, okay, let's see here... right... We have an AMEX we

share for the points. The account here shows that Joe took an Uber."

"Can you read me what it says?"

"UBER *US MAYXX HYFJM – HELP.UBER.COM, CA"

"Okay. Is there any more information? A reference number?"

Travers heard Harlan repeat the question. Shortly after, he said, "Yes, in the drop-down. Here it is: Reference: 3201727409309611136."

Travers wrote down the number. "Okay. This is helpful. Let me chase this down. Oh, and while we're at it, are there any other charges in Miami?"

"Actually, yes. There are. There's a charge at Saks Fifth Avenue. $102.23. Doesn't say what for. And there's also another Uber charge. Shall I read it to you?"

"Hold on a second. Can you just have Meg email me the information on all of those charges? Along with the AMEX card number? That might be more efficient."

"Yes, of course. It'll be with you shortly, Detective..."

"Try not to worry," Travers said, reading the man's thoughts. "We're going to use this information to construct a timeline of Joe's whereabouts. Two Uber pick-up and drop-off points and a shopping receipt is a very good start."

DAY EIGHT

Saturday, May 5, 2018

Saturday morning at sunup, Susie and Roy headed back across the Straits to Miami. The weather was as forecast, with waves roughly the same height as they were two days before when Roy made the crossing to Bimini. Although now, sitting up on the flybridge, it felt as though they were gliding across glass, but for the occasional rogue wave that kicked spray up into the helm.

Roy set the autopilot on the Sunseeker to the waypoint: Entry to Biscayne Channel. Then, he sat back at the helm with Susie cuddled up next to him, wrapped in a blanket against the early morning chill.

They were cruising at twenty-six knots. Though it wasn't horribly loud on the flybridge, between the wind and the sound of the boat running through the water, and the thrum of the engines, it was too loud for comfortable conversation. So, they both simply enjoyed the view, each wrapped in their own thoughts until Susie dozed off.

They reached the house at 9:30, docked the boat, and began to organize and unload their things.

Since they'd been gone for a week, Susie told Roy that she needed to go to the store to get supplies.

While Susie was gone, Roy performed a detailed inspection of the Yellowfin to see if they had missed anything of importance. He paid particularly close attention to the coffin box and surrounding deck area. It was immaculate. No stains. Nothing.

Nevertheless, Roy went over the boat one more time from top to bottom. He knew the crew would be by later in the week to clean, but he still ran a hose all over, from bow to stern, just in case. Running the water also helped eliminate any stray hairs that they might have missed.

Susie was gone about an hour and a half, and returned with milk, fresh fruit, vegetables, a couple of steaks, and some smoked salmon.

Roy took a quick shower and then joined her for lunch on the terrace, where he cooked the steaks on the grill.

* * *

Detective Rosa Pérez was working from her apartment in Wynwood, an artsy, up-and-coming Miami neighborhood. She was sitting in front of her laptop playing catch-up with the aid of a glass of pinot.

Her Friday had run long, and she'd spent most of the day Saturday with friends.

And now she had another case on her to-do list: the disappearance of Joe Harlan Jr., for which she had reluctantly opened a case file.

She typed up a summary of her visit to the Intercontinental Hotel, then she ran three entries through the MDPD database—Joe Harlan Jr., David Kim, and Cruise Capital.

Joe Harlan Jr. came up blank.

David Kim, on the other hand, had been the victim of a homicide in 2003. Clearly not the David Kim she was looking for.

Cruise Capital also returned a hit.

Several years back, a file had been opened in the case of Liam Bareto. There wasn't much information available as the case hadn't gone far, but one of Cruise Capital's directors, a certain Roy Cruise, had been questioned in connection with the matter.

Rosa picked up her mobile phone and dialed the cell

number for the detective listed on the file, Eddie Garza. She was feeling lucky.

"Go for Eddie."

"Eddie! It's Rosa Pérez, here. How are you?" she asked with a big smile.

Rosa and Eddie had crossed paths a few years back. They'd never worked together, but knew each other well, which was one reason why she hadn't hesitated to call so late.

After some chitchat, Rosa finally brought he conversation around to her reason for the call.

"Listen, Eddie, I need a favor. I see that you worked a file a while back that popped up in connection with something that's just landed on my desk. Liam Bareto. Does that ring any bells?"

"Holy shit! Bareto, again?"

"What do you mean, again?"

Eddie told Rosa about the call he'd received from Veronica Rios a few weeks back.

"Your search have anything to do with my friend Veronica?" Eddie asked.

"I don't think so. Liam Bareto came up when I did a search on Cruise Capital, owned by a Roy Cruise. Sound familiar?"

"Sure. I questioned him and his wife in connection with the case. You read the file? Sad case. He was in the hospital for a while after being involved in a head-on with their daughter. She was pronounced dead at the scene. Bareto was in a coma for a while. Died later. His mom thought there was foul play."

"What do you think?"

Eddie sighed. "Fuck. There were some odd circumstances around the case, for sure. But nothing to do with Cruise and his wife. They were out of town when it happened."

Rosa nodded as if the man was in the room with her. "What're they like?"

"Rich. She used to be on TV—Susie Font, hardcore reporter type turned anchor."

"Oh yeah! I've heard of her."

"Yep. Him… Professional. Smart. Likeable guy. They

lawyered up for the interview, but then, they're both lawyers themselves, so... you know."

Rosa harrumphed.

Many people believe that hiring a lawyer for a police interview is a sign of guilt, and opt to show up alone and "cooperate." Lawyers, on the other hand, know that having a lawyer at an interview makes no difference as far as guilt or innocence is concerned, and might save you from a wrongful prosecution, and possibly even a wrongful conviction. Lawyers know from experience and education what most could learn from watching videos on YouTube such as "Don't Talk to the Police."

"File's closed though. What's the favor?" Eddie asked.

"Honestly, I'm swamped. You know how it is. And then I get this call from Texas?"

Rosa told Eddie about her call with Travers and her visit to the hotel.

"To be perfectly honest, I'm up to my neck in it and really don't think there's much there. But I was wondering... if I could hand this off to you, since you already know this Cruise guy and there's this connection, I'd owe you..." she said, wrinkling her face and holding her breath as she waited for answer. When the line went quiet, she quickly added, "I mean, I don't mind helping out, but if you could run point, you know I'd be eternally grateful, Eddie." She batted her eyelids, pointlessly.

"Ay, Rosita, Rosita, Rosita," Eddie groaned. "You young cops, always trying to shirk responsibility."

Rosa laughed. She wasn't much more than two years his junior.

"Fine. Give me the gringo's number. I'll call your cowboy and take lead. But you owe me. You owe me big time."

"Sure, Eddie," she said as calmly as she could when what she really wanted was to get up and do a little victory dance.

Eddie hung up and called Travers. He introduced himself and shared that Detective Rosa Pérez had brought him up to speed.

Travers didn't have much more to add other than that he'd now ascertained that Kristy Wise had an alibi—she'd been at a martial arts class. He was having someone verify her alibi as well as that of her parents, but had no reason to believe any of them were in Miami at the time of Harlan's disappearance.

Eddie shared that he was expecting to get a copy of the surveillance video from the hotel first thing Monday and that he'd be going through it as soon as it arrived.

* * *

Often, a short trip to a place that differs significantly from one's day-to-day life can afterwards feel otherworldly. In the case of their vacation in Bimini, Roy had also been sleep-deprived at times. And, of course, the main focus of the trip had been so foreign from his daily life as to be almost surreal. It stood in stark contrast to his work-a-day Miami living. Thus, it did not surprise me when he later confessed that, at times, the whole thing seemed like a dream.

Upon returning from Bimini, he craved normality.

Roy went back to work on Monday.

He and David touched on the Harlan situation at their morning catch-up meeting, but swiftly moved on with the rest of the agenda.

From his research, Roy knew that it would take the police some time to get their act together. All they had at this point was a missing twenty-something male with a history of partying who'd flown to Miami for a business meeting but never showed up.

It would take a while for the police to begin to truly suspect foul play. And, they would need to coordinate across two jurisdictions—Austin, Texas and Miami, Florida—further complicating matters and slowing things down.

Roy knew that with time evidence would get stale. Security camera footage would be erased or filmed over. Any potential witnesses who may have seen something—Roy and Harlan walking around near the marina, the Yellowfin in the bay—would already be forgetting it. The more time that went by, the less anyone would recall.

As you know, Roy had planned everything carefully, but he acknowledged that there was no way of controlling or accounting for the unknown.

However, one thing was certain. The longer it took the police to get into gear, the better.

What Roy didn't know was that the police were about to pick up the pace.

CHAPTER THIRTY ONE

West Lake Hills—shortened by locals to Westlake—is an Austin suburb minutes from downtown. It lies on either side of the Colorado River and claims some of the most beautiful homes in the city.

Although it sits in the midst of a city of over 1.5 million people, Westlake has managed to retain a green, natural, unspoiled feel. Raccoons, opossums, squirrels, owls, and snakes (occasionally of the poisonous variety) are common. Deer can be seen on most mornings, grazing in the yards—a blessing in the eyes of some, large rats in the eyes of others.

In Westlake, the banks of the Colorado River rise relatively quickly in parts, creating hills with beautiful views to the west and to downtown. The area is hilly, and the community boasts a wide range of construction styles and property sizes.

Simon Robles was driving down a street in one of the older parts of Westlake. The homes were a mix of ranch and colonial style, most of them sitting on half-acre lots. He parked in front of a corner house and got himself organized.

Being a postal worker was in some ways monotonous, no question about it. Day in and day out, driving the same streets, pushing paper through the same mail slots. If you didn't approach it with the right frame of mind, you could end up like a Bartleby.

There were a lot of upsides, too. First, you were a federal civil servant. In other words, even Trump couldn't fire you. Also, parking for lunch was never a problem—you could put your mail truck anywhere and no one would bother you. The walking kept you in great shape. And, if you landed a good route, the scenery was beautiful.

Westlake was one of those routes. Some of the younger carriers would also have appreciated the human scenery in the area—the soccer moms going to and from yoga or spin class in their spandex "whatevers" were something to see.

Simon was a bit old for that stuff. Not too old for sex, but most of the moms in the area were the same age as his daughters. They looked like little girls to him.

He was always polite—greeting and smiling at people. And he liked most of the neighbors on the route. They were friendly and always pleased to see him. Some were even famous.

For a while, Simon had delivered mail to Michael Dell's house—the Dell Computer founder and billionaire. The actor, Dennis Quaid, was on his route for a time, and he'd actually handed Mr. Quaid his mail personally, once. Same for Lance Armstrong—as far as Simon was concerned, the poor guy got a bum rap on all that doping stuff. Then there was Dan Rather. Simon actually had a selfie he'd taken with Dan Rather—a real nice guy.

There were also lots of local celebrities. The "Attorney that Rocks," the mayor of Westlake, and State Senator Joe Harlan Sr. He was one of many politicians that lived in the area.

Of all of them, Harlan was the one who most stood out to Simon. Not because of his political position, but because of his son—the one who had been on trial for that rape. The postman had spotted him on several occasions. Seemed normal enough. Guilty, not guilty. Who knew?

Simon whistled as he approached the Harlan house and arranged their mail in a bundle—electric bill, Valu-Pak junk mailer, a couple of postcards from Realtors, and other correspondence that meant nothing to him.

The house was nice, one of Simon's favorites. It was an imposing white colonial. Well-maintained with a neatly manicured lawn and an American flag hanging from a thin pole attached to one of the porch columns. It looked like a politician's house, with knock out roses planted along the drive. Beautiful when they were in bloom.

Simon was so busy looking at the pretty flowers that he

almost tripped on the single step up onto the porch.

He pushed the mail through the slot in the door. When he straightened, though, he caught sight of something hanging on the front door at about eye level. It looked like some kind of decoration. He stepped closer, tilting his head up so that his bifocal glasses could focus better on what he was seeing.

When he realized what he was looking at, he stepped back in shock and lost his balance as he went off the single porch step, staggering and tripping onto his backside, undelivered mail spilling out of his bag onto the grass. As he sat on the ground, eyes still glued to the *thing* on the front door, he reached for his mobile phone and dialed 911.

Given the notoriety of the homeowner, dispatch sent out multiple police vehicles. And the news media, forever scanning police radio traffic, picked up on the call almost instantly. They arrived on scene minutes after the patrol cars.

By the time Travers arrived, forensics was already there, doing their thing. He checked in with the crime scene investigator in charge, Natalie Bates. Sharp girl. Cute in that librarian kind of way.

"A postal worker made the discovery. Around 10:15. Called 911. We've secured the area. Lab techs are working it. There's no one home."

"Anything?" Travers asked, referring to clues, evidence, and so forth.

"Not really. Pretty clean site."

"You guys contacted Harlan yet?"

"No. We wanted to get a better sense for what we were looking at first."

"Mind if I talk with the lab techs?"

"Be my guest."

Travers spoke to the head lab tech on site and got a rundown of what they knew so far, which wasn't much. Tests would need to be run before they could confirm anything.

Travers circled back to Natalie. "Who's making the call?"

"I don't know. But," Natalie indicated the media trucks with her head, "someone better, before he finds out on TV."

CHAPTER THIRTY TWO

Thursday had been a long day, and Roy was just wrapping up work and getting ready to head home.

It had been quiet. No news was very good news.

Every day that went by without hearing about Harlan increased the likelihood that the murder, if it were ever ruled as such, would go unsolved.

Roy was just walking out of his office when he saw David emerge into the hallway, looking flustered. "Roy, come here! Quick!"

When Roy walked into David's office, he was back at his desk, peering at his computer screen.

"What's up?"

"Fuck, fuck, fuck, fuck," David said. "Check this out."

Roy patiently crossed the room and looked over his colleague's shoulder as he clicked to play the video on his screen.

It was a news segment. A young blonde woman in a grey pantsuit and white blouse was standing in front of a large white house. At the foot of the screen, the caption read:

Thursday, May 10, 2018, Austin, TX

The blonde spoke.

At approximately 10:30 this morning, a mail carrier called 9-1-1 after making a grisly discovery right here at State Senator Joe Harlan Sr.'s residence. The discovery was a male sex organ, and it was nailed to the front door. Police arrived on the scene shortly after and removed the organ, which is being subjected to DNA testing.

The Harlans made the headlines several years ago when the senator's son and namesake, Joe Harlan Jr., was charged and then acquitted of sexual assault.

Shortly after, Harlan Jr. was attacked at a local Whole Foods by real estate investor Tom Wise, the father of the young woman involved in the alleged assault.

Today's discovery is just another twist in an already convoluted tale.

Senator Harlan was not available for comment, though a spokesperson indicated that he is naturally shaken and disturbed by the incident and is cooperating with authorities.

The camera cut to the on-set news anchor, who asked,

Beth, I guess that, at this stage, there is no indication who would do something like this or why?

At this point, Bob, we have been unable to get a clear answer to that question. The police tell us that DNA testing is underway and results will be available shortly. That will at least reveal the origin of the... discovery. However, both the police and senator's representatives are not giving away much else at this time. Although, it is worth noting, Bob, that when asked about the whereabouts of Joe Harlan Jr., both the police and the senator's office refused to comment—which, of course, only fuels mounting speculation that the, um, appendage may well belong to someone close to the senator.

The video ended.

"Fucking crazy, right?" David asked.

But Roy could only stare in slack-mouthed shock. If it was in fact Harlan's dick, how the fuck had it gotten there? And if it wasn't, who the hell did it belong to?

Of course, it could mean nothing at all—have nothing to do with the kid. The man was a senator for Christ's sake. He must have enemies. But the sinking feeling in Roy's stomach told him that this was all related, very related.

"Hey, you alright?" David asked. "You look white as a sheet."

"Yeah. No. I 'm fine. I mean, it's just that... that's fucking nuts. Shocking. I mean, poor kid."

"Right? You think that's his dick? Right? If it is, he didn't stick around Miami long. That is way fucked up, man!"

"Yeah. He must have gotten back somehow," Roy uttered, absentmindedly. Then, snapping out of it, he added, "Anyway, thanks for that, I've, um, I've got to go."

Roy made for the exit without looking back.

David looked after him. "Sure, man, any time."

CHAPTER THIRTY THREE

"Go for Eddie."

"Eddie, it's Art Travers."

"I know that, Tex—caller ID. You still living in the twentieth century? What's up?"

If Art was tiring of the Miami detective's sense of humor, he didn't show it. Instead, "We've got a homicide," he said.

"You sure?"

"Pretty sure. We'll get a confirmation in a few days. They put a rush on forensics testing. DA's a friend of the senator."

"I don't get it. Confirmation of what?"

"It's on the news here already. Don't know if it'll bubble up in Miami or if it already has. This morning, a postman found a dick nailed to the senator's front door."

"A dick—as in a pee-pee dick?" Eddie asked. "Ouch."

"Yeah. Not pretty. I'm sending you a photo."

"Geez, man. Thanks. That puts a new wrinkle on things." Eddie laughed.

"You're fucking sick, Eddie." Travers laughed a bit too, though. Gallows humor.

"It's a real pisser," Eddie added.

"Eddie, stop."

"Okay. Sorry. So, it's a homicide. Our guys are working on the security camera footage. You got anything on the Uber and the shopping at Saks?"

"Nothing yet. I've got some folks working that as well as chasing down alibis. I've been out of the office all day dealing with this latest development. The senator was not happy, needless to say."

"Who made the call? Was it you?"

"Yeah," Travers responded, grimly. He didn't have much time for the senator, but nobody deserved that.

"Was it *hard*?" Eddie scoffed.

"Dude, stop it."

"Sorry, that just popped up out of nowhere."

"Seriously, Eddie. Come on..." And before the man could say anything else, he added, "So, listen. We should have the DNA results early next week. How about I call you then? You know. Compare notes. That'll also give us some time to chase down these other leads, double-check alibis, et cetera. The senator said he wants to help in any way, which means we should be able to get the kid's phone records.

"I had one of my guys do a write-up on everything we know about Junior. I'll email it to you. Read the summary, think on it all, sleep on it. Then we can try and make some sense of this. Also sending you the photo. You gotta see it. Puts this thing in a new perspective. We're not disclosing this to the press yet, but there's writing on it."

"Damn. Okay. I'll have a look," Eddie confirmed. "Hey, listen. It occurs to me... if you don't mind, I'm gonna share your info with a psych profiler we have down here. He's good. Does a lot of work with this kind of stuff. Specifically with sexual mutilations and so forth. I think we could use some support there. At least get a perspective on a type."

By *type*, Eddie meant the type of killer that would be inclined to this sort of mutilation.

"That sounds great, Eddie."

"So, what are you thinking, Art? The kid made it back to Austin and got whacked there? No pun intended. Or he got knocked off here and someone FedExed his dick back to Texas? Or maybe even drove back with it?"

"I dunno. It may not even be his, but I'm expecting forensics to shed some light on that. "

"If they don't cock up the test."

Travers sighed. "Later, Eddie. I'll call you when I've got more. Okay?"

"You got it, Art," Eddie laughed then disconnected the call.

* * *

Eddie hung up with Travers and dialed Emile Van der Put. Eddie had worked with the doctor on a few occasions. He was skilled at tying crime scene clues to criminal motivation.

Van der Put had published an in-depth case analysis of serial killer Danny Rolling, who in 1990 killed five college students in Gainesville, Florida. Also called the "Gainesville Ripper," Rolling killed his victims by stabbing. He'd then mutilated their bodies, dismembering them in parts—even decapitating one—and posed them in a disturbing tableau.

Van der Put's analysis of mutilation and motivation was widely studied in the criminal forensics world and had earned him the nickname "Dr. Van der Parts."

Eddie got right to the point. He provided the doctor with a summary of the key elements of the case. He provided no suspect names or information since the doctor insisted on not being provided information that might in any way affect how he processed facts. If he was given information about possible suspects, this could force preconceived notions into his analysis. And he didn't like that. Instead, he insisted on letting the facts define the profile and was meticulous about avoiding any information that might, even unconsciously, allow him to shape the profile to fit a suspect.

Eddie concluded, "When the case went from a simple disappearance to a likely homicide and dismemberment, I thought of you. If you could help us work up a psych profile for the kind of sicko that would do something like this, that would be great."

"Absolutely, Eddie. This is certainly a curious case. The severed penis raises a number of interesting psychological questions. Normally, I'd be thinking some sort of paraphilic disorder consistent with a lust murder, but there are other factors at play here. There appears to be some premeditation involved, which isn't necessarily inconsistent with lust murderers. And yet, in the context of what you've told me about the young lady he possibly assaulted, perhaps this is simply a case of revenge. That could be the simplest and most likely direction. But that doesn't mean that typical paraphilic considerations wouldn't apply.

"Very interesting, indeed. I do believe I can be of assistance. The young man in question was from Austin, Texas, you say?"

"Yeah, Doc."

"You need a quick turnaround, I assume? I can work on it this weekend if that's the case."

"That would be great, Doc."

"Okay, Eddie. Feel free to email me whatever information you have and I will get right on it. But, remember, just facts. Nothing about suspects."

"Will do, Doc. Thanks."

CHAPTER THIRTY FOUR

As Roy drove home, he ran through scenarios. If the penis belonged to Harlan, there was only one explanation. Susie had removed it. But how?

After they'd killed him, Roy had gone to the aft for the Quikcrete and left her to wrap the body in the anchor chain. Roy remembered that she'd snapped at him when he offered to help her. When he'd returned, she'd finished, but he recalled that the body had been sideways in the duffle bag.

She would have to have acted fast, but the bleeding would have been manageable given that the man was already dead—no heart pumping blood to all extremities. Whatever the case, that was the only point at which she could have done it.

What the fuck, Suze?

There were other possibilities, but none seemed likely.

One was unthinkable. That Harlan's body had somehow been recovered, and the penis removed. Unlikely, but not impossible.

Another possibility—which he hoped was the case—was that it was simply someone else's dick. Someone taking advantage of the disappearance to send a message. But who knew that the boy was missing? And where the hell would you get a human dick? A morgue?

It could possibly belong to an animal of some kind. Were there common animals with dicks like humans? Maybe a sheep. Roy had heard about farmers screwing sheep because their vaginas were approximately the size of a woman's vagina—in England, Ireland, Arkansas—these things happened, right? Roy knew this bordered on the absurd, but the other options were so improbable that he continued the train of thought.

If sheep vaginas were the size of human vaginas, it stood to reason that sheep dicks were approximately the size of human dicks. Maybe it was a sheep dick that had gotten nailed to the senator's door?

He had absolutely no idea.

If it *was* Harlan's dick, and Susie had removed it, there was a bigger question to be answered. How had she gotten it onto Harlan's front door? It was impossible for her to have gone to Austin and back without him knowing. That meant that she would have had to have an accomplice in Austin. The most likely options there were Tom and Deb Wise. Who else would be motivated enough to risk nailing the dick to the senator's front door? Who else would want to?

When Roy got home, Susie was in the dining room working at her laptop.

"Hey, babe," she greeted him without looking up.

Roy watched her, but she didn't look up to meet his gaze. She just kept tapping at her laptop.

"Anything you want to tell me?" he asked.

Susie paused her typing and looked up at him. He noted the look of concern on her face, and of understanding. She'd seen the news. She knew that he knew. And she had done it.

Shit, thought Roy. *That's not a sheep dick.*

Roy glared at her. "I'm going to change."

While he was upstairs changing, Susie came into the bedroom. Her body language was conciliatory.

"Sorry?" she offered.

"How the fuck could you, Suze?"

"I knew you wouldn't let me. So, I figured I'd ask for forgiveness rather than for permission."

Roy sat down on the bed. He rubbed his temples with both hands. "Have you got any fucking idea what you've done? Do you know what this means?" he asked, voice quivering with anger. "It's going to accelerate everything. Now they know they've got a murder on their hands. Or, they will as soon as they confirm it's his."

Susie leaned up against the wall, arms akimbo.

"They're going to turn up the heat on this whole investigation. He's a senator's fucking son, for Christ's sake! They're going to start identifying suspects. That means they start looking into Harlan's last days, which means they're going to start looking into David. And by association, that means Cruise Capital and me."

"Babe, you planned the perfect crime," Susie began, her voice calm, as if her husband hadn't just told her that she'd put the whole plan at risk. "There is no way they're going to get to us. Having the dick appear in Austin just confuses things even more. Think of it that way. It sends a message. It ties it all back to the rape. Who else would nail his dick to his dad's front door? And what do we have to do with the rape? Nothing. If anything, it takes the attention away from us. Misdirection."

She was probably right about that, but Roy was in no mood to make concessions.

"When did you decide to do it? How?" He glared at her.

This is where she had decided she would have to lie, a bit.

"Deb Wise called me. She had my contact info from Colorado. She called me from a payphone about a month ago. She wanted to apologize, for Tom—for both of them. She said that they'd been out of line. Too much stress. I told her not to worry about it. And I got her address. I told her I'd be sending her a package. That she'd know what it was and what to do with it."

"That's bullshit!"

"No, Roy. It's true."

"You're telling me that this was your idea. That you, what— FedExed the guy's fucking dick to Austin..."

"UPS. It was cheaper, and they didn't ask about the contents. And I used a fake name. Paid cash."

"Fine, you UPSed the dick to Austin, and you had no idea what she'd do with it? You just hoped for the best?"

"That's pretty much it."

"Did you send a card, too? 'With love, from the Cruises?'"

Susie laughed but she noticed that her husband was not amused. This didn't surprise her. It was exactly what she'd expected.

"Look, Suze. I may not be the brightest guy in the world.

And I know I have a blind spot when it comes to you. But this is one hundred percent bullshit." He paused. "Why the fuck are you lying to me? Don't you know that I would do anything for you? Hasn't this whole mess proven that? What more do you need, Susie? I thought we were a team."

There was genuine pain in her husband's eyes, but she didn't feel compelled to put her arms around him. It was best to wait it out.

Roy stood. "This whole thing is starting to stink. Right back from the beginning. Now I'm starting to wonder about all of it. We meet this woman 'by chance' in Colorado, and her husband asks us 'by chance' to kill someone for them. Out of the fucking blue!

"You push me and push me until I finally agree to do it. Then you insist on killing him before we throw him in the ocean— ice pick or Hefty. Because 'we' should do it, not the ocean!

"Then, she calls you out of the blue again, a month before we do the deed, and you ask her for her address, and tell her she'll be getting a surprise package? And it's all just a coincidence?

"Come on, Susie. Do you think I'm a fucking idiot?"

He headed for the bedroom door but stopped in the doorway and looked at her. "You know," he began, voice shaking with something Susie didn't recognize, "after everything. Everything we've built. Everything we've been through. After Camilla. After this whole Harlan mess. I deserve better."

With that he was gone, leaving her gaping after him.

Susie remained motionless for a while as she processed what she'd just heard.

Shit. She wanted a cigarette. He was right. She'd have to come clean. She needed to tell him more. Not everything. She wouldn't tell him everything about her relationship with Deb. That was too much.

Still, she needed to clear the air.

CHAPTER THIRTY FiVE

Tom Wise was driving home. He had been on a construction site all day with a large crew, and with crappy cell reception. As he turned onto MoPac, his phone rang.

He frowned, sighed, and then answered. As he did, he unscrewed the top on a container of Pepcid chewable antacids and popped two more. Lately, these things were his main source of calories.

"Hello."

"Hello, darlin'," Deb answered.

"Hi, Deb. Finally on my way home."

"Great. Traffic alright?"

"Not too bad, yet. We'll see when I get to 290."

Deb and Tom lived in an area called Tarrytown, located just west of downtown Austin; it's an upscale neighborhood that is about eighty percent renovated or rebuilt. The remaining twenty percent is still original 1940s vintage. Tarrytown is locked between State Highway 1 on the east (which runs parallel to the Missouri-Pacific rail lines, and which everyone calls MoPac) and the Colorado River to the west. Traffic into Tarrytown at rush hour is, consequently, hellish.

"Sounds good, Tommy. You hungry? I hope so, 'cause I've got roast filet for dinner."

Deb's roasted filet mignon was a specialty.

"Yep. Always got room for filet."

The two were dancing around the conversation topic that they both wanted to address. They were both just too cautious to discuss it explicitly by phone.

They had both been up since 4:00 a.m., though it was

Tom who'd made the special delivery to the Harlan address. He had dressed in running clothes, then driven to Westlake and parked by Red Bud Isle—no security cameras, and about a ten-minute jog from the Harlan house. He'd worn a small fanny pack in which he'd carried a Ziploc with all that remained of Joe Harlan Jr. The fanny pack also contained two powder-free latex gloves, a small pin hammer, and two extra two-inch box nails, just in case.

Harlan Sr. was an early riser who left home for the office at 5:15 a.m. every day. Tom and Deb had gleaned this from an online article from a few years back profiling the senator, which made a point of the fact that he arrived at his office every morning before 7:00 a.m. after swimming at the Y.

The Wises simply backed into what time the senator would have to leave home in order to keep to that schedule. Then, Tom had gone running by the Harlan house on two occasions to confirm their estimate. He had seen the senator's black BMW 7 Series make the turn onto Forest View Drive both times at about 5:20 a.m. He'd hoped that today would be no different.

It hadn't been.

The senator had turned onto Forest View a little early, at 5:17 a.m. Once his car was out of sight, Tom put on the latex gloves (inconspicuous flesh-colored) and jogged down the street. Then, he casually walked up to the senator's front door, opening the fanny pack as he approached. He'd unzipped the Ziploc, and, when he reached the door, brought out the penis in one hand and the hammer in the other. He had prepared for the moment by putting a two-inch box nail through the organ in advance, at the same time they had written "4 Kristy" on it.

He had positioned the trophy against the thick wooden door and given the nail two solid whacks. Then, he'd turned away, placing the hammer in the fanny pack, removing and placing the latex gloves next to it. After that, he continued his run. The whole maneuver had taken less than fifteen seconds.

Given the skill with which Tom executed this task, it would be easy to think that he had relished it. The reality was quite different. Tom wasn't happy about the stunt. It seemed excessive to him. But

Deb had insisted. He'd reluctantly complied, but was now sulking, trying to strike the fine balance between letting his wife know he was unhappy while at the same time trying not to piss her off.

The filet was her feeble attempt at an apology.

"So, everything good otherwise?" he asked.

"Yep," Deb answered. "All good, Tommy. All very good."

CHAPTER THIRTY SIX

Detective Art Travers texted his counterpart in Miami on Monday morning. The DNA results were back. They'd scheduled a phone call for later that afternoon.

"Go for Eddie."

"Hey Eddie, it's Travers. How's it going?"

"Good. Good. Got a lot of good stuff here. Been working this baby hard! You?"

"We've made progress."

"Cool. Hey, listen. I'm putting you on speaker 'cause I got Rosa here with me—she's still helping out some." Art noted the change in audio when Eddie switched to speaker—more echo.

"Hi, Rosa."

"Hello, Art," the female voice echoed back.

"Okay. So, I'll start," Travers said. "The DNA is back. Positive. It's Harlan's penis. So, it's definitely a homicide. The ink on the dick is just standard Sharpie permanent marker. The cut at the stump was clean. A sharp knife, probably. Interestingly, they also found traces of fish DNA and sea salt. So, probably a fishing knife."

"Sh-it. So, he gets killed here," Eddie said, "dick gets cut off and sent to Austin. Someone writes '4 Kristy' on it in Sharpie, and nails it to the senator's front door."

"Yep. Well, that's one scenario," Travers answered. "There's no way to tell if it was cut off when he was alive or dead. The cut was clean, like I said, meaning he likely wasn't struggling, but he could have been drugged."

"Okay. What else you got?"

"Now, come on Eddie, I showed you mine. Time for you to show me yours, right?" Travers asked with a smile, knowing the detective would appreciate the humor.

They were working the case together; they didn't have a choice due to jurisdiction and geography. So, there was no real reason to get territorial. But old habits died hard.

"Sure. I'm not shy," Eddie answered. "We got Harlan landing in Miami more or less on time per American Airlines. Then, we've got him on the hotel's security camera a few times.

"We've got him at 2:27 p.m. at check-in. The airport's about twenty minutes from the Intercontinental Hotel. There are no credit card transactions for transportation. So, he probably took a taxi. Probably paid cash.

"Then, we've got him leaving the hotel again at 4:14 p.m.

"Coming back to the hotel at 5:25 p.m.

"And we've got him leaving the hotel one last time at 5:47 p.m.

"That's everything we have of Harlan on video. From that point on, there's nothing related to him or the case until when the hotel manager let Detective Pérez into the room."

"Okay," Travers said. "That's consistent with the credit card info we got. We've got him in an Uber from the hotel to Brickell City Centre at 4:12 p.m. He goes to Saks and buys a pair of boat shoes at 4:58 p.m. Then takes an Uber back to the hotel at 5:11 p.m.

"Boat shoes? Eddie—pull up that last video," Rosa said. "The last time he leaves the hotel." There was silence for a few moments.

"What do y'all see?" Travers asked, wondering what they were looking at.

"Hold on," Eddie said.

Travers heard them talking on the line. Eddie asking Rosa, in a low voice, "What do you think?"

"Could be—definitely changes shoes—not what he was wearing in the prior video," she responded.

Eddie said, "Looks like he may be wearing the boat shoes when he heads out. Hold on." Travers heard paper shuffling. "Yeah, there's no boat shoes listed on the inventory from the hotel room, either. We got a pair of Pumas and some loafers, dress shoes. No shoe box, either. Maybe housekeeping made a pass before we got there. I'll check."

"Okay. Good. So, he buys the shoes, then wears them to go out. What else?"

"That's it. Depending on what we decide today, we'll start canvassing. See if we can find any eyewitnesses," Eddie answered.

"Okay. So, we went through his phone records. Some useful stuff—fills in some gaps. I'll go through these in order of occurrence. First, about an hour after he checks in, he calls Sweet Miami."

"Whoa. Hold on," Eddie said. "Let me cover Rosa's ears."

Rosa rolled her eyes, but said nothing.

"So," Travers continued, "apparently, he was booking some female company. Then, at 3:44 p.m., we have an incoming call from a Seattle phone number. Call lasts just over one minute.

"A few minutes later, he calls Sweet Miami again. I took the liberty of contacting them. They said they had no record of any calls. I tried to see if they had a booking or a cancelation in his name; they weren't very cooperative."

"I bet," Eddie commented. "I can follow up with them. Although... escort services aren't known for their record keeping. At least not here in Miami."

"Great. Then, at 5:40 p.m., we've got an outgoing text from Harlan to David Kim."

"The plot thickens," Eddie commented.

"The text says: 'Sorry you can't make dinner. See you in the morning.' At 7:57 p.m., Kim responds: 'Joe. Did you mean to text me? What dinner? See you at 10.'

"We tried to get location data from the carrier, but Harlan had location services turned off. Normally, that would be unusual, but the guy's already been accused of rape once. And he's calling hookers an hour after landing in Miami. So, not that surprising, I guess.

"Also, in between those two text messages, he gets another call from the Seattle number—at 5:56 p.m. This one really short. Less than a minute," Travers clarified.

"You got anything else on the Seattle number?" Eddie asked.

"Yeah, that's interesting. We checked Harlan's contacts by accessing his iCloud data. He had the Seattle phone number listed in his contacts as Marty McCall—the former roommate from Austin. Lives in Seattle now. So far, that makes sense—Seattle number, Seattle resident.

"Then we had the team pull all of Harlan's iCloud back-up data. That way, we could see when the contact was created. According to his back-up files, that contact was created on May 2, 2018 at 3:47 p.m.—while he was in Miami."

"So, he's contacted by McCall for the first time while he's in Miami?"

"Maybe. But that's not all. When we checked the back-up data, we found that the contact was not only created that same day, but when it was initially created, he listed the contact as 'Cruise Captain.' Later that evening, at 8:12 p.m., the contact was edited to 'Marty McCall.'"

There was silence on the line.

"You still there?"

"Yeah, yeah. Just thinking. So, is it Cruise, as in Cruise Capital? Or is it Cruise as in a cruise—like a boat, like a cruise ship? There are dinner cruises here in Miami, 'tour the bay' kinds of things. There are also major cruise lines. That would put the two together."

"Okay. That's good."

"But," Rosa chimed in, "why change it later to McCall?"

"And who changed it?" Eddie asked. "Harlan, or the killer?"

"If it was the killer," said Rosa, "then you're dealing with someone who is very meticulous. And, you're dealing with someone who didn't want 'Cruise Captain' showing up in Harlan's contacts. Are the C's capitalized?"

"In 'Cruise Captain' you mean?" Travers asked. "Yep, both capitalized. Most of his contacts are. But that could just be auto-formatting."

There was a pause.

"The contact change could be based on new information," Rosa suggested. "I mean, in that Harlan got new information. What if he initially receives a call, and it's Cruise or a boat captain of some sort, so he lists the contact as 'Cruise Captain,' right? Then, later, he learns that the call was made from someone else's phone—McCall's. So, he changes the contact?"

"Following that thinking, if it's Cruise as in Cruise Capital, that would tie Cruise and McCall together. Using the same phone," Travers added to Rosa's thought.

They paused, reflecting.

"Gotta think on that," Eddie replied. "What else?"

"That's all for now," Travers said.

"Did you call the Seattle number?" Rosa asked.

"Yeah, right. Yes, we did. No answer. Tracked the number to a mobile carrier. The number was assigned to a prepaid phone. It's only been used twice, to call Harlan. Both times, the calls came from Miami cell towers. No other activity on the line.

"The physical phone, we traced back to Target—they bought it as part of a batch from a company in Korea. We've traced it to part of a shipment of phones received at a Target distribution center. We're still trying to see if we can track the specific phone to a specific Target store and see if we can get a final sale date on the phone itself. I won't go into all the details, but it's not that easy to trace a phone—the hardware, I mean."

There was another pause in the discussion. Travers could hear Eddie and Rosa speaking again before he broke in and started summarizing. "Okay. So, persons of interest. I've got the Wises—Tom, Debra, Kristy—and Marty McCall, David Kim, and possibly Roy Cruise."

"Yep."

"Anyone else?" Travers asked.

"We read through your write-up on Harlan," Eddie answered. "All the Wises definitely have a motive. McCall—with the lawsuit, yep, I get that. The oddballs here are Kim and Cruise.

"I mean, Kim's on the list because Harlan came to town to see him, and there's the weird text message, I guess. Cruise, because he owns the company Kim works for, and the 'Cruise Captain' contact. But, we need to know more if we're going to find a motive for Kim and Cruise."

"Yeah," Travers confirmed, "I agree. Let's stick with the basics. Motive first. The Wises? Clearly, revenge. Any one of them has a motive. McCall—the lawsuit could get you there, I suppose. If we put McCall and Cruise together with Kim, that could work. Especially if there's something related to the lawsuit or the business."

"Money, sex, or revenge," Eddie said, naming the three classic motives. "We got alibis for the Wises. We need alibis for the other guys."

Travers responded, "On that, I have a bit more—all confirmatory."

"Ooh," Eddie said. "Fancy word."

"We followed up on the Wises. The girl, Kristy, we've got in Austin. Confirmed she attended a martial arts class. Spoke with the owner of the studio.

"Dad—we contacted his dentist. Excellent dental hygiene; he was there that day.

"The mother's tennis alibi checks out, as well. Playing doubles with three other ladies, and a lunch at the club after.

"I haven't done anything further on McCall—wanted to wait until after we talked today. Same with Kim and Cruise. I think we look for a money connection there somewhere."

"We need more info," Eddie confirmed.

"I think we should make an initial contact with McCall, Kim, and Cruise. Keeping it general and very nonspecific. Just ask about their whereabouts. If they've got alibis, we short-circuit a lot of this. If they don't..."

"Okay," Eddie agreed. "How do we do it?"

"Why don't you pay the Miami guys a visit? I'll give McCall a call. Again, let's not give them any details—just go fishing and find out where they were, see what they say."

"Got it. Okay. What else?"

"What about the dad?" Rosa asked. "He's a politician and the kid's caused him a lot of headaches. Wants to get rid of his son, so he arranges for him to disappear?"

"It's possible," Travers said. "I'll add him to the list. I can check on his alibi, too."

Eddie added, "Meanwhile, we'll keep chasing leads here. We'll get some folks to walk Saks, talk with the Uber drivers—see what more we learn. We can also call the few bay cruise and dinner cruise outfits we have down here—the commercial ones—and see if there's anything there. I'll call Sweet Miami myself and see if there's any more information to be had on that end."

"What about marinas near the hotel? If he got on a private boat of some sort, he could have walked there," Travers said.

"Or someone could have picked him up in a car and driven him to any marina anywhere in South Florida, but yeah, sure. The hotel's near Bayside—there's a marina there. We can send someone down there, show Harlan's picture around, see what we find."

"Sounds good," Travers said.

"Okay. I think that's it," Eddie said after a moment.

"What about the psych profile guy?" Travers asked.

"Oh, right. I'm meeting with Van der Parts this afternoon," Eddie said. "I'll email you the profile and anything interesting he has to say after."

"Okay," Travers said. "Looks like there's quite a bit to work on. Let's keep in touch."

CHAPTER THIRTY SEVEN

Travers sat back and reviewed his notes.

He added Harlan Sr. to his list of persons of interest. He'd been wrong not to—preconceived notions. Like it or not, over the course of his years spent dealing first with the rape trial and then with the assault on Joe at Whole Foods, he had gotten to know the senator. He'd formed certain opinions about the man. The senator was first and foremost interested in himself. His career was his life. He had not remarried after his wife died. And, although there were rumors about him and his assistant, Meg, Travers believed them to be just that. Harlan was dedicated to politics one hundred percent. And to his son. Which was why he hadn't instantly seen him as a possible suspect.

During the rape trial, the senator had stood by Joe Jr. unfailingly. No matter how much the trial was tarnishing his relatively squeaky-clean reputation, he'd refused to distance himself from his son. He could have spun some bullshit story about his having some kind of addiction and banished him to rehab until it all blew over, but he didn't.

To Travers, that was very telling.

Then there was the look in the man's eyes when Travers had gone to interrupt his lunch at Abel's on the Lake. They were alone in the booth when Travers shared the gruesome details about finding the penis on the door. The senator's hard-ass composure melted away and the man disintegrated into a blubbering mess. Either he was an incredible actor or he was a man who had just faced the undeniable probability of his only son's death. And not just any death, but most likely a rather painful and gruesome death.

But Travers was a professional. He would keep the senator on his list until all lines of inquiry were complete and he was completely satisfied that the man was not involved in the disappearance of his son.

In the meantime, he reviewed the notes from his telephone call with Eddie Garza and Rosa Pérez.

TRAVERS' NOTES

Timeline

May 2, 2018

1:47 p.m.	airplane lands in Miami (Source: American Air lines)
2:28 p.m.	check-in at hotel (Source: Surveillance video)
3:22 p.m.	phone call to Sweet Miami (Source: Phone records)
3:44 p.m.	call from Seattle number (Source: Phone records)
3:47 p.m.	phone contact created (Source: Phone records)
	- "Cruise Captain"
3:48 p.m.	phone call to Sweet Miami (Source: Phone records)
4:12 p.m.	Uber to Brickell Centre (Source: Credit card/Uber)
4:14 p.m.	leaves hotel (Source: Surveillance video)
4:58 p.m.	shoe purchase at Saks (Source: Credit card/Saks) (buys boat shoes)
5:11 p.m.	Uber to hotel (Source: Credit card/Uber)
5:25 p.m.	arrives at hotel (Source: Surveillance video)
5:40 p.m.	sends text to D. Kim (Source: Phone records) "Sorry you can't make dinner. See you in the morning."
5:47 p.m.	leaves hotel (Source: Surveillance video) (in boat shoes)
5:56 p.m.	call from Seattle number (Source: Phone records)
7:57 p.m.	text from D. Kim (Source: Phone records) "Joe. Did you mean to text me? What dinner? See you at 10"
8:12 p.m.	phone contact edited (Source: Phone records)
	- "Marty McCall"

Other:

        Penis in Austin
        Cut with sharp instrument
        Fish DNA
        "4 Kristy" in Sharpie

        Seattle phone (206-576-1324)
        number listed as McCall.

        Prepaid phone
        Purchased in Seattle

Persons of interest:

        Tom Wise, Debra Wise, Kristy Wise
        Marty McCall
        David Kim
        Roy Cruise
        Harlan Sr.?

CHAPTER THIRTY EIGHT

Eddie Garza arrived at Dr. Van der Put's office at 3:45 p.m. He was fifteen minutes early and the doctor's assistant showed him into a small conference room containing a round table with four chairs. Eddie took a seat and looked around. The doctor had remodeled since the last time he'd been there. The office was now decorated in muted tones and natural woods.

On the wall hung a number of framed degrees, titles, and licenses. There was pan flute music playing over the speaker system. Or was that Enya? He wasn't sure. Whatever it was, it was making him feel sleepy. Eddie stood up to try to stay awake and alert.

Thankfully, Dr. Van der Put entered the room a few minutes later. He was wearing a cardigan and carrying a thin manila file folder. He shook hands with the detective and then sat across from him at the table.

"So," Eddie began, sitting up in his chair and giving his head a shake, "what have you got for me, Doc? Hard one, right?" he asked with a grin.

Dr. Van der Put didn't react to the dark humor; instead, he went straight to his findings. "Well, Eddie, you would think so. At first blush, there doesn't seem to be a lot to go on here. But the lack of evidence in this case is actually evidence, at least from a psychological perspective."

Eddie scowled and leaned forward. "How so, Doc?"

"Well, due to the dismemberment of the body, and the part that was removed, the case can be categorized as a 'lust murder.' Mutilation, dismemberment, posing the corpse—all of a sexual nature—these are signatures to this type of crime. Psychologically, it would fall under sadism—paraphilia, technically. But, the gist of it is that the killer is acting out a fantasy of a sexual nature. And that fantasy includes the severing of the penis."

"Taking a trophy, right?"

"Exactly. Now, there are two typical lust murderer profiles. Organized and disorganized. Your murderer falls into the first category," Van der Put paused, "precisely because there is no evidence." He looked up from the folder with a supercilious grin on his face.

Eddie could see that the doctor thought he had come up with a very clever analysis, and was being intentionally cryptic. Eddie just wanted to get the damned profile and go, so he played along. "Okay Doc. So, tell me, how can 'no evidence' be evidence?"

"Your classic organized offender is going to be very smart; high IQ. And he is going to methodically plan his crime. He is cunning. He often kills and moves the body to muss up the crime scene. Confuse the forensics. This individual takes great pride in considering himself smarter than the police."

"So, you're saying that because we haven't got a body or a crime scene, that our guy's an organized offender, and based on that you can tell me what a typical organized offender is like?"

"Exactly!" Van der Put exclaimed. "Very good, Eddie. The typical organized offender chooses his victim carefully. Usually, a stranger. He likes to hunt far from his home or work. He thinks he's smarter than the police. He even likes to flaunt his crime at the authorities—a sort of 'catch me if you can' mentality.

"I think the penis nailing incident here fits the bill. He's saying, 'Look at me, everybody. Look what I can get away with,' to the police and to the world, all while making his point."

Dr. Van der Put opened the manila file folder he'd brought in and slid a document across to Eddie entitled "Clinical Assessment." Eddie skimmed through the document, which captured much of what the doctor had shared but in greater detail.

"So, when you say 'all while making his point,' I'm assuming you're referring to the revenge angle? Someone avenging an alleged rape for example? No sex fantasy or anything, just payback."

"I see no reason why that can't fit into this analysis.

Organized offenders carefully choose their victims. They look for certain types of profiles. Your killer here may have sought out the victim because he was abused himself. Or possibly someone close to him was abused.

"But, this is not a crime of passion. This is a well-thought-out and meticulously-planned murder. The victim was selected carefully. Most likely lured into a trap. He was probably tortured—I suspect the penis may even have been removed while he was alive. Then, the killer disposed of the body and used the victim's member to announce himself to the world."

"By nailing the dick on the door."

"Precisely."

"So, how'd he get it to Austin?"

"I suspect he drove it there, and that he lives near there. The killing in Florida was designed to throw you off the scent. Young Harlan disappeared on a Wednesday. The penis appeared on the door the following Thursday. Why so long?"

Eddie chuckled.

Van der Put was oblivious to his own pun and plowed on. "That is more than enough time for our killer to have driven back to Austin."

"And how did he know our guy was coming to Florida?"

"Ah, Detective. Now we leave the world of my expertise and enter yours. Who knew he was coming to Florida? Who did young Harlan tell? That may very well be the key to your entire case."

Eddie read through the profile again and pondered. "Interesting, Doc. Very interesting, as always," he said with a big grin.

***

Back at his office, Eddie scanned the assessment and emailed it to Travers with a note:

Art:

See attached. We have a new suspect—Lust Murderer in Austin.

We need to find out who knew Harlan was traveling to Florida. Eddie

Attachment
(Garza.Harlan.pdf)

CLINICAL ASSESSMENT
DR. EMILE VAN DER PUT

Case Facts:

A twenty-four-year-old male disappeared after leaving his hotel room in Miami, Florida. The following week, the victim's penis was found nailed to the door of the victim's father's house in Austin, Texas. On the penis in indelible ink was hand-written the phrase "4 Kristy."

The victim had previously been accused of sexually assaulting a woman named Kristy. After trial, the victim was acquitted. There was speculation that the victim's father, a politician, may have had a hand in having the conviction set aside.

Assessment:

A homicide that includes sexual mutilation can be categorized as a Lust Murder. Lust murders can be categorized as organized or disorganized.
The typical organized psychopathology would involve a structured killing, including torture and severing of the penis as a part of the murder.

In the case of a disorganized offender, the crime scene would present signs of uncontrolled rage, with the victim likely succumbing to a violent and rapid attack, followed by post-mortem mutilation and a possibly symbolic posing of the corpse.

Lust murders of both types are often associated with necrophilia.

Normally, crime scene forensics provides information that allow for distinguishing between organized and disorganized offenders.

The instant case is utterly devoid of crime scene forensics as a crime scene has not been located. Nor has the victim's body, other than the penis.

These facts point to an organized offender, as only an organized offender could successfully execute such a crime without leaving a crime scene. The dearth of evidence in the instant case leads to this assessment.

The organized offender is cunning and typically plans his crime carefully and in great detail. He is of above average IQ. He is methodical in his thinking and in action. The organized offender typically kills far from his home or place of work. He is often mobile, owning a vehicle in good working order.

For the organized offender, victim selection is a process. This type of killer does not kill randomly, but selects his victim in advance and based on specific criteria. If he kills more than once, his victims will share similar criteria. The victim is typically a stranger—which is consistent with the lust murderer's focus on escaping detection and arrest.

The organized offender knows full well the nature and illegality of his crime. He considers himself smarter than the police and believes he can flaunt his crime without risking detection or arrest.

The organized offender has strong social skills and will use these to get the victim into a position where he can execute his criminal plan. He will usually use his own weapon in committing the crime and often move the body from the scene of the crime to confuse police.

He likely takes a souvenir or trophy from the murder. He enjoys the cruelty of the act and may have tortured the victim. The organized offender will follow news stories concerning the crime.

CHAPTER THIRTY NINE

Travers had traded calls and voicemail messages with Marty McCall until they finally managed to schedule a phone call for 2:00 p.m. on May 17th. It was a Thursday. Travers called on schedule, and this time Marty answered. After briefly introducing himself, Travers dove right in.

"I'm calling about your former roommate, Joe Harlan Jr."

"What about him?" McCall asked.

"He's disappeared," Travers said, bluntly. "We suspect, actually, that he's been murdered."

"Are you kidding?"

"I rarely joke about homicide," Travers said.

"What happened? Is that dick—I mean, penis—the penis thing I saw on the news, was that his, after all?" McCall asked. Then he added, "Wait, what's that got to do with me? You do realize you're calling Seattle, right? I'm halfway across the country. Wait. Do I need to call my lawyer?"

"Take it easy, Mr. McCall, I'm just checking boxes. You have nothing to worry about right now."

"Right now? What do you mean, *right now?*"

"Look, Marty. Can I call you Marty? I'm not at liberty to discuss the details of the case. You'll appreciate that. Right now, I just need some preliminary information. Can you help me with that?" Travers waited for a response.

Finally, McCall said, "Okay. What do you want to know?"

"Can you tell me if you've travelled lately? Outside Seattle, I mean."

"Shit. I haven't been to Austin since I left. I'm going to be down there in about a week to give my deposition in the lawsuit but it's the first time in almost two years," McCall added quickly. "I'm assuming you know about the lawsuit?"

"So, you haven't traveled outside Seattle lately?" Travers asked again, keeping the conversation where he needed it.

"No. I have not."

Travers waited, but McCall didn't volunteer anything further.

"Can you tell me if you've been to Miami lately?"

"Detective, I've already told you that I haven't been anywhere."

"No, Marty, you said you haven't been to Austin. I want to know if you've been to Florida lately." Travers waited for an answer, but none came and his patience was wearing thin. "Look, I can always arrange for the local PD to stop by, pick you up and take you in for questioning if that's easier," Travers said, seemingly indifferent.

"Florida? No. I haven't been to Florida," the man finally said. "Why would I go to Florida?"

"I don't know. Aren't you fundraising for your company?"

"Yeah, but what's Miami got to do with all this?"

"Can you tell me where you were from May 1st to May 4th—what you were doing on those days?"

"I was here. In Seattle, I mean."

"Doing what?"

"Living life, Detective. What do you think?" the man snapped.

"Can anyone verify just how you might have been doing that?" Travers asked.

"Sure, lots of people."

"Could you give me names and contact information?"

"Happy to," McCall answered. "Hold on."

Travers heard clicking in the background. Not the fake clicking that you hear when you call AT&T and they try to make you think that the automated voice is actually typing on a computer. This was real clicking and typing.

"Okay. You got a pen?" McCall asked.

"Go ahead."

McCall provided a list of names and phone numbers. During the days in question, he had had coffee with three different people in Seattle. He'd had lunch with someone different every day. He'd had two dinner meetings, and one dinner at home with his girlfriend. He also volunteered the fact that his office building was fitted with state of the art security and that his key card would verify when he had come and gone from work on those days. He gave Travers relevant contact details for the security office in his building.

After all this, McCall added, "If you call any of these folks I met with, can I ask that you be... I don't know, discreet? No offense, but I'm trying to build a business here. We're still fundraising. Some of these folks are potential investors. I moved out here to get away from Joe and Frank. I don't need them tainting my business now."

"Sure," Travers answered. "I'm not interested in causing you any problems, Marty. I'm only interested in the facts. I promise to be discreet."

"I appreciate it. Thanks."

"You mentioned that you were coming to Austin soon. I assume you would be okay with meeting me while you're down here, just for a few follow-up questions?" It was always better to interview witnesses live. Body language was completely lost over the phone. If Travers could interview McCall live, it would be much more valuable to the investigation.

McCall paused, and then eventually and somewhat petulantly, Travers thought, replied with, "Whatever. Sure. That's fine."

CHAPTER FORTY

Roy's intercom burst to life.

"Roy?"

"Yeah, Eve?"

"Marty McCall on line two."

Roy picked up, injecting a smile into his voice even though he already suspected what this call was about. "Hey Marty. How's it going?"

"Hello Roy. How are you doing? Staying out of trouble?"

Roy hesitated. *Well, not quite.* "Sure am. You?"

"Good. Listen, I've been thinking about your proposal, and I just don't think your valuation number is fair."

McCall then launched into a long-winded explanation as to why TrueData was worth more, much more, than Roy had proposed paying. They'd been through all this before, though. McCall wasn't adding anything new.

And, as we know, Roy wasn't even considering investing. He never had been. The offer he'd made to Marty had all been a ploy, part of getting Harlan down to Miami. Now, it no longer mattered. McCall was just giving him an easy out by refusing to lower his price.

McCall summed up, "So, I'd like you to think about investing, but just going with the price I initially proposed. Take some time. Sleep on it. Think about what I've said. Then let me know."

"Alright, Marty. Well, sorry you feel that way. I'll talk to the team and get back to you, though, okay?"

Roy was about to hang up, when McCall took the conversation in an unexpected direction.

"Cool," McCall said and then added, quickly, "Also, on another note. You probably heard about Joe and all that stuff on the news?"

Shit.

His response was somber. "I did. Horrible stuff."

"Well, I just talked to the cops. Nothing to worry about. Just standard procedure—since we're involved in this lawsuit, I assume they needed to talk to me. I guess you could say that I could benefit from Joe's disappearance."

He didn't just disappear, Marty, Roy thought.

Marty cleared his throat and continued, "Nice guy. The cop—Travers. Art Travers. He was mainly interested in where I was. You know, checking my alibi and all that. I guess. I'm good though, of course. I was in Seattle the whole time. Shitload of witnesses. And I haven't talked to Joe in forever. And, um, I don't really have anything to hide."

McCall paused giving Roy enough time to wonder *why the fuck is he telling me all this shit?*

"I'm going to get interviewed again, though," he finished.

"Is that right?" Roy forced himself to remark. There was silence at the other end of the line and he waited for a long time, all while his leg bounced nervously, impatiently under his desk.

"Yeah," McCall finally continued, thoughtfully. "I fucked up and told him I was going to be in Austin for the lawsuit. You know, my deposition. So, now he wants to meet in person." The man's tone had changed. He seemed agitated, yet at the same time smug. "I assume Detective Travers is going to ask more questions. Odd thing is, he asked me if I'd been in Miami lately." McCall paused. Roy said nothing. "Which is a 'no,' I haven't. But he mentioned it in connection with 'fundraising.' That seemed odd to me. Strange. But it did get me thinking about you."

"Really? How so?" Roy asked, as casually as his nerves would allow. He now suspected what the little shit was implying.

"Do you know anything about Joe being in Miami, Roy? I mean, I just assumed he got whacked in Austin. But then when I thought about it…"

"Marty, I don't know if we should be talking about this, under the circumstances," Roy heard himself saying.

"Really? Why not? We've got nothing to hide, have we, Roy? I mean, it sure is messy. Anything to do with cops. It's like skunk piss. I can't tell you how long it took me to get the stink of that whole rape shit off me."

"Marty—"

"Anyway, I just wanted you to know that when Art, the detective, asked me about Miami and fundraising, I thought of you. My guess is that it's bound to come up again when I meet with him next—Miami and fundraising. And, of course, if he asks how we met, I'm just gonna have to go ahead and tell him the truth. Just tell him how we met. What we discussed. You know. Just tell him how we met at the Trace. How we talked business. You really liking my company. How you were looking really hard at investing." Marty paused. "Of course, we never discussed Joe. His name never came up."

Roy sat silent, for a moment, choosing his words carefully, then answered, "Sure, Marty. You know that the truth is best—"

"Anyway, that's all I got, man. Sleep on my proposal and let me know. The sooner the better, of course. In fact, let me know before I go to Austin. I'm going to take advantage of my trip to do some fundraising down there. You don't want anyone jumping the line ahead of you, right? Especially given how excited you were about the company when we last met. I think we could work really well together. Right?"

"I will think on it, Marty," Roy said reluctantly. "And I have to say, you're a good negotiator. I know there's a lot of interest in TrueData here."

"Cool. Talk to you later. And... stay out of trouble."

"Goodbye."

You little fucker.

This was not how Roy had planned things, and he was starting to feel the pressure bearing down on him like a giant boulder of shit.

He took some time to gather his thoughts. He resolved,

at least for the time being, that the best strategy with McCall was simply to delay.

CHAPTER FORTY ONE

Harlan had "disappeared" May 2nd. The penis was found on the door about a week later. From that point, the Miami investigative contingent took about a week to run down their various leads.

Garza had two officers canvas Brickell City Centre. They carried with them a headshot of Harlan, as well as a still image taken from the surveillance video showing how he'd been dressed when he'd left the hotel.

At Saks, they were able to identify the clerk who'd sold him the boat shoes. She remembered him. Cute. Kind of flirty. He'd been alone. Hadn't said anything she could remember about what he was doing or where he was going.

Aside from Saks, they came up empty.

The marina and surrounding shops they approached differently. First, they obtained a list of all of the boats with slips at the marina, as well as the names of their owners. Most of the boats were titled under individual names. A few were titled under entities—corporations or limited liability companies. They chased these down to find owner names. None matched any of the names on their list of persons of interest, or even had any connections to any of those individuals.

Garza emailed the boat owner list to Travers, who in turn emailed it to Senator Harlan. Harlan reviewed the list, but told Travers that none of the names meant anything to him.

Rosa had the idea that maybe "Cruise Captain" referred to the name of an actual boat—a boat name with the word "cruise" in it. It was a good theory, but they drew a blank there also.

One of the boat slips was rented out to a Frank Cruz.

Further investigation, though, determined that he owned a sailboat, and that the boat hadn't even been in the marina at the time of the disappearance. It had been up at Norseman's Boatyard having its hull repainted.

Rosa took on the job of contacting all the sightseeing boat companies in the area to see if anyone by the name of Harlan, McCall, Kim, Cruise, or Wise had chartered a cruise or been onboard. She compiled a list of twenty-three companies that provided bay tours or dinner boat rides. Two had the word "cruise" or some variant in their company name. Over the course of two days, she contacted each and every one of them and verified all associated records.

Nothing.

Having found no leads through their preliminary investigation of the marina, they took to the pavement. Eddie and Rosa walked the marina. They questioned employees, flashed Harlan's photo.

Nothing.

They inspected fuel receipts—most boaters paid for their fuel by credit card. The police compiled a list of names, but nothing jumped out at them. There were three cash purchases of fuel from the day of the disappearance. They questioned the employees who had been working the pumps that day, but it had been over two weeks since the disappearance. "You know how many boats come through here in a day? At a certain point, they all just run together, man." That was the stock answer, and it was maddening.

Next, they expanded their canvassing efforts to include shops and restaurants around the marina. They went store-by-store, starting in the morning and returning in the evenings, in order to be sure to question as many of the employees who worked on the day of the disappearance as possible.

Nothing.

One Starbucks barista said she thought she remembered seeing a guy who fit Harlan's description. He'd been alone, standing outside the shop. It had been slow at the time, so she'd been watching him. He'd just been standing around. They'd even made eye contact a couple of times she thought. Hard to tell because he'd been wearing sunglasses. She'd assumed he was waiting for someone but wasn't sure. She was a firm believer in *"See something, say something..."* She'd been watching him, but then someone had come into the shop and ordered a latte. When she'd finished with that customer, the guy outside was gone.

Rosa logged her name and contact information.

After leaving a couple of messages and getting no return phone call, Eddie and Rosa made a personal stop at Sweet Miami's headquarters, a surprisingly respectable office space in Miami Shores. He spoke with a lady named Carmen. After identifying himself and doing a bit of cajoling, she checked her records and confirmed that a guy calling himself Joe Smith had made a date with one of their escorts for 6:00 p.m. at the Intercontinental, Room 576. However, he'd called back later to cancel. He was listed as a "cash pay" on the record.

Other than that, the name, and his phone number at the hotel, there was nothing else to tell. Carmen told the detectives that she had personally taken the call. She remembered that this Joe guy had been looking for a Latina, minimum D-cup. Nothing else. It was most likely Harlan, but all in all, it wasn't much to go on.

The Uber drivers had little more to offer. One didn't remember Harlan at all. And when presented with the record of the trip and the photos, the driver shrugged and said, "Just another fare."

The other remembered Harlan. He recalled that the young man asked about "the marina near Bayside." The driver had told him it was about a ten-minute walk from the hotel and given him directions on how to get there on foot. He'd offered to drive him, but the man had said he wanted to walk and see the sights.

The driver remembered because the guy had tipped him in cash. This at least indicated that Harlan had been interested in the marina, and that it had possibly been his destination that evening.

CHAPTER FORTY TWO

Travers wasn't surprised when McCall asked that the interview take place at his lawyer's office. He was coming to Austin in connection with the Procurex-TrueData lawsuit, so it was logical that he would mention Travers' call to his lawyer, and equally logical that his lawyer would highly recommend being present—if for no other reason than to run up some fees.

McCall's lawyer's office was in the One Congress Plaza building. They met in a conference room overlooking downtown on May 25th. Travers sat on one side of the table, McCall and his lawyer, Gerald Woodfield, on the other.

Travers began by questioning McCall about any recent contact with Joe Harlan Jr. McCall claimed to have had none since leaving Austin, other than through his lawyer in connection with the lawsuit.

Travers then asked about contact with the Wises. McCall replied that those were even further removed. His last contact with Kristy preceded the rape case. And, he had never had any contact with Debra or Tom.

Travers next read through a prepared list of names, asking McCall to tell him if he was familiar with any of them. This was the list of boat owners from the marina. He watched McCall as he went through the list. Travers knew that it was unlikely that McCall would know any of them, though he needed to be sure. Reading through the list also gave Travers a chance to see how McCall responded when being totally honest. He wanted to be in the best position to judge McCall's reaction when he asked about Cruise and Kim. He saved those two names for the end.

"Alan Hughes."

"No."

"Kelly Whittaker."

"No."

"Arturo Saenz."

"No."

"Roy Cruise."

McCall's eyes lit up. "Yes. I've met him."

"What about David Kim?"

"No. No David Kim."

"Okay. That's the end of the list. Can you tell me about Cruise?"

"Sure. He's a VC type. He's interested in investing in my company. We had drinks—a couple of months ago."

"Where was this?"

"Seattle. At the Trace—a hotel bar."

"How was it that you got in contact with him?"

"He contacted me, actually. Said he was going to be in town talking to some startups and that a time slot had opened in the evening. He wanted to hear more about my company."

"Do you know the exact date?"

"Sure, hold on." McCall picked his phone up off the table and manipulated the screen. "Wednesday, April 11th."

"Okay. And what did you discuss?"

"The company. The business. What we're trying to build. And our current Series A."

"Is that a software program?"

McCall smiled. "No. It's a fundraising round. You know— Seed, Series A, Series B. Anyway, our software is done; the platform is all built. We have clients. We're doing a Series A fundraising round so we can hire some marketing folks and really grow the company."

"And did you get the investment?"

Woodfield piped in, "Hold on, Marty. That's company confidential information, Detective. What does it have to do with this case?"

"Motive. There's a lawsuit pending."

"Correct," responded the attorney. "Pending. It's still there.

Hasn't gone anywhere. If getting rid of the lawsuit was a motive, that hasn't happened."

"The victim is a witness in the lawsuit, and a party to the case."

"If you're saying that my client is a suspect, then this interview ends right now."

Travers held up his hands in a calming gesture, thought for a second, and then said, "Okay, let me ask a different question, then. Did Harlan come up in the conversation?"

"No," McCall answered. "Why would he?"

"In connection with the lawsuit?"

"No. I mean, he mentioned the lawsuit in passing. Cruise did. But he was familiar with TrueData, with what we've built. He'd done his homework. I think he just saw it as a nuisance case, like I do. We didn't dwell on it. He did ask about Frank, but Joe didn't come up."

"Not at all?"

"Nope. Not at all."

"Okay," Travers answered. He paused, reviewing his notes. "One last subject. Are you familiar with this phone number?" He slid a sheet of paper across the conference table.

McCall looked at the paper first and then at his lawyer. Nothing registered on his face. He looked up back at Travers and said, "No."

"Any idea why it would be on Joe Harlan's mobile phone, under your name?"

McCall's face darkened. He looked back at the sheet of paper, then at his lawyer, who shrugged, and then back at Travers. "Is this some kind of trick? You've got my mobile number. You've called me on it. This is my phone," he said, holding up his phone for all to see. "I changed my number when I moved to Seattle. It's the only one I have. I don't have a landline, and you've got my office number—and that ain't it."

"Well, that's what we found on Joe's telephone. Your name, and this phone number. And—what's worse—he received two calls from this number the day that he disappeared—which is probably the day he died."

"Well, I have no idea. Someone trying to set me up, maybe? Have you tried calling it?" McCall asked, sarcastically.

"We have. It's a prepaid phone. No one answers. We checked with the carrier. Only two calls have been made from it, ever. Both to Harlan. Both the day he disappeared." Travers left out the fact that both calls had been made from Miami.

McCall shrugged. "You got me, man."

Travers paused for a few moments, reviewing his notes, and then said, "Thanks very much for your time, Marty. I think that's all for today."

All three men stood.

As they did, McCall asked Travers, "I guess the dick turned out to be his after all. Right?"

Woodfield cringed. "That really doesn't matter, Marty."

"Just wondering, man. That really sucks. I mean, we had our differences and all, but getting your dick cut off. That's just fucked up."

"Yes," Travers nodded pensively. "It sure is."

CHAPTER FORTY THREE

There is more than one way to skin a cat. Or so the saying goes. Not that I particularly care for that expression. But the point of it is that one way of doing something isn't necessarily better than another. People are different, which means that we approach things differently. Police work is no exception.

Detective Travers' style was very methodical. Logical. Some might even say plodding. If police work were like World Cup soccer, Travers would be like the German team. Structured, predictable.

Detective Travers closed most of his cases not necessarily because of any particular originality, but because of the systematic way he followed up every lead and documented every fact. Leaving nothing out.

Detective Eddie Garza could be described as more of a freestyle specialist. Eddie went where his intuition took him. If Eddie were a World Cup soccer team, he'd be Italy, or maybe Brazil. He claimed to have an underlying method to his madness. Though, to an outsider, what Eddie did appeared to be more madness than method.

Eddie's favorite part of the process was interviewing suspects. He felt that this was where he outshone other cops. He believed that human psychology was stacked in his favor. His favorite book was Dostoyevsky's *Crime and Punishment*. He loved the book because it was a case study on the typical human reaction to committing homicide. He believed that murder was contra-natural, and that murderers were plagued by guilt complexes and that even the most brazen, sociopathic killers subconsciously wanted to get caught.

This hypothesis was the foundation for his philosophy of interrogation. He believed in pressuring his suspects by giving them the impression that the case against them was made. That their capture and punishment was inevitable. He operated from this premise, and then sprinkled in other psychological tactics.

Detective Eddie Garza arrived at Cruise Capital at 10:20. His meeting with David Kim was scheduled for 10:00. Arriving late was one of his tactics. He believed it put him in control of the situation.

It also played with the interviewee's state of mind.

Eddie believed that tension would increase until the agreed upon appointment time. Then came uncertainty, or maybe even hope that the *interrogation* might be postponed. And, of course, as the appointed hour passed, the suspect would begin to experience relief, maybe even relax. Then, Bam! Eddie would show up and put them right back in the hot seat. At least, this is what Eddie thought.

However, this time, when he arrived at Cruise Capital, it was he who was made to wait, for the grand total of a whole half hour.

At 10:50, Eve showed him into the main conference room. It was empty. But the power seats were taken—the seat at the head of the conference table, and the first one next to it. They were already occupied—a legal pad in front of one, and a phone and file folder in front of the other. Eddie moved the folder and phone and sat at the head of the table.

"I am so sorry to keep you waiting, Detective," David Kim offered as he rushed into the room.

Eddie noticed that David looked twice when he realized that his things had been moved.

David was accompanied by another man. He introduced himself as Mark Moran.

Rich guy has lawyered up. Shocker.

"You were obviously running late, so I took advantage and jumped on another call which ended up dragging on longer than expected."

Eddie nodded and mustered a fake smile. "No problem, Mr. Kim. So, given that we're all running late, if it's okay with you, I'll just jump straight in." David nodded. "So, could you tell me how exactly you know Mr. Harlan?" He leaned back in his chair and stopped short of putting his hands behind his head.

"We met briefly in Austin at a pitch meeting. Then—"

David's attorney shook his head, and David stopped.

"Then what?" Eddie asked.

David sat down at the opposite head of the table, ignoring the fact that his stuff was in the middle. His attorney stood to his right, casually looking out of the window.

"Then we spoke later, by phone."

"Why did you fly him down to Miami?"

"We were interested in possibly hiring him."

"For?"

"Consulting."

"For?"

David frowned and glanced at his lawyer.

"What kind of consulting, Mr. Kim?" Eddie clarified.

"For Cruise Capital."

"Look, David," Eddie said, glancing at the suit by the window and leaning forward, "I get that you've got your lawyer here and that you don't want to say something stupid that's going to get you into trouble. And I get that your lawyer probably told you not to volunteer anything."

David half-smiled.

"But I'm just trying to get some basic information here today. If I thought you'd killed this guy, I'd be here with a warrant, and the whole 'tenor,'" he made air quotes with his fingers, "of this meeting would be very different. So, if you want to keep playing lawyer games, I can be a dick, too." The suit looked at him, but Eddie carried on, "I can go get a warrant and drag you down to the station to one of our interview rooms. Bad coffee. Shitty view… Or, you can be cooperative, help me do my job, and we'll probably never see each other again."

Moran seemed bored, as if he had witnessed this patter many times before, and said, "Detective, my client has every right to—"

"Hold on. Hold on." David raised his hand. "Look,

Detective. I'm happy to cooperate. Trust me. I think what happened is terrible, but I too have to follow company policy," he said, and nodded at the lawyer. "Ask your questions, and I'll answer to the best of my ability. I'm sorry, I didn't even offer you a beverage. Where are my manners? Would you like something? Tea? Coffee?"

"I could use a coffee. Thanks. So, I'll ask again, then. What'd you want to hire Harlan for?"

"He was part of a company—a startup—in the government procurement space," David said as he poured coffee into a cup. "Procurex is the name. We believe that the sector has got a lot of upside. He knew the space. And, he had contacts. Well, his father did. Does. We wanted to explore bringing him on to consult for us on companies in this sector."

"Why him? Why not his partner, Stern? Or this guy McCall from Seattle?"

"Neither of them had the contacts. And, in government, contacts go a long way."

"And the dad, why not him?"

"I don't think he can—he's a sitting senator. I think that's illegal?" David looked at his lawyer, who nodded.

"Why not meet with him in Austin? Discuss it there?"

"It was cheaper to have him come in and meet with our team here, rather than for us to go to Austin. And we thought his schedule was probably more flexible. That way things could move faster. Sugar?"

Eddie shook his head. "Black please. So, he was meeting with multiple people here? Who?"

"Me and Roy Cruise, the founding partner. But, later that changed."

"What do you mean?"

"Well, initially it was going to be me and Roy, but Roy had something else come up, so in the end it was just going to be me."

"What came up?"

"Um, he took a trip. With his wife. To Bimini, I believe," David said, rising from his seat and placing the coffee cup in front of the detective.

"So, the cost savings kind of evaporated, huh?"

"Well, we flew Harlan down economy, and we didn't have to cover all his meals, so technically it was probably still cheaper to have him come here," David said, resuming his seat, situating his tie and brushing invisible lint from his blue shirt.

"What happened with dinner?"

"How do you mean?"

"If you want to get this guy to work for you, isn't it typical to wine and dine him? You know, take him to dinner. Show him a good time?"

"Um, yes. Sort of. The plan was to meet here at the office in the morning. Then, go to lunch. And, if things went well and seemed positive, we would then roll that into dinner. At least, that was the plan," David added, soberly.

Eddie drank from his cup. "So, we have records showing a text message from him to you about dinner plans. What was all that about?"

David nodded. "Yes. I know exactly what you're talking about. I thought you'd ask." He took a sip of his coffee. Then, "I have no idea. After I received the text message, my first thought was that he had written to me by mistake. That he was having dinner with someone else and that it got cancelled. I wrote back to him saying as much.

"But, then, the more I thought about it, the more I started to think that maybe he was offended. You know, because I hadn't offered to take him to dinner. I assumed he had in some way expected it and was being sarcastic. But it did seem like kind of an odd way to make that point. It's still somewhat baffling to me."

"Baffling?"

"Yes. As in confounding, confusing."

Eddie sighed. "Yes, Mr. Kim, I understand what it means. And I agree, 'tis somewhat *baffling*. So, let me give you my take on it. If you'll indulge me for a second, David," Eddie said in his best snobby voice. "It sounds to me like three of you were planning on having dinner together—Harlan, you, and someone else—let's call him Percy.

"Percy sets up dinner. A nice place. Maybe on the water. You know, somewhere fancy. But then, for whatever reason, you back out. You decide not to attend. You let Harlan know. But Harlan still goes ahead to have dinner with Percy. He then writes to you that message saying, 'Sorry you can't make it, David. See you tomorrow.' Percy then meets Harlan, kills him, cuts off his dick, and nails it to his dad's door. What do you think of that version?" Eddie asked stone-faced, before taking another sip from his cup.

David squirmed in his seat for the first time since the meeting started and looked at his lawyer, who responded with a shrug.

David turned back to the detective, who had now crossed his hands on the table, and was watching him with keen eyes. "Well," David began, "can't say I care for that version very much, but I can say that I don't know anyone named Percy." He picked up his coffee cup to take a drink.

"What if Percy was Marty McCall? Or Roy Cruise?"

David paused, then put the cup down without drinking from it, returning it to its saucer with a loud clatter. "I guess a scenario like that is consistent with the message he sent. But I can only tell you what I know, Detective. There was no dinner plan. From the outset, the only plan was to meet in the morning. The next day."

"And, as far as you know, was Harlan planning on having dinner with Cruise, or McCall?"

"I..." David paused. "I don't know what to tell you. If Roy had planned a dinner, I would expect he would have told me. After all, I was the one who set everything up with Harlan. And Roy was in Bimini anyway. At least as far as I know. He wasn't even in the country. So, if I were to hazard a guess, I would say that he doesn't fit into your theory. And McCall, what would he be doing in Miami? Was he in Miami? I... I have no idea."

"Why do you say, 'as far as you know' Roy was in Bimini?"

"I'm trying to be precise," David said, glancing at his lawyer. "Roy said he was going to Bimini. I spoke to him by phone while he claimed he was in Bimini. I have no reason to think that he *wasn't* in

Bimini. But I have no way of verifying that. So, I can only tell you what I know. I'm not trying to be difficult, Detective—just precise."

Eddie held the man's gaze for an unnervingly long time before nodding. "Okay. Got it." Then he drank more coffee before continuing. "So, since we're talking about what you can and cannot actually tell me. Why don't you go ahead and tell me exactly where you were that night? You know, the night before your meeting with Harlan that never happened?"

"I was at home. I had a ton of work to do. I was reviewing due diligence documents on a company we're looking at investing in. I had a conference call with the founders."

"Alone?"

"Well kind of. It was just me in my study. On Skype. I did order food. Sushi Maki—from Uber Eats. And, I do have an alarm system at home. I set that before I went to sleep. But, I was alone, working."

"You ever meet Marty McCall?"

"No."

"But you know the name?"

"I do. He works in the space—government procurement software. TrueData is his company."

"And you know where he lives?"

"I know his company is based in Seattle. I assume he lives there or nearby."

"You ever spoken with him?"

"No."

"But your friend and colleague Roy Cruise has?"

"Yes. He told me he had."

"What about?"

"About the business, I suppose, but you'd have to ask Roy. I only know what he told me."

Eddie thought about this and then stood abruptly. "Okay. Thanks very much for your time and for the coffee. Very nice by the way. Never did care for the shitstant crap."

With that, the detective glanced at the lawyer and left the room.

CHAPTER FORTY FOUR

The whole point of the first meeting with David was to get his alibi info from him. Where had he been on those critical days? The detective's objective was to find out while giving away as little information as possible. And he felt he'd succeeded.

But Eddie wanted to use the opportunity for a little more. He wanted to take a measure of David Kim. How nervous was he? Did he seem guilty? Could he have done it?

He also wanted to keep David on edge. Hence the scenario—painting a picture of where the case was heading without disclosing any evidence that supported the theory.

As David had told him where Cruise was, there was no point in meeting with Cruise until they had more information. Chasing down Roy Cruise's alibi took almost two weeks. The Bahamian government was always very cooperative, but they were also slow.

When the Bahamian government finally responded, it confirmed that Roy Cruise and Susie Font arrived in the Bahamas on April 28th. They passed through customs in South Cat Cay. A Sunseeker yacht, a jet ski, a paddleboard. Destination—Resort World Bimini. There was no exit information. None was required.

Eddie checked with the Customs and Border Protection in Miami. Susie and Roy had reported their re-entry to the United States using the CBP's ROAM app. They were both cleared for re-entry without video interview on May 5th, at 8:27 a.m.

Resort World Bimini was equally cooperative. The Sunseeker had arrived on April 28th. It had stayed for a full week, departing on May 5th. Records were not kept of every entry and exit—so it was possible that the boat had left Bimini, maybe even come back to Miami, during that week.

Eddie obtained a list from the harbormaster's office of all boats docked in Fisherman's Village Marina for the full week.

Then began the slow process of contacting them all one by one. He and Rosa split the work, questioning the boat owners about their stay, and about the Cruises' Sunseeker. Had they seen anything unusual? Had they in fact seen or spoken to Cruise or Font?

They started with the boats docked closest to the Sunseeker, and worked their way outward. Almost immediately, they hit on Roland Obregon. He and his wife had taken a short vacation to Bimini, and had been in the slip right next to the Sunseeker for three days.

While Roland hadn't seen anything, his wife Toni was a cop's wet dream. An insomniac, she was the typical next-door neighbor with the proverbial twitching curtains, keeping tabs on everyone.

It was Rosa who initially questioned Toni by phone. Based on the information she'd obtained, they agreed that it would probably be worth Eddie's time to make a trip to Fort Lauderdale to meet with her.

Eddie wasn't crazy about travelling so far north. In his mind, there was an imaginary line, but a very real border, up at around NE 167th Street, where you left Miami and entered the United States. He preferred staying in Miami. But from time to time, he "traveled abroad"—mostly for work. Never for leisure.

CHAPTER FORTY FIVE

Susie confessed to me that the penis was Deb's idea. The way Deb explained it to Susie was that Kristy's version of what happened would always be in doubt. And if, as they hoped, Harlan's body was never found, then what had happened to him would always be in doubt, as well.

The dick on the door told the world that Harlan was dead, and why. It brought closure to the entire episode and it told the world that Harlan had been in the wrong.

While Susie didn't fully agree with Deb's argument, she could see the logic to it. It was twisted, but it was there. And Susie firmly believed that if she was careful—as she had been—there would be no tracing it back to her. No one would be able to except for Roy. She also knew that, once the penis was discovered, Roy would know she'd been involved and would suspect a stronger connection between Susie and Deb than just that chance meeting in Colorado.

I believe that Susie wanted to tell Roy about her history with Deb—at least some of it. She would most likely have wanted him to know that it was Deb who had killed Liam Bareto, and that Camilla, like Kristy, had been avenged. I think that's why she went along with Deb's idea regarding Harlan's penis.

Once the penis was "out," Susie knew that she would owe Roy some amount of truth about Harlan. If she didn't offer it, he would most certainly demand it. And to explain Harlan, Susie needed to explain Bareto. To do that, she would need to come clean about her relationship with Deb—but how much should she share? That was a difficult question.

It pained her to lie to him, to withhold information. It really did. But she had been doing that to some degree since they'd met.

So, while she didn't like doing it, for her it was just a fact of life. As long as she was with Roy, there would always be certain things about her past that she would never be able to share. Certainly not with him. This was her cross to bear and she was willing to live with it.

Now, though, Susie needed to explain to Roy how she knew Deb. How they met. That wasn't complicated, but the details were the problem. How could she explain the relationship that their early friendship evolved into? Susie's relationship with Deb was tainted very early on, almost before it began. When they'd met again on the cruise ship, they reconnected like old friends. Things blossomed from there.

For Susie, Deb was the gasoline to her fire. Being with her made her feel things that nobody else ever had or could. She thrilled Susie. She also frightened her. She'd seen the extremes that Deb could go to, and could make her go to. It was because things had gotten so extreme so early on that Susie kept her distance from Deb. Deb was dangerous.

Like a moth to the flame, Susie was drawn to her. She loved Deb. Both physically and mentally. Yet, unlike a moth, Susie *knew* that if she got too close she would burn. She was afraid of Deb.

There was a cruelty to Deb that Susie thought bordered on the sociopathic. The flipside was that Deb had a moral clarity about her that, ironically, could only come from a complete lack of morality.

Deb knew very clearly what she wanted and whom she loved. These things were "right" in Deb's version of morality. Anything that got in the way of them or threatened them was an obstacle to be eliminated. Of course, Deb's approach to the world was very liberating. In Deb's world, the only thing that mattered was what Deb wanted. Anything that got in the way of that was disposable.

When Susie was with Deb, she felt that same clarity. That certainty. It was powerful, intoxicating. That feeling that anything was possible, anything was acceptable, so long as it got you what you wanted.

And it was extremely useful. When Deb called Susie after

Camilla's death, Susie knew that the deal was done. If Deb said she was going to kill Bareto, she was going to do it. Period. But it wasn't just that she *would* do it. Susie knew, even then, that if she had pushed, she could have gotten Roy to do it. It wasn't about the willingness to commit the act.

To Susie, what was so powerful about Deb was that, for Deb, it was a given that Bareto had to die. That it needed to be done was simply fact. In Deb's moral balance, Bareto had hurt someone she loved, and therefore he needed to be eliminated. It was that simple.

It was this clarity that was so dangerously addictive to Susie.

Susie felt that same sense of justice, but she didn't feel the same moral clarity. Susie also thought about Liz Bareto, a mother like her who would also lose her child. Susie took into account the collateral damage killing Bareto would cause. Deb saw none of that.

Susie had to agonize her way through the situation before concluding that Bareto should die. Deb didn't. That was the difference.

In some ways, Deb reminded Susie of Roy, in the sense that like Roy, she also bent the world around her to her will. But where Roy had very specific ideas about what he wanted, and thought things through and listened to Susie, Deb didn't. Deb didn't think things through. She didn't plan. She simply acted. For Deb, her desires were the only things that mattered. Her "people" were the only ones of value.

Susie couldn't share all of this with Roy. But as she worked all this through in her mind, she decided on what she could tell him.

With that in mind, Susie invited Roy into their study.

As he entered, he found her sitting at the desk with a small lockbox in front her.

Roy sat down, arms folded across his chest, body language clearly projecting the barrier that still existed between them. He was still sulking. Angry. He had been since the whole penis thing came to light.

"Roy, you're right," Susie began. "I've been thinking about everything you said, and you're right. You deserve better. You deserve so much better than what I have given you.

"So, I want to tell you some things. You're not going to like them. I wanted to tell you all along. I planned to tell you all along. I just didn't know exactly when. The timing is always the hard part, you know?" She spread her palms out on the desk in front of her. "So, here's the thing. You nailed it. Colorado wasn't an accident. Deb and I met a long time ago. When we were kids. We haven't really stayed in touch. Life took us in very different directions.

"But when Camilla died, she called me out of the blue. It was right in the middle of my whole breakdown. When I was pushing for us to kill Bareto."

Susie raised the lid on her lockbox then placed a small, white plastic strip on the table in front of Roy.

```
Liam Bareto
PT 06730574    RM# 472
AD 03/30/2015  AB-
M   18Y        DOB 11/27/96
```

A hospital patient's ID bracelet.

"Where did you get this?" Roy asked.

"Deb."

"She's the lady-finger?"

"Yep."

"And you have this why?" Roy raised his voice. "You need to shred this thing!"

He shook his head, eyes narrowed, jaw muscles flexing. Then he stood up.

"For fuck's sake, Suze! If they show up with a warrant looking for Harlan stuff and they find this, do you know what would happen?" He began pacing, looking at the bracelet and then at his wife.

"I do. We'll shred it now. I just kept it to show to you. I could have just told you she did it, but I wanted to show you. This is why we had to kill Harlan. For Camilla, too. But also—we owed it to Deb. Do you understand?"

Roy stopped pacing and gawked at her. Then, through

gritted teeth, he said, "I understand that you manipulated me. I understand that you faked the meeting in Colorado, and what... was Tom in on it, or was Deb lying to him, too? Getting him to ask me to kill Harlan?"

Roy's voice was getting progressively louder. "What the fuck, Suze? I mean, this is really twisted. Why couldn't you just be honest with me? Why all of this manipulation? Now, you're telling me that we didn't kill Harlan for Camilla, but we did it as a favor for one of your old buddies? An old buddy who killed Bareto for us? And then gave you fucking evidence as a souvenir that you've kept in our home. All, this, this, *Strangers on a Train* bullshit can still get us caught, Suze!

"I mean, is this traceable? Your contact with Deb? How often do you talk? You realize that, if the cops make the connection, we're screwed, right? As in *jail* screwed? As in death penalty fucking screwed!"

Now Roy was yelling. Susie responded in kind.

"Goddammit, Roy, you're not listening. In the last ten years—longer, probably—I've spoken to Deb twice. That's it! There's no connection to make." Susie was lying, of course. As she continued, she lowered her voice, hoping to bring his tension down, as well. "There's nothing there. I promise. I swear it."

Roy was pacing again, shaking his head as he struggled to process everything he had just learned. This changed everything. All of his planning... for what?

Eventually, he stopped and leaned against the desk. "You have nothing linking you to her? No contact in your phone? No address? No letters, email?"

Susie reached into the box and handed Roy a small photo—a 3x5. It was a picture of Deb and Susie when they were very young. At camp. On the back of the photo was written, *Deb and Susie – 4 ever.*

He stared at the photo silently. Finally, Susie broke the silence. "That's all there is," she said softly. "And we can shred it, too."

Roy didn't acknowledge her. Instead he asked, "You look so

young. How old?"

"Thirteen."

"I didn't know you went to camp."

"Just one year."

After angling her head so that she could see her husband's face, Susie noticed that his eyes were glistening with tears. He was in pain.

She mistakenly surmised it was pain caused by her lies.

She reached out and took his hand.

"Why?" he asked.

"Why what?"

"Why just one year?"

"A girl died. My parents didn't think it was safe."

Seconds drifted by. Outside, a sports car rumbled by.

"Susie, we have to shred this. All of this. It isn't safe."

"Let's do it right now," she agreed.

* * *

Roy's head was spinning. They shredded the ID bracelet, and the photo. The photo made his belly sink.

4 ever

4 Kristy

Deb had killed Bareto.

He and Susie had killed Harlan.

And the bracelet and the photo put it all together. At least now they were gone. The evidence destroyed.

But so was his trust in his wife. Well, maybe not destroyed, but severely damaged?

His head ached.

He didn't believe his wife. He couldn't believe her. Sure, she had come clean—sort of. She had tried to dispel his concerns.

Tried to make things right. But he just knew, he felt in his gut, that something was missing. She was holding back. What exactly? He didn't know.

But he knew how to find out.

Not yet though. The timing wasn't right. They had other things to worry about right now. But if this whole Harlan thing blew over, if they got away with it, he swore to himself that he would get to the bottom of it all. He would get to the truth.

CHAPTER FORTY SIX

"Go for Art."

"Very funny," Eddie said.

"Hey, caller ID—I knew it was you." Travers was having a good day. It was sunny in Austin. Clear but cool. The full heat of summer hadn't yet arrived.

"So, you ready to talk?" Eddie asked.

"Yep. What you got?"

Eddie ran Travers through everything they had uncovered. As he did, Travers updated his timeline.

The last piece of new information he shared was the Toni Obregon interview. Toni had seen Cruise and Font come and go from their boat multiple times, and she confirmed that the boat never left the slip while they'd been there.

She had a very clear memory of the day of Harlan's disappearance because it was their last day in Bimini. Font was up early that day and left the Sunseeker at around 4:00 a.m. Obregon hadn't seen her come back during the day, but emphasized that she'd been out and about during the day and well into the evening, playing poker.

Late that night, Mrs. Obregon had smoked a cigarette with Susie Font. This was the night of Harlan's disappearance, before the morning meeting he'd never showed up for. According to Obregon, Roy Cruise had been suffering from food poisoning most of the day—that was what Susie Font told her that night. Obregon didn't recall seeing Roy the whole day. But, again, she had been out.

Finally, one last tidbit. She'd offered that, on the morning they'd left for Fort Lauderdale, when she'd been casting off, she'd said goodbye to Susie. As they'd been leaving, she'd noticed that the jet ski they'd had tied up next to their boat was gone. She'd thought it odd that Mr. Cruise would be up so soon after being so unwell, and out on a jet ski. But, she'd also been quick to point out that the jet ski could have simply been tied up on the other side of the boat. She hadn't bothered to look.

Travers' team hadn't been idle in Austin. Based on Rosa's insight, Travers had followed up on the Harlan Sr. angle. After a few awkward moments, the senator admitted that his alibi was his secretary, Meg. He'd spent the night at her apartment *in flagrante delicto*. Travers had spoken with Meg and she validated the senator's story.

"The senator and his secretary, huh? That's original." Eddie scoffed.

"Yep. Now that I'm looking at him, I suppose if he wanted to eliminate the kid, it would make sense to get him out of Austin— do it somewhere far away," Travers admitted. "But that's pure speculation. No evidence."

"Yeah," Eddie sighed. "We're running up on a bunch of dead-ends. Alibis everywhere. If we're thinking contract killing, then we could look to the Wises and McCall, and maybe the dad. They've all got motives. But there's no evidence that this was a contract hit."

"Eddie, there's no evidence of shit! It's been almost a month since the kid disappeared and all we've got is a dick with an extra hole in it." Travers sighed.

"What if it's someone we're not even looking at?" Eddie mused. "Someone who's dropping little clues out there in front of us to cover something else? What about LM?"

"Huh?" Travers asked.

"Lust murderer. Dr. Van der Put's theory. You got the psych profile I emailed you?"

"Oh, yeah," Travers responded. "Interesting read. Puts a completely different spin on this thing. What did you think of it?"

"There are definitely parts that fit. I mean, we got no body, no crime scene, and a traveling dick. Somebody went to a lot of trouble to make that happen. Smart. A planner. Careful. A lot of it makes sense," Eddie said.

"It helps with the profile, but if we're looking at LM, and not someone who knew Harlan, it's 'needle in the haystack' time."

"What do you mean?"

"Well, after getting your note, I talked to Frank Stern. Informally—he was in Austin, by the way. Solid alibi. He knew Harlan was going to Miami. Joe was completely up front with him about the contact from Cruise Capital. So, I asked him who knew Joe was going to Miami—who he had told. Stern didn't tell anyone. But then he took out his phone, and on his Facebook page he showed me a post by Harlan the Monday before the trip. It said something like 'Big meetings in Miami this week' with some hashtag things after it. Stern claims Harlan had over a thousand Facebook followers. And that doesn't include reposts of people who saw 'likes' and such."

"Shit," Eddie said.

"So, if some unknown killer targeted him, there's a list of a thousand people we could start with that all knew he was going to Miami," Travers concluded. "We're all out of leads. And we're up to our asses in alibis. The Wises have strong motives. McCall a weak motive. Cruise and Kim—weird facts and no motive."

"Okay. So, I think we've done all we can in terms of forensics and canvassing. We've got what we've got. I think it's time we interview the rest of them and see if anything shakes loose," Eddie offered.

There was a long pause, and then Travers sighed. "Alright. Let's do it."

CHAPTER FORTY SEVEN

Roy's office intercom squawked with Eve's voice. "An Eddie Garza on line two. He says you'll know what it's about?"

"Sure. I'll take it." Roy put his earpiece in and then pushed a button on his phone to connect the call. "Detective Garza, how are you?"

"I'm well, Mr. Cruise. It's been a while."

"That it has. How can I help you?"

"Well, I'm sure you spoke with your buddy, David. You had to know you were on our list of favorite people."

"Is this about Joe Harlan, then?"

"The one and only."

"And what can I do for you?"

"Well, I'd like to sit down for a chat. How's this afternoon?"

"Well, Detective, as you know, we have a protocol here."

"Yeah, yeah. I know. Talk to your lawyer and call me back with a couple of dates. Sooner rather than later."

"I'll pass your request on to my lawyer and let you guys sort out all the details, how's that?"

"I guess that'll be fine."

"Okay. Thank you, Detective."

"No, Thank you."

If Roy detected the sarcasm in the detective's tone, he didn't acknowledge it. Instead, he hung up and dialed his lawyer.

* * *

Tom Wise sat at his kitchen counter. He was sipping on a beer—a Pilsner Urquell. Tom favored light tasting beers—lagers, pilsners—he couldn't stand the hoppy ales that all the craft breweries were cranking out. Ales are easier to brew because ale yeast feeds at the top of the wort—the lazy man's beer. Pilsners and lagers are made with bottom-feeding yeast that requires more care, greater complexity.

Deb was drinking red wine while she made dinner—a large roasted chicken, steamed green beans, and quinoa. She wasn't happy. Tom had just told her that Art Travers had contacted him about doing an informal interview with each of them—Tom, Deb, and Kristy. Tom had already spoken to Harold Riviera, their attorney, about the request.

"Travers just said it was about Harlan," Tom said. "I'm guessing the DNA results are in and they know it's his. And they want to interview us because we have a motive."

"So, what did you tell him?"

"I told him that I needed to talk to my lawyer, and that I'd let him know."

Deb took a healthy swig from her glass, opened the fridge, and poured herself a refill. She liked her wine cold.

"What do you think we should do?"

"Well, I think that cooperation—agreeing to the interview—is the best way to put them off the scent. Not without a lawyer, of course, but I think that if we refuse it looks like we've got something to hide."

Deb took the lid off the pot where she was steaming the green beans, fished one out while being careful not to burn herself, and bit it to check for doneness. Satisfied, she turned the burner off and put the lid to the side to keep the green beans from overcooking in residual heat.

"What did Harold have to say?"

"He's a bit on the fence. He says that if we cooperate and give an interview, it will work to clear us and hopefully shut down any future inquiries. And we have nothing to hide. But he says that the only way he would recommend doing it is if he's there to push back on them and make sure we don't answer any questions that we shouldn't."

"Why doesn't that surprise me? At five hundred dollars an hour, of course he wants to be there. I'm not saying he's wrong. It just pisses me off to pay that kind of money.

"So, Tom, here's what's going to happen. Kristy has been through hell, and I'll be goddamned if I'm going to let another douchebag moron ask her questions about this fucking mess. So, you can tell Travers that if he wants to question her, he can come and fucking arrest her. And the same for me.

"If you want to appear on behalf of the family, that's up to you. If you think it'll somehow satisfy them, by all means. Maybe if they hear from you, they'll be happy and leave us alone. All our alibis are rock-solid. They've already verified them, for God's sake. Half the girls I play tennis with have gotten calls to confirm I was at the club. This sounds like a last ditch attempt to try and scare us into saying something stupid, and that just ain't gonna happen.

"If you decide to do it—and just in case I haven't made it clear, I don't think it's a good idea—but if you do, for God's sake, be careful."

* * *

Travers answered his mobile phone and recognized the husky voice as Meg, Harlan's assistant. "Hello, Art. Are you free to speak with the senator?"

"Sure, Meg."

"Okay. I'm putting him through."

There was an almost imperceptible *clok* sound on the line.

"Detective Travers."

"Hello, Mr. Senator. Thank you for returning my call. I just wanted to give you an update—we're still chasing down some leads and are in the process of setting up interviews with a number of witnesses."

"Who are you going to interview?"

"That's what I was calling about, Senator. As of right now, we are looking at interviewing all of the Wises, David Kim, and Roy Cruise. Obviously, Cruise and Kim's interviews will need to be done in Florida. And all of this depends on everyone agreeing to be interviewed, of course."

"Well, why wouldn't they agree? If they've got nothing to hide, they shouldn't be concerned."

"That's true, Senator. In fact, along those lines is the reason I called—you know we are working this case jointly with Homicide in Miami. So, it's always a balancing act. They have jurisdiction; we have jurisdiction. It can get complicated sometimes."

"Get to the point, Art. You're dilly-dallying."

"Yes, sir. Detective Garza is going to be coming from Florida for the interviews here. And..." Art paused, "he would like to sit down with you to formally take your statement." Travers closed his eyes and cringed, waiting for the backlash.

There was an agonizingly long pause.

"Art, we've known each other a long time. You know me, and my family. You know everything we've been through." Harlan's voice was increasing steadily in volume. "Are you saying that this man Garza suspects me of somehow being involved in Joe's death?"

"Not at all, Senator," Travers said, lightly. "He just wants to talk to you himself. Clarify some points. That's all."

"You know what, Art..." the senator growled and Travers braced himself, but then the words trailed off and there was silence on the line once more.

When the senator spoke again, his tone was calm. He chuckled, "Well, what's good for the goose is good for the gander. Of course, I'll meet with Detective Garza, Art. I'm happy to cooperate. The most important thing here is getting to the bottom of this and finding out who..." the words dried in the senator's throat. Then he cleared his throat and continued, "who killed Joe."

When Travers hung up, he noticed that his hand was shaking

slightly. He sent Garza a text message: *Harlan OK for interview.*

In any normal situation, Travers would have handled the interview. But pushing a Texas state senator's buttons to see if he had anything to do with his only son's murder could have a deleterious impact on Travers' career. So, they had agreed to let Garza take the heat.

Harlan wasn't stupid. He'd seen through it. But, at least this way any personal animus wouldn't be directed against Travers.

Interview of The Honorable Joseph Alan Harlan Sr.
06.15.18

Present:
Art Travers
Edward Garza
Joseph Alan Harlan Sr.
Attorney Alan Fletcher

(On the record. 7:00 a.m.)

Garza: Good morning, Mr. Senator.
            My name is Detective Eddie
            Garza. I work Homicide in
            Miami,Florida. I know we've
            been introduced, but could
            you state your name for the
            record?

Harlan: Joseph Alan Harlan Sr.

Garza: Thank you. We're here to
            briefly review the incidents
            leading up to your son's
            death. Let me begin by saying
            you have my sincere
            condolences.

Harlan: Thank you.

Garza: Mr. Senator, when did you
            last see your son, Joe Harlan Jr.?

Harlan: May 1st of this year. The
            night before he flew to Miami.

Garza: Did you know why he was going
            to Miami?

Harlan: To meet with a Mr. David Kim at
            Cruise Capital.

Garza: Do you know Mr. Kim or Mr. Cruise?

Harlan: No.

Garza: Do you know of any reason why they
            would wish your son ill or harm?

Harlan: No.

Garza: Do you know if they had anything to
            gain from your son's disappearance?

Harlan: No.

Garza: Do you know of anyone who would?

Harlan: Have something to gain? Not really.
            Joe was... I don't know of anyone
            that stood to gain.

Garza: Now, your son had some issues...
            legal issues... in the past.
            Correct?

Harlan: He did.

Garza: Could you tell me if those issues
            were in any way embarrassing to
            you, being a politician and all?

Harlan: Yes.

Garza: Were you concerned about a possible
            repeat of these issues? You know,
            say in the future? That he might
            cause you further embarrassment?

Harlan: Look, Detective. Let's cut to the
             chase. I've spoken at length to my
             lawyer about this. And...

Fletcher: Please do not divulge anything we
             have   discussed, Mr. Senator. All
             of thos discussions are attorney-
             client privileged.

Harlan: Thanks, Alan. I won't. Detective,
             I understand that you have to cover
             all your bases. I understand that
             you are also going to look to
             everyone as a possible suspect.
             You're going to look for motives
             wherever you can find them. And...
             hell, anyone that watches CSI
             knows that you guys always look
             at those closest to the victim as
             suspects.

             Yeah - Joe's problems in the past
             gave me a lot of headaches, but I
             love my son.

             Loved.

             But, yeah... he wasn't perfect. He
             got himself into trouble recently,
             as you know. With the Wise girl.
             Yes, it was problematic for me, as
             a politician. Did I wish it hadn't
             happened - you bet I did.

             But that doesn't change the fact
             that he was my son. I loved him. I
             still do. I would never wish him
             any harm. He was my boy, and...
             and...

Fletcher: Do you need a minute, Senator?

Garza: Should we take a short break?

Harlan: No. No. I'm fine. It's just all
              still raw. As I was saying.
              I know you need to cover bases. So,
              I will tell you for your record.
              I loved my son. And I will do
              anything, I mean anything I can
              to help you find who killed him so
              that those sons of bitches can be
              brought to justice. All you need
              to know is that it wasn't me. I
              was in Austin that entire time.
              Working. And with my female
              companion, Meg Watts. I believe you
              have already spoken to her.

(A discussion was had off the record.)

Garza: Senator, can you tell me if
              you've made any significant cash
              withdrawals recently?

Harlan: None.

Garza: Would you have any problem sharing
              your bank records with us in that
              regard?

Fletcher: I'm afraid...

Harlan: No. No, Alan. Please. No. I have no
              issue with that, Detective. Just
              tell me what you want to see.

Garza: Have you traveled to Florida
              recently?

Harlan: No.

Garza: Art? Anything else?

Travers: No. I think we're finished.

(Off the record at 7:17 a.m.)

Interview of Thomas Wise
06.15.18

Present:
Art Travers
Edward Garza
Thomas Wise
Attorney Harold Riviera

(On the record. 10:08 a.m.)

Travers: Please state your full name.

Wise: Thomas Kincaid Wise.

Travers: Mr. Wise, can I call you Tom?

Wise: Sure.

Travers: Thanks, and feel free to call
             me Art. I know this feels a bit
             formal, with the stenographer and
             all, but I really just need to
             clarify some points.

Wise: Okay.

Travers: You are represented today by your
             attorney, Harold Riviera, correct?

Riviera: That is correct, Detective.

Wise: Yes.

Travers: It's kind of warm in here. At least
             I am. Are you okay, Tom?

Wise: I'm fine.

Travers: Summer's definitely arrived. I think

it's going to be a hot one. Can I
get you some water?

Wise: I'm fine, Art.

Travers: By the way, how is Mrs. Wise, and
           Kristy?

Wise: Fine.

Travers: Kristy is what, a senior now?

Wise: She's...

Riviera: Detective. It's my understanding
           that we're here because you have
           some questions for Mr. Wise
           regarding Joe Harlan Jr. If that's
           the case, then let's please get to
           them. The good cop chat thing is a
           waste of your time and ours. So,
           please, just get to the heart of
           the matter.

Travers: I'm sorry. I apologize. I just
           wanted to be polite. I just want to
           clarify a few points. This doesn't
           need to be confrontational.

Riviera: Art, Mr. Wise is here to clear the
           air as to his alibi. That's it.
           Let's just deal with that and move
           on.

Travers: I'm sorry. Do you feel that way,
           too, Tom?

Wise: Art, I want to be accommodating,
           and I'm happy to help however I
           can, but I do need to get back to

work, so...

Travers: And your wife. I understand she
            didn't want to meet with me...

Riviera: Hold on. Please. I represent Mrs.
            Wise as well as Mr. Wise. And
            Kristy Wise. I already told you
            that neither she nor Kristy agree
            to be interviewed. Now, on the
            record, I'm telling you again.
            Neither Deb Wise nor Kristy
            Wise agree to meet with you for
            an informal interview. We are not
            going to discuss why they made that
            choice.

            Get on with it, Art. These folks
            have been through enough. Tom's
            agreed to talk to you just so
            you'll move on and leave them
            alone. Please try and respect that.

Travers: Alright. Thank you. So, Tom, we're
            here to talk a bit about Joe Harlan
            Jr. I know you know who that is.
            You guys have a long history.

Wise: Yes.

Travers: Since the altercation at Whole
            Foods, apart from the trial, have
            you seen Joe?

Wise: No.

Travers: What about his father, Senator
            Harlan?

Wise: I don't believe so. Possibly on TV.

But, in person, no.

Travers: As you probably know, Joe disappeared last month. He was on a trip to Miami. At least that's where he was last seen. You are aware of that?

Wise: I was not aware of that. I knew about a penis being found on his father's door.

Travers: You are not aware of Joe's travel or disappearance?

Wise: No. First I'm hearing.

Travers: How did you hear about the penis?

Wise: In the news, I believe. I think in the *Austin Herald.*

Travers: Did you discuss that news with anyone?

Riviera: Tom, don't share any discussions you had with me, Deb, or Kristy. Anything else is fine.

Travers: Why is that, Counselor?

Riviera: I want to be sure not to waive any possible privilege, spousal, etcetera.

Travers: But, with Kristy? What privilege would there be?

Riviera: He's not going to answer, Art. He's not on trial here. This is an accommodation. We'll choose the questions we answer and those we don't.

Travers: Okay. Tom, other than Deb or Kristy, did you discuss either the finding of Joe's penis or his disappearance with anyone?

Wise: Only you. When you came by my office and asked me about my recent travel.

Travers: Tom, when I came to see you, I'm pretty sure I didn't say anything about Joe.

Wise: No. You didn't. But I assume now that that's what you were asking for. What you were asking about. That's why you were interested.

Travers: When I came by your office, did you already know that Joe was missing, from some other source?

Wise: No.

Travers: Are you sure?

Wise: I'm sure.

Travers: Then why do you consider our meeting back then a discussion about his disappearance, if I didn't even mention it?

Wise: I recall thinking that it might have something to do with him in general. But I had no idea what.

It could have been about vandalism.
Or something else.

Travers: So, you were aware of vandalism
             involving Joe Harlan? What kind
             of vandalism? A penis nailed on a
             door,maybe?

Wise: Art, you're twisting my words.
             I'm speculating. I mean, I was
             speculating. When you came to see
             me, I assumed it had something
             to do with him. Or his dad. The
             only thing that connects us... you
             and me... We met... because of the
             whole situation with Harlan. I've
             never had any brush with the law
             other than that. When you showed
             up asking me... basically looking
             for my alibi, I assumed someone
             had done something to Harlan or his
             dad, and you were checking to see
             if it could have been me. I didn't
             think murder or anything extreme.
             Vandalism came to mind.

Travers: So, when I came to see you, did you
             or did you not think it was about
             Harlan?

Wise: I assumed it was, because that is
             the only thing we have in common.
             But I did not know that it was for
             a fact.

Travers: I'm guessing you know the rest of
             the story?

Wise: I'm not sure what you mean.

Travers: Shortly after I came to see you,
            his penis was found nailed to his
            father's front door. The door of
            his house in Westlake Hills.

Wise: Yes. I saw some of that on the
            news.

Travers: Would you call that vandalism?

Wise: No.

Travers: Did you know about that when we
            met?

Wise: No.

Travers: Are you sure, Tom? Because I'm
            getting the feeling that there's
            something you're not telling me.

Wise: I'm sure, Art.

Travers: How did you feel about it? His
            penis being nailed to his father's
            door?

Wise: Art. I...

Riviera: No, no, no. Hold on. Detective
            Travers, my client is here to
            answer questions about his
            whereabouts. About his alibi. That
            is what you asked for. That's why
            you said you wanted this interview.
            I've been fair, overly really,
            letting your questions run far
            afield. But you are not going to
            start asking him about how he feels
            about the guy or what allegedly

happened to him.

Tom, you only answer questions
about facts. About where you were.
That sort of thing. No questions
about your thoughts, or how you
feel... or felt. None of that.

Travers: Tom, I don't think that's fair.
            I just... I know how I would feel
            if it were my kid. I just... I
            mean, you punched the guy in
            public. I'massuming there was some
            satisfaction. Some feeling of just
            desserts?

Wise: Art. Ask me where I was. That's
            what I'm here for.

Travers: Tom, no one will fault you if
            you're happy about what happened to
            him.

Riviera: And, we're done.

Travers: What?

Riviera: You're totally out of bounds,
            Travers. Totally.

(A discussion was had off the record.)

Travers: You live kind of close to the
            senator's house, don't you?

Wise: I...

Riviera: Hold on. Hold on. Do we have the
            senator's address? Have you shared
            that with us, Art?

Travers: He lives in Westlake.

Wise: I was going to say. I think on
             the news they said Westlake. We
             live in Tarrytown. So, we're not
             neighbors, but... so...

Travers: Yes?

Wise: That's all.

Travers: So, you do live close?

Wise: I don't know where the house is if
             that's what you're trying to get
             at.

Travers: Tom, I've been able to verify your
             whereabouts from your dentist, and
             others. Around May 2. Did you have
             anything to do with the death of
             Joe Harlan Jr.?

Wise: No.

Travers: Do you know who did? Do you know
             who killed him?

Wise: No.

Travers: Where were you May 10th?

Wise: What? The tenth?

Riviera: Detective, I thought Harlan
             disappeared the second?

Travers: Do you recall, Tom? May 10th?

Wise: I... I think... Here, in Austin, I
           think...

Travers: Did you have any meetings? Anything
           I can check on?

Wise: I can check my calendar...

Riviera: Hang on a minute...I thought...

Travers: I am asking Mr. Wise about his
           whereabouts. We agreed that was
           fair game.

(Discussion was had off the record)

Wise: According to my calendar, I was in
           Austin May 10th. Regular workday.
           Had some meetings.

Travers: What was your first meeting of the
           day?

Wise: Let's see. I had to view a property
           with some clients. Downtown Austin.
           Around 10:00 a.m.

Travers: Nothing before that?

Wise: Nope.

Travers: So, how did you spend that morning?
           Before the meeting. Do you recall?

Wise: Could we take a break?

Travers: Sure, but first, if you could
           answer...

Riviera: Let's go off the record.

Travers: No. Wait. I want him to answer...

Riviera: We're taking a break. Restroom,
             Art. Five minutes.

(Off the record at 10:54 a.m.)

(On the record at 11:07 a.m.)

Travers: Can you answer my question now, Mr.
             Wise?

Wise: Could you repeat the question?

Travers: How did you spend the morning of
             May 10th?

Wise: Like most mornings. I got up, got
             ready for work, went into the office.

Travers: Did you at any time on the morning
             of May 10 go by or near the house
             of Senator Joe Harlan?

Wise: Can you define "by or near" please?

Travers: I thought you said you didn't know
             where he lives?

Wise: I... I don't... I mean... I know
             it's Westlake. But when you say "by
             or near," I don't...

Travers: Go on, Tom. Why'd you stop? You
             "don't..." what?

Wise: What I was trying to say is that I
             don't know how to answer if I was
             "by or near" because I don't know

where the house is. If you consider
driving through Westlake on my way
to work, which I do every day, as
"by or near" then the answer might
be yes, but I just don't know.

Travers: Then why didn't you just say "I
don't know"?

Wise: I guess I should have.

Travers: Tom, look. I know that you have
been through a lot. Your family has
been through a lot. I get it. Hell,
the jury got it, didn't they? When
you got tried for punching Harlan,
they let you off easy because we all
get it. No one would blame you.

Level with me, Tom. I know you know
something. What is it? Do you know
who killed him? Who nailed the
penis to the door? I can see in
your eyes that you know. Tell me,
Tom.

Riviera: Detective, way too many questions
in there. Could you pick one,
please?

Travers: Will you tell me what you know,
Tom?

Riviera: Are you alright, Tom?

Wise: (nods)

Riviera: Should we take a break?

Wise: No. I'm fine. There is nothing

to tell, Detective. If I knew
anything, I would tell you. But I
don't.

Riviera: You're not saying anything
           Detective. Do you want to take a
           break?

Travers: No. No. Just disappointed. I
           expected more from you, Tom.

Riviera: You are totally out of line,
           Detective.

Travers: A kid is dead, Harold. I'm trying
           to get to the bottom of it and your
           guy is lying to me. It's plain as
           day. You can see it too.

Riviera: We're going to take a break so you
           can collect yourself, Detective.

Travers: I don't need a break. Tom, do you
           know who Marty McCall is?

Wise: No. Wait - was he one of Harlan's
           roommates? I think I read about a
           lawsuit or something. Is that him?

Travers: Have you ever spoken to Marty
           McCall?

Wise: No.

Travers: Have you communicated with Marty
           McCall in any way?

Wise: No.

Travers: David Kim?

Wise: No.

Travers: Roy Cruise?

Wise: I... yes.

Travers: How do you know Roy Cruise?

Wise: I don't.

Travers: I don't understand.

Wise: I know who he is. I think I do.
            I think he's an alum - a Texas alum
            - runs a venture capital firm...
            something like that. There was
            an article in *The Alcalde*. The UT
            alumni magazine. Is that the guy?
            That's the name, I think.

Travers: You have a good memory. When did
            you see this article?

Wise: I don't know. Six months ago? A
            year?

Travers: That's a long time to remember a
            name from an article.

Wise: Is that a question?

Travers: Why did the name stand out? Why do
            you remember him?

Wise: Just his story. Transitioning
            from law to business. It was
            interesting.

Travers: Have you ever spoken to Mr. Cruise?

Wise: No.

Travers: But wait. I just asked if you had
             ever communicated with him, and you
             said yes. Which is it?

Wise: Oh. Communicated? No. I thought you
             asked if I knew him. Or knew of
             him.

Travers: Okay. Are you sure? Never spoken to
             him?

Wise: Pretty sure.

Travers: Why just pretty sure?

Wise: I talk to a lot of people. We're
             always looking for investors.
             I also go to a lot of alumni
             events. Is it possible I've spoken
             with him? Yes. But I have no
             recollection of having spoken to
             him, or of ever meeting him. I
             remember the name from the magazine.

Travers: Have you made any large cash
             withdrawals from your bank account
             lately?

Wise: I don't...

Riviera: Whoa. Detective. What does that
             have to do with where Mr. Wise
             was... with his alibi?

Travers: It's a simple question. Have you...

Riviera: That has nothing to do with my

client's alibi.

Travers: It has to do with opportunity, and that's a part of alibi.

Riviera: Opportunity? That's BS Travers, and you know it. Do you have any other questions about Mr. Wise's whereabouts?

Travers: I think that asking whether he or Mrs. Wise have moved any large sums of money is perfectly...

Riviera: Do you have any more questions about his whereabouts, or just the bank accounts? From where I sit, it looks like you're at the end of your notes.

Travers: The money is the last topic. If you'll just let me...

Riviera: No. Art. No. This is bullshit. We agreed alibi. Only alibi. If you've got evidence of something, probable cause, get a warrant. Get a judge to give you a warrant. But you're not... man, my guy's here trying to cooperate, and you're taking advantage. You're on a fishing expedition now.

It's not going to happen. Do you have a warrant? Do you?

Travers: I'm just trying to...

Riviera: Is my client free to go, or do you have a warrant?

Travers: There is no warrant.

Riviera: Then this interview is over.

(Off the record at 11:36 a.m.)

CHAPTER FORTY EIGHT

The incoming number on Eddie's mobile phone looked familiar, but he couldn't place it. Eddie was horrible about managing his contacts. Technology...

"Go for Eddie."

"Hello, Detective Garza. Veronica Rios here."

After the usual pleasantries, Veronica asked, "So, a little bird tells me that you're rattling Roy Cruise's cage again? Interviewing him in connection with another murder?"

"I don't know where you get your information, Ms. Rios, but I cannot comment on an ongoing investigation." Eddie sounded stilted, formal.

"Come on, Eddie, off the record?"

"I'm sorry, Veronica. I'd love to help you, but I can't," he responded, more casually—friendly.

The telephone conversation ended shortly after. Veronica was disappointed. Then, she wondered if Liz Bareto might know something about the new case.

* * *

Both Roy and David were wanted for questioning. Their lawyer, Mark Moran, had spoken to Detective Garza—a courtesy call. Garza said that neither was a suspect, but Moran wasn't buying it. The police clearly didn't have enough for a warrant or an arrest or they would have done that. But this was more than just an alibi check.

Moran sat Roy and David down and talked them through everything having to do with Harlan in detail. From what David and Roy told him, he understood the following.

David initially met with Procurex about a possible investment. Roy heard about TrueData and included drinks with Marty McCall on his trip up to Seattle. Given the pending lawsuit, Roy and David thought that if they brought Harlan on board, they could buy into TrueData on the cheap, then make the lawsuit go away and use Harlan's contacts to help grow TrueData, making a killing (money-wise) based on their low cost of acquisition.

David arranged for Harlan to come to Miami on the pretext of discussing a consulting position. They arranged for Harlan's flight, but he never showed up for the meeting.

David shared with both Roy and Moran the details of his interview with Garza. The only two areas of interest were the odd text message from Harlan about dinner and Garza's "Percy scenario."

Moran explained the rules of the game to Roy. He'd been through this before a couple of times for depositions in civil lawsuits, and once when he and Susie had been questioned by Garza about Bareto's death. The Bareto interviews had been very short, as both Susie and Roy had been out of state. Roy hoped that this interview would be just as short.

Moran cautioned against that expectation, however, as in this case Garza had already showed his hand by laying out a theory of the case, albeit a weak one, that included Roy.

David summarized for them what he remembered of Garza's scenario from his first meeting with the detective.

"Someone sets up dinner with Harlan. Then I back out and tell Harlan. Harlan goes ahead to have dinner with Mr. X—who I assume Garza was suggesting is Roy. Then Harlan writes to me, saying, 'Sorry you can't make it, David. See you tomorrow.' Then, Roy meets up with Harlan, kills him, et cetera."

"But I was in another country," Roy said. "The guy's nuts."

"He's fishing," Moran corrected. "It's typical. They have no evidence, so they're hoping you were somehow involved and that they can scare you—shake something loose."

Regardless, the rules of the game were simple.

Answer the question that you are asked.

Do not volunteer any information.

You can't be charged with a crime based on something you don't say. But lots of people get into hot water by opening their big fat mouths.

Less is more.

The interviews were scheduled for June 29th at Moran's office. Moran planned to bring in a court reporter to take a record of the interviews so that there would be no question later as to who said what.

As part of the preparation for the interviews, Moran asked Roy for copies of all documentation related to their Bimini trip. Roy brought in their immigration and customs paper copies. He also made copies of their passports, each stamped with their Bimini arrival date. Roy also brought credit card statements showing charges in Bimini, and made a copy of their slip receipt from Resort World Bimini—which showed charges for electrical and water hookups, as well as for their slip, from April 28th to May 5th. Roy mentioned that they'd been to the casino and were likely on security video, but Moran indicated that there was no point in going after that kind of information… yet.

* * *

The day of the interview, Roy and David walked over to Moran's office an hour before the scheduled start time for the interviews. David would be interviewed first, then Roy. There had been an argument between Moran and the detectives, as Garza wanted to interview Roy and David separately. Moran had already told the detective that that wasn't going to happen. In the end, they settled on allowing each to be present at the other's interview.

Roy and David met with Moran in a small conference room down the hall from where the interviews were to take place. Both Roy and David were asked to review the documents they had given Moran to refresh their memories.

At the agreed time, the three headed down the hall to the main conference room. Already present were a court reporter, seated at the head of the table, and on the side of the table facing the windows were Detectives Garza, Travers, and Pérez.

Roy later mentioned to me that he had noticed something odd between David and Detective Pérez. He couldn't quite put a finger on it at the time but he did figure it out later.

Interview of David Kim
06.29.18

Present:
Art Travers
Edward Garza
Rosa Pérez
Roy Cruise
Attorney Mark Moran
David Kim

(On the record. 10:12 a.m.)

Travers: Please state your full name.

Kim: David Kim.

Travers: No middle name?

Kim: No.

Travers: Your address?

Kim: Home or office?

Travers: Both.

Moran: Excuse me, sir. If you need to
              contact either Mr. Kim or Mr.
              Cruise, you have my number. Any
              other contact information is
              irrelevant. Please, move on.

Travers: I'm just trying to confirm what I
              have.

Moran: Then show them. Just show him.

(Mr. Travers passes a paper to Mr. Kim.)

Kim: Those are correct.

Travers: Where are you from, Mr. Kim?

Kim: I was born...

Moran: No. No. No. We are not going
            down that path. We are not doing
            a Genesis to present examination
            here. We are here as a courtesy
            to provide you with information
            regarding the unfortunate
            disappearance of Joe Harlan Jr.
            That's all we'll be discussing
            today.

(A discussion was had off the record.)

Travers: Mr. Kim, you are aware that
            we are here investigating the
            disappearance and likely death of
            Joe Harlan Jr., correct?

Kim: Yes.

Travers: When did you first meet Joe Harlan
            Jr.?

Kim: I've only spoken to him by phone.

Travers: Okay. When did you first speak to
            him?

Kim: That would have been on April 13th.

Travers: Was that a...

Kim: My calendar shows Friday.

Garza: Friday the thirteenth? How

appropriate.

Moran: You're way out of line, Detective.

Travers: Please, Eddie.

Garza: Just saying.

Travers: How did that conversation come
            about?

Kim: I called him.

Travers: Why did you call him?

Kim: To discuss the possibility of
            him working with us. With Cruise
            Capital.

Travers: What did you want him to do for
            Cruise Capital?

Kim: We...

Moran: Hold on. Hold on. Excuse me. Mr.
            Kim is not going to get into
            specific details about business
            strategy or plans of Cruise
            Capital. He'll discuss the
            role they had for Mr. Harlan at a
            high level, but he's not going to
            give away company secrets here.

Travers: Mr. Moran, if you're going to keep
            interrupting...

Moran: I don't plan on doing so but you
            need to understand that we are here
            to cooperate. We're here to assist.
            Mr. Kim is going to do that. But

he's not giving away company secrets. No corporate strategy. Go ahead, David.

Kim: Like I said. We wanted him to consult. We're interested in the government procurement space. He had knowledge about that space. So, we wanted to explore the possibility of him working with us in that regard. We... I think, yeah, that covers it.

Travers: Did you discuss that idea with Roy Cruise?

Kim: Yeah. We discussed it.

Travers: Whose idea was it? Yours?

Kim: I... That's a good question. Thinking about it now, I don't remember. I think it just kind of bubbled up. We were interested in the space. Thought he could be helpful.

Travers: So, it wasn't your idea?

Kim: It bubbled up. I don't know... It bubbled up.

Travers: Why did you arrange for Mr. Harlan to come to Miami?

Kim: Expense. It was cheaper.

Travers: Cheaper than what?

Kim: Than us flying to Austin.

Travers: But you go there a lot, don't you?
             Why not just include him in your
             next trip?

Kim: Timing. We wanted to meet with him
             sooner than that.

Travers: In the end, though, only you were
             going to meet with Mr. Harlan,
             correct?

Kim: No. It was going to be me and an
             other partner. Melody Kranz.

Travers: Melody Kranz?

Kim: Yes.

Travers: What about Mr. Cruise? Was he part
             of the meeting?

Kim: He was going to be at first, but he
             was out of town. Out of country.

Travers: When did you find out that Mr.
             Cruise was going to the Bahamas?

Kim: I don't remember. Before.

Travers: Before scheduling the visit? I
             mean, before arranging for Mr.
             Harlan to come to Miami?

Kim: I don't remember. I know it was
             before the meeting. I think it
             may already have been scheduled,
             though.

Travers: Had you planned to have dinner with

Mr. Harlan?

Kim: No.

Travers: Is that unusual?

Kim: No. We were meeting in the morning.
                At 10:00. I was planning on taking
                him to lunch.

Travers: Then didn't it seem strange to
                you when he texted you? Hold on.
                Here it is. Mr. Harlan texted you,
                "Sorry you can't make dinner. See
                you in the morning."

Moran: Excuse me. Is there a question
                there? Because you started, then...

Travers: You're right. Sorry.

Moran: ...you just read the text.

Court reporter: Please, gentlemen. One at a
                  time. I can't take you all
                  down if you talk over each
                  other.

Travers: Yes. Sorry. Let me ask again. Mr.
                Harlan texted you, "Sorry you
                can't make dinner. See you in the
                morning." You received that text?

Kim: Yes.

Travers: Didn't it seem odd to you? If there
                was no dinner, that he was writing
                to you about a dinner?

Kim: We discussed this before - I mean -

with Detective Garza.

Travers: I understand. I just need to make
a complete record. Could you answer
the question, please?

Kim: Yes. It seemed odd.

Travers: You responded to him: "Joe. Did you
mean to text me? What dinner? See
you at 10."

Kim: Yes.

Travers: Why did you wait so long to reply?
His message came in at 5:40 p.m.
and you didn't respond until almost
8:00 p.m.

Moran: Excuse me. Can we have the exact
time, please?

Travers: 7:57 p.m.

Moran: So, before 8:00.

Travers: Yes. Why did you wait so long?

Kim: I don't know. I don't recall
waiting. I think I responded when I
saw it.

Travers: Are you usually away from your
phone for that long? Almost an hour
and twenty minutes? I would think
a busy man like you has his phone
on hand and checks messages
regularly.

Kim: I don't know what to tell you. I

> responded when I got it. Maybe I had it on vibrate. I really don't remember.

Travers: What did you do on the night of May 2nd?

Moran: Just a second. Just so we can speed things up. The security logs... they show entries from Mr. Kim's security card. May 2nd, leaving the office at 5:37 p.m. He was probably driving when the text came.

Kim: I did drive home.

Moran: And we have a receipt from Sushi Maki. Order placed on Uber Eats. Receipt for sushi rolls, edamame, so on, delivered to the residence at 9:12 p.m. We also... well. That's all. Let's mark them as an Exhibit please.

(EXHIBIT A was marked.)

Travers: Can I? Thank you. Okay. So, you left the office at 5:37 p.m. Where did you go?

Kim: Home. I drove home.

Travers: In your car?

Kim: Huh?

Travers: I mean, you drove. You didn't take an Uber or...

Kim: Oh. Yeah. No. I drove my car.

Travers: Okay. Is there any security or
             surveillance in your building?

Kim: Camera. Yeah. We...

Moran: We have asked the building for a
             copy. We... I was going to say
             earlier. We have seen the footage.
             He... Mr. Kim is on the camera
             getting... arriving at the
             residence at 7:20, more or less. We
             are getting a copy.

Travers: Could I get a copy when...

Moran: Sure.

Travers: Thank you. Do you know what Mr.
             Harlan did in Miami?

Kim: No.

Travers: Well, you know what time he
             arrived, don't you?

Kim: How? How would I know that?

Travers: Well, you booked the flight?

Kim: Oh. No. I mean, yes, we did. The
             firm booked the flight. But my
             assistant did that. She
             coordinated it. I just told her
             economy. You know. Expenses. But
             she booked it based on his
             schedule. She coordinated with him
             to...

Travers: Yes?

Kim:	Nothing. That's all.
Travers:	So, your assistant would have spoken with Mr. Harlan?
Kim:	Yes.
Travers:	What is her name?
Kim:	Eve Jones.
Travers:	We may want to talk to her.
Moran:	We can discuss that off the record.
Travers:	Okay. So, going back to the text message.
Kim:	Yes.
Travers:	Didn't it seem odd to you that Mr. Harlan was texting you about dinner?
Kim:	That's why I responded the way I did.
Travers:	Doesn't it sound like he thought there was a dinner planned that included you? And that he found out you weren't going to be there?
Moran:	Objection. Mr. Kim...
Travers:	Objection? We're not in court.
Moran:	I'm sorry, but I thought I made it clear. Mr. Kim is not here to speculate about what Mr. Harlan thought or to interpret Mr.

Harlan's thoughts. Ask him about facts, please. Only facts. Don't speculate, David.

Travers: Are you going to answer the question?

Kim: I really don't know what he was trying to say. Like I said, that's why I responded how I did. I thought he was writing to someone else and texted me by mistake.

Travers: Someone else that he was not having dinner with that night, but seeing the next morning? When he was supposed to be with you?

Kim: No. We were meeting at 10. All he said was "morning." I dunno. Maybe he was having coffee with someone before.

Moran: Don't speculate, David.

Kim: Sorry. I don't know.

Travers: What happened when Mr. Harlan didn't show up?

Kim: What do you mean? Nothing. We couldn't meet with him without him.

Travers: Right. Stupid question. I mean, what did you do?

Kim: Oh. Well, I let Roy know that he was a no-show.

Moran: Hold on. It's... Here you go, sir.

(handing document to Mr. Travers)

Travers: I'm going to read this out loud for
             the stenographer:

             11:37 a.m.

             Kim: Harlan no-show.

             Cruise: Really? No phone call?
             Nothing?

             Kim: *Nada*. Called his mobile twice.
             Got voicemail. Didn't leave a
             message...

             Cruise: Give him a couple of hours.
             Maybe he went out and partied?
             Overslept?

             And then there is a thumbs-up
             symbol or icon from Kim.

Travers: Can you tell me what this is?

Kim: Text messages between me and Roy.
             Mine first, then back and forth.

Travers: When were the others sent? There's
             only a time for the first message.

Kim: Right...

Moran: That's what the phone shows. It
             only shows the first time stamp.

Kim: ...after.

Travers: Sorry?

Kim: I was saying. The messages were
           one right after another. Back and
           forth. Like in real-time.

Travers: Okay. So, you never met Mr. Harlan?

Kim: No.

Travers: At what point did you begin to
           suspect that something might be
           wrong?

Kim: His dad called and said that he
           hadn't caught the return flight.

Travers: Did you do anything after he didn't
           show for the meeting?

Kim: Other than text Roy? No.

Travers: Why not?

Kim: He didn't show up. I don't know.
           What else was there to do?

Travers: Give me a second.

(A discussion was had off the record.)

Travers: That's all I have.

(Off the record at 10:56 a.m.)

Interview of Roy Cruise
06.29.18

Present:
Art Travers
Edward Garza
Rosa Pérez
David Kim
Attorney Mark Moran
Roy Cruise

(On the record. 1:12 p.m.)

Travers: Please state your name.

Cruise: Roy Cruise.

Travers: You were born Roy Diaz, correct?

Cruise: Yes.

Travers: And changed...

Moran: Again, sir...

Travers: ...your name...

Moran: Excuse me. We are here to answer
            specific questions. My client and I
            would very much appreciate it if
            you would focus on the matter at
            hand.

Travers: Mr. Moran, I am trying to get
            background information. Just so we
            can confirm records.

Moran: Please move on.

Travers: Mr. Cruise, your twin died, leaving

> you an only child, is that correct...

Moran: No. I'm sorry. We're done. We're done here. Let's go, Roy.

(Off the record at 1:14 p.m.)

(On the record at 1:21 p.m.)

Travers: Mr. Cruise, let's discuss Joe Harlan Jr.

Moran: Please, let's.

Travers: Mr. Cruise. When did you first become aware of Joe Harlan Jr.?

Cruise: Sometime in April of this year.

Travers: How?

Cruise: We were looking at his company and TrueData as possible investments. I don't think we knew it was his company at the time.

Travers: Did you ever meet with him or Frank Stern?

Cruise: No.

Travers: What about TrueData? Marty McCall?

Cruise: Yes.

Travers: How did that come about?

Cruise: I was scheduled to be up in Seattle meeting with several companies. I was coming back on the

> late flight, so I had some time available in the evening. So, we set up drinks. I met Marty for drinks.

Travers: Was that before or after you became aware of Mr. Harlan?

Cruise: Before, I think.

Travers: What did you discuss with Mr. McCall?

Cruise: He was... is in the process of raising a Series A. He pitched me his company.

Travers: Did Mr. Harlan come up in the conversation?

Cruise: I don't think so.

Travers: What did you decide?

Cruise: About what?

Travers: About the investment.

Moran: No way, Art. Roy, don't answer that. We're not going to get into Cruise Capital's confidential business information. Investment decisions are a critical part of that. That's completely off-limits Mr. Travers. Completely.

Travers: Did you do any shopping while you were in Seattle?

Moran: What does this have to do with

anything?

Travers: Please answer, Mr. Cruise.

Cruise: No.

Travers: No, you didn't do any shopping, or no, you won't answer?

Cruise: No. No shopping.

Travers: Have you seen this phone number before? (handing witness paper) 206-576-1324.

Cruise: I don't know. It doesn't look familiar. But, you know, with smart phones - who knows phone numbers these days?

Travers: But you don't think you recognize it, correct?

Cruise: I don't recognize it.

Travers: Do you have any idea why it would be listed under your name on Mr. Harlan's phone?

Cruise: No.

Travers: Have you made any large cash withdrawals recently?

Cruise: No.

Travers: Would you have a problem sharing your financial records with us?

Moran: Hold on. We'll take that under

advisement. We can discuss that off the record, Detective.

Travers: Mr. Cruise, how is it that Mr. Harlan came up as a potential consultant for your company?

Cruise: I don't remember. I know we were interested in his contacts. And his father's contacts. As far as building a procurement business.

Travers: Were you planning on having dinner with Mr. Harlan while he was in Miami?

Cruise: No.

Travers: When did you decide to go to Bimini for the week of April 28th?

Cruise: My wife came up with the idea. I don't recall when.

Garza: You guys seem to have a convenient habit of being out of town when bad things happen.

Moran: Excuse me, Detective. We agreed to have only one person questioning the witnesses.

Garza: I'm just saying. Bareto dies; you're out of town. Harlan dies; you're out of town. Very convenient.

Moran: Sir, you are out of line, sir. Completely out of line. You should...

Travers: Hold on, hold on...let's just all
             calm down. Okay.

Garza: You're the one that's out of line,
             Moran!

Moran: Come on. We're done, Roy. We're
             done

Garza: Sure. Just run away. You can run,
             but you can't hide, Cruise.

Travers: Hold on. Mark, hold on. Eddie, stop
             it.

Moran: Come on, Roy. We're going.

(Discussion was had off the record.)

Travers: Mr. Cruise, do you know who Kristy
             Wise is?

Cruise: Yes. I believe she is the young
             woman that Harlan was charged
             with... raping, I guess... and then
             he was acquitted.

Travers: Have you ever met her?

Cruise: No.

Travers: What about her mother, Debra Wise?

Cruise: No.

Travers: And the father, Tom Wise, do you
             know him?

Cruise: No.

Travers: Are you sure?

Cruise: I believe so. I meet a lot of
            people. And I am in Austin quite a
            bit. But, I don't recall him.

Travers: Just to be absolutely clear, are
            you sure you have never met Tom or
            Debra Wise?

Moran: Detective Travers. This is getting
            repetitive. He's answered the
            question. Move on.

Travers: I just want to be sure, Mark. This
            is important. Mr. Cruise, are you
            sure?

Cruise: I am as sure as I can be. Like I
            said, I meet a lot of people.

Travers: Would it surprise you if I told you
            Tom Wise says he knows you?

Cruise: It...

Moran: Wait a minute... Wait a minute. If
            you have any evidence that shows
            that Mr. Wise knows Mr. Cruise, lay
            it on the table, now. Show it to
            the... to Mr. Cruise. If not, don't
            speculate. Roy, don't answer the
            question. He's already said he's
            never met them. That's his answer.
            That's it, Detective. Move on.

Travers: Mr. Cruise, could you just answer,
            would it surprise you to learn that
            Mr. Wise says he knows you?

Moran: Roy...

Cruise: I am going to take my attorney's
            advice on that. Do you have any
            more questions?

(Discussion was had off the record.)

Travers: Okay. Mr. Cruise. There are some
            unusual pieces of evidence tying
            you to Mr. Harlan. I'm hoping that
            you might be able to help me with
            getting to the bottom of them.
            First, your name was on his phone,
            listed under the Seattle number I
            showed you. Have you ever owned a
            phone with that number?

Cruise: No.

Travers: Do you have a captain?

Cruise: Excuse me?

Travers: You own two boats and a jet ski,
            correct?

Cruise: Ah. Got it. No. No captain.

Travers: You run your boats yourself?

Cruise: Yes.

Travers: Do you know any captain with that
            phone number?

Cruise: Which one? That Seattle number? I
            don't know any captains from
            Seattle. At least not to my
            knowledge.

Travers: Did you run your Sunseeker to Bimini?

Cruise: I did. We did. Susie and I together.

Travers: Did you take the jet ski?

Cruise: Yes.

Travers: Were you in Bimini all week?

Cruise: Yes.

Moran: Mr. Travers. Here is a copy of Mr. Cruise and Ms. Font's entry papers into Bimini. Also, here is a copy of their passports, stamped by the Bahamian government at time of entry. I also hand you a copy of receipts from Resort World Bimini for the slip, electrical, and water for their boat the entire week. Here is a copy of a receipt from an ATM – withdrawing cash on Bimini at the Resort ATM on May 3rd. Last, this is an AMEX credit card statement, redacted, but showing charges all week in Bimini.

Travers: Thanks for that, Mark.

Moran: They were there all week, Art.

Travers: As I said. Thanks for that.

Moran: Let's go ahead and mark all of these as an Exhibit?

(EXHIBIT A was marked.)

Travers: You didn't come back to Miami at
              all?

Cruise: From Bimini? At the end of the
              trip, obviously. But during the
              week? No.

Travers: Any idea why Mr. Harlan would have
              bought boat shoes the day he
              arrived in Miami?

Moran: Don't speculate, Roy.

Cruise: I honestly don't know, Detective.

Travers: Did you have any stomach problems
              when you were in Bimini?

Cruise: Stomach problems?

Travers: Yeah. You know... Diarrhea?
              Vomiting?

Cruise: Yeah. I did actually. I forget
              which day. I think it was
              Wednesday? Maybe Thursday? It
              started late at night, after
              dinner. Bad sashimi, I think. Went
              into the next day. Wow. You
              guys have really done your homework.

Travers: What were you doing that night? The
              night of May 2nd? What did you do
              that night in Bimini?

Cruise: If I have the timeline right, I
              think I was on the toilet a lot. If
              that was the night. But we went
              to the casino one night, too.
              Maybe we were there. The days kind

of run together down there. Island
time, you know?

Travers: Okay. But, this is important. Do
you remember that specific night?
May 2nd. What you were doing? Was
that the night you were sick?

Cruise: I think so. But, honestly, it's
been almost two months. I'm just
not sure. I'm sorry. I want to help
here, but it's been a while. I'm
just really not sure.

Travers: What about jet skiing?

Cruise: What do you mean?

Travers: You took a jet ski to Bimini,
correct?

Cruise: Yes.

Travers: Did you use it?

Cruise: Yes.

Travers: Before or after you got food
poisoning?

Cruise: Before, for sure. After, I don't
recall. Again, it's been almost two
months.

Travers: About six weeks, actually. What
do you remember doing the days
after you were sick? The balance of
your trip after you got food
poisoning?

Cruise: Again, Detective. Island time. I
             know we went to the casino - I
             think before. We went to the pool
             at the hotel. Dinners. But, it all
             kind of runs together, you know?

Travers: What if I told you that a witness
             says your jet ski was missing the
             day you say you were sick?

Cruise: I don't...

Moran: Hold on. Just a second. Which day,
             Detective? And what witness? If
             you want Mr. Cruise to review
             someone's testimony and comment,
             show him. But I am not going to
             have him responding to witnesses
             who aren't here based on your
             representation of what they
             supposedly said.

Travers: Will you answer, Mr. Cruise?

Cruise: Sorry, Detective. I have to follow
             my lawyer's advice.

Travers: Did you... Hold on.

(A discussion was had off the record.)

Moran: Detectives, would you like to take
             a break so you can talk in privacy?

Garza: Screw you, Moran.

Moran: Just trying to be cordial, Freddie.

Garza: It's Eddie, and you know it.
             Asshole.

Moran: Apologies, Eddie. You remind me of
              a Freddie I know.

Travers: Come on, guys. Cut it out. Mr.
              Cruise, did you do any fishing?

Cruise: When? That day? May 2nd?

Travers: No. In Bimini.

Cruise: No.

Travers: Do you have a fish knife?

Cruise: I... maybe? Yes? I don't know how
              to answer that. At home? On the
              boats? How do you define a fish
              knife? I guess the answer to the
              question as asked is "probably."

Travers: Okay. Yes, that's kind of broad. Do
              you have a knife on either of your
              boats that you use for gutting fish?

Cruise: There's not any one knife. Those
              things are pretty cheap. There's
              always a knife around.

Travers: Would you mind providing us with
              any knives you have on your boats?

Cruise: I suppose I...

Moran: Are you kidding, Travers? No, Roy.
              Don't say anything. We'll take that
              under advisement, Detective.

Garza: Gentlemen, may I? I think I can cut
              this whole thing short. Save us a
              lot of time?

Moran: We agreed on only one...

Travers: Eddie, we discussed...

Moran: ...person asking questions.

Travers: ...this.

Garza: I think I can short- circuit this.
              Get to the crux. Can we go off the
              record?

(A discussion was had off the record.)

Garza: Hello, Mr. Cruise. We've met
              before, correct?

Cruise: We have.

Garza: You're a pretty sharp guy, right? I
              mean, you've built this big
              company. Made a lot of money.

Cruise: Is there a question in there you
              want me to answer?

Garza: I'm getting there. You've done well
              investing in businesses, right?

Cruise: I can't complain.

Garza: Because you get them. Businesses.
              You understand how they work,
              right?

Cruise: I have a sense for that, yes.

Garza: So, look, just like you got a good
              sense for business, I got a good
              sense for murder. I can tell, in

my gut, when something's on the up-and-up, and when something's fishy. You like that pun, fishy?

Cruise: I don't understand.

Garza: Really? Fishy. As in fish knife. You don't understand? Because your lips are saying no, but your eyes are telling me that you do.

Cruise: Again, is that a question?

Garza: So, here's what I think happened. I think you killed this kid. You and your sidekick, the boy wonder over there. (indicating Mr. Kim)

I don't know if you did it. Or if he did it. Or if with all your money you hired someone to do it, but it was you putting it all together.

You got this kid Harlan down here to Miami, and you killed him, cut off his dick, and got it back to Austin where it got nailed to his dad's front door.

(Mr. Garza placed a photo on the conference table.)

You see that? That's his dick. It says "for Kristy" - Madame Court Reporter, that's a four as in the number 4, space, Kristy.

4 Kristy

You guys got the kid to come down
here. Hell - you paid his way.

We've got this kid texting your
sidekick about a dinner that you
both claim to know nothing about.
Strange, I think.

Then, we've got a Seattle phone
number saved on the kid's phone
using your name.

But, you got all sorts of decoy
stuff going on here, don't you, Roy?
Misdirection.

You got the dick in Austin with the
girl's name on it.

You got the Seattle number changed
to McCall's name. Someone changed
that. You? Your sidekick?

All very clever. (Mr. Garza clapped
his hands - applauding.)

Very well done. And, you know what,
I think you're going to get away
with it.

Very well planned. Very well
played.

But me, see, like I said, I'm good
at what I do. I got a good sense
for murder. And, sitting here
watching you, I think you did it.

So, just between us girls. Look me
in the eye, Roy, and tell me the

truth.

Come on, Roy. Just between us
girls. Did you kill him? Did you
kill Harlan?

Cruise: No, Detective Garza. I did not.

Garza: You're lying, Roy. I can't prove
it, but you're fucking lying.

Moran: Okay. That's quite enough. The
grandstanding is over. Roy, don't
say another word. Detective Garza.
Detective Travers. Get a warrant.
We've cooperated. We're here in a
spirit of cooperation, doing our
civic duty. This is abusive. It's
unprofessional. Mr. Cruise has
taken time out of his day, and Mr.
Kim, to cooperate. But, if you...

Cruise: Mark...

Moran: ...want to accuse upstanding
citizens falsely, get a warrant.
We're done.

Cruise: ...hold on. Hold on, Mark.

Moran: Roy, you are under no obligation to
do or say anything here.

Cruise: Yeah, I understand. But, I... I
want the officers here to get what
they need and leave us alone.

And, hopefully, find the person who
did this. That's why I just want to
be clear.

I want to respond to Detective
Garza's monologue. So the record is
clear.

Detective Garza, I wasn't even in
the country when all of this
happened. And David has a solid
alibi based on his building
security and all the other
documents he gave you.

Regardless of all of that, the
critical question here, Detective
Garza, Detective Travers, is why?

You're right. I am good at
business. When I look at buying
a business, I always want to
understand the company story.
Why is it going to succeed where
others have failed? What makes it
different? What drives the team? Why
are they doing what they're doing?

In startup companies, more than
ninety percent of the battle is
motivation, persistence. And that
comes down to belief. To faith.
You've got to believe in what
you're doing. You've got to have a
reason that makes you do it. A
powerful motivation.

In this current situation, I'd
advise the good officers here to ask
the same question. Why? Why in the
hell would David or I want this guy
dead? What is our motivation?

Like you said, Eddie, I'm a rich

guy. I don't need more money. I could quit work tomorrow and still live like a king for two lifetimes. So, there's no amount of money that would motivate me to kill someone.

So, why would I risk all of that – everything I have and everything I've built – to kill some kid I've never met?

The answer is – I wouldn't. There is no good reason.

Look, David and I saw the possibility for collaboration between us and this kid, Joe. Unfortunately, now we will never know if that was a real possibility.

But, for us, he was valuable alive as a consultant. Dead, as unfortunate as the circumstances may be, he can't help us. He's useless to us.

And the last thing we would want to do is make him useless to us.

I am very sorry, Detectives, if that doesn't fit with what you need or hoped to hear today.

But that is all there is.

And now, I am done.

(Off the record at 2:37 p.m.)

CHAPTER FORTY NINE

Eddie sat back in his chair. It was his favorite piece of furniture; a brown leather recliner. It was well-used. Comfortable. He'd taken many a good nap in this chair. He hoped that he'd die in it. Literally, in his sleep. Best way to go.

As a homicide detective, death is a part of everyday life. Death is your business. So, you tend to think about it a lot. And that inevitably leads you to think about your own death. Not the consequences—the "what will they do without me" part of death—but the actual event. The passage from a living being with hopes, worries, and aspirations to an inert corpse. The *how* of that transition is something that homicide detectives deal with more than people in any other profession. And, they think about it a lot.

When people think of death and careers (everyone does, don't they?) they tend to think of morticians or doctors.

This is not quite accurate, though. Morticians deal with death as a given.

He died of a heart attack.

She committed suicide.

This is death as past tense. By the time the corpse arrives at the funeral parlor, it's been dead a long time. Death has done its work and moved along.

Morticians don't deal with death. Death is an event. A moment.

Morticians deal with the aftermath. The preparation of the corpse; all the rituals. All of that really has nothing to do with death or even with the dead. The mortician's work is really focused on those who remain behind. Morticians basically throw a party for the living, aimed at helping the attendees adjust to a new state of affairs in which a usual member of the party is absent—permanently.

Doctors don't deal with death, either. For them, death is a failure mode. A bad outcome. Death is the enemy to be defeated. A potential lawsuit to be avoided.

Only homicide detectives deal with death in all its facets. Why would anyone want him dead? How did it happen? Where was the killer standing? How many knife wounds are there? Which one was fatal?

On his desk across the room there was a stack of four different case files. All homicides. Eddie was intimately familiar with each. He knew the ins and outs of every killing. He had researched and read up on the victims. He understood who had a motive, who would want to see these people die. Deconstruction of each victim's last days, hours, minutes—all leading up to the moment of death... that was Eddie's job.

Morticians and doctors? They know nothing about death.

Eddie had just finished reading the last piece of this particular file—Joe Harlan Jr.

He was in the process of closing out files. Dead cases, he called them. He liked the irony. Unsolved cases that would probably remain unsolved. As was his habit, before shutting a file down, he read through it one last time. You never know. Something might jump out at you. You might see things from a different perspective. It had never happened to him, but there's always a first time.

In this file, there was nothing new. Some anomalies. Some weird facts. But nothing more than circumstantial evidence pointing at foul play. Who did it? Who knows?

The biggest issue with the case was the complete lack of a crime scene. Odds were high that the kid had been killed in Florida. Assuming that to be true, alibis eliminated most of the prime suspects.

The Wise family was the most fertile area for investigation. Alibis, all. Every one of them in Austin. A contract killing? It was possible. Though there was no evidence to support the theory.

The father, the honorable Senator Harlan? He didn't stand to gain much from his son's death. Though he did stand to avoid potential future scandals. That's sort of an incentive. But, again, verifiably in Austin.

Frank Stern? No motive. In Austin.

Marty McCall—possibly a motive, financial—but even farther away, in Seattle.

Did Eddie think Cruise did it? Or him and David Kim both, together? He'd pushed them hard at their interviews to try and make them crack. They hadn't flinched.

And, as Cruise had pointed out—they had no motive.

That was the clincher. Although they had the closest ties to Harlan near the time of his disappearance, and there were some weird facts—that strange text message, especially—to put someone away for murder, you had to convince twelve people off the street that the accused wanted someone dead enough to actually make it happen. If you had no motive, no reason for killing, nothing to be gained, you had no case. No motive, no case. And with Kim and Cruise, as Cruise had pointed out, there was no motive.

That left Dr. Van der Put's Lust Murder theory. Someone unknown to Harlan singled him out for murder. And crucified the dick to show off how clever he was. It was possible. Stern had said most of Facebook knew about Harlan's travel plans. It was possible.

Eddie sighed, putting Roy Cruise's interview transcript back in the file.

Good news was, with the possible exception of his father, no one would miss Joe Harlan Jr. And no one thought that seeing his dick hanging from his own front door was a terribly wrong outcome. A bit crude, perhaps.

But Eddie thought of his little girl, asleep down the hall. If what had happened to the Wise girl happened to his little Maggie, God forbid, he wouldn't think twice.

As Eddie reached for the next file, his phone rang. The caller ID showed "Liz Bareto."

During the investigation of Liam Bareto's death, he'd gotten to know Liz. She'd been grieving. Everyone does it in their own way. He'd felt for her. Tried to be compassionate.

They had connected somehow. After the flurry of initial

activity investigating Liam's death, they'd continued to talk from time to time.

She still called him every couple of months, ostensibly for updates on Liam's case. There was never anything new to report. But they'd chat a little. Catch up.

She was a nice lady. Elegant. She didn't deserve what had happened to her.

Since the last time they'd spoken, he'd heard from Veronica Rios. Liz was still beating the bushes—still looking for justice. And in the meantime, all this Harlan mess had gone down.

Eddie thought for a second. While it would have been out of school to discuss an ongoing investigation, he had literally just closed the file on the Harlan case. It couldn't hurt to update Liz, seeing as Cruise was involved. It was odd—Cruise seemed to be out of town when people connected to him died. So, he decided to give her a full rundown on the Harlan case.

Eddie picked up his phone and stepped out on his balcony so as not to wake his wife. Maybe there was a little guilt at play there, too. Liz was an attractive woman in her way. Elegant.

"Go for Eddie."

CHAPTER FIFTY

In the physical universe, we have the law of conservation of energy, which essentially states that energy persists—it is neither created nor destroyed. It simply changes form.

The billiard table provides the classic example. Two balls sit on the table. One ball is pushed into the other. Upon impact, the first ball (the mover) transfers its energy to the second ball—the ball it hits. The second ball begins to move. The first ball abruptly stops. No energy is lost; it is simply transferred from the first ball to the second. This is how the physical world works, according to Newton.

But, if we consider, as physicists now claim, that everything is energy—everything we see, everything we think, everything we do—then it is just possible that this same law of conservation of energy applies to questions of morality. A conservation of moral energy, a maintenance of equilibrium... a balance exists and must be preserved. If an action is taken that disrupts that balance, then an action similar in kind and degree is required to restore equilibrium.

This seems instinctive to man.

In fact, the earliest existing expression of human law operated from this premise of moral conservation of energy. Hammurabi's Code, a Babylonian code of laws written in approximately 1750 B.C., states:

> 196. Anyone destroying the eye of another shall suffer the loss of an eye as punishment therefor.

> 197. If anyone fractures the bones of another, the guilty one, upon conviction, shall have his bones fractured in punishment therefor.

> 200. If anyone knocks out the teeth of one, his equal [in

rank], his teeth are to be knocked out, upon conviction of the offence.

Eye for eye... tooth for tooth.

It is called *lex talionis*—the law of talion—and it requires punishment of an injury by inflicting a similar injury on the offender, an injury similar in kind and degree.

Children instinctively gravitate to this concept of justice. We see this in play. One child is injured. He begins to cry. The offending party, seeking to avoid punishment by the adults, reverts to this primitive, instinctive sense of justice: "Hit me back. Then we're even." And note that, in this situation, it is not "the law" that imposes punishment. In fact, "the law"—the adults—is precisely what the offender wishes to avoid. The children seek to resolve the issue amongst themselves, and mete out punishment to restore balance and keep the game going.

Childhood games teach that any game is only as good as the rules that circumscribe game play. If the rules are followed, everyone has fun. However, when someone cheats, the game breaks down, the fun ends, and chaos reigns. Isn't this why, to children, being a "cheater" is such a bad thing? The cheater ruins the game for everyone.

If man is indeed Hobbesian, as Roy thinks, then he imposes laws on himself and his fellows because otherwise anarchy would reign. In a Hobbesian world, man creates civilization by creating laws. Laws establish order, and enforcement of laws aims to maintain order. In this type of world, the legal system enforces the laws to preserve itself—to protect its own existence.

Perhaps there is a balance that preexists man's law. And maybe all of our social rules—our laws—have been designed by us, consciously or not, with another aim in mind. Not to create balance, but to preserve it: to keep a preexisting moral universe from spinning violently out of control. Conservation of moral energy.

If that is the case, then the rules we "make" for society simply define a preexisting field of play. We do not so much make the rules as we simply recognize that they exist. We discover them.

And just as the rules preexist us, the balance that they protect also preexists. We can do as we like... within the boundaries. So long as we stay within the lines, the balance persists, and we are safe.

We are also free to break the rules, but only at a cost. A price must be paid for coloring outside of the lines. For every bad act that is committed, another similar action must be taken to rectify it—every bad act requires a punishment. There is a cost, and that cost must be exacted—whether by a legal system that steps in and imposes punishment, or simply by the players who take action to restore balance.

Murder, then, is doable. It can be committed without detection. It can be committed without the offender being subjected to the laws that punish such acts.

Yet, murder disturbs the equilibrium. It fucks with the balance. And, in life, when you fuck with the balance, bad things happen. And a price must be paid.

I'm not talking about a heaven and hell, fire and brimstone kind of price. *Please.* We finished with fairy tales and the Brothers Grimm back in Chapter Fourteen. No, I am talking about a more fundamental *what goes around comes around* kind of price.

Balance is disturbed. Balance must be restored.

Take our current situation. In our little game, there are three billiard balls on the table: Roy, Susie, and Deb. All three have been bad. All three have broken the rules. All three have been directly involved in murder. But, let's be honest. They've been bad to very different degrees.

If we proceed in reverse order of disappearance, we begin with Joe Harlan Jr., of whom we can say: *He needed killin'.* What he did to Kristy—his evil—was intentional, not accidental. Removing Joe from the playing field was fun. And the dick on the door thing—come on. Admit it. You kind of liked that part, too. Even a New Testament God would have a hard time faulting us for Joe's death and the penile crucifixion.

Liam Bareto is a little trickier. His act was not intentional. It was carelessness that caused the death of an innocent, Camilla. That same carelessness left Liam in a physical state where it was questionable whether he would have recovered his faculties or remained a vegetable. I have it on good authority that, in fact, he had sustained severe brain damage, and would have remained a vegetable for the balance of his life, had he even awakened from his coma. So, while he didn't need killing the way Joe did, the taking of what remained of his life—a vegetable state—balanced against the "evil" (a highly charged, religiously tainted word that serves as a substitute for the word "imbalance") he caused Camilla… well, an Old Testament God, at least, would probably pat us on the back for that one.

Arguably, both Joe Harlan Jr. and Liam Bareto were killed to restore the balance—because each of their acts had created imbalance.

No. The real imbalance in our little universe was caused by the death of poor young Joan. And, incredibly, if ever there was a stumbler of a murder, that was it. No planning. No premeditation. No well-conceived cover-up. No real motive. Stupid, really. Very true to life.

What happened to the piece of wood Deb hit her with? Was it found? Was there any blood on it? Was there any blood on the ground where her shoe was found? Did she really even die from that blow?

Or did she die from the fall?

Think about it. Two kids in the dark. Scared, trying to take a pulse. She was probably still alive when they threw her off the cliff. It was most likely the fall that killed her.

What had little Joan done wrong? Nothing, really. She didn't deserve to die. And, if we consider the "consequences" had she made it back to the main cabin and ratted Susie and Deb out, it wasn't even really worth killing her. Nobody is happy that Joan died. That just wasn't fun.

Joan's death was the murder of a child, an innocent, for no good reason.

And that, my friends, is a punishable offense. New Testament, Old Testament, Torah, Koran, Hammurabi. That kind of a killing fucks with the balance. It messes with the equilibrium.

CHAPTER FIFTY ONE

Sixteen Months After Harlan's Disappearance

Deb felt uneasy.

The call had come in earlier that day from UNKNOWN. She'd thought it was Susie. Big, big surprise... it was Roy. He was in Austin. And he needed to see her "about Susie."

"Urgently."

Deb was concerned—what could be going on with Susie that Susie herself wouldn't call her about? Maybe she was sick? Cancer? But Susie would have contacted her for something like that, right? So, it had to be something to do with Harlan.

It had been over a year since the senator's son had disappeared. After a few months of activity, everything quieted down. Deb couldn't imagine that anything new could have cropped up in connection with that.

Could it have something to do with Bareto? That was even further in the past. Even more remote.

She had considered calling Susie. She'd almost dialed her twice. But something told her to wait, to hear Roy out.

He'd suggested meeting at the Austin Animal Center in the parking lot. Just a quick, discreet talk.

Deb was intrigued. And, the more she thought about it, the more she liked the idea. She'd hatched a plan—brilliant in her estimation. This meeting was going to pay off big for her if it worked out. She'd discussed her plan with Tom. As usual, he'd hemmed and hawed, and waffled, and finally she'd just had to tell him what the fuck to do.

The location made sense. It wasn't highly trafficked. The odds of seeing anyone they knew were very low.

She parked as far away from the main building as she could without being obvious—about four spaces from the farthest parked car. A lone car in the farthest corner of the lot might attract attention, or get some notice, at least.

It was almost 7:00 p.m.

A car pulled into the lot and parked one space away, to Deb's left. It was Roy. Deb did a quick check. There was no other activity in the parking lot. She pressed a button on the console of her Jaguar and the locks snicked open.

Roy looked around discreetly. There was nobody else in the parking lot. He was in jeans and a short-sleeved shirt, with a light jacket to hide the Glock. He had brought it with him from Miami— in checked baggage (which is perfectly legal).

He walked around the front of Deb's car and slid into the seat next to her, closing the door.

"Long time, Roy," she said with a wry smile.

"Listen, Deb. I want to be quick," he said, snatching a glimpse at the parking lot around them.

"I'm listening," she said. Turning her body so that she could face him better.

Roy paused, holding her gaze for a few seconds before he began.

"Susie told me about you two. Everything. And I mean everything. As you'd expect, I was pissed at first. But, I get it. I mean, of course, I wish you'd both been more honest. You certainly had me fooled, back in Colorado. And, of course, I really appreciate the whole Bareto thing. Susie was in a bad place. I think she would have done something stupid if it hadn't been for you," Roy said, earnestly as he gazed out of the windshield. "So, thank you for that."

This wasn't what Deb had been expecting, and it irritated her. She pulled a face. "Roy, you said this was about Susie. That's the only reason I'm here. And you know better than I do, meeting like this isn't smart, so get to the fucking point, will you? What about Susie?"

"You're right. I'm rambling," Roy said, scratching the stubble on his chin and then looking Deb in the eye. "I want you to stay away from Susie. No more calls. No more contact. Nothing."

Deb scoffed and turned to the steering wheel. "Sure, Roy. I agree. Now, get the fuck out of my car."

That wasn't quite the response Roy was expecting. He was trying to get Deb riled. He had the sense that if he pissed her off enough, he might be able to get information from her. Information that he was convinced Susie was holding back.

If not, there was always the gun.

"I'm serious, Deb. Whatever you two had in the past, that's over. There are way too many connections between us now. It's too risky. I did the Harlan thing for Susie. Because *she* needed it. Now, I have to wonder if she really needed it for Camilla or for you. Regardless, I did it for her because I love her. But she's mine. We're done with you. Our debt is paid. So, now, please, just stay away."

Deb stared ahead, nostrils flaring. Then she shifted in her seat to face him once more. "Where the fuck do you get off telling me what to do? You don't know what love is, Roy. You think doing this little thing for her proves your undying love? It doesn't. You did it because you're weak, and always have been. You're not good enough for her. You never were good enough for her."

Roy's eyes flashed at her. "If I'm no good, Deb, then you're rotten. Rotten to the core. You convinced her to get me to kill Harlan, but you knew that if it went south, I'd be the one on the hook. And even that wasn't good enough for you. No. You had to add that bullshit—nailing the guy's fucking dick to the door. Why? He's dead. You almost screwed the pooch on that. And it was my ass on the line. But it's over, and I win. And you're going to be out of the picture from now on. Understand?"

"You know nothing, Roy Cruise. You failed Susie. You left her hanging. When she really needed you, you were missing in action. You have no sense of family. No sense of loyalty. Bareto killed your daughter, and what did you do? Go to work! What the fuck kind of a man does that? What kind of man cares so little for his own child? His own blood? Even Harlan had more balls than you!"

Deb paused, waiting for reaction. But Roy knew he had her fired up. He stayed silent, looking at her and shaking his head slowly from side to side.

Then he scoffed, "You're pathetic."

"Me? I'm pathetic? You're the walking definition of that. If Susie wasn't pulling your strings, you'd be nothing but a limp-dicked puppet."

"You failed your family, Deb. You failed to protect your little girl."

"Fuck you, Roy. You motherfucking asshole!" She poked a manicured finger into his chest. "Fuck you and everything about you!"

"You're so pathetic, Deb. You had to hang the dick on the door to appease your conscience. 'Cause you didn't have the balls to avenge your daughter. You know why? Because you only care about yourself."

"You don't know shit about me!"

"Sure, I do. The only thing that matters in your life is Deb. And it's a good thing, because no one else gives a shit about you."

"Oh, fuck you! You don't know anything about me. And you have no clue who you're married to, Roy. You know nothing! And sure, I care about Suze because we're meant to be together. It's me she loves, not you, and it's always been me. You're just an afterthought. A meal ticket."

"Am I? Seems to me she's made her choice."

"Choice? You think we had a choice? You think she chose you? If it hadn't been for that little bitch at camp, we'd probably be together right now!" Deb was leaning into him now. He could feel the heat of her breath on his face as she shouted.

"What? What little bitch?" he asked, surprised. "What are you talking about?"

"Well shit, Roy. She didn't tell you?" she spat. "You stupid motherfucker! And you think she loves you?" She raised her hands, waving them in unison with her mocking in a sing-song voice, '*Oooh, Susie loves me. She told me everything, everything...*' Obviously not.

"But I'll tell you..." she said, eyes narrowing, maliciously. "It was love at first sight. Me and Susie. We knew it the moment we met. We could barely keep our hands off each other. And it was fucking amazing! I bet you've never had that kind of sex with her. You ever heard her whimper when she comes? Have you? I bet not.

"We were meant to be together right from the beginning, but then that little bitch came along threatening to ruin everything. She was going to turn us in. I mean, I didn't give a shit. She was just another self-righteous little cunt. I just wanted to shut her up. Did I want to kill her? No. But, hey, shit happens.

"And Susie stuck by *me*. She helped *me* cover it up. We got rid of her body together. It's always been *me*, Roy. Don't you get it? We were meant to be together. You're just window dressing.

"When we reconnected on the cruise ship. That was amazing. I swore I'd never lose touch with her. I never will. And when all this blows over, we'll be together again. And, you'll be nothing but a bad memory. Now, please get the fuck out of my car!"

Roy was silent.

"Her... her name was Joan," he stammered, eyes welling with tears.

"What? Yeah. So?"

"The little cunt, Deb. She had a name. Her name was Joan. Joan Diaz."

CHAPTER FIFTY TWO

The shock of Joan's death—finding out what really happened to her—hit Roy, hard. When he first told me about it, his pain was obvious.

Ironically, he didn't want to discuss it. I think he just wanted to say it out loud. He wanted someone else to know, and to know that he knew. And I say someone else, because he didn't tell Susie— not right away. That was his cross to bear.

Roy kept his knowledge of Joan's death—and Susie's involvement in it—from her, for some time.

What he didn't know was that at around the same time, Susie learned a secret too. About him. One that she planned to confront him with. She just needed to find the right moment.

Shortly after his confrontation with Deb in Austin, Roy sprung a surprise on Susie; a vacation in Spain. She was ebullient.

Susie had been out shopping for the trip when, as she was driving home, her phone rang. It was Roy.

She pressed a button on her steering wheel and spoke to the cabin, "Hey, babe."

"Hey, Suze. You coming home soon?"

"Yep. I'm in the car. Should be there in about fifteen."

"Okay. I'm starting up the grill. David and Rosa are already here. See you soon!"

"Love you. Bye."

Susie was happy. Life was falling back into place. Things were working as they should. And her marriage to Roy had never felt so strong. There was no doubt that everything that happened had brought them much closer than they ever had been before.

The last year had been incredible. Their lives had completely changed. They were going out again, attending social functions. Things that neither of them would ever have entertained after Camilla. And they travelled, extensively.

It bonded us at a whole new level—one that's really hard to understand unless you've been there.

Susie would not recommend murder therapy without reserve; it wasn't for everyone. Still, given the totality of their circumstances, she felt that it had worked for them.

Back home, she hurried in the front door laden with bags from her shopping and called out "Hellooo!"

"In the kitchen, Suze!" Roy responded.

Susie dropped her bags in the foyer and tossed the car keys in the key bowl. She could hear Roy and company laughing in the kitchen. Before joining them, she decided to quickly flip through the mail.

She stopped when she reached a large manila-colored envelope. It was addressed to her, from a law firm in Austin, Texas.

She ripped it open. Inside, there was another smaller envelope. Her name was written on it in blue ink. She recognized the handwriting instantly.

She detoured to the study, where she closed the door, leaned up against it, and read.

July 12, 2018

Dearest Susie,

> *I'm dead.*

> *If you are holding this letter, it's because that's what's happened. I asked my lawyers to send it to you as a part of my last wishes. I asked that it be sent unopened, but you can't trust anyone these days. So, I can't tell you everything I'd like, but I think you'll understand, all the same.*

> *I hope that this letter finds you happy. You deserve to be.*

> *I have to say that I've enjoyed my life. I've been fortunate to have found love, and to have been loved in return. You know what I mean.*

> *There are obviously things that I would change about my life— things I did early on that probably kept me from enjoying your love and*

friendship as much as I could have. But that's all water under the bridge.

I just wanted to send you a note to tell you that I love you. That I will always love you, no matter where I am.

I'm glad that I was able to help you out when you needed it.

And I thank you from the bottom of my heart for returning the favor. You and Roy both. I can't imagine all that it took. But it's made a big difference in all our lives.

If you can, keep an eye on Kristy for me. She's not like us. She's fragile. And on Tom. He means well, and he tries hard. But he's no Roy.

Well, that's it. I've never been much of a writer. You know that.

Big kiss, girl. Be good. And sorry for all the headaches.

I hope I went in my sleep. I always thought that's how I would want to go. Not that I deserve to. But it would be nice, you know?

Love always,

Deb

It was a joke. A sick joke. It had to be.

Susie wiped the tears from her eyes.

Susie crossed the room, opened the safe, and pulled out her burner laptop. She opened the TOR browser and searched "Debra Wise obituary."

9/17/2019

Debra Wise. Mother, wife, friend. Debra was taken from us unexpectedly. She was a loving mother ....

No details as to how.

Susie refilled the search bar "Debra Wise dead Austin" and hit ENTER again.

9/12/2019

Alleged Rape Victim's Mother Found Shot

A woman found shot dead in her car outside the Austin Animal Shelter this morning has been identified by police as Debra Wise. Police suspect the victim was killed in a robbery gone bad.

Mrs. Wise was the mother of Kristy Wise, who was allegedly assaulted by Joe Harlan Jr., son of State Senator Joe Harlan, in 2015. Harlan Jr. was tried for the assault and acquitted.

Harlan Jr. later went missing while in Miami, Florida on business. His whereabouts remain unknown, though he is presumed dead.

Mrs. Wise was found dead in her car by an officer on patrol. She was not known for her love of animals, and police refused to comment on what the mother and wife was doing at the shelter.

Wise suffered a single gunshot wound to the head that police say killed her instantly...

The story went on, but the rest was unimportant. Deb was gone. Susie was stunned, and she broke down.

She cried as she had for Camilla. Deep, heart-wrenching sobbing. A part of her was missing, gone.

Poor Deb...

Susie read the letter again. It had been written shortly after the whole Harlan thing. Well over a year ago.

Had Deb intuited that something was going to happen? Or was there a prior version that she'd updated after Harlan?

For Susie, it felt like someone had torn another chunk from her. As if she had lost another member of her family.

Their relationship had always been long distance. They'd never been able to be friends, or more, the way normal people were. That had been impossible after Joan, at least for Susie. Yet, in their own way, they had been closer than they might have been otherwise. Closer friends than most people could hope to have in a lifetime.

Susie carefully folded the letter.

She took it and the burner laptop, and put them back in the safe. She put the letter in the lockbox where she had kept Bareto's hospital band and the photo of her and Deb at camp.

All the box contained now was the letter from Deb.

As she was closing the safe, Susie paused. Something seemed wrong. A bit off. She wasn't quite sure what.

She stood there looking at the contents of the safe thinking.

And then she saw it. Or, better said, she didn't see it.

Roy's Glock 26. The handgun that always sat on the center shelf in the safe. It wasn't there. It was gone.

Her legs buckled underneath her, but she caught the wall for support. After a few moments, she moved over to the bar and poured herself a scotch. She drank it all in one gulp. Then, she pulled her mobile phone from her purse and collapsed on the sofa.

She opened her calendar and navigated to 9/12/2019—the day Deb was shot.

Roy Traveling — Austin

She left her seat and made for the kitchen. She would ask him. That was all. She'd know. Just by how he reacted.

As she entered the kitchen, she hesitated. Roy was standing on the other side of the island. David Kim and Rosa Pérez were there with him, drinking beer.

David and Rosa had started dating shortly after his interview regarding Harlan's disappearance. It was a complication, to be sure.

Rosa was laughing at something one of the two men had said.

David saw Susie first. "Hey, TV lady!" He smiled.

Roy looked up at her and smiled, "Hey, babe."

She looked at him. His face registered that she'd been crying. It also seemed to her that he knew why.

She could ask him.

He might tell the truth. He might lie.

She thought she'd be able to tell the difference. Then again, would it matter? Deb was gone. Water under the bridge. The damage was done. Susie couldn't get her back.

If he didn't want her to know, he would never tell. That, she knew. But could she figure it out? Could she see through him? Before Harlan, she'd have answered yes, definitely. Now, she wasn't so sure.

She had seen him in action. Roy was not a stumbler. He was a planner. If he'd done it, he'd planned it. And if he'd planned it, there'd be no proving it.

Deb was gone, but Roy was still here and no one would take

him away from her. Not for Harlan. And not for Deb.

Because of all of *Roy's Rules for Murder*, he knew the most important one.

No singing bones.

EPILOGUE

Now you know how the whole mess began. Well, at least you understand the background. You see, it didn't end with Deb's death. That was just the beginning.

For the rest of the story to make sense, I need to tell you a bit about me. My involvement in all this began innocently enough. Just another day at the office. A pretty average day, in fact. A Thursday. I always reserve Thursdays for new patients. It was time for my three o'clock appointment, and in walked Susie Font. Veronica Rios had referred her to me.

It was just a few months after Camilla died. Susie was struggling to deal with Camilla's death. She was sleeping over eighteen hours a day. She was neglecting herself and her marriage. She was blaming herself. She was blaming Roy.

She was a mess.

Clinically, she presented anxiety, empty mood, and feelings of hopelessness, coupled with pessimism and irritability. In lay terms, she was a mother grieving the untimely loss of her child. Nothing out of the ordinary.

Diagnosis—Adjustment Disorder with mixed anxiety and depression, ICD: F43.23.

I told her at the time, filching from Lewis Carroll—one of my favorite authors—*Susie, you're entirely bonkers. But, I'll tell you a secret. All the best people are.*

She laughed through her tears. It seemed to make her happy. I seemed to make her happy.

We connected.

She was distraught. But, under all the pain, there was

a tough, resilient woman. I could tell. There was still a sense of humor in there, fighting the depression. She was self-aware. She was reflective. She knew that she needed help and she was open to guidance. In short, there was hope and a clear path to adjustment and resumption of normal life activities.

And so began our work together. We met regularly—thrice per week initially. At my suggestion, she started meditation exercises. I spoke to her doctor, with her consent, who prescribed some medication. Light stuff—Xanax—to take the edge off.

She tried it, but told me that she didn't like the way it made her feel. She didn't use it much. I found out later what she did with the leftovers.

She fought the depression. She also tried to communicate with her husband, Roy, to open channels.

I was very impressed with Roy. He was supportive. Very concerned. Open to any solution. I was pleased by his devotion to her. He was extremely diligent. Followed up on everything we discussed. They even attended a few group sessions with other grieving parents. We made progress. Slowly at first.

Eventually, we made breakthroughs. Bit by bit, Susie stabilized. She seemed more content. She left her job in television. She took up advocacy work to help her cope with the loss of Camilla. To make her feel that she was *doing something* for her daughter. She called it "vocational therapy."

After almost three years of working together, I felt that we were coming to a point where we could begin to reduce the regularity of our meetings.

That's when I started to see another side of Susie. I don't know if she was initially reticent to share everything with me, or if she was simply toying with me. Seeing if I could—when I would—figure it all out.

She started dropping small clues, hints, during our sessions. A little here. A little there. As I started to piece it together, well, at first, I couldn't believe it. When I was pretty sure, and prepared to confront her, she beat me to the punch.

She confessed. She told me that the peace she had found—

and the stability I believed I had helped her achieve—was the result of her having orchestrated the murder of Liam Bareto.

She was a bit vague at first. She told me that she had connected with "a friend"—someone in "that sort of world," and that she had arranged it all. I was shocked. I couldn't imagine her taking such drastic steps. I didn't press for details, though in the end she told me everything.

At the time, naively, I told Susie that she should consider surrendering herself to the authorities.

She laughed at me. It was not a Lewis Carroll kind of laugh.

She was also quick to remind me of my oath, and my obligation to maintain all of our discussions confidential, as they'd all been had in the context of Susie seeking medical treatment—mental health treatment.

Don't forget that Susie trained as a lawyer. She made it perfectly clear to me that she was aware of her rights, and my duties as a psychologist.

I refreshed myself on the law, just to confirm what I already knew. She was right. She had confessed a past crime. I was prevented by the law, and my oath, from disclosing anything.

In fact, I was obligated not to.

I did, however, adjust my prior diagnosis of Susie to include a moderate amoral personality disorder. ICD: F60.3

Even then, I believed, maybe convinced myself, that what she'd done to Bareto was situational. And in my professional judgment at the time, given the circumstances, Susie didn't appear to present an ongoing danger to herself or others.

I missed the boat on that one.

Literally.

I clearly recall Susie and Roy's trip to Bimini about two years after she confessed to the Bareto killing. It wasn't long after the third anniversary of Camilla's passing, shortly after the interview she did on Roni's radio show. It was a time that I thought might be challenging for Susie.

You see, patients recovering from trauma sometimes relive the incident at certain trigger points. A trigger can be a similar situation or event. Sometimes even a smell can recall a past trauma. Obviously, the anniversary of a traumatic event can be a major trigger.

When Susie told me about her plans, I thought the vacation in Bimini was a good idea. Time to disconnect. To heal.

Susie passed that anniversary without incident of any sort that I could detect. None that she shared with me, or that was apparent in our sessions.

At that time, I thought that her mental health was strong. While the Bareto confession was disturbing, I had concluded that what she'd done was contextual, and that Susie had—through our work together—moved on. I believed that we might begin to cut down on our sessions, maybe even stop altogether. Although, if I'm perfectly honest, there's no doubt that a part of me just wanted to wash my hands of her.

In retrospect, I think that in some way I must have been telegraphing this to Susie. Just as she had the first time I'd considered reducing our time together, Susie once again had additional information to confess.

It was at this point that Susie told me all about Joe Harlan Jr. This time, I did ask her for specifics, and she didn't hesitate. She walked me through it all in detail.

Needless to say, this second confession was really discouraging. I felt like I was useless to her, medically. The Bimini murder was committed *while she was under my treatment.* She killed Harlan *after I had determined* that she was not a threat to others. Was I even doing her any good?

About a week after Susie's big Harlan confession, I received a visit—unannounced—from Roy. He was very pleasant. He told me that Susie was really happy with me and with our work together. He said that he had seen tremendous improvement in her, in their relationship, and in their life as a whole. He asked me to keep up the good work, and said that he believed that Susie "should continue to benefit from my support for years to come."

He also told me that he was interested in "a bit of therapy" himself. He said that he had found our previous joint sessions—his and Susie's—very helpful and thought maybe he could benefit from more regular "contact."

Something made me think that it wasn't a good idea to say "no."

And so, my work with Roy began soon after. In our early sessions, he complained mainly of work-related stress. We discussed career, marriage, family life. All very generic.

Once he got comfortable with me, he opened up.

He told me that he didn't want to talk about his youth, and that he thought a lot of what I did was "bullshit," but that he was trying to keep an open mind. He went on to share that he was having anxiety issues related to killing Harlan. He described having what sounded to me like a panic attack at a restaurant.

As I slowly and carefully delved into Roy's past, I concluded that many of his issues stemmed from his parents' divorce and the loss of his twin sister. Relationships between twins are by default extremely close. Roy lost Joan just as he was becoming a teenager, and then lost his parents shortly after as a result. Two terrible traumas at a critically formative moment.

We delved further into this. Bit by bit, I felt that we made progress, slowly healing these past wounds.

And that's when things took a turn for the worse.

I was stupefied, speechless when Roy shared with me that Susie was involved in his sister Joan's death. He told me how he had learned this in a face-to-face meeting he'd had with Debra Wise in Austin. When I tried to explore the subject further, he asked me to "let it be"—for now. He said that he was still "processing."

As you can imagine, I worried about the potential impact that this "processing" might have on their marriage. I really worried about what Roy might do vis-à-vis Susie.

Then, Susie sprung on me that Deb Wise was dead, and that she (Susie) believed Roy had killed her. She even had me Google Mrs. Wise's obituary, and then shared with me the calendar entry on her phone showing that Roy was in Austin at the time. She also told me about the missing gun.

I obviously didn't tell Susie what Roy had told me about

meeting with Deb, but what Susie shared was consistent with Roy's confession to me regarding how he'd learned the details of Joan's death.

For me, this had strayed way beyond the bounds of normality—not to mention morality.

These two killers were now keeping secrets from each other. Pretty nasty secrets. I was worried that they might "hurt" each other—physically I mean.

And, of course, I started to fear for my own life. I was, after all, the sole custodian of their respective secrets. The only so-called *loose end.*

At that time, right after Deb's death and her revelation regarding Joan, the position that Susie and Roy had put me in began to weigh very heavily on me. My own anxiety increased exponentially.

Without divulging names or inappropriate details *in any way*, I discussed my feelings and impressions, and the impact of all of this on my own well-being, with my therapist. I explained that I was not comfortable treating two active murderers.

I wanted out.

In the end, we (my therapist and I) reluctantly agreed that the best course of action was to continue to maintain my physician-patient relationship with both.

This conclusion rested on two points.

The first was about professional ethics. I was more familiar with these two people than another physician could hope to become without significant investment of time and development of trust. My therapist thought I should stick it out since I was the only one with any chance at making headway and hopefully preventing further killings. While I didn't disagree, that standing alone wasn't enough to keep me involved.

What made the decision for me was the second reason. We were concerned (my therapist agreed with my assessment) that if I terminated their treatment, I might be putting myself in danger. If I was no longer useful to them, but still knew all their secrets, my life might be in jeopardy.

There was no way around it. I was stuck with them.

So, I worked to manage my own stress issues through therapy and with medication. My therapist also recommended that I write this journal as a form of therapy.

In this journal, I've included everything I've learned from Susie and Roy through their confessions. I have also included supplemental information gleaned from my own research.

I must admit that I've found the rewriting of Roy and Susie's revelations cathartic. Writing has helped me to cope with the anxiety that continuing to treat Roy and Susie has generated.

And, while that is all well and good, this journal has also served another purpose—and one that, to me, is even more important.

Insurance.

You see, Roy stopped by not long ago to thank me "for everything." He does that. Random acts of gratitude. He brought me a bottle of Macallan 18. And he seemed truly grateful. In fact, he ended by saying that we should all get together and go out on his boat sometime.

I didn't have the guts to ask which one.

After thinking on it, though, I sent Roy a thank you note. It read as follows:

Dear Roy,

I wanted to send you a long overdue "thank you" for the bottle of scotch and for the kind invitation to go out boating. It is a pleasure to work with you and Susie. I am very pleased with our progress and am happy to be here for both of you for as long as you desire.

However, please rest assured that, should you ever wish to change therapists, I have taken copious notes to ensure a seamless transition in treatment. Furthermore, please know that should anything happen to me, I have taken great care to ensure that these same notes fall into the right hands, in order to ensure your continuity of care.

Warm Regards,

C.J. Martin, PhD

This journal was to be my *buried bone*, and if something

"happened" to me, it would *sing*. But, if no one ever read it, which I hoped would be the case, that would mean that we—Susie, Roy, and I—all lived happily ever after.

That was my initial plan.

As a psychologist, however, I am not a big believer in happily ever after.

I strongly believed that if I was going to ensure that I survived Susie and Roy, that they didn't want me dead, I needed something more. More than just the threat of disclosure if something "happened" to me.

I was sick of feeling beholden to them.

I was sick of living in fear.

That's when a solution occurred to me.

And that's where the real story begins.

Turn the page for an exclusive preview!

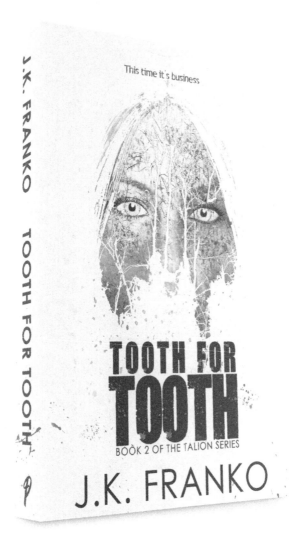

This time it's business

J.K. FRANKO

TOOTH FOR TOOTH

TOOTH FOR TOOTH

BOOK 2 OF THE TALION SERIES

J.K. FRANKO

Book 2 in the Talion Series
OUT HALLOWEEN 2019

PROLOGUE

I have come to believe in choices—the power of decision.

Though I have said elsewhere that, as a psychologist, I am not a big believer in "happily ever after," my thinking has evolved.

Happiness depends on your point of view.

Living "happily ever after" is a choice, because ultimately, happiness is a choice.

This is a scientific fact.

From a psychological perspective, happiness is best thought of as an emotional state brought about by positive thoughts, feelings, and experiences. We psychologists refer to it as a "positive affect."

A significant percentage of what makes one happy is controlled by the individual. Indeed, some research indicates that only 10% of happiness is based on circumstances—external events. A much greater part of happiness depends upon how one processes external events.

How you see, process, and react to reality determines whether or not you will be happy.

This means that our experience of reality ultimately is what we choose it to be.

For the first time in years, I can finally say that I am happy. It has not been for want of trying. But, at first, it was difficult to process everything that I was exposed to in a way that made me happy.

After all, it's hard to put a positive spin on murder.

At first, it was impossible for me to see what Susie and Roy were doing through rose-colored glasses. I found it hard to accept that two seemingly normal people could be capable of such evil. That my patients, one of whom I had treated for years, were capable of murder.

Try as I might, I found it hard to compartmentalize the information. Their actions haunted me.

But, even more so, I was overwhelmed by the fear that they might turn on me.

I was not just a loose end.

I was *the* loose end.

They had shared everything about their crimes with me—and only me. And I mean everything, in meticulous detail. It was no secret that I was the weak link. The one thing that could bring them down.

Being in such close proximity, and in the confidence of, two active killers was very disturbing to me.

Try as I might, I could not initially find a way to be happy with these circumstances.

But, as I said before, happiness is a choice. Who we are and what we do with our lives is a choice.

We create our happiness.

This is the key nugget of wisdom I have taken away from all of this.

We are not what happens to us.

We are what we choose.

Ultimately, it was a choice that I made that finally brought an end to my torment. That choice put me in a place where I can once again be happy.

For you to understand that choice, I must share with you something that happened years ago at an ostensibly happy event. I say ostensibly because it was a happy night for almost everyone concerned. There were two people there that night who figure in our story—in my story.

The first is Sandra Bissette. For her, the night in question was the beginning of what would become a successful career in politics and the law.

For the other, Billy Applegate, the night would end in tragedy.

1974

Everybody loves a party.

And there's nothing quite like a political party. I don't mean "political party" as in Democrats or Republicans. I mean political party as in a party about politics: in this particular case, an election night celebration.

What do you need to throw a successful party? Well, the usual: food, drinks, and a lot of music of course, but most importantly? People. And it's not just the "who," but the "why."

People best enjoy a party when it has a purpose. Wakes, birthdays, and anniversaries all have a purpose and feature a guest of honor, but an election night celebration is a completely different animal.

An election night party isn't about any one person or couple. It's about a group of people: the guests.

The people who gather to watch election results are all of one mind. Of one spirit. They are like pack animals. All of the same skin. All focused on the same outcome. They all share the same heroes and the same enemies.

If their candidates win, they win.

In a sense, an election night party is similar to a sports-watching party. But in sports, when one team wins, there is no benefit to the fans.

A win in politics, however, equates to real-world changes for constituents—such as tax benefits, government spending, judicial appointments. And, if we're talking about a high-level election party, a national election where candidates and top donors are present, then the stakes are even higher. A victory not only means change but, more than likely, money for the victors.

This particular election party took place in Maryland in 1974. To be precise, because I can be, this party was held the night of the 1974 midterm elections, on Tuesday, November 5th.

It was a good year for Democrats. This was the first national election after Watergate. Nixon's resignation had severely damaged the Republicans' chances in the election. Gerald Ford was just three months into his presidency, having taken over from Richard Nixon a few months earlier. And, of course, having pardoned Nixon in September, Ford destroyed his chances for re-election and added to the national animus against Republicans.

This election-night party took place in a spacious colonial-style home that had been decorated in red, white, and blue, with American flags hanging from the windows and banisters. It featured a large living and dining area. The kitchen was good-sized and well-equipped. There was a generous backyard with a comfortable deck and a terrace around the pool. All of the four bedrooms—aside from one guest bedroom—were upstairs.

There was a "pin the tail on the donkey" game set up near the bar, for those with a sense of humor. No one actually played.

This house belonged to Daniel and Annette Applegate, two proud and active members of the Democratic party in Maryland.

Dan's family had always been active in politics. His grandfather had been a state representative. His father served as county judge for most of his career. Dan—born Daniel Parsons Applegate IV—was the fifth generation of Applegates admitted to the Maryland bar. While he would never actually serve in public office, he understood well the value of political contacts and actively cultivated them.

This party was a part of that effort.

Dan was dressed in a beige suit with the large lapels, oversized shirt collar, and wide tie that were fashionable at the time. The tie was burgundy. Annette was wearing a pant-suit. Sky blue. Colorful, yet apropos. Their twelve-year-old son, Billy Applegate, was in dark green overalls with a white shirt. He wore blue Keds and had short hair.

Billy was an only child. His parents doted on him, as did his grandparents as he was the only grandchild in both families. Even so, Billy was a good boy and knew to stay out of the way when his parents had guests, though he stayed close enough to be in the mix and see what was going on. He was at the age where he still enjoyed watching the grown-ups. Spying on them. In fact, he was familiar with many of the faces that night from other events of this kind. It was a small community.

Tonight, Tuesday night, the guests were arriving early, many coming over straight after work and before polling places were even closed.

It was going to be a long night.

The band was playing. Alcohol was flowing. Anticipation was in the air—and excitement at the prospect of big Democrat wins. After everything Nixon had put the nation through, how could voters not want a change?

A black and white TV in the living room announced results as they came in. Dan was loitering by the green phone mounted on the kitchen wall that periodically rang with live information from a few Democrats charged with providing up-to-the-minute results from county polling.

Remember, this was back in the days before computerized voting machines. Back then, voters went to the polling place in their precinct and used a machine to punch holes in their ballot. These were then collected and transported to a central counting center. Precinct ballots were run through a counting machine, and results were tabulated and released to the public.

As the results came in, Dan relayed them to his guests, with each round bringing more good news. More cheering. More drinking.

It was a good year to be a Democrat.

In between announcements from Dan and updates on the TV, the guests mingled, danced, and drank. At peak, there were over 250 guests in and around the property.

The party overflowed onto the street, which was not a

problem. Most of the neighbors were in attendance. And these were all good white folk. The police were kind enough to block off both ends of the street and make sure that those who'd had too much to drink made it home safely.

Inside the house was a political orgy. Supporters rubbed elbows with candidates. Candidates rubbed elbows with incumbents. Incumbents rubbed elbows with donors. And lobbyists rubbed elbows with everyone except each other.

On the public servant side, a number of judges were in attendance. Several city council members were hovering by the buffet, and a few state representatives were sprinkled through the crowd.

It was into this whirlwind of excitement that Sandra Bissette arrived.

At a time when men still ran everything in politics, Sandra hoped to make a name for herself. The fact that she was a Yale-graduated lawyer didn't hurt, nor did the fact that she had both the figure and the looks of Jackie Kennedy.

Sandra was the daughter of lifelong Democrats, and her father happened to be the county sheriff. Although Sandra was not a part of the elite set in Maryland, she was making her way. She was two years into working as an associate at a top law firm after high-level summer internships in D.C.

That night, Sandra was particularly interested in meeting two people: Dan and Annette Applegate. She knew that both were active in the Democratic party in Maryland, although Dan had a reputation as a snob—always riding on his family's coattails. Annette was the nicer of the two, according to Sandra's information. And Annette knew everyone. Sandra hoped to build a connection with the wife.

Someone else Sandra had added to her charm offensive was Harrison Kraft—another young Yale lawyer who, unlike her, was connected in all the right ways.

A few years ahead of her in law school, Harrison was running for state representative. He checked all the right boxes—family pedigree, education, professional credentials. There was no doubt the man was going places. Sandra had heard good things about him as a person, and was interested in seeing for herself.

It was a little after 9:00 p.m.—Dan had just announced the results from Precinct 4 in Montgomery County when Sandra saw a good opening.

Annette was by the buffet chatting with Howard Patrick, an older lobbyist. He was handsy, and a bit of a bore. Sandra straightened her back, raised her chin, and approached.

"Hello Howard," she said with a big grin.

"Sandra, hello my dear. Don't you look beautiful tonight?"

"Why, thank you, Howard. Ever the charmer," she said, allowing him to kiss her hand.

"Have you met our hostess, Annette Applegate?"

As Sandra turned to greet Annette, she noticed that the woman was looking past her, over her shoulder.

"Um, excuse me, young man!" Annette said, eyebrows raised, pearly white teeth dazzling.

Sandra turned and followed Annette's gaze to a young boy in green overalls filching shrimp from the buffet.

"Aw, crap," said Billy through a mouthful of shrimp.

"Come here, you," Annette said, narrowing her eyes in mock disapproval.

Billy hesitated as he took in the young woman, the fat old man, and his mother who stood waiting for him, expectantly now, with her hands on her hips. He'd never seen the young woman before. She was new.

Unconsciously, he slowly moved to return the three shrimp in his little hand to the platter.

"*With* the shrimp, silly," his mother said, shaking her head.

Billy moved toward her, chewing rapidly so he could stuff the other shrimp in his mouth.

Howard put his hand against the small of Sandra's back, a little too low, and harrumphed to her under his breath, "Better seen, not heard. That's how it used to be."

Sandra tried to smile and fought the instinct to pull away. Howard's breath smelled of scotch and cigarettes.

Annette overheard but ignored the old lobbyist's comment.

"I suppose I don't need to ask if you've had dinner? I left meatloaf for you in the kitchen."

"I know. But mom, these shrimp are amazing."

"And the meatballs?" asked Annette, looking over Billy toward the platter on the buffet.

Billy blushed, "Those too."

"Well, it's getting a bit late for you," Annette said, ruffling her son's fair hair and then kissing him on the forehead, making him squirm. "Finish up the shrimp and get to bed."

"What about dad?" Billy asked, looking around.

Annette sighed. "I'll send him up for a goodnight kiss. But you come along young man, now," Annette said, putting her hands on Billy's shoulders and steering him towards the stairs. "Excuse me for a moment," she said over her shoulder.

Shit. Thought Sandra. She twisted politely away, getting the old lobbyist's hand off her lower back as he struck up a conversation. While she tried to focus on what he was saying, it was all she could do not to stare at the green thing wedged in between the man's tar-stained teeth.

It took her ten minutes to extricate herself from Howard thanks to Alan Watts—a decent enough guy. His family ran a small chain of grocery stores. He had asked her out a while back, and though she'd declined, he still had hopes—she could tell. Alan came up to chat with her and Howard, and after a few more minutes of polite conversation, Sandra went to "old reliable."

"Excuse me gentlemen," she said smiling, "Ladies room... "

Once she was sure she had escaped, she continued to work the room. About half an hour later, as she accepted another glass of white wine from a passing waiter, she felt a hand pressing low on the small of her back.

Oh fuck, not again.

"Yes, Howard?" She turned, fake smile firmly in place, to find Annette Applegate standing behind her.

"Gotcha," laughed Annette.

Sandra laughed, both from relief and from delight at the inside joke made by the woman to whom she'd hoped to ingratiate herself.

This is going to be a great night.

* * *

While Sandra and Annette chatted amiably, getting to know one another, many other members of the party were well beyond civility.

Substances were being abused.

The drinking had begun five hours earlier. A lot had been consumed. But there was more than just alcohol flowing.

Some drugs. Discreetly, of course. While most were partaking solely for recreational purposes, there were a few ingesting more heavily.

Most hazardous of all, given that it was infecting everyone and was in ample supply, was the potent and dangerous combination of two stimulants: victory and power.

You see, politics doesn't attract only "normal" people. As in every part of society, there is a spectrum. And politics, too, has its outliers. The smug and the superior. The arrogant and the snide. The sociopaths.

Not to be taken with alcohol or drugs.

For a select few, this combination of alcohol, drugs, and victory combined with power was toxic. It created a euphoria that knew no rules. No limits. No fear.

Upstairs, Billy had fallen asleep.

He was awakened by light spilling into his room, accompanied by the rhythm of music and the chaotic chatter of voices as his door suddenly opened and then closed.

He was groggy and didn't try to open his eyes. Instead, he just spoke out to the room.

"Dad?"

He felt the bed sag as his father sat next to him in a cloud smelling of alcohol and cigars.

Then he felt dry lips on his forehead. The kiss made him smile, sleepily.

A hand stroked his head and his hair. He snuggled into his pillow, drifting back towards sleep.

Suddenly, the same hand that had been stroking his hair gently clamped over his mouth. It was a man's hand, but it was soft. Clammy. It was not his father. Billy tried to sit up, but the hand squeezed hard, the man leaning into him, pushing him down and pinning him to the bed.

Billy suddenly felt a second hand, groping, touching him. He didn't know what to do. He was terrified. He opened his eyes, but it was too dark. He couldn't see anything other than the shape of the form pressing down on him. He could smell the booze on the man's warm breath.

Tears came as the vise over Billy's mouth forced him to suck air noisily through his nose as the groping continued, searching, finding, fondling, stroking, then reaching, penetrating. He felt pain. He hurt inside.

He tried to fight, but couldn't. The hands were too strong. The body too heavy. He felt sick. The stench of cigars and alcohol on fetid breath was nauseating. And he was scared.

Bile rose in his throat. But the hand over his mouth prevented him from vomiting. He swallowed everything back down. His body began to convulse.

As it did, the second hand stopped.

The man's weight eased on top of his body, no longer pressing him down. The hand over his mouth loosened slightly, and Billy felt the other stroking his hair. He wanted to move, but he was paralyzed with fear.

The whole ordeal had lasted maybe five minutes. Maybe ten.

Then the man leaned over and Billy heard him whisper, "Sleep. Sleep. You were dreaming. Go back to sleep."

The weight lifted from the bed, and as it did the hand fell away from his mouth, leaving him shivering in the aftermath.

The door opened and in came the light and the babble of music and voices. That was when he saw the broad profile of a man. The image burned itself into his memory. The image of a stranger whose identity he would eventually learn.

As the door closed, the crowd cheered as the band started playing—*You Ain't Seen Nothing Yet.*

Alone in the dark, Billy Applegate cried until exhaustion claimed him in a fitful sleep.

ACKNOWLEDGEMENTS

In addition to dedicating this book to her, I have to start by thanking my wife Raquel. For over twenty years, she has gently and consistently pushed me to write fiction. Thanks for all your support over the years, for reading all the drafts of this book, and all the others that came before, for your great ideas on story, character, setting, and on the business side of this project as well. This would not exist were it not for you. I love you. You are amazing.

Thanks to our three children, Pi, Coco, and Jay for being so interested in storytelling, and so creative. Thanks for listening to my ideas, concepts, and generalized rambling for different scenes and providing feedback. And thanks also for sharing your ideas and projects with me.

I want to thank all of my early readers and supporters—Raymond Rodriguez, Mark Moran, Dr. Melvin Martinez, Clarissa Monell, Anne and Roman Pérez, Carla Cavero, Kyle Lawson, Sara Bensadon, PhD, Richard Grant, and Mercedes Perote. Thank you for your input and encouragement.

Thanks also to my focus group participants—Francesca Marturano Pratt, Anna Pratt, Daniella Roxanne Pratt, Cheryl Green, Renee Freeman Owens, and Lisa Hall—who devoted a significant chunk of their time to providing feedback leading to significant improvements in the story.

Thank you to author, designer, artist, and marketing guru Tony Marturano, who started out as the cover designer for "Eye for Eye" and ended up contributing significantly to editing the book and running the entire book launch.

I would also like to acknowledge one source of material for this book—which is mentioned and quoted from—Roy's PHI. This book was also relied on the develop Dr. Van der Put's Lust Murder analysis. Geberth, Vernon J. Practical homicide investigation: *Tactics, procedures, and forensic techniques*. CRC Press, 2016.

The Talion Series

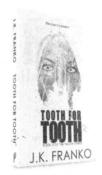

OUT NOW   **OUT HALLOWEEN 2019**   **OUT 2020**

If you enjoyed

EYE FOR EYE
Book 1 of the Talion Series

**Please leave an Amazon review
so that others may enjoy it also.**

To find out more about J.K. Franko, the Talion series and for access to exclusive additional content, register now at J.K.'s official website.

www.jkfranko.com

Made in the USA
Las Vegas, NV
08 February 2021